Medicus and the Disappearing Dancing Girls

R. S. DOWNIE

MICHAEL JOSEPH
an imprint of
PENGUIN BOOKS

IAEL JOSEPH

by the Penguin Group

Penguin Books Ltd, 80 Strand, London WC2R ORL, England
Penguin Group (USA) Inc., 375 Hudson Street, New York, New York 10014, USA
Penguin Group (Canada), 90 Eglinton Avenue East, Suite 700, Toronto, Ontario, Canada M4P 2Y3
(a division of Pearson Penguin Canada Inc.)
Penguin Ireland, 25 St Stephen's Green, Dublin 2, Ireland (a division of Penguin Books Ltd)
Penguin Group (Australia), 250 Camberwell Road,
Camberwell, Victoria 3124, Australia (a division of Pearson Australia Group Pty Ltd)
Penguin Books India Pvt Ltd, 11 Community Centre,
Panchsheel Park, New Delhi – 110 017, India
Penguin Group (NZ), cnr Airborne and Rosedale Roads, Albany,
Auckland 1310, New Zealand (a division of Pearson New Zealand Ltd)
Penguin Books (South Africa) (Pty) Ltd, 24 Sturdee Avenue,
Rosebank, Johannesburg 2196, South Africa

Penguin Books Ltd, Registered Offices: 80 Strand, London WC2R ORL, England

www.penguin.com

First published 2006

1

Set in 13.5/16 pt PostScript Monotype Garamond
Typeset by Rowland Phototypesetting Ltd, Bury St Edmunds, Suffolk
Printed in England by Clays Ltd, St Ives plc

A CIP catalogue record for this book is available from the British Library

HARDBACK
ISBN-13: 978–0–718–14929–1
ISBN-10: 0–718–14929–7

TRADE PBK
ISBN-13: 978–0–718–14943–7
ISBN-10: 0–718–14943–2

Medicus and the
Disappearing Dancing Girls

To Andy, with love.

O diva . . .
serves iturum Caesarem in ultimos
orbis Britannos.

[Oh Goddess . . .
safeguard Caesar as he sets off for the remotest
regions of the Earth – Britain.]

Horace

Acknowledgements

People whose names are not on the cover helped with this book, and I am heavily indebted to the friends and family who offered encouragement in the face of my frequent assertions that it was going Very Badly.

A few people deserve a special mention. Richard Lee and the Historical Novel Society helped to conjure the early chapters out of a very different story. Peta Nightingale and Araminta Whitley encouraged me to finish it — something I failed to do until the good folk at BBC Scotland threatened to come and inquire after its progress. Mari Evans at Michael Joseph and Gillian Blake at Bloomsbury USA provided much-needed guidance — and, thank goodness, a title.

Bill Hancock supplied the quotation from Horace. Nina Palmer, Guy Russell, Kate Weaver and Dr Martin Weaver were all kind enough to read through the text and saved me from much of my own ignorance.

Three books provided particularly fascinating background: David J. P. Mason's *Roman Chester, City of the Eagles*, Ralph Jackson's *Doctors and Diseases in the Roman Empire* and Alan K. Bowman's *Life and Letters on the Roman Frontier*.

Needless to say, none of the above is responsible for any factual errors, misinterpretations, deliberate tweakings or wild flights of fantasy that readers may encounter in the following pages.

Characters

Inside the fort at Deva

The men of the Twentieth Legion (Valiant and Victorious) plus their officers' households, and including:

Hospital staff

Gaius Petreius Ruso	A doctor with debts
Valens	A doctor with ambitions
Priscus	The ultimate administrator
Albanus	A diligent clerk
Decimus	A hospital porter, man of strong passions
The mortuary assistant's assistant	A man doing his best
The signaller	A soldier with a secret
First Dog	An uninvited guest

Others

Second Spear	A formidable officer
Second Spear's daughter	A young lady with prospects
Duty Regional Officer	A man not in love with his job
Centurion Rutilius	Better at controlling men than women
Centurion's wife	A hostess
Rutilia the elder	Their daughter, a young lady burdened with a sister
Rutilia the younger	The sister
Woman with chins	A gossip
Justinus	A whistler

Secundus	A builder
Quintus Antonius Vindex	A confused recruit
Second Dog (with puppies)	A leftover from a previous tenant
Mice	More uninvited guests

Outside the fort

(and mostly only here because of it)

Tilla	A slave
Claudius Innocens	A sleaze-bag
Lucius Curtius Silvanus	A (relatively) respectable slave-trader
Tadius	A house-slave, much put upon
Merula	Keeper of a disreputable bar
Bassus	A veteran of the Legion, now Merula's Head of Security
Stichus	Another veteran, assistant to Bassus
Chloe	
Daphne	
Saufeia	A selection of Merula's girls
Asellina	
Mariamne	
Lucco	Merula's kitchen boy
Phryne	A native girl who wishes she had never left home
Barber	Another veteran settled near his old comrades
Barber's wife	A local woman
Barber's son and his friends	Seekers after knowledge (and cash)
Barber's mother-in-law	A trial
The signaller's girlfriend	A local girl with plenty to say
Brothel-keeper on the Dock Road	A man with low standards
Elegantina	His security guard

In the countryside

The old woman in the village	A tribal elder
Sabrann	Her assistant

Across the sea

On the way to Rome

Publius Aelius Hadrianus	The new Emperor

On the way into the shadows

Trajan	The old Emperor

In Gaul

Lucius	Long-suffering brother of Ruso
Cassia	Lucius' wife, a motherly soul
Their children	Four of them – so far
Ruso's stepmother	A woman with a lot to answer for
Ruso's half-sisters	Girls who have no interest in him whatsoever

Back with her parents, perhaps?

Claudia	Ruso's ex-wife

I

Someone had washed the mud off the body, but as Gaius Petreius Ruso unwrapped the sheet there was still a distinct smell of river. The assistant wrinkled his nose as he approached with the record tablet and the measuring stick he had been sent to fetch.

'So,' said Ruso, flipping the tablet open. 'What's the usual procedure here for unidentified bodies?'

The man hesitated. 'I don't know, sir. The mortuary assistant's on leave.'

'So who are you?'

'The assistant's assistant, sir.' The man was staring at the corpse.

'But you have attended a post-mortem before?'

Without taking his eyes off the body, the man shook his head. 'Are they all like that, sir?'

Ruso, who had started work before it was light, stifled a yawn. 'Not where I come from.'

The description should come first. Facts before speculation. Except that in this case much of the description was speculation as well.

Female, aged . . . He spent some time frowning over that one. Finally he settled on *approximately 18–25 years. Average weight. Height . . . five feet one inch.* At least that was fairly accurate. *Hair: red, scant.* That too, although it might not be very helpful if no one had ever seen her before without a wig. *Clothing: none found.* So no help there, then.

Three teeth missing, but not in places that were obvious.

Someone would need to know her very well indeed to give a positive identification from that.

Ruso glanced up. 'Did you go over to HQ for me?'

'I told them we'd got a body and you'd send the details over later, sir.'

'Did you ask about missing persons?'

'Yes, sir. There aren't any.'

'Hm.' This did not bode well. Ruso continued working his way down the body, making notes as he went. Moments later his search was rewarded. 'Ah. Good!'

'Sir?'

Ruso pointed to what he had found. 'If somebody turns up looking for her in a month's time,' he explained, 'we'll be able to tell them who we buried.' He recorded *Strawberry birthmark approximately half an inch long on inside of upper right thigh, eight inches above the knee*, and sketched the shape.

When he had completed the description, Ruso scratched one ear and gazed down at the pale figure laid out on the table. He was better acquainted than he wished to be with the dead, but this one was difficult. The water had interfered with all the signals he had learned to look for. There was no settling of the blood to indicate the position in which the body had been left, presumably because it had rolled over on the current. The limbs were flexible, so that meant . . . what? Men who died in the stress of battle often froze and then relaxed again much faster than was normal. So if the woman had been frightened or struggling . . . On the other hand, how would the aftermath of death be affected by cold water? He scratched his ear again and yawned, trying to think what he could usefully write on the report that would not cause more distress and confusion to the relatives.

Finally he settled on *Time of death: uncertain, estimated at least 2 days before discovery* and gave his reasons.

He glanced up at the assistant's assistant again. 'Can you write legibly?'

'Yes, sir.'

He handed the tablet and stylus across the body.

'*Place of death*,' he dictated, then corrected himself. 'No, put *Location of body*.'

The man laid the tablet on the end of the table, hunched over it and repeated, 'Location . . . of . . . body' as he scraped with awkward but determined obedience.

'Found five hundred paces downstream from the pier, in marshes on the north bank,' said Ruso, wishing he had carried on writing himself.

'F . . . found . . . five hundred . . .' muttered the man, suddenly breaking off in mid-sentence to look up and say, 'She could have drowned a long way upstream and come down on the river, sir. But then, she might have gone in further along and come up on the tide.'

'Pardon?' Ruso blinked, taken aback by this sudden display of initiative.

Moments later it was apparent that, although this soldier knew nothing about hospital administration and very little about writing, he had devoted his spare time to learning everything there was to know about the local fishing. The assistant's assistant's detailed description of all possible points of waterborne departure which might end in an arrival in the marshes on the north bank of the River Dee left Ruso baffled, but one thing was clear. In a land where coastlines shifted in and out and rivers flowed backwards twice a day, anything that floated could end up a very long way from where it fell into the water.

'Point of entry into water unknown,' he dictated.

The man paused. 'I didn't get the bit before that, sir.' Ruso repeated the location of the body. The man wiped a scrape of wax off the end of the stylus with his forefinger, flicked it away and began to write.

There was a bird chirruping in the hospital garden, and a murmur of voices. Ruso glanced out of the window. On the far side of the herb beds an amputee practised with his crutches while orderlies hovered at each elbow, ready to catch him. A soft breeze wafted in, fluttering the flames of lamps that had been placed on slender black stands around the table, burning for the soul of the unknown figure laid out beneath them.

The flames lurched wildly as the door was flung open. The assistant's assistant looked up and said, 'It's not her, Decimus,' but the intruder still hurried to the table to look for himself.

Ruso frowned. 'Who are you?'

The man clasped both hands together and carried on staring at the body.

'Have you lost someone?'

The man swallowed. 'No. Not like this, no, sir.'

'Then you'd better leave, hadn't you?'

The man backed towards the door. 'Right away, sir. Sorry to interrupt, sir. My mistake.'

Ruso followed him across the room and barred the door before turning to the assistant. 'Is there a missing person that HQ don't know about?'

The man shook his head. 'Take no notice of Decimus, sir. He's just one of the porters. He's looking for his girlfriend.'

'In the mortuary?'

'She ran off with a sailor, sir. Months ago.'

'Why look in here, then?'

The man shrugged. 'I don't know, sir. Perhaps he's hoping she's come back.'

Ruso, not sure if this was an attempt at humour, tried to

look the man in the eye, but the attention of the assistant's assistant remained firmly on the writing tablet.

Ruso looked down at the body. 'Write "Cause of death".'

The stylus began to scratch again. 'Cause of . . .'

'We'll start from the head down.'

'We will start . . .'

'No, don't write that.'

'Sir?'

'Just write "Cause of death". Nothing else yet.'

He frowned at the girl's head. The fishermen who brought the body in had sworn that they had done nothing to it, but he was at a loss to explain the girl's hair. At first he had thought she was simply unfortunate: now, on closer examination, he realized the patchy baldness was not natural. He ran one finger across the bristly scalp.

'Is this some sort of a punishment, do you think?'

'Perhaps she cut it off to sell it, sir,' suggested the orderly.

'This isn't cut, this is practically shaved.'

'Nits, sir?' suggested the orderly, suddenly sounding hopeful. 'Maybe she went down to the river to wash out the nits and drowned.'

Ruso took a deep breath of fresh air before bending down and holding the lamp closer to the body.

'She didn't drown,' he said, lifting the girl's chin with the tip of one finger. 'Look.'

2

Ruso was still pondering the body in the mortuary as he walked out of the East Gate of the fort. He was barely aware of his progress until he was abruptly recalled to his surroundings by a shout of 'Get up!' from further along the street. A man with a large belly was glaring at a grimy figure lying across the pavement just past the fruit stall. A woman with a shopping-basket put down the pear she was examining and turned to see what was going on.

The man repeated the order to get up. The woman stared down at the figure and began to gabble in some British dialect. The only word Ruso could make out was 'water'.

'Burn some feathers under her nose,' suggested the stall-holder, bending down to retrieve a couple of apples that had tumbled off the edge of his display.

Ruso veered into the street to avoid the commotion and narrowly missed a pile of animal droppings. He frowned. He must try to concentrate on what he was doing. He had come out for a walk because he was unable to sleep. Now he was walking, he was having trouble staying awake.

At the open shutters of Merula's he ordered the large cup of good wine he had been promising himself for days. When it came it was nothing like the Falernian it was supposed to resemble. He scowled into its clear depths. At that price and in this place, he supposed it was as good as could be expected. In other words, not very good at all.

The doorman watched as he drained the wine almost un-watered and asked him if he would like to meet a pretty girl.

'Not before I've been to the baths,' grunted Ruso. 'Are you still serving those oysters?'

'Not today, sir.'

'Good.'

'I'm sorry, sir . . . ?'

'So you should be.'

Ruso wondered whether to explain that a dish of Merula's marinated oysters was the cause of his present unkempt state and uncertain temper. He decided not to bother.

Yesterday, strapping a poultice round the foot of a groom trampled by his horse, he had composed an imaginary notice for the hospital entrance: 'To all members of XX Legion Valeria Victrix. While the Chief Medic is on leave, this hospital has three officers. The Admin Officer has gone shopping in Viroconium and taken his keys with him. One doctor has severe food-poisoning. The other is doing his best, despite having no idea what's going on because he has no time to attend morning briefings. Until reinforcements arrive, non-urgent cases and injuries resulting from drunkenness, stupidity or arguments with drill instructors WILL NOT BE TREATED.'

Before the sun had fully risen today he had been presented with a seized back, a dislocated elbow, three teeth in the hand of a man who wanted them replaced and the body. When he pointed out that the body was beyond his help, he was told that they didn't know what else to do with it.

Mercifully Valens – a paler and thinner version of the Valens who had eaten the oysters – had reported for duty this afternoon. Peering at Ruso, he announced, 'You look worse than I do. Go and get some rest.' Ruso, who had been desperate to sleep for the past three days, suddenly found himself unable to settle.

A group of youths with Army haircuts was sauntering

across the street towards Merula's. As they entered Ruso murmured, 'Don't touch the seafood.' He was gone before they could reply.

Passing the bakery, he realized he could not remember the last time he had eaten. He bought a honey cake and crumbled it against the roof of his mouth as he walked along.

Ahead of him, a babble of excited voices rose in the street. He recognized the fat man, still shouting orders in a thick Gallic accent. The female who had collapsed had now attracted a sizeable crowd. They seemed to be carrying her to the fountain. Ruso tossed the last fragments of cake to a passing dog and strode on in the direction of the amphitheatre. It was nothing to do with him. He was not, at this moment, a doctor. He was a private citizen in need of some bath-oil.

He took a deep breath before diving into the perfumed dusk of the oil-shop. He had placed his flask on the counter and was naming what he wanted when the shopkeeper's attention was caught by something behind him. The man snatched up a heavy stick and leaped out from behind the counter, yelling, 'Clear off!' The dog that had finished Ruso's cake shot out from behind a stack of jars and scuttled off down the street.

The shopkeeper replaced the stick under the counter. 'Somebody ought to do something about those dogs.'

'Are they dangerous?'

'Only when they bite. Now, what was it you were after?'

Outside, half a dozen pairs of hands were dragging a limp body along the pavement to where the fountain, a large and ugly stone fish, was vomiting water into a long rectangular tank.

The shopkeeper glanced up from the pouring-jug. 'Something going on over there.'

Ruso heard a splash as he said, 'A woman fainted in the street.'

'Oh.' The man twisted the stopper into the flask and wiped the side with a cloth. Ruso handed over a sestertius. As the man counted out the change more people were crowding round the fountain. Voices drifted across the street.

'Get up, you lazy whore!'

'Give her another dunk!'

'If you burn some feathers –'

'Stand her up!'

'Lie her down!'

'Lie her down? She does nothing but lie down!'

Ruso dropped the coins into his purse and emerged into the fresh air. He was not going to offer help. He had been caught like that before. Poor people, like stray dogs, bred huge litters they couldn't look after and latched on to you with the slightest sign of encouragement. As soon as the whisper went round that some doctor was treating people for free, every case of rotten teeth and rheumatism within a thousand paces would be rounded up and thrust under his nose for inspection. He would be lucky to get away before nightfall.

A voice whispered in his memory: a voice he hadn't heard for almost two years now: a voice accusing him of being cold-hearted and arrogant. He silenced it, as he usually did, by recalling other voices. The Tribune's praise of his 'commendable single-mindedness' (of course Valens had to ruin it later by explaining, 'He meant you're boring'). Or the officer's wife who had smiled at him over her sprained ankle and said, 'You're really quite sweet, Petreius Ruso, aren't you?' That memory would have been more comforting, though, if she hadn't been caught in the bed of the Chief Centurion a week later and been sent back to Rome in disgrace.

Raising his fingers to sniff the smear of perfumed oil, Gaius Petreius Ruso headed back the way he had come.

The sharp crack of a hand on flesh rang down the street.

'On your feet! Move!'

A pause.

'Throw some more water on her.'

A splash. A cry of 'Hey, mind my new shoes!'

Laughter.

Ruso pursed his lips. He should have stayed up at the fort. He could have helped himself to some of Valens' oil and used the hospital baths. Now he would sit in the steam room wondering what had happened to the wretched woman, even though he wasn't responsible for it.

'Wake up, gorgeous!'

More laughter.

If he managed to revive her, those comedians would take the credit.

'Turn her over!'

If he didn't, he would get the blame.

There was a sudden gasp from around the fountain. Someone cried, 'Ugh! Look at that!'

A child was pawing at her mother's arm, demanding, 'What is it? I can't see, tell me what it is!'

Ruso hesitated, came to a halt, and promised himself it would only be a quick look.

The military belt was an accessory with magical powers. Several of the onlookers disappeared as soon as it approached. The rest parted to let its wearer through, and Ruso found himself staring down at his second unfortunate female today. This one was a skinny figure lying in a puddle by the fountain. She was still breathing, but she was a mess. The rough grey tunic which covered her was the same colour as the bruise under one eye. Blood was oozing from her lower lip and forming a thin red line in the water that still trickled down her face. Her hair was matted and mud-coloured. She could have been any age between fifteen and thirty.

'We're giving this girl some water, sir,' explained someone with an impressive grasp of understatement.

'She's fainted,' added someone else.

'She always faints when there's work to be done,' grumbled the man who had been shouting at her. He bent as far down as his belly would allow and yelled in the girl's ear, 'Get up!'

'She can't hear you,' remarked Ruso evenly. His gaze took in the copper slave band around the girl's upper right arm. Below the elbow, the arm vanished into a swathe of grimy rags. The pale hand emerging at the other end was what had silenced the crowd. It was sticking out at a grotesque and impossible angle. Ruso frowned, unconsciously fingering his own forearm. 'What happened to her arm?'

'It wasn't us!' assured a voice in the crowd. 'We was only trying to help!'

The grumbler turned his head to one side and spat. 'Silly bitch fell down the steps.'

'Fell down the steps, *sir*,' corrected Ruso, restraining an urge to seize the man by the ear.

'Yes, sir. Didn't look where she was going, sir.'

'It should have been set straight away.'

'Yes, sir.'

'Get it done.'

'On my way now, sir.'

The girl groaned. The man grabbed her good arm and hauled her to her feet. She fell against him. Caught off balance, he struggled to stay upright.

Ruso was uncomfortably aware that he was now at the centre of this entertainment. Whatever he did, he must not admit to being a doctor. Nor did he intend to waste his afternoon being soaked and muddied by dragging a sick slave around.

'You there!' He pointed to a greasy-haired youth who was lolling against a wall trying to dislodge something from his ear with his forefinger. 'Yes, you! Give him a hand.'

The youth withdrew the finger, opened his mouth to argue, then thought better of it. He slid a reluctant hand under the girl's arm. He and the girl's owner began to drag the limp body along the pavement.

Ruso scowled at the crowd, which began to disperse.

'The fort's the other way!' he shouted after the owner.

No reply.

He overtook them, blocking the path. The trio paused. The girl slumped lower.

'She needs to go to the fort hospital. Now.'

'Yes sir,' agreed the owner, 'but the thing is, sir . . .'

The thing was that he was short of cash. The girl's last owner had driven away with a cartload of best-quality woollens and palmed him off with a slave who was lazy and useless. Now she had gone and broken her arm, and he couldn't even sell her on. A harder man would have thrown her out into the street, but everyone knew Claudius Innocens was a man too soft for his own good. He knew the hospital at the fort had an excellent reputation – 'Get on with it!' prompted Ruso – but it was too expensive for a poor trader. He had heard there was a good healer on the Bridge Road. He was going there now.

'I just have to do a little business on the way, sir,' he added. 'So I can pay for the treatment.'

Ruso had only been stationed in Deva for four days but already he knew that the local healer wouldn't be able to do anything with that arm. He said nothing. It was not his problem. He had only come out for a drink and a flask of bath-oil. The girl's face was horribly pale: she probably didn't have long left anyway. The healer would have henbane, or mandrake. Perhaps some imported poppy-juice.

Ruso glanced round to make sure no one was looking, then undid his purse and placed two sestertii into the hand of Claudius Innocens. 'Take her there now,' he ordered. 'Buy her a dose of something for the pain.'

'You're a kind-hearted man, sir!' Innocens' jowls bulged outwards in a smile that failed to reach his eyes. 'Not a lot of gentlemen would see a poor man in need and –'

'See to it!' snapped Ruso and walked away, checking that his oil-flask was still tied to his belt and had not been subtly removed by someone in the crowd. He was not feeling like a kind-hearted man. He was a man who was deeply exasperated. He was a man who needed a good night's sleep. And before that, he needed a trip to the baths.

In a few minutes, stretched out on a warm couch with a soft towel beneath him, he would forget the merchant's slimy gratitude and the grisly shape of his slave-girl's arm. He would forget the screams of the recruit this morning as his elbow was put back into shape. Distracted by the splash of the cold plunge and the murmur of gossip, his thoughts would drift away from the puzzle of that unknown woman lying in the mortuary. The perfumed oil would clear the stench of decay from his nostrils. The masseur's practised hands would pummel away the tension of problems which, when he thought about them logically, all belonged to other people.

There was no sign of the young soldiers at the tables in Merula's. The doorman pretended not to recognize Ruso. He must have overheard the warning about the food.

An elderly slave was limping past the place where the girl had collapsed. The stink of the two buckets swaying on the pole over his shoulders was unmistakable. The man stopped to scrape up the pile of dung Ruso had almost trodden in earlier.

Half the world, decided Ruso, raising his fingers to his nose again, spent its waking hours engaged in clearing up the mess made by the other half. That girl's owner, like whoever had dumped that corpse in the river, had been a mess-maker. Not fit to be in charge of a dead dog. That disgusting bandage had been on for days.

Ruso stopped so suddenly that a child running along behind him collided with the back of his legs, tumbled full-length on the paving stones and, refusing his offer of help, ran off howling for its mother.

That girl hadn't fallen down any steps. She had raised the arm to shield herself from the blows that had blackened her eye. The wool-trader would pocket the money and leave town, and before long another unclaimed body would be found floating down the river. Gaius Petreius Ruso had just been swindled out of two sestertii.

It did not take long to find the unattractive trio again. The wet trail led away from the fountain and down a side street, weaving unsteadily round the legs of scaffolding poles. The scrape and slop of shovels mixing mortar announced yet another row of new shops. Ruso strode around the far side of the building site, entered the street from the opposite end, picked his way down past a burned-out building awaiting demolition and came face to face with the shuffling threesome.

'The Bridge Road is the other way!' he shouted over a sudden burst of hammering, stabbing his forefinger in the direction they had just come.

The girl opened her eyes and looked at him.

She couldn't see him, of course. It was an illusion. The eyes were blank; like the eyes of a sleepwalker. For the first time Ruso noticed the delicate shape of her nose, the tiny dimple in an ear-lobe where jewellery had once hung. And those eyes. The colour of – what were they the colour of? Like . . . like the clear, deep waters of . . . Ruso's tired mind groped for a description that didn't sound like the work of a bad poet and failed to find one.

The merchant was still talking. The youth was examining the toe-straps of his sandals. Only Ruso seemed to be interested in the girl.

'If you don't get help for her soon, this slave is going to die.'

He realized it was a mistake as soon as he had said it. The trader bent forward and dragged down the girl's lower eyelid with a dirty thumb. Then he forced her jaw open and peered into her mouth. He was clearly not a man to waste two sestertii on dying livestock.

'It's not the state of her teeth you want to worry about.'

Innocens turned and looked at him curiously. 'You wouldn't be a medical man yourself, by any chance, sir?'

Ruso glanced up, wishing he believed in the sort of theatrical gods who swooped down from the heavens at difficult moments and set humanity to rights. But the gods, if they were watching, were hiding in the grey British clouds beyond the scaffolding poles, leaving him to his fate. And then, as if inspired by something beyond himself, Ruso had an idea.

'You said she isn't worth anything.'

Innocens paused. 'Well, not the way she is, sir. After she's had a bit of a clean-up –'

'I'll take her off your hands.'

'She's a good, strong girl, sir. She'll perk up in a day or two. I'll knock a bit off the price for that arm.'

'What price? You told me she was lazy and useless.'

'Useless at cleaning, sir, but an excellent cook. And what's more . . .' Innocens raised his free arm to steady the girl as he leaned forward in a haze of fish sauce and bellowed over more hammering, 'Just the thing for a healthy young man like yourself, sir! Ripe as a peach and never been touched!'

'I'm not interested in touching her!' shouted Ruso, just as the noise stopped.

Someone sniggered. Ruso looked up. A couple of men were leaning down over the scaffolding. One of them said something to the other and they both laughed. The youth holding the girl glanced up and grinned.

It would be all over the fort by morning.

You know that new doctor up at the hospital? The one that's been telling the lads to stay out of whorehouses?

What about him?

Hangs around back streets. Tries to buy women.

Innocens was smiling again. Ruso suppressed an urge to grab him by the neck and shake him.

'What would you like to offer, sir?'

Ruso hesitated. 'I'll give you fifty denarii,' he muttered.

Innocens' jowls collapsed in disappointment. He shrugged the shoulder not being used to prop up his merchandise. 'I wish I could, sir. I can hardly afford to feed her. But the debt I took her for was four thousand.'

It was a ridiculous lie. Even if it wasn't, Ruso didn't have four thousand denarii. He didn't have four hundred. It had been an expensive summer.

'Fifty's more than she's worth, and you know it,' he insisted. 'Look at her.'

'Fifty-five!' offered a voice from the scaffolding.

'What?' put in his companion. 'You heard the man, she's a virgin. Fifty-six!'

Innocens scowled at them. 'One thousand and she's yours, sir.'

'Fifty or nothing.'

The trader shook his head, unable to believe that any fool would offer all his money at the first bid. Ruso, remembering with a jolt that payday was still three weeks away, was barely able to believe it himself. He should have put more water in that wine.

'Two hundred, sir. I can't go below two hundred. You'll ruin me.'

'Go on!' urged the chorus from the scaffolding. 'Two hundred for this lovely lady!'

Ruso looked up at the workmen. 'Buy her yourselves if you like. I only came out for a bottle of bath-oil.'

At that moment the girl's body jerked. A feeble cough emerged from her lips. Her eyelids drifted shut. A slow silver drool emerged from her mouth and came to rest in shining bubbles on the sodden wool of her tunic. Claudius Innocens cleared his throat.

'Will that fifty be cash, then, sir?'

3

'What are you doing in here?'

Ruso opened one eye and wondered briefly why he was being addressed by a giant inkpot. Opening the other eye to find himself in fading light and surrounded by shelves, he realized he must have fallen asleep in the records office. He hauled himself upright on the stool and yawned. 'Catching up on some notes. How are you feeling?'

Valens grinned. 'Better than that thing in room twelve. It looks as if it's just crawled out of the sewer. What is it?'

Ruso reached for the writing-tablet before Valens could make out: *Female, history unknown, fracture to lower right arm, pale, dry cough, weak, no fever. Note: Launder bedding, treat with fleabane.* He snapped it shut and slid it into the Current Patients box.

'That thing is a sick slave with a broken arm.'

'Whose?'

'Her own.'

'Very funny. Whose slave?'

Ruso scratched his ear. 'Couldn't say, really.' He had entertained a faint hope that his purchase might be claimed by the lovestruck porter and taken off his hands, but the man had not recognized her.

'I leave you on your own for a couple of days,' said Valens, 'and you fill the place with expiring females.'

'A couple of fishermen found the other one already expired. The town council clerk wouldn't let them dump her outside his office, and they couldn't think what else to do with her.'

Valens shrugged. 'Of course. We're the Army, we'll deal with everything. If somebody doesn't identify her soon I suppose we'll have to bury her, too. So who said her friend could die in one of our beds?'

'She isn't dying,' argued Ruso, seizing the chance to side-step the question of who had brought her in.

'That's not what I heard. She on your list?'

He nodded.

'No hope for her, then.' Valens glanced out into the corridor, pushed the door shut and lowered his voice. 'Five says she'll be dead by sunrise.'

Ruso pondered this for a moment. Payday seemed further away now than when he had foolishly offered all his remaining cash for a slave he didn't want. If he could just keep her alive until tomorrow, he would salvage some of his dignity and come out of it with money in his purse.

'She isn't dying,' he repeated with more confidence than he felt. 'Five says she's alive when they blow first watch.'

'If she were a dog, you'd knock her on the head now.'

'Well she isn't, and I shan't. So push off and find some patients of your own to annoy.'

The hollow cheeks of the patient in room twelve looked distinctly yellow against the white of the blanket that had been draped over her. The injured arm, secured across her chest in a crisp linen sling, rose and fell gently with each breath. The draught had done its work. She was asleep. Her doctor placed a cup of barley water on the table beside the bed and went to the shrine of Aesculapius.

*

The hospital entrance hall was empty save for a smell of fresh paint and roses. Aesculapius leaned on his stick and looked out from his niche with a quiet dignity that somehow transcended the inscription 'WET PAINT' chalked underneath him. The God of Healing needed more maintenance than most of his colleagues: the touch of his eager supplicants tended to damage his paintwork. Today the faithful had left a bunch of white roses and a couple of apples at his feet, hoping to be saved from their ailments. Or, more likely, from their doctor.

Usually Ruso spared the deity no more than a passing nod. Now he paused to stand in front of the niche and murmur a promise of two and a half denarii should the girl in room twelve survive until morning.

Having thus enlisted extra help for the cost of only half his winnings, and with nothing to pay if the god failed to perform, Ruso headed back to room twelve to see what more could be done to improve his chance of winning this unexpected and probably illegal wager.

4

'Are you – sure he's – dead?' asked Ruso, the words punctuated by grunts as he struggled to manoeuvre his end of the stretcher through the door.

'Positive, sir,' said the surgical orderly, deftly kicking the door shut behind him. 'The man who told me heard it from someone who got it from one of the kitchen staff in the Legate's house. It'll be announced at parade this morning.'

'How do the kitchen staff know?'

'The despatch rider popped along for something to eat while the Legate read through the message, sir.'

Ruso suppressed a smile. 'I suppose you know the cause of death?'

'Not sure yet, sir. All we know is, he had a funny turn on the way back from sorting the Parthians out.'

They lowered the stretcher on to the table. 'Do we know who's taken over?' asked Ruso, sliding out one of the carrying poles.

'The Army are backing Publius Aelius Hadrianus, sir.' The orderly slid out the other pole and stacked them both in the corner. 'I'm told he's a very generous man when it comes to bonuses. Double the going rate is what I hear.'

'Does anybody know what the going rate is?' asked Ruso. 'Half the Army wasn't even born when Trajan took over, let alone on the payroll.'

'Hard to say, sir,' agreed the orderly, 'But in nineteen years it's bound to have gone up, isn't it?' He bent over the table. 'Just lie on your left, now.' As they rolled the girl first to one side of the table and then the other, slipping the stretcher sheet out from beneath her, he observed, 'Nothing of her, is there?'

When they had settled the girl the man hurried out to refill the water-bucket, complaining that someone else should have refilled it last night. 'You can tell Priscus isn't here.'

Ruso waited, hearing distant voices. The clump of boots on floorboards in the corridors. The usual clatter from the kitchen. Window-shutters crashing open to let in the new day. A day the anonymous girl in the mortuary would never see. Ruso, who did not like to inquire too deeply into matters of religion, wondered vaguely if she and Trajan would meet each other on the voyage into the shadowy world of the departed. He eyed the girl lying on the table in front of him. It might have been kinder to let her join them.

Laid out under a crumpled linen gown that smelled faintly of lavender, she looked smaller. And younger. He wondered how old she was. She must have a name: a tribe: a language. The trader had been yelling at her in Latin, but the words she had mumbled as the poppy-juice carried her into oblivion sounded British.

That was the only time he had heard her speak. When he had put his head round the door of room twelve just after dawn and said, 'Morning! Did you sleep well?' (She was alive! He must go and tell Valens . . .) she had looked at him with those eyes that were the colour of – well, whatever it was – as if she did not understand the question.

The eyes were open again now. The pupils had been shrunk to small black dots by medicine he had given her. She was staring up at the dust-motes floating in the sunshine that streamed in from the high windows. She showed no curiosity about where she was.

She did not seem to have grasped the purpose of the gleaming instruments laid out on the cloth beside the empty water-basin. She was not alarmed by the rolls of bandage stacked on the shelves, nor did she seem to be wondering what so many empty bowls might be there to catch.

Ruso was pleased with himself. Deciding the right amount of poppy-juice to administer had been a tricky business. The borrowed works he had hurriedly consulted last night had implied that, in all respects which would matter this morning, women were the same as men only smaller. In Ruso's experience, however, there was much about women that was dangerously unpredictable, and one of the attractions of Army life was that he was no longer expected to live with one.

'Everything all right, sir?' The orderly was back, splashing clean water into the basin.

Ruso nodded. 'I think she's about ready.'

The orderly began to buckle a leather strap across the girl's legs. She lifted her head slightly.

'Nothing to worry about,' said the orderly, who was a practised liar.

The girl's head fell back. She closed her eyes and appeared to be drifting off to sleep.

The door opened. Valens' head appeared, then retreated. 'Sorry! Didn't know you were in here.'

Ruso called after him, 'What about that five denarii?'

Valens reappeared, glanced at the body on the operating table and grinned. 'You must have cheated.'

'I could do with some help.'

'I'm supposed to be doing the rounds. What have you got?'

As the girl continued to doze while the orderly strapped her down, Ruso jerked a thumb towards the bandaged arm lying on top of the linen. 'Compound fracture of radius and ulna about halfway down. Probably three or four days old. I redressed the outside last night but it was too dark to operate.'

'I like a challenge,' said Valens and closed the door behind him. 'Have you heard? Trajan's dead.'

'I know,' said Ruso, who had private reasons to mourn the Emperor's passing. 'Sounds as though it's Hadrian.'

Ruso began to remove the bandaging he had put on last night. The girl's body jerked as she tried to raise herself. The orderly gripped her shoulders and held her down.

On the other side of the table, Valens stroked her good hand, leaned over and said gently, 'We're going to see to your arm. We'll be very quick.'

Ruso wished he had remembered to say that himself.

They began to soak off the rag that had been stuffed into the wound.

'I met him once,' mused Ruso.

'Hadrian?'

'Trajan. In Antioch.'

'I suppose he'll be the divine Trajan soon.'

'No doubt,' agreed Ruso. At least, none that he was foolish enough to express in public.

'May he rest among the gods,' added Valens.

'Among the gods indeed, sir,' echoed the orderly.

Ruso left a brief silence that could have been respect or rebellion, then murmured, 'Water.'

The orderly refilled the jug.

'Think Hadrian'll try and take the North back?' asked Valens.

'Why not?' Ruso said. 'He'll be wanting to make an impression. Britannia's big enough to count, but remote enough not to matter.'

'He'll have to send more legions if he's serious about it. We're spread pretty thin here.'

'He might not go for it. He's Trajan's man. He might just carry on the divine Trajan's policies.' Ruso glanced at the orderly. 'No doubt the kitchen staff will let us know. Here it comes . . .' He lifted off the rag and dropped it into the waste-bucket.

Both men leaned forward to peer at the swollen and blood-caked mess that had once been an arm.

Valens brought one hand down over his own elbow with a chopping motion, and raised his eyebrows in question.

Ruso shook his head. 'It looks clean. The wrist's intact.'

Valens strolled round the table, looking at the injury from a different angle. 'I wouldn't,' he murmured. 'You'll only make a worse mess and end up taking it off anyway.'

'It might work. If you broke your arm —'

'I'd pray I didn't get some would-be hero like you.'

'I think we should try.'

There was a pause.

'She's my patient,' added Ruso.

Valens shrugged. 'Fine. She's your patient. So, do we know how much Hadrian values his loyal troops?'

'He'll be doubling the usual bonus, apparently.'

'How much is that?'

'Not a clue.'

As they began to clean the wound, the girl gasped. Her face twisted into a grimace of pain.

'Try and lie still,' said the orderly, tightening his grip and glancing to check that all the straps were fastened.

'We'll be very quick,' promised Ruso, wishing he could make patients believe it the way Valens did.

'My friend's famous for being quick,' added Valens. 'Ask all the girls.' He glanced at Ruso. 'What's she called?'

25

'I don't know.'

'Ruso, only you could round up two women and not know the names of either of them.'

'Next time,' said Ruso, 'I'll tell them my friend would like to be introduced.' He picked out a stray thread of rag with the tweezers. The girl gave a low moan.

'Shush now,' said the orderly.

Ruso hoped she wouldn't be a whimperer. Whimperers were worse than screamers. Screamers made him cross, which made him work faster. The sound of a whimperer trying to be brave was a distraction.

The girl didn't whimper. She clamped her teeth on to the leather strap the orderly offered her and didn't make another sound.

There was a rap at the door.

'What?' snapped Ruso. A very young soldier appeared, swallowed and announced, 'Urgent message for Gaius Petreius Ruso.'

'That's me.'

'Sir, there's a man at the East Gatehouse. He says you promised to pay fifty-four denarii first thing this morning.'

'It was fifty,' said Ruso, not looking up. 'And I'm busy.'

The youth did not reply. He was staring at the operating table.

'Tell him I'll be down later,' said Ruso.

The youth swallowed again. 'He said to tell you the extra is the tax and the cost of drawing up the documents, sir.'

Ruso nodded towards the mangled mass of the girl's arm. 'If you don't get out right away, I shall do this to you too.'

The youth fled.

Ruso aimed the tweezers at the waste-bucket, missed and said, 'I think that's clean.'

Valens laid a hand on the girl's forehead. 'We like this

26

arm so much, young woman, we're going to put it back together for you.'

The orderly leaned down until his face was almost touching the girl's. 'Breathe deeply now,' he ordered. 'Ready? In, out, in, out . . .'

Ruso had rehearsed his speech all the way down to the gatehouse, but when he got there he found his time had been wasted. Instead of the wool-trader, the guards presented him with an elderly slave with no teeth who made it clear that if he failed to return to his master with the right money, his life would not be worth living. Ruso, who had neither the time nor the inclination to queue at the tax office, paid up. He also sent a message to say that if Claudius Innocens ever showed his face in Deva again he would be instantly arrested but he doubted the slave would have the courage to deliver it.

The clerk of the Aesculapian Thanksgiving Fund gave him a receipt for the two and a half denarii which Valens had borrowed from someone who had borrowed them from someone else who had very possibly borrowed them from the Aesculapian Thanksgiving Fund in the first place.

Ruso went to thank the god personally. Standing in front of the statue, he fingered the two receipts tucked into his belt. One said that in gratitude and fulfilment of a vow, Gaius Petreius Ruso had paid the Aesculapian Thanksgiving Fund two and a half denarii. The other confirmed Gaius Petreius Ruso as the new owner of an injured and sickly girl with indescribable eyes and a name that seemed to be a series of spelling mistakes.

Ruso gazed up at the statue of the god who had answered his prayer. For the first time he noticed that the painter had not just performed the usual touch-up over the rough bits.

27

The god had been completely repainted. Ruso stood to take a closer look and as he gazed into the brown eyes of Aesculapius he had the distinct impression that the god of healing was looking back at him, and laughing.

5

Ruso lay on the borrowed bed and stared into the gloom that hid the cracks in the ceiling plaster, reflecting that Socrates was a wise man. Surveying the goods on a market stall, the great one was said to have remarked, 'What a lot of things a man doesn't need!'

What a lot of things a man doesn't need. That thought had comforted Ruso over the last few months. The more you own, he had told himself, the more you have to worry about. Possessions are a burden.

The kind of possessions which needed to be regularly fed were a double burden. They were only worth having if they earned their keep by doing the laundry, or barking at burglars, or catching mice, or carrying you somewhere, or chirruping in a way that your ex-wife used to find entertaining. It was a pity Socrates hadn't thought to add, *which is why I never shop after drinking on an empty stomach.*

'As far as I'm concerned,' Valens had said, carefully lowering the lid back on to the beer-barrel so as not to tip the stack of dirty dishes which had been there when Ruso moved in, 'if there's no one waiting for the room and you're not using much staff time to nurse her, you can leave her there.'

Ruso took the dripping cup of beer and wondered whether to clear up the dishes, or whether to wait and see how long it would be before Valens did. 'She'll need proper nursing for a few days.'

'Fair enough. But the other one's got to be out of the

mortuary tomorrow, claimed or not.' Valens tossed a broken fishing-rod into the corner to clear himself space on the couch. As he sat down, three puppies scuttled out from underneath. The puppies were a legacy from the previous occupant, whose lone and portly terrier bitch Valens had agreed to look after while the man was seconded elsewhere. 'Gods, I'll be glad when Marius gets back to pick this stuff up. It's not all my mess in here, you know.'

Ruso, who had shared quarters with Valens before, made no comment. The offer of free accommodation had been too good to turn down, but he had known there would be a price to pay.

'To tell you the truth,' said Valens, 'I thought you'd be bringing a servant or two. You used to have lots.'

'Claudia had lots.'

'Ah.' Valens squinted into his own beer, rescued something with a forefinger and flicked it over his shoulder. A rush of inquisitive puppies followed its course.

'How long have you been a beer drinker?'

'I'm not. Some native gave it to me as a thank-you for treating one of his children.'

Ruso frowned into his drink. 'Are you sure he was grateful?'

'Smells like goat's piss, I know. But you'll get used to it.'

Ruso tried another mouthful and wondered how long getting used to it would take. He said, 'Can't the Legion give us somebody to help keep the place straight?'

Valens winced. 'If you want some squint-eyed misery who makes a ridiculous fuss about a little bit of mess.'

Ruso deduced that this had already been tried. 'What about a private arrangement? It wouldn't cost much between us.'

'The servants here aren't much better than the beer, I'm

afraid. The first one we tried had a bad back. The next one kept sitting on the floor and crying and we didn't have the heart to beat her, so we sold her. At a loss, of course. Then we tried hiring in a local girl, but Marius saw her kick the dog, so she had to go.' Valens leaned back and indicated the size of the room with a sweep of his arm. The motion sent beer slopping over the side of his cup. 'This isn't a big house, is it?' He transferred the beer to the other hand and wiped his wet fingers on the couch. 'It can't be much work. I mean, we don't even use that end room.' The beer slopped again, indicating the direction of the corner room which had been abandoned as impossibly damp and was now growing several fine blooms of strange-smelling mould. 'There's only the two of us to cook for,' he continued, 'and half the time we eat across at the hospital. Here, can your girl cook?'

'At the moment she can't even stand up.'

'No matter. We don't want one in a splint anyway. We want some nice healthy lass who's handy with dogs and cleaning.'

'And wants a challenge,' observed Ruso, glancing through the open door into the earthquake zone that was Valens' bedroom. 'Where would we put this healthy lass?'

'In the kitchen, I suppose. When your furniture turns up she could have the mattress off that bed you're using.'

Ruso did not reply.

'We could always get rid of her later if your girl shows promise,' Valens added.

'I won't be keeping her. I'll start looking for a buyer as soon as she can be moved.'

'You'll just have to hope Priscus doesn't come back in the meantime.'

Ruso frowned. 'Doesn't anybody know when he's coming?'

'Doubt it. He likes to take people by surprise. He thinks it keeps them on their toes. He's not keen on private patients unless they pay well. By the way, that other dog isn't yours as well, is it?'

Ruso said, 'What other dog?'

'I didn't think it was. I'll tell them to get rid of it.'

Other dog?

Ruso yawned. The girl in the mortuary was not his problem, but if he didn't get the live one out of the hospital soon, not only would he get off on the wrong foot with Chief Administrator Priscus, but he would be saddled with every other passing stray for whom no one else wanted to take responsibility.

Somewhere beyond the ill-fitting shutters of his bedroom window a trumpet sounded the change of watch. He rolled over, wriggled to avoid the lump that always seemed directly under his shoulder no matter how many times he turned the mattress or shook the straw around and closed his eyes. He was just dropping off to sleep when he heard a knock on his door and Valens asking if he was awake.

'No.'

'Are you busy in the morning?'

'Yes.'

'Pity. Somebody's going to have to go down to Merula's.'

'Uh. Send an orderly.'

'It ought to be somebody official, and I'm on duty.'

'Can't it wait?'

'No. One of the men's identified that body.'

6

The shutters had been pushed right back to let in the autumn sunshine. Beyond them, Merula's was almost empty. Benches were upturned on the tables. A lad of eight or nine was shovelling ash out of the grate under the hot drinks counter. A young woman with lank hair pushed behind her ears was pushing sawdust into a grey pile with limp strokes of a broom. A buxom girl was barefoot on a stool, displaying a dainty silver chain around one ankle as she reached above a lamp bracket to wipe at the smuts on the wall. Ruso looked at the girl with the ankle-chain. He thought of the discoloured figure stretched out on the mortuary table. He wished he hadn't.

A door opened somewhere at the back of the bar and a third girl, this one heavily pregnant, emerged carrying an oil-jar. From somewhere in the shadows a gruff voice said, 'Morning, Daphne.'

Daphne came to an instant halt on the far side of one of the tables. Ruso had the impression she was holding her breath as the taller of Merula's two doormen stepped up close behind her.

'Just got out of bed, have we?' inquired the doorman. The pregnant girl flinched as he leaned round to peer into her face.

From the doorway Ruso noticed the cloth dangling unheeded in the hand of the girl standing on the stool, who had turned to watch the encounter. The lank-haired one shuffled away to sweep under the stairs.

The doorman was shaking his head despairingly. 'Daphne, Daphne, what am I always telling you about conversation? When a gentleman says hello, you say hello back. Good morning, Daphne.'

If Daphne made any reply, it was covered by the screech of the shovel being slid into the fireplace.

'Very nice. Now come here.'

He seated himself behind her on the table, placed his hands on her shoulders and manoeuvred her back towards him until she was standing trapped between his knees with the oil-jar propped awkwardly against her swollen belly. 'You want to be more careful,' he said, his large fingers retying the loose braid in her hair with a surprisingly deft touch. 'You could have lost that ribbon, couldn't you?'

She did not answer.

He gave her a rough shove forward. 'Run along, then. The mistress don't want to see you standing around chatting.'

As Daphne approached Ruso, her face was expressionless. She stood on tiptoe to fill the lamp on the bracket by the shutters. When she had finished, she wiped first her nose and then the neck of the jar with a cloth and made her way back towards the kitchen with the sway-backed walk of a woman working to counterbalance a heavy weight.

Ruso stepped forward on to the red tiles, avoiding a pile of sawdust. A broad figure emerged from behind the shutters to block his path. He recognized the fading ginger hair.

'We're closed,' said the man in a tone that suggested he too remembered Ruso's last visit, but not fondly.

'Is the manageress in?'

The solid shoulders rose just enough to indicate that the man's job was to know nothing, see nothing and be as unhelpful as possible, and he was intending to do it to the best of his ability.

Ruso looked him in the eye. He was saying, 'Would you like me to repeat the question?' when he heard another voice behind him.

'Who wants to know?'

He turned. The doormen had positioned themselves so that he was caught between them. 'Gaius Petreius Ruso,' he said to the second man, who seemed to be in charge. 'Medicus with the Twentieth.'

The man folded his arms. 'Whatever it is,' he said, 'it didn't come from here. All our girls are clean. You want to try down by the docks.'

The man's bearing would have said *ex-legionary* even without the telltale scar where the scarf had failed to stop the armour chafing his neck. Ruso said, 'What's your name, soldier?'

The man assessed him for a while longer, then said, 'Bassus. He's Stichus.'

'Bassus. I'm here from the hospital to see your mistress on an official matter. It's confidential and it's urgent. So if you don't know where she is, you'd be wise to find out.'

The crease between the doorman's eyebrows deepened. 'Why didn't you say so?' He turned. 'Lucco!'

The boy paused with the shovel in one hand and a brush in the other.

'Go and tell the mistress there's an officer to see her. Chloe, get the officer a seat.'

Ruso said, 'I'll stand –' but the girl with the ankle-chain had already stepped down from the stool. She heaved a bench off one of the corner tables and swung it over to land on the tiles with a clatter. 'Take a seat, sir,' she said, gesturing towards it as if he might not know what it was for. 'What would you like to drink?'

Ruso declined. In the circumstances, it hardly seemed appropriate.

Bassus went back to whatever he was doing behind the counter. Stichus seated himself in the corner with the air of a man who had spent long years honing the skill of waiting for action.

Ruso's gaze ran along the loops of gold braid that had been painted at waist-height along the deep red of the wall beside him. Similar loops ran along the adjacent wall. A large tassel bloomed in the corner, probably inspired by the painter's discovery that the two braids – which must have been started at opposite ends of the walls – weren't quite going to meet up.

The boy Lucco reappeared at the foot of the stairs, and assured him – with more optimism than accuracy, as it turned out – that the mistress would not be long. The girls went back to cleaning.

Merula evidently took just as long as all other women to get ready. Ruso was pondering why, when seated at a bar table, the average soldier felt compelled to carve his initials into it, when a female voice from the top of the stairs snapped, 'Chloe!'

The girl with the ankle-chain looked up in alarm.

'Don't rub so hard, you stupid girl! You'll have all the paint off!'

The figure sweeping down the stairs was, he assumed, Merula.

Ruso had no idea what that silky material was called but he knew it was expensive because his wife had needed something like it for a dinner party and then managed to lean across a brazier and burn a hole in it. Merula looked like a woman who would be more careful. The fabric was draped to make the most of an elegant figure. Hair which

36

could almost have been naturally black was pinned back, leaving little tendrils of curl framing her face. As she reached the foot of the stairs, Ruso observed that the eyelids were dark, the lips red and the cheeks subtly pink. It was well done. Only the lines that ran between nose and mouth suggested that Merula would not look quite as good in daylight.

The lines deepened round something approaching a smile as she greeted him.

'Gaius Petreius Ruso,' he announced, standing. 'Medicus with the Twentieth.'

'Gaius Petreius. Ah yes, the new doctor. Did my girls offer you a drink?'

He nodded. 'Is there somewhere we could talk in private?'

Merula clapped her hands and called, 'Out!'

Instantly the girls stopped what they were doing. Chloe threw the cloth down and beckoned the lad to follow her into the kitchen.

Merula said, 'Thank you, boys.'

Bassus and Stichus glanced at each other, then retreated to stand guard outside.

'Now, Doctor.' Merula seated herself opposite him. 'What can we do for you?'

Ruso scratched his ear. There were good reasons why he was now facing the task of breaking bad news to this woman. Principal amongst them was that Valens was busy with morning clinic and the junior Regional Officer on duty, whose job it surely was, was already late for a meeting. 'You know the sort of thing,' the man had explained from the back of his horse, swinging one leg forward so the groom could tighten the girth. 'Just show them we take it very seriously but whatever you do, don't promise we'll do anything about it.'

Ruso cleared his throat again, reminded himself that the woman wasn't a relative, and began. 'I'm afraid I have bad news.'

Merula stared at him for a moment, then lowered her head and shaded her eyes with one manicured hand.

'It's about –'

She said, 'Saufeia.'

'Yes.'

'I was afraid of this.' The woman sighed. 'No matter how many times you try to tell these girls, some of them just don't listen.' She looked up. 'What happened to her?'

'Her body was found in the river the day before yesterday and brought into the hospital. She was identified late last night.'

'She had only been with us for ten days,' said Merula, inadvertently explaining why none of the hospital staff, many of whom would be intimately acquainted with the local tavern girls, had recognized her. 'Did she drown?'

'There were, er –' Ruso hesitated. 'There was some bruising around the throat,' he said, 'and her neck was broken.'

'I see.' Merula paused, then shook her head. 'Poor, silly Saufeia.'

Poor, silly Saufeia, who had ended up naked and muddy and practically bald, unmourned until a gawper who shouldn't have been in the mortuary at all recognized the birthmark on her thigh.

'Was there any family?'

Merula shook her head.

'I don't suppose you have any idea who might have –?'

'Who might have taken advantage of a girl looking for business with no protection? Outside an Army base?'

There was no need to answer.

Merula glanced through the open shutters to where one

38

of the doormen was leaning against the wall of the bakery opposite, eating. 'The boys will blame themselves, but they can't watch them day and night.' A bitter smile twisted the red lips. 'After we realized she'd gone, the girls were hoping she'd run off with a customer. It does happen.'

'You didn't report her as a runaway?'

'We were busy. I suppose we might have passed her name on to a slave-hunter sooner or later, but to be honest I doubt she would have been worth the recovery fee. She wasn't really suitable for this kind of work.'

'When did you last see her?'

'Five days ago. Early in the evening. She must have sneaked out when nobody was looking.'

Ruso said, 'She appears to have died quite soon after that.'

Merula understood. 'I shall make the funeral arrangements as quickly as possible.'

Relieved, Ruso got to his feet. He acknowledged the woman's thanks with a nod. Her composure had made a difficult task much easier than it might have been.

The girls emerged from the kitchen with a promptness which could only mean they had been listening behind the door. Ruso was passing Stichus in the doorway when a voice called, 'Sir?'

He turned. Chloe, with the lank-haired girl hovering behind her, said, 'You don't know who did it, do you, sir?'

Ruso shook his head. 'I don't,' he said. 'But if you remember anything suspicious, you should go to the fort straight away and ask for the duty Regional Control Officer.'

7

She ran for the door. The fat one got there first. She dodged back behind a stack of barrels. He came in after her. She tried to scramble out. The barrels were crashing down and rolling across the floor. She tried to leap free but her feet slipped in something wet. The smell of beer mingled with the stink of the fat one's breath as he loomed above her, raising the crowbar, his mouth twisted with the shouting. She tried to shield herself. The crowbar swung down. She heard the crack. Felt herself jolt with the blow.

She was in the white room again. The familiar pain was pulsing through her arm, but instead of her own bones looking back at her, the arm was hidden inside a thick bandage and strapped across her chest.

So. She was still in this world.

The door was opening. She closed her eyes. A hand was laid on her forehead. In the ugly sounds of Latin the man announced that it was not a fever.

'She's having bad dreams,' he said, apparently talking to someone else. She pretended to be asleep, trying not to flinch as the bandages were tweaked and tidied while two men talked about post-operative fevers and swelling and things she did not understand.

Bad dreams.

She must have called out. She hoped she had not spoken in Latin. She tried to remember, but her mind had been travelling in strange places, fleeing from the pain and the bitter medicine the man kept making her drink. He had told her she was safe from the fat one, but what did he know? When the medicine gave her sleep, the fat one returned.

There were other dreams, too. A man dressed in green who held her down and whispered in her ear while wolves tore at her arm. Voices echoing behind closed doors. Birds singing. The sun with four corners –

No. She must try to think clearly. *The sun has no corners. The white room has a square window in the outside wall. I am in a white bed. A tall, thin table stands beside the bed. A black cup and a jug are on the table. Behind the door is a stool.* The man who brought the medicine had pulled the stool up to the bedside and sat down to ask, '*Quid nomen tibi est?*' as if he were talking to a small child.

When she had failed to answer, he repeated the question. She had continued to stare at his dark eyes, at his unshaven chin, as if she could not understand what he was saying. His Greek was easier to ignore because she genuinely did not understand it. She did not recognize his third attempt at all until, reciting it in her mind after he had given up and left, she began to suspect that it could be a mangled version of her own tongue, impossible to grasp unless you had first heard him ask in Latin: What is your name?

She had not heard her real name spoken since she was captured. For two winters she had been 'girl' at best, the Northerners at first deliberately refusing to honour her with the use of her name and later, she supposed, forgetting what it was. When the other slaves had asked what to call her, she had invented something. She had spoken to them – to everyone – as little as possible. But Romans were full of questions.

How old are you? Where do you come from? Do you understand what I'm saying? Does it hurt when I do that? Do you need to pass water? Did you really fall down the stairs? Do you know a girl with red hair? They seemed to have lost interest in the girl with red hair now. But they persisted with the other questions. *Quid nomen tibi est?*

She was not about to offer her name up to a stranger. It was almost the only thing she possessed that nobody had stolen.

A voice was asking, 'How much poppy are you giving her?'

The left side of the bed heaved as the blanket was tucked in. 'No more until nightfall.' She felt herself rolled the other way as he tucked in the opposite side. 'I want her awake enough to eat.'

8

Ruso was considering trying a different poultice on an infected thumb that he didn't much like the look of when Valens knocked on the door to announce that the *Sirius* was coming in to dock on the midday tide.

The *Sirius*! After three months, Ruso and his possessions were about to be reunited. The last time he had seen them was when he had left Africa, fully expecting to return to his comfortable rooms after his leave. Instead, he was sharing condemned lodgings at the opposite end of the Empire with the untidiest medic in the Army.

He said, 'I'll get down to the docks when I've finished ward rounds.'

'I'll go down now,' Valens offered. 'Make sure they don't drop anything.'

Several patients later, Ruso finally escaped from the hospital. As he nodded to Aesculapius on the way out, he thought he heard the patter of claws on floorboards. He turned to see something brown and hairy and just above knee-height vanishing around the corner of the front entrance. When he got outside, there was no sign of it.

There was no time to investigate. He hurried along the Via Praetoria to the cashier's office, where the chief clerk beckoned him past the queue and into the office to tell him that the donation to the Aesculapian Fund was very generous.

'Donation?' Ruso frowned, wondering if the man was being sarcastic about his two and a half denarii.

'From the owner of Merula's bar, sir. In gratitude for the hospital's services to the deceased.'

Ruso remembered. The grim-faced Bassus had arrived early this morning with a cart to carry away the body of poor, silly Saufeia. Afterwards he had mentioned making some sort of contribution to the hospital fund, and Ruso had told him to go to the pay office. 'Do you know where that is?'

'Know it?' Bassus had snorted. 'I built it.'

Ruso, encouraged by the size of the gift Bassus had delivered and the clerks' apparent belief that he was the cause of it, increased the size of the loan he had come to request. No doubt the clerks would talk, but with luck the rumours of his cash problems would not travel too far before they were brought to a halt by Hadrian's promised double bonus. As the trumpet was blaring the change of watch he emerged from the West Gate of the fort with an advance in his purse that was enough to redeem his possessions many times over.

On the way to the docks he passed a couple of bars that made Merula's look like a high-class establishment for country gentlemen. Glancing at a rusty cage hung outside a door, he saw a bird with scraggy feathers and a vicious-looking beak. He thought of Claudia's singing bird, the pampered pet released by a hired slave-girl in a misguided fit of kindness. The next morning a noisy bunch of squabbling sparrows had been shooed away to reveal the little songster bedraggled and lifeless on the pavement. Claudia's fury had been vented on Ruso, since he had sent the slave back to her owner with a demand for compensation before Claudia had a chance to punish her.

Saufeia, it seemed, had understood no more about the dangers of freedom than the hapless songbird. She must have been very naive indeed to abandon the protection of Merula's graceless but efficient 'boys' to take her chances on the narrow streets of a military port like Deva. It struck him that whoever was charged with tracking down the culprit was going to have a difficult job. She would have been a target not only for vicious customers, but for the owners of businesses who did not want the competition.

Between the baths and the riverside warehouses, one of those businesses was displaying its merchandise. White shoulders and big earrings and fat ankles gleamed in the late September sunshine. Other establishments relied upon lurid paintings beside an open street door, but perhaps the owner of the fat-ankled and big-earringed couldn't afford a painter. Either that, or he believed the valiantly grinning females sprawled across the bench outside his crumbling walls were genuinely tempting. Ruso wondered how long a man would have to be at sea before he would agree.

His mood lifted as he approached the wharf, passing an altar to Neptune and a couple of surprisingly elegant houses probably built by traders wanting to enjoy the sight of the sea god safely delivering their latest cargoes. Ahead of him, a light breeze was lifting the broad river into a glitter around the silhouettes of fat-bellied merchant ships and a scatter of fishing boats. A slender trireme was moored at the distant end of the wooden jetty. Ruso paused to watch as a fishing boat which had turned in from the main course of the river dropped its sail and began to row in under the stern of the trireme. The shriek of gulls rose above faint shouts of orders and a chant of *One! Two! Three!* from a team shifting something heavy.

A man who had seen little of the world might think this

was a beautiful view. A man who had never stood by a sea that was translucent, under a sky so brilliantly blue it hurt the eyes, would probably think this was a grand place to be.

Scanning the painted merchant ships tied up along the jetty, Ruso wondered which had brought the remains of his belongings, and how many years it would be before he could load them up again and have them sent to a posting back in civilization. The bars and the whorehouses would be the same wherever soldiers were stationed, but they didn't have to be set in a chilly place where grey sloppy waves retreated twice a day to leave the land and water separated by glutinous brown mud flats. No wonder the hospital was stocking up on cough mixture for the winter. Unfortunately the nature of the Britons was such that the Army wouldn't let him prescribe a mass transfer of the legion to a healthier climate.

Valens' letters had made Britannia sound entertaining. The islands, apparently, were bursting with six-foot warrior women and droopy-moustached, poetry-spouting fanatics who roamed the misty mountains stirring up quarrelsome tribesmen in the guise of religion.

His own observation of Britannia now led Ruso to suspect that Valens had deliberately lured him here to relieve the boredom.

The bizarre movements of the British seas had been a novelty, but not one with which he desired a better acquaintance. When his ship had docked in Rutupiae the captain had offered him the chance to stay on board and sail round to Deva. He had declined, taken a lift as far as Londinium with an eye surgeon who was on the way to operate on the Governor's wife, then hired a horse and spent several days riding north. He had, he now realized, probably passed Chief Administrator Priscus travelling in the opposite direction on his way to discuss contracts for Army medical supplies. Had he but known, he would have seized Priscus and wrested the hospital keys from his grasp. As it was, the trip had been an interesting introduction to his new province.

It had been hard to imagine the lush meadows and busy little towns of Britannia as the setting for the ghastly massacres witnessed by the old and toothless who could remember the rebellion. But by the fifth day of travelling, the hills had become steeper, the military traffic heavier and the towns less welcoming. Here, it was easier to see the problem with keeping order. The road passed through stretches of dark woods where the occasional column of smoke in the distance might have signalled charcoal-burning or someone cooking breakfast or an unwary tax-collector being ambushed. The farmland was rich still, but the houses were primitive: mud-plastered round huts squatting under mushrooms of thatch and not a window or a water-tap in sight. At one point he passed a knot of grim-faced civilians being marched along the road under guard from a squad of auxiliaries, and half a day's ride further north there was a double crucifixion at the roadside. More civilians huddled weeping underneath the bloodied figures, while a military guard gazed on with studied indifference, and an officer's horse, the only creature at the scene who was definitely innocent, raised its head and whinnied to Ruso's mount in the apparent hope that someone had at last come to take it away.

The only trouble he had encountered on the journey north was a minor brawl in a roadside inn, but the civilians Ruso met on the road looked as sullen as the weather when they stepped aside to let him pass. And these were supposed to be the friendly tribes. Still, many a man had made his reputation at this moist and chilly frontier of empire, and Ruso, who had needed a change for reasons he wasn't intending to confide to anyone here, was happy to let it be thought that he considered Britain a smart career move.

'Fresh fish, sir?' A woman who was out of breath from pushing a cart up the slope lifted a cloth to display glistening silver bodies. She grinned, showing a gap where her front teeth should have been. 'Just landed in time for dinner!'

Ruso shook his head.

In the space of a hundred paces he also declined a bucket of mussels, a jar of pepper, a delivery of coal, a dinner set, an amphora of wine, a bolt of cloth to make the finest bedspread in Deva, some indefinable things in the shape of small sausages, and an introduction to an exotic dancer. Stepping on to the quay, he dodged a trolley being pushed by a small boy who couldn't see over it. Behind him a voice shouted, 'Tray of plums, sir?'

It was comforting to know that he still had the appearance of a man with money to spend.

The quay stank of fish and weed with undertones of sandalwood. Somebody must have dropped something expensive. The crews were rushing to load cargoes while the tide was in, shifting crates and sacks and baskets of whatever it took to maintain civilization in this corner of the Empire before the tide forced the captains to move their vessels further out or be stranded on the mud. Ruso wove his way between carts and trolleys, skirting a pile of slate that must have come from the western mountains and would probably be someone's roof by the end of the week. The stack of jars labelled 'Salinae' would be loaded up and shipped out. He knew that not because he was interested in exports but because one of the legionaries guarding the salt-springs had somehow managed to impale himself on a fencing spike, and Ruso had made him talk about his duties in great detail as a distraction from the efforts to remove it.

A wide-eyed brown monkey peered at him from a crate, its childlike fingers wrapped around the bars of its prison. Further along he passed a pale group of chained slaves. They looked even less thrilled to be here than the monkey was. A couple of them seemed to be gazing at the green weed heaving against the legs of the jetty and wondering whether to fling themselves into it. He hoped they would have enough sense to realize that since they were chained, they would only be fished out again and revived to have 'Tendency to suicide' written on their sale tags. A warning to buyers that might as well read, 'Please work me to death.'

None of the ships moored along the quayside was the one he sought. Ruso turned and added his footsteps to the dull thunder of boots making their way along the jetty.

The second ship out bore the name *Sirius* in jaunty blue letters, and beside it Ruso recognized the figure leaning back on a chair with his feet on a small, upturned table.

'Bad news,' said Valens, rising to greet him. 'Some sort of cock-up.' He waved one hand towards the carved chair he had been sitting on. It was facing two large trunks, on top of which the table had been upended. Ruso saw his name, and the words 'LEG XX DEVA BR' chalked on each item. 'You'll have to talk to them,' said Valens. 'I can't get any sense out of them. They keep telling me this is all there is. Jupiter knows where they've sent the rest of it.'

Ruso knelt and checked the seals on the trunks. 'No, it all seems to be here.'

Valens looked blank. 'Where's your furniture?'

'Termites,' explained Ruso, who had anticipated the question. 'Africa's full of them.'

'Termites?' Valens scratched his head and stared at the table. 'Termites ate the Lucky Earthquake Bed?'

Ruso shrugged. 'Turn your back for a moment over there and the damn things eat everything.' Of all the items that were gone, he would miss that bed the most. It had been a reminder of a time when he had, briefly, been mistaken for a divine being. Now the divine being was reduced to telling lies to explain his lack of furniture.

Valens was leaning down and peering at the locked trunks. 'You don't think you've brought any with you, do you?'

'They'll have fumigated it,' Ruso assured him. 'They'd have to. Long voyage, wooden ship . . .'

'I'll go and get a cart,' Valens offered, moving hastily away from the articles that looked like trunks but could turn out to be Trojan horses.

Ruso lowered himself into his chair to wait and wondered who was now sleeping on the Lucky Earthquake Bed. It had been a wedding present from his father and stepmother. In conventional respects it hadn't been a great success. The only time the earth had truly moved in it for him and Claudia, it had also moved for the rest of Antioch. They had clung to each other under the heavy oak frame while roof-beams smashed down on top of it and tiles shattered all around them. When the shaking seemed to be over, they crawled out to find that others had not been as lucky. All around was confusion: screams of pain, shouts for help, people scrabbling at piles of rubble, calling the names of their loved ones, and the smell of smoke in the dusty air as fires took hold in the ruins. Had he but known it, the earthquake had signalled the final collapse of his marriage.

He managed to send Claudia to safety with friends who were heading for the countryside. Then he headed back towards the nearest Army base: they would surely be organizing rescue parties.

Moments after he set out, the earth shook again. He flung

himself to the ground with his hands over his head and hoped Claudia was somewhere out in the open.

The shaking stopped. For a moment all was silence, save the creak and rumble of more buildings collapsing. Ruso lifted his head. A man close by was calling for help.

No one else seemed to have heard the voice, which was coming from an ornate building that was still partially standing. Squinting through the dust and cupping one hand over his nose, Ruso picked his way around the ruin. The only door he could find had most of a wall collapsed against it. Finally he managed to squeeze himself in through a small window.

The room stank of burning oil. Black smoke was seeping through cracks in one elegantly painted wall. A smartly dressed body was sprawled on the floor. Blood was seeping from beneath a heavy cabinet that lay where the head should have been.

'Over here!' called the voice. 'Under the table!'

Through the murk, Ruso saw a corner of a table sticking out from under a pile of plaster and brick. Trying to move quickly without pulling more masonry down on top of himself, he managed to clear a way through to the gap beneath. A figure grey with dust crawled out, grabbed his arm and started to thank him just as the floor gave a sickening heave. 'Move!' yelled Ruso, dragging the man across the room and pushing him head-first out of the window before scrambling after him.

Behind them, what was left of the building seemed to groan in despair before finally crashing in on itself. They were still peering at it through the clouded air when a voice cried, 'Your majesty! Oh my lord, you're safe!' and someone fell at the feet of the man Ruso had just rescued. The man reached down and helped the servant up, still staring at the ruin from which he had so narrowly escaped. That was when Ruso realized why he looked vaguely familiar. It wasn't a half-remembered patient after all. He had just rescued the Emperor Trajan.

Over the next few days and nights the tremors had continued, claiming more victims from the rescuers trying to reach people trapped under the rubble. Ruso struggled to save the dying and patch up the injured with no equipment, no water, no sleep and nowhere to turn for advice. Rumours abounded: that the whole country had been devastated, that nowhere outside the city had been hit, that the Army was bringing elephants to clear the streets, that plague had broken out, that Antioch was being punished by the gods, that a man crushed to death had come back to life and that a mysterious being, surely a god, had entered the building where the Emperor Trajan was trapped and spirited him out through the window. It never occurred to Ruso to try and set the record straight. For the first time in days, he had found something to laugh about.

Claudia, with whom he unwisely tried to share the joke, later cited it as one of her reasons for leaving. Following *You abandoned me in the earthquake!* was *You had a chance to make something of yourself with the Emperor and you refused to do anything about it!*

Three weeks after Claudia moved out, Ruso had signed up to a fresh start in Africa with the Army. Now he stared at his pathetic collection of furniture and wondered if his wife had been right.

Valens was back, bringing a gnarled creature who had evidently spent all his money on blue tattoos and couldn't afford to bathe.

'I suppose you'll want to carry on using the spare bed, then?' inquired Valens as the tattooed one moved the table aside, lifted both trunks at once and set off with them down the jetty.

Ruso picked up the chair. 'Just until I get sorted out.'

Valens reached for the legs of the table and swung it up over his head like a large sunshade. 'With what these people charge,' he said, 'we ought to give up medicine and take up shifting furniture.'

They reached the end of the jetty. The trunks had been loaded on to a cart that smelled of old fish and appeared to be held together with greasy twine and dirt.

Valens wrinkled his nose and stepped back from the cart. 'Were you serious about those termites?'

'The smell from that cart should finish them off.'

'You're not in some sort of trouble, are you?'

Ruso watched the man roping down all that remained of his furniture and said, 'No, of course not.'

'You won't find much to buy over here, but we've got a few decent carpenters. I'm thinking of having a proper dining suite knocked up.'

'In that house?'

'No. I told you, that one's supposed to have been flattened weeks ago. I mean in my new rooms. The ones I'll get when they make me up to CMO.'

'So he's definitely not coming back?' Ruso was aware that no one expected the hot springs of Aquae Sulis to rejuvenate the present Chief Medical Officer, but so far there had been no official word of his retirement.

'He's bound to go before long,' said Valens. 'I'll save him the bother of trailing back up here and have his things sent on.'

'And you think they're making you up to CMO?'

'Why not?'

'Because they might choose me.'

'Bollocks.'

'I've got combat experience.'

'But you don't know anybody yet, Ruso. Anyway, you don't need the money like I do.'

'No?'

'I thought you were supposed to inherit from your father? Aren't you the oldest son?'

'There were a lot of expenses,' said Ruso. 'You know what funerals are like.'

'Didn't he have land over in Gaul?'

'My brother's looking after it. The farm has a lot of people to support.'

'Giddup!' The carter gave one of the beasts a flick with his stick and the cart lurched forward. They followed its creaking progress up the slope.

'What you need,' said Valens suddenly, 'is a rich widow.'

Ruso noted this suggestion to add to his list of things he didn't need at all. He had no intention of explaining to Valens that what he *did* need was either the CMO's pay packet or a collection of lucrative private patients and some peace and quiet to get on with his writing. Now that he was living in a backwater with no earthquakes or family members or ex-wife to distract him, he hoped to complete the work he had already started and abandoned several times. *G. Petreius Ruso's Concise Guide to Military First Aid* would be detailed enough to be useful in the field, and short enough to be copied on to very small scrolls which would fit into a soldier's pack. The copying would be expensive, but once those copies had been sold, there would be a double profit – one in cash and one, he felt sure, in lives and limbs saved. What he didn't need was Valens making helpful suggestions, or worse still, taking up the idea himself.

'Did I tell you,' Valens continued, recalling Ruso to the

subject in hand, 'I'm thinking of proposing to the Second Spear's daughter?'

'Is she a rich widow?'

'Gods, no. She's sixteen. Rather attractive, actually, considering what her father looks like.'

Whatever the Second Spear looked like, he must have been on centurion's pay for some years before he had been promoted to a command in the top cohort. He would be a wealthy man.

'Only child, I suppose?' ventured Ruso.

Valens grinned. 'Divorce has turned you sadly cynical, my friend.'

'Not divorce,' said Ruso. 'Marriage.'

9

Ruso lay in the darkness and listened to the scurry of the mice in the dining room, and then to the patter of the dog. There followed some skidding and squeaking and a crash, then a long silence. It was finally broken by the wail of third watch being blown, and the creak of his bed as he rolled over and vowed to move out of this madhouse as soon as he could afford it.

By the time he woke again, Valens had gone on duty. The house was quiet. As soon as he had breakfasted and bathed (there would be no time later), he would be able to make some progress with his writing.

Ruso wandered into the kitchen and picked up half a loaf of bread and a chunk of cheese that had been left out on the kitchen table. There were, he observed with relief, no mouse-droppings on the table this morning. Then he glanced across at the little box on the window-sill and saw that the pile Valens was collecting had grown considerably. Abandoning the food, Ruso strode back to his room, pulled on his overtunic and went across to the hospital.

The girl was still asleep. He did not wake her. Valens would check her over during ward round.

The words 'Closed for improvements' had now been chalked on the main fort baths for so long that they had grown faint with age. Apparently half the builders had been called away on more pressing peacekeeping duties. The rest were clearly determined not to be accused of rushing their work. The height of the weeds growing round the feet of the scaffolding struts suggested to Ruso that it would be weeks before they got round to fixing the hospital roof. Months until they demolished the old centurion's house in which he now lived, which Valens had somehow persuaded them to leave standing when the adjoining barrack block was flattened ready for rebuilding. The rebuilding hadn't even been started. The reopening of the main military baths was surely far more urgent, but even that didn't seem likely to happen this month – let alone this morning.

Using the hospital baths was out of the question. The thought of being trapped naked with a roomful of patients comparing their symptoms made him shudder. He would go out to the public baths. This early, there would be no queues. With no mistreated slave-girls to distract him, he should soon return clean, invigorated and ready to make progress with *The Concise Guide to Military First Aid*.

First he needed a decent breakfast. Recent disappointments at other shops had confirmed that it was worth the trouble of walking across to the bakery opposite Merula's, where he savoured the smell before handing over his cash for a fresh roll. The crust crackled as he tore it. Steam rose into the cool morning air. He sat on the bench, leaned back with his legs stretched out over the pavement and took a mouthful.

The streets were as quiet as was usual in the mornings: so quiet that he could catch the occasional bellow of orders from the parade ground, where most of the legion would be sweating their way through daily training. So far his name had not appeared on the training rota, an oversight that would no doubt be rectified when the Chief Administrator returned.

A couple of women called into the bakery to load their

shopping-baskets. A small boy passed down the street, bumping along a cartload of apples cushioned in straw. A settled hen squawked in annoyance as a woman emerged from the doorway where it was sitting and batted it out of the way with a broom. Across the street the shutters were still closed. Ruso gazed idly at the advertisements on Merula's whitewashed walls.

Beneath a picture of a bowl and a jug 'Best Food in Deva' and 'Fine Wines, Low Prices' had been daubed in red for long enough to fade and be refurbished – not very accurately, so the faded paint still appeared at the edges of some of the letters. He was surprised to see Saufeia's name still listed under 'Beautiful Girls!': a bizarre memorial in sharp fresh paint. Asellina and Irene had evidently moved on and been wiped away with a single coat of white which left them still faintly legible. Mariamne and Chloe were listed, but not the nervous and pregnant Daphne. Customers had scrawled comments next to the names. Most were predictable. Something that looked very much like 'Juicy!' was inscribed next to Chloe. Someone had attempted to scrub off Saufeia's only testimonial but it was still possible to make out the faint scrawl of 'Snooty bitch'.

An elderly man with one leg was lurching towards the bakery on crutches, managing to balance despite a bulging sack tied over one shoulder. Seeing Ruso's interest in the bar he called, 'You're too hasty, boss!'

Ruso turned, but his scowl failed to stop the cackle of laughter and the announcement that, 'Them girls don't get up till it's time to go to bed!'

The last thing Ruso wanted this morning was a close encounter with them girls, or indeed with anything female. He was about to leave when another handcart came rumbling along the street. It paused outside Merula's. Its owner, a whistling man in a paint-spattered tunic, unloaded a box and put it down in front of the shutters.

'Don't get up till it's time to go to bed, hah!' chortled the legless one for the benefit of anyone who had missed it the first time and lurched off down the street.

Ruso sat down again. For reasons he could not articulate he wanted to see the dead girl's name removed from that wall.

The painter fetched a cloth out of the box and cleaned the word 'Saufeia' and the scrubbed patch next to it. Then he stepped back and surveyed the rest of the wall.

Ruso stepped across to join him. 'You need to take that name off, not clean it up.'

The painter squinted at the wall. '"Mariamne bites". That'd better go and all.' He stepped forward again and rubbed at the words, which had been scratched on with charcoal. 'Keeping me busy, this lot are. Can't keep the staff, see?'

He bent over the box and lifted a brush. He paused to finger a silver charm in the form of a phallus which was slung around his throat, then with one stroke he reduced Saufeia's name to a red shadow showing through the white.

'Bad luck, having that up there,' he observed. 'Might as well finish off the other one, too.'

'Other one?'

'The one that run off with the sailor.' He reached up and obliterated the faint outline of 'Asellina' with a fresh brushload of white paint. 'She won't be back.'

'I think I've met somebody who knew her,' said Ruso. It had not occurred to him that the porter's missing girlfriend might have worked in a place like this.

The man grinned. 'Round here, you'll have met quite a few.'

Asellina had probably weighed up the offers of several admirers, and the luckless porter had not come top of the list.

The painter stepped back and squinted at the wall. 'Looks a bit patchy, don't it? I told 'em the whole lot wants doing again, but her inside won't part with the money. Knew that Saufeia, then, did you?'

'No.'

'Something funny going on there. I reckon she had a premonition.'

Ruso, who spent much of his professional life battling against superstition, could not resist asking, 'Why?'

'I never took much notice at the time, but she stuck her head round the door while I was working, took one look and said in that posh voice of hers, "You've spelled me wrong." I'd gone and put two f's in, see? So I went to put it right and she said, "You really needn't bother, I shan't be here much longer."'

The man touched the charm again, then recharged the brush and ran it across the wall again. In its wake, Saufeia's name, correctly spelled with one 'f', grew fainter still. ''Course, I changed it anyway,' he said. 'I like to do a proper job.' He put the brush back in the pot. 'Might as well not have bothered.'

He picked up the red brush. 'Here's something to cheer the lads up.' In the space where 'Mariamne Bites' could still faintly be read, he sketched out the words 'NEW COOK'.

'Merula says I got to put it in big letters,' he explained, 'so everybody knows. She don't want a bad name after them oysters.'

'She's sacked the old cook?' said Ruso.

'Packed her off to the dealer. Lucky that doctor didn't drop dead, or they'd all be facing the inquisitors.'

'How many people were ill?'

'Just the one,' replied the painter, frowning with concentration as he led the brush down the first stroke of the 'N'. 'That were lucky, weren't it?'

'Not for the doctor.'

'That's what they're saying,' agreed the painter. 'Peculiar, like, just him and no one else. Anyway, won't happen again. New cook, see?'

It had been a day where everything was more complicated than it should have been. When he reached the baths Ruso found he was the wrong sex and had to wait outside ('Women only till the sixth hour, sir – it *is* on the door, sir . . .'). This afternoon a signaller who had been sent to have a head cut stitched turned out to have tripped over something he hadn't seen. Alerted by the young man's reluctance to meet his gaze, Ruso had insisted on checking his eyesight after the wound was treated. Within seconds he had discovered not only the advancing shadow of cataract in both eyes, but some inkling of the desperate and complex cover-up undertaken by the man and his comrades. Blindness would be the end of any soldier's career, but a signaller with failing eyesight would be invalided out sooner than most.

'I can manage all right, Doc.'

'Really?' Ruso gestured towards a notice on the surgery wall. 'Read me some of that.'

The man turned and stared: not at the notice, but at the blank wall to its left. Then he moved his head and eyed the periphery of the notice from the other side. Finally he said, 'The light's not very good in here, is it?'

Ruso said nothing.

The man lowered his bandaged head into his hands. 'My girl thinks it's an illness,' he said. 'She thinks I'll get better.'

'Have you spoken to any of the other medics?'

The man shook his head. 'I don't need to,' he said. 'I watched this happen to my father.'

It was too early to disclose the idea forming in Ruso's mind. He said merely, 'I'll have a word with my colleague.'

The man gave a bitter laugh. 'Does he work miracles? Because if he does, you tell him I've got a little lad of two and a pregnant girlfriend to support.'

Ruso said, 'What about other family?'

'None of mine. Her people want me to go for promotion so we can get properly married.' He paused, not needing to explain the irony. He would never be promoted now, and the medical discharge that would free him for marriage would also render him an undesirable son-in-law. He looked up. 'We need the money, Doc. Can't you just . . . keep quiet for a bit?'

Ruso frowned. 'If you're sent out into the field you'd be as much danger to us as to the enemy.'

'I've managed so far.'

'And who's been covering up for you?'

The signaller said nothing.

Finally Ruso said, 'You've had a serious bang on the head. I'm recommending you stay here for two days for observation.'

Ruso sent the man down to one of the wards. As soon as the rest of his patients were dealt with he went straight to the records room and scrawled an urgent letter to the eye specialist he had met on the ship. He was not optimistic. Even if the specialist agreed to take the case, the delicate surgery required would be terrifying for the patient and difficult for the doctor, and would possibly hasten the blindness it was supposed to cure.

On the way back to his lodgings Ruso glanced across at the builders working on the roof of the bath-house. He wished he had chosen a trade where almost anything that went wrong could be fixed with a hammer.

He was about to turn the corner when a voice called after him, 'Sir?'

He stopped. One of the hospital orderlies was hurrying after him. 'You're wanted, sir!'

'Officer Valens is on duty now,' said Ruso, who had been hoping to get on with the *Concise Guide*.

'No, sir, it's you who's wanted.'

'Who by?'

'The Second Spear, sir. You're to report to him straight away at the Regional Control office.'

'Stand easy, Doctor.' The Second Spear settled into his seat, rested muscular arms on a desk that seemed too small for him and gave Ruso the kind of look that said nonsense would not be tolerated.

Ruso decided he did not envy Valens the challenge of persuading this man to hand over his daughter in marriage.

'We've had a complaint,' continued the Second Spear. 'About a body.'

'Sir?'

'A girl from a bar.'

'Yes, sir. Merula's.'

'You took it in?'

'Yes, sir. Nobody knew who she was at the time.'

The Second Spear nodded. 'Probably just as well. It might have been somebody's wife. Most of us keep our women well guarded but you always get the odd one who thinks she knows better. So then what happened to it?'

Ruso explained. His pauses were punctuated by grunts of assent from across the desk, followed by, 'Right. So who cut the hair off?'

'I don't know, sir. It was like that when she was brought in.'

'And you didn't think to warn the owner?'

'No, sir.'

'Well, they're not happy. They got a bit of a shock when they saw it and they want to know if we did it.'

'Absolutely not, sir. You can check with the gate guards.

She was found by a couple of fishermen. You could ask them.'

The Second Spear shook his head. 'Doesn't matter. As long as we can't be blamed for it. I'll send someone over to calm them down. And tell them to forget any ideas about compensation.'

'Thank you, sir. Any luck finding the culprit yet?'

'No. Don't expect we ever will. We'll keep an eye open, of course, but I doubt much will turn up. No witnesses, of course. It's the usual story: these people are quick enough to complain, but blind, deaf and dumb when you start asking questions. Turns out the girl was offered protection and chose not to take it.'

'She might not have understood the dangers, sir. She'd only been here ten days.' It was about the same length of time that Ruso had been here himself.

'Hmph. Not what you'd call bright, these locals. Did she think they'd got two of our lads down there on security for fun?'

Ruso said nothing.

'This will knock a bit of sense into the rest of them,' continued the Second Spear. 'At least for a month or two. Bloody nuisance, all of them. Haven't been here long, have you?'

'No, sir.'

'In a civilized country – even parts of Britannia – we'd leave the town council or tribal elders or what-have-you to sort this kind of thing out. Round here, just because they're living on Army land, they expect us to wipe their backsides for them. If it was up to me, I'd have a curfew and flog anything that moves after dark. Still, we should have a bit of peace and quiet for a while. You won't find many women hanging around the streets tonight.'

'No, sir,' agreed Ruso, who had not planned to look for any.

The Second Spear leaned back in his chair and folded his arms. 'When I was up with the Ninth,' he said, 'one of the medics took in a body. Thought he was being helpful. The natives got the idea he was cutting it up for anatomy lessons. Caused a riot. Ended up with a whole lot more bodies, three of them ours. My advice, Doctor, is not to get involved with the locals if you can help it.'

'Yes sir,' said Ruso, glad the Second Spear did not know who was in Room Twelve.

I 2

Ruso had discharged his duties for the day. There was nothing further he could do about the signaller's cataracts. His superiors would make any decisions about the dead girl, and he had left orders that he was to be called if there was a crisis with the live one. Alone in his bedroom, he was free to get on with drafting the next section of the *Concise Guide to Military First Aid*. Unfortunately, it was proving more difficult than he had expected.

He had imagined that once his reference books arrived, he would get straight back to work, freshly motivated after so long a break. Instead, he was sitting in his room scowling at a writing tablet on which he had written a title and two lines of notes before delving into the trunk to look up something which turned out to be in a different scroll from the one he expected and to be less relevant than he had remembered it. The bed was now scattered with unravelled scrolls and note tablets and a few scraps of broken pot on which he had scribbled passing thoughts when nothing else had been to hand, and he was still stuck on line three. His mind, apparently unwilling to apply itself to ordering his work, seemed to be seizing every chance to wander off. It was futile and unproductive to wonder why a slave with a posh voice and the ability to read her own name had been working in a bar in the first place. No wonder Merula had said she was not suited to the job. But then why –

A shout of laughter from beyond his bedroom door recalled Ruso to his task. He reread what he had written, picked up the stylus, then paused to glance over his notes again. It didn't help that Valens was on call this evening, unable to leave the house unless summoned by duty. Across in what passed for a dining room (they had not bothered to shut the door, of course), his colleague was discussing horses with a couple of friends who had loud voices and even louder laughs. Valens had invited him to join them, but as soon as he explained that he had work to do they seemed to forget all about him.

At least they didn't keep popping in to ask how it was going. The *Concise Guide* had been conceived – the only thing that was, thank the gods – during his marriage to Claudia. It had been a welcome retreat. The early work had progressed fluently, but several chapters in, it had occurred to him that he was no longer being concise. Instantly, the flow of words seemed to dry up. While he waited for inspiration to return, he went back to the beginning and edited the first chapters to half their original length. That was when Claudia asked to see how much he had written.

'Is that all?'

'It's supposed to be concise.'

'So is it finished now?'

'No.'

'Well when will it be?'

'Later.'

'You ought to talk to Publius Mucius if you're stuck. He writes books.'

'I am not stuck!' To prove it, he had begun to devise an Overall Plan. This was what he should have done in the first place. He had entangled himself too early in the detail.

Ruso stared gloomily at the four versions of the Overall Plan, which he had removed from the trunk and stacked on the corner of his writing table. Each version had made good the shortcomings of its predecessor, but some new drawback had soon become apparent. He had kept all the versions in case he wanted to refer to them later – it would be a nuisance to find he'd rubbed something flat only to have to rewrite it – but incredibly, considering the hours he had spent poring over each one, he could not now remember which was which. He did not know whether the tablet claiming to be 'latest version' really was, or whether he should be working from 'NEW'. And what was 'Amended' amending?

Ruso sighed. The truth was, despite all the hours he had spent on it, the Overall Plan was a waste of time. Maybe the whole project – no, he couldn't abandon the *Guide* after all this work. Any fool with a stylus and a modicum of education – even Publius Mucius – could write a book, and plenty of them seemed to make money at it. Unlike most of them, he actually knew something worth passing on. He must simply get on with it. He picked up the stylus, frowned at the title 'Treatments for Eye Injuries', and began to write.

One of the dogs was scrabbling at his door. Ruso reread what he had just written and realized he had missed out a vital word. He upended the stylus and flattened the wax.

There was another shout of laughter from outside. When it died away there was a brief moment of peace, then the scrabbling started again. Ruso made a conscious decision to ignore the dog, rewrote line three and mentally arranged the essential points of 'Treatments for Eye Injuries' into the right order.

The scrabbling stopped. A plaintive whine came from under the door. Ruso wrote 'Next, check for . . .' With the writing end of the stylus poised above the wax but no patient in front of him as a reminder, he realized he couldn't remember what to check next. He flung the stylus down and made for the door, managing as he went to stub his toe on the corner of a trunk that didn't quite fit under the bed.

When he opened the door the terrier bitch rushed in and then stopped dead, sniffing, while several small shapes bounded past her and disappeared beneath the bed. Ruso narrowly missed treading on another one in the doorway.

One of Valens' friends, a veterinary surgeon, was waving his arms in the air, demonstrating the height of a jump taken by a filly with the potential to be one of the best horses in the province.

'Ruso!' Valens paused to pick out a date from a bowl propped on the arm of the couch. 'Want to buy a horse?'

'Not today.'

'How's the work going?'

'Well, the dog was keen to read it.'

'Oh, sorry!' Valens gestured towards Ruso's room with the date. 'I meant to tell you . . .' Ruso waited while he bit one end off the date. 'I think you've got a mouse in there. She was at the door this afternoon. If you leave her she'll flush it out for you.'

'Right.'

'Something else bothering you?'

Ruso leaned against the doorpost. 'Tell me something,' he said. 'If you were buying a girl to work in a bar, would you choose someone with a respectable accent and some education?'

Valens shrugged. 'Why not? She could help with the books.'

'Add a bit of class,' suggested the owner of the filly.

'Might pull in one or two officers, I suppose,' added another voice. Its owner was prone on the floor next to a jug of wine. Ruso recognized the man from Regional Control who had been too busy to break bad news to Merula. 'Personally, Ruso, I'd think twice. Invest in a bar by all means, but don't get involved in running it. It won't go down too well higher up.'

'I'm not running a bar, I —'

'He's just collecting women,' Valens explained. 'Which reminds me. We need a girl who can cook. Anybody who finds us one gets an invitation to dinner.'

Ruso returned to his room. Hastily whisking a valuable scroll away from the nose of a curious puppy, he tidied all his work back into the trunks and fastened the lids. He piled everything else that was chewable on to the top of the cupboard. Then, since he had no money and nowhere else to go, he headed for the hospital.

Ruso lit the lamps in the records room, closed the door quietly and lifted the box labelled 'Current Patients, Rooms VI to X' on to the desk. He pulled up a stool, seated himself, leaned on his elbows and stared at 'Current Patients'. A true philosopher would not give way to exasperation at the waste of an evening. A true philosopher, a man determined to apply the power of reason to every circumstance, would welcome this chance to catch up with his records.

There were footsteps outside the window. The low murmur of conversation. As the sounds faded, the smell of fried chicken sidled in through the shutters.

Ruso flipped through the record tablets with his forefinger until he reached room nine. He removed and opened the first one. 'Crush injury to left foot.' After consulting his rough notes, he dipped his pen in the ink and scrawled, 'Day 3, still swollen, extensive bruising visible, no mobility in toes, henbane, repeat compress.' Putting it aside to dry, he consulted his notes again and wrote, 'Day 4, breathing improved,' on a chest infection.

The smell of chicken was still there. Reminding himself

how much money he had saved by dining on hospital stew, Ruso recorded the symptoms of a blacksmith who had been admitted this afternoon with an unfortunately located boil which he would be lancing in the morning.

Outside, men were strolling about with their comrades, eating fried chicken. Inside, Ruso was spending his free evening writing about other people's boils. A less philosophical man would have been depressed.

The slave-girl was sitting up in bed. On the table, the lamplight glinted on the contents of a bowl of broth which must have sat there untouched for several hours. Ruso's greeting of 'Good evening. How are you feeling?' met with the usual serious stare and silence. The lack of response was beginning to irritate him. She was lucky to be alive. Once her arm had healed and she had been properly cleaned up and fed, she could be worth money. But her value would be limited if she remained silent and uncooperative. So, instead of pointing and saying, 'How is the arm?' as a prelude to his usual inspection of the hand and check of the bandaging, he sat on the end of the bed.

'So. Tell me why you haven't eaten your dinner.'

As he scrutinized her, he had the uncomfortable sensation that she was doing the same to him. He wondered how long she had been a slave. There must have been a time when she – or her owner – had been rich enough to afford jewellery for the pierced ears. Just as someone in Saufeia's past had thought she was worth the bother of teaching her to read. He supposed the fortunes of slaves rose and fell, just like those of their owners. But unless he could find some way of communicating with this one, he would never find out how she had slid low enough to be dragged about by Claudius Innocens.

73

'I know you can speak,' he insisted, although if he had not heard her shout out in the poppy-induced dreams he would have begun to wonder.

No response.

'Are you always this quiet?'

No response.

'Well, silent one,' he said, 'my dining room is full of horsemen and my bedroom is full of dogs. So a little peace is a welcome change.'

He took out his own writing-tablet and opened it up. The space under 'Treatments for Eye Injuries' seemed even emptier than before. He sniffed. He glanced across at the girl. 'How long is it since you had a trip to the baths? In fact, have you *ever* bathed?'

Moments later Ruso nudged the sign aside with his foot and opened the door of the hospital bath-house with the hand that wasn't supporting the girl. Inside, he lowered her on to a bench and went back out to find a light. On the way back in he repositioned the sign against the foot of the wall: 'CLOSED'.

The changing room was still warm, although the fires would have been banked up some time ago. Ruso began to light the lamps. The girl was watching him, clutching her arm, breathing the air, which was thick with damp and sweat and perfumed oil. She was taking in the blue-painted walls, the niches and hooks for clothes, the white piles of discarded towels. He considered collecting up the towels himself, then realized how inappropriate that would look. The master tidying for the slave.

'Wait there.' His voice echoed around the room as he made the gesture that Valens made when telling the dog to 'sit'.

He only lit one lamp in the cold room: just enough to pass through. Ladies did not need a cold plunge. Claudia had always been very firm about that. Presumably slave-girls could do without, too.

The atmosphere in the warm room made his tunic stick to his skin. He tripped on a discarded wooden shoe and almost turned his ankle. The lamp he was carrying swayed and spat as the oil spilled out on to the floor. He sent the shoe clattering across the tiles towards the hot-room door, where the rising light revealed an empty rack looming over a jumble of discarded footwear. Another used towel dangled over the side of the massage couch. A strigil, edge glistening with the last oily scrapings of dirt, skin and hair, lay on the rim of the tub. Ruso, who never used these baths and had never thought to inspect them, was willing to bet they didn't leave this sort of mess when the Chief Administrator was around. Evidently they weren't expecting him back before morning.

He wiped the strigil on the towel, then dropped the towel to mop up the spilled lamp-oil. The light caught an end-of-the-day rainbow sheen dappling the surface in the tub, but at least the water was still warm. He sniffed the contents of a couple of bottles that had been left on the shelf. Spice. Lavender. The girl could take her pick.

The coals in the brazier of the hot room were almost out. The room smelled of overheated men. He had barely stepped inside when something landed on his head. He flinched and shot up a hand to brush it away, then realized, shook his head and smiled. This was not Africa. There were so few biting and stinging creatures here that the hospital didn't even have its own poisons expert. What he had felt was only condensation dripping from the ceiling.

Ruso abandoned the hot room, guessing the girl would not linger in there.

When he went back he found she had edged along the bench and was huddled in the corner. She looked bewildered. It struck Ruso that since she had been unconscious when he carried her in, this was the first time she had seen anywhere outside room twelve.

He turned to find her a clean towel, only to find himself facing an empty shelf. He did the 'sit' gesture again and stepped out into the corridor just as an orderly was passing with a tray of water-jugs.

'Where's the clean linen kept?'

'Third door on the left, sir.' The orderly disappeared into a side corridor.

Ruso flipped the latch and collided with the door, which had failed to open as expected. He rattled it to no avail, then realized there was a key-hole. When the orderly reappeared with an empty tray he said. 'Where's the key?'

'Officer Priscus will have it, sir.'

'He took the key to the *linen cupboard* as well?'

'Officer Priscus is in charge of all the keys, sir.'

'That's ridiculous!'

The orderly was too wise to comment. Ruso was wondering what to do next when he heard a familiar voice.

Evidently Valens' social evening had been interrupted. He found him arguing about racing teams with a grizzled veteran whose leg was swathed in bandages from the hip downwards. Ruso said, 'How do we get hold of clean linen when the admin officer's not here?'

Valens glanced up. 'He usually leaves enough out to last till he gets back. There'll probably be some up from the laundry in the morning.'

'Surely he can't just bugger off like this?'

'Excuse me a minute,' murmured Valens and left the man's bedside.

As they approached the door, Ruso heard a dog bark somewhere inside the hospital building. 'Did you hear that?'

'What?'

Ruso wondered if he was starting to imagine things. 'Never mind.'

'Priscus has a system,' explained Valens. 'Jupiter knows what it is, but nobody likes to interfere because as long as he's left alone, everything turns up more or less when you need it.'

'I need it now. Why the hell isn't he here, anyway?'

'Apparently he went to Viroconium to negotiate a contract for delivery of hospital blankets.'

'Blankets? Gods above, surely any peasant with a couple of sheep and a wife can knock up a few blankets?'

'Ah,' agreed Valens, 'you and I might think so. But they have to be the right specification to fit hospital beds.'

'Does anyone really believe that?' said Ruso.

Valens shrugged. 'You'll have to pinch what you want from someone else.'

Back in the corridor, Ruso contemplated the silent door of the linen cupboard. He had yet to meet Officer Priscus, but already he hated him. The man seemed to have turned hospital administration into an art form – something incomprehensible, overpriced and useless. In the meantime, a sick girl was huddled in a corner of the changing room facing a pile of wet towels.

Ruso stood back, contemplated the latch for a moment and moved. A splintering crash echoed down the deserted corridor. He helped himself before anyone could arrive to see who had just bypassed the hospital administration with a military boot.

*

'Towels!' he announced, presenting them to her with a flourish.

She seemed less impressed than he had hoped. He took her good arm and helped her up. As he opened the cold-room door she tried to pull away. He tightened his grip. 'You need to bathe,' he insisted, walking her through into the warm room. He thought again how thin she was as he lifted her on to the edge of the massage couch. As he approached with the cleaned strigil and the two bottles of oil, her eyes widened. She raised herself up with her good arm and tried to shuffle away down the couch.

Ruso did the 'sit' gesture again. 'Stay still.' He walked around to the other side of the couch, leaned across and began to untie the sling that was knotted behind her slim neck. He felt her shoulders tighten, and remembered how the pregnant Daphne had frozen at the touch of the door-man. 'It's all right,' he assured her. 'You're safe here. Nobody is going to hurt you.'

He had carried this girl in through the East Gate. He had put her to bed and dressed her in the washed-out grey tunic she now wore. He had already seen the protruding ribs, the breasts shrunken by hunger, the yellowing bruises that shouldn't be there. He knew the sight of her body would arouse nothing in him but anger. Unable to explain that to her, he tapped the splint and said, 'Don't get water on the bandages,' then put the towels over her good arm and told her he would come back later.

He had finished his records and there was not enough time to settle into 'Treatment for Eye Injuries', so Ruso strolled down to the nearest of his wards. He looked at an abscess, got a concussed man to count the number of fingers he held up, ordered another poultice for the crushed foot, listened to a worrying cough, chatted to the signaller, checked up on recent surgical patients and told the surprised staff not to expect this every night. In a small side room he examined a veteran centurion who had been brought in after collapsing and decided he had been right this afternoon: it was pneumonia. The man was sixty-six. There was little they could do beyond trying to make him comfortable.

He dared not leave the girl for too long in case she fainted in there. When he had made sure the gasping centurion was propped up on his pillows and had instructed the orderlies to check him every hour, he made his way back down the corridor to the bath-house.

His announcement of 'It's the doctor!' echoed through the rooms. The only response was the flicker of the lamps in the draught from the door.

He found her perched on the side of the warm bath wrapped in a towel, skinny legs dangling, matted wet hair dripping down her face. 'Enjoy that?' he asked, more out of habit than in any hope of an answer. He stood in front of her and frowned at the rough surface of the tangled hair. 'Time we sorted this out,' he announced. 'Can't have you harbouring lice.' The girl's eyes met his. She showed no sign of understanding.

He reached behind him for the shears he had tucked into his belt. They were usually used for cutting clothes off accident victims, but they were fairly small and sharp and he knew he had a steady hand. He lifted one side of the mat away from her ear. 'Keep still.'

'*No!*'

The shriek echoed around the empty blue walls.

Ruso paused with the shears in mid-air. In his surprise he had let go of the hair. The girl was bent double, her good arm shielding the back of her head.

The sound of the scream died away. The girl began to

79

rock backwards and forwards, making a soft moaning sound.

'I'm not going to hurt you!' Ruso insisted, hoping no one had heard the scream and wishing he had left this for another day. 'I'm cutting the tangles out so you can tidy it up and let it grow back.'

The rocking continued. The moaning formed itself into, 'No, no, no.' The sniff which followed led Ruso to suspect that she was crying.

'Oh, for goodness' sake!' He tucked the shears back into his belt. He was never sure how to deal with crying women, who roused within him an uncomfortable mixture of guilt and exasperation. The 'No, no,' had finally died into silence by the time it dawned on him that she might have overheard and understood something about the state of the girl dumped in the river.

'Nobody here is going to hurt you,' he repeated. 'But you can't leave your hair in that mess. What do you want to do about it?'

The girl sat up. She gave another loud sniff and rubbed her eyes with the back of her hand. Then she squared her shoulders and looked him in the face.

In a voice lower and hoarser than he had expected, she said, 'I want to die.'

13

An orderly was helping the blacksmith down from the treatment table early the next morning when Ruso put his head out round the door to investigate the cause of the raised voices and running feet. The corridor was blocked by a crowd of cavalrymen. An unconscious man was being dragged along, his comrades simultaneously yelling for help and shouting at each other to get out of the way. Ruso was grabbed by a wild-eyed rider who insisted, 'You'll look after him, right? There wasn't nothing we could do, I'm really sorry, right?'

He learned later that they had been practising a close-formation gallop when the patient's horse had stumbled. He had fallen under the hooves of the animals behind. There was, as the unfortunate rider had said, nothing the other men could do. There was nothing Ruso could do either. Despite everyone's efforts, the youth was on his way into the shadows even before they hauled the chainmail off to check his injuries.

Ruso had hoped to spend any slack moments of his duty with the girl. Instead, the crushed foot was looking worse, the old centurion was putting up a determined fight to die as slowly as possible, and he had to put a frightened patient in an isolation ward until Valens could confirm his diagnosis of leprosy. By the end of the afternoon he had managed only to hand the girl a bowl of porridge and a comb and say, 'I'll be down later. I don't want to see that food when

I come back,' before heading back to the records room to write up his part of the fatality report.

He was reaching for the pen when he distinctly heard something that was not human pattering across the tiled entrance hall. He dropped the pen, leaped up from the desk and flung open the door. The corridor was empty. He took the few strides to the corner, round which he caught sight of Decimus the porter strolling in through the main doors.

The man paused. 'Can I help you, sir?'

'I could have sworn I heard a dog.'

'Dog, sir?'

'Running across the entrance hall.'

The man looked around as if the dog might leap out from behind Aesculapius. 'Across the entrance hall, sir?'

Ruso sighed. 'Don't repeat everything I say. You were told to get rid of it.'

The man eyed him for a moment, evidently weighing up what to say next. Finally he settled on, 'I know we should have, sir, but me and some of the lads –'

'We've got enough to cope with here. We don't need a dog running round the hospital.'

'Ah, but it's not an ordinary dog, sir. It does tricks. Cheers the patients up. And it's a champion ratter. We don't want rats running round the hospital either, sir, do we?'

'You were told you couldn't keep it here.'

'Oh yes, Officer Valens told us what you said, sir.'

'What *I* said?'

'Only he doesn't much mind it himself, sir. So we thought if it didn't get in the way . . .'

'I've seen it. That's enough. And it barks.'

'But it never gets in the way, does it, sir? Me and the lads feed it on scraps. It's a grand dog, sir. It'd be a shame to get rid of it.'

Ruso closed his eyes. He had had to explain to a bunch of distraught and disbelieving cavalrymen that there was nothing he could do for their comrade. Now he had to go over it all again in writing. He was not in the mood to discuss the comparative desirability of dogs and rodents, and he could hardly point out that Officer Valens was using him as an excuse to wriggle out of giving an unpopular order. It seemed that the porter, having mislaid a woman, had replaced her in his affections with a dog. Perhaps it was a sensible exchange. When he opened his eyes the porter began again.

'Sir . . .'

'Just keep it out of the treatment rooms and out of sight, you understand? The minute it's a nuisance, it goes.'

'Right-oh, sir,' agreed the porter. 'You won't have no bother with it. It'll be an invisible dog.'

'Well if it becomes visible to Officer Priscus, you're on your own.'

Ruso thought he detected a slight hesitation before, 'It's not true, then, sir, that he's got a posting with the Governor?'

'Not as far as I know. Now push off. I've got work to do, and I suppose there is a faint chance that you have as well.'

'Sir?'

'What now?'

'You don't happen to know when he's coming back?'

'I haven't a clue,' said Ruso. 'Go and make sure the room lists are up to date in case he turns up this afternoon.'

Ruso shut the door of the records room and sat down again. Just as he picked up the pen, the latch clicked and Valens strolled in. He helped himself to the spare chair before inquiring whether Ruso had seen the younger sister of a recently appointed centurion. 'She is *stunning*.'

'Even more stunning than the Second Spear's daughter?'

Valens grinned. 'That's a long-term project.' He settled himself in the chair. 'I heard you had a problem?'

Ruso gave him a short run-down of the afternoon's events, leaving out the dog.

'Not good,' summarized Valens, putting his feet up on the desk and treating his friend to a display of gleaming hobnails surrounded by dried mud. 'By the way, I dropped in on your Tilla just now. Since you were too busy.'

Ruso frowned. 'My what?'

'Tilla,' repeated Valens. When there was no reply he shook his head sadly. 'Gods above, Ruso, you are hopeless. What have I told you? First rule with women: get the name right. Anyway, it looks as though you've got away with that arm. Too early to say whether it'll be any use, of course.'

'Are you sure she's called Tilla?' persisted Ruso. 'It doesn't look anything like that on the sale chit.'

Valens shrugged. 'She said that's what you called her.'

'I didn't call her anything. I can't pronounce her name. It's got about fifteen syllables stuffed with g's and h's in odd places.'

'She seems to think you told her she'd be Tilla from now on. She seemed quite cheerful about it.'

'Did she?' There was no justice in the ways of the world. Ruso, who had saved the girl's life, was rewarded with weeping and 'Let me die.' Valens, who would have fixed her broken arm with a sharp saw, was granted a pleasant chat.

'Well, she was smiling.'

'Good,' said Ruso, with as much grace as he could muster.

He should have guessed that Valens' idea of a medical check-up would include an attempt to charm the patient with his boyish good looks and his smooth bedside manner. He would probably smarm his way into the CMO's job in the same fashion. Even without any combat experience. Ruso folded his arms and leaned back against the wall. 'I had an interesting conversation myself just now,' he said. 'Did you tell the staff they could keep that dog?'

Valens scratched his head. 'I may have said it didn't bother me. I can't remember.'

'Thanks very much. You're not the CMO yet, you know.'

'I did tell them what you'd said.'

'Only I hadn't, you had. And anyway they completely ignored it. Do we really want animals running round the hospital?'

'Don't be miserable, Ruso. It's only a dog. Which reminds me . . .' Valens reached out one foot and kicked the door shut before leaning closer. 'Speaking of miseries, have you heard this rumour about Priscus getting a posting down with the Governor?'

'Just now. Is it true?'

'You'd better hope so. Then he might not find out you've demolished his linen cupboard.'

'Gods above, he's only a pen-pusher! Who runs this place?'

Valens pondered that for a moment and then said, 'He doesn't interfere with the medical decisions.'

Outside, there was a clank of buckets. Someone called out something about stocking up dressings, and footsteps trod down the wooden boards of the corridor.

'*Uti*la,' said Ruso suddenly. 'Useful. Her Latin's a bit shaky. She got into a bit of a state last night. Thought she was never going to get better and wanted to be off with the ancestors, or something. I told her she'd be *utila* to me.'

'Well, that must have been a big comfort. So you aren't going to sell her, then?'

'Of course I am. I don't need her.'

85

'She's cleaned up rather well, don't you think? A bit skinny, but surprisingly good teeth. Why don't we hold on till she's mended and give her a try?'

'No.'

'So how is she going to be useful to you?'

Ruso reached for the pen. 'How much would you say an attractive female slave would fetch here?'

Valens' face betrayed his amusement. 'Claudia would never have approved of this line of business, you know.'

'One of childbearing age?' persisted Ruso.

Valens shrugged. 'Two thousand, if you can find the right buyer? Three or four maybe, if she can actually do something.'

'Exactly,' said Ruso, and dipped the pen in the inkpot.

Finally alone, Ruso started the fatality report. The first stroke of the first letter slid down the sheet and ended in a quivering black blob. He rested the pen on the edge of the desk while he blotted the page with a soft rag. A glance at the shelf told him there were no spare sheets. Of course not. The Chief Administrator had probably taken the key to the stationery cupboard, too. Ruso held the sliver of wood over the lamp flame to hurry the drying of the blot, and wondered what the girl's smile was like.

The blot was obliterated by a scorch mark. He swore.

This time the stroke started well enough, but the ink began to falter halfway down. He pressed harder. The nib scraped down the wood, leaving a blank indentation like a dry river bed. The dead cavalryman deserved better than this. He dipped the pen in the inkpot and tapped it against the edge.

Gods, Ruso, you are hopeless.

He wasn't *completely* hopeless. He'd managed three years

of marriage. Whereas Valens was still single at thirty-two, and any woman willing to marry him would need her sanity examined. So would the Second Spear, if he gave his permission.

A fine, neat stroke this time, cutting across the sepia edge of the scorch mark. That was better. He was making progress now.

The pen jolted between his fingers and stopped working. A second attempt at the stroke made an inkless scratch. Ruso lifted the pen to eye-level and squinted at the nib. It was bent at an impossible angle. He flung it into the corner where it made a splash of black as it bounced off the plaster, missed the waste bin and rolled across the floor.

Claudia would never have approved of this line of business, you know. He must stop showing an interest in slave-girls. He would become a source of amusement.

The next pen had a nib that wobbled about. The third proved to be an inky stick with no nib at all.

Ruso sent the stool crashing back on to the floorboards, wrenched open the door and roared, 'Can't anybody get anything organized in this bloody place?' to an empty corridor.

14

A thrush was singing its early song in the hospital garden. The girl who had decided they could call her Tilla lay with her eyes closed, letting the music lift her above the dull ache of her arm. The bed was comfortable. She felt clean for the first time in weeks. It occurred to her that she was happy.

The feeling was followed by a flush of shame. She had no right to be happy. This white room with the square window was only a temporary resting-place.

The Roman healers had, for reasons that were not clear to her, chosen to delay her arrival in the next world. Three times now she had allowed her thirst to defeat her resolve, reached out her good hand and drunk the barley water they had left in the black jug. When the serious one had sat on the bed and fed her with a spoon like a child, she had accepted a few mouthfuls of salty broth. After he had gone, she had struggled out of the bed, picked up the bowl and tipped the contents out of the window.

She opened her eyes. This morning's bowl of meal was still untouched on the table. This time there was a plain bone comb beside it. She swung her feet down on to the wooden floor and paused with her head bowed until the giddiness passed. Moments later, the thrush's song died as the latest meal slid out of the bowl to join the others under the lavender bush.

By the time she fell back on to the bed she was sweating and exhausted. She closed her eyes and leaned back against the white wall. She must not weaken. In the next world, the others were waiting.

15

Ruso paused in the doorway of the admissions hall and eyed the three very young soldiers who were standing stiffly against the wall. Over the murmur of conversation that echoed around the hall he enquired, 'Are you here for me?'

'Yes, sir,' they chorused in badly timed unison.

'Ah.' It struck him that this answer was less than helpful since everyone in the hall was there for him in one way or another. 'So, you're the new bandagers who are supposed to be following the doctor about this morning?'

'Yes sir.'

'Good. Keep your eyes open and your mouths shut and you might learn something. I'll try and make time for questions afterwards.'

There were about twenty patients already lined up on the three benches. Half a dozen still stood in the queue at the orderlies' table by the main entrance, waiting to be processed. Each man already seated had been assigned to a bench depending on the apparent urgency of his case. Several of the men on the nearest bench were slumped forward with their heads in their hands. A couple were clutching at injuries with bloodstained rags – one eye, one foot – and one was shivering and coughing.

'Not so busy this morning,' observed Ruso, eyeing the empty seats.

'Word gets round, sir,' said one of the trainees.

Ruso turned and raised his eyebrows. The other two shrank back as if they were hoping to melt into the wall.

'I mean, sir,' the lad stumbled, 'only the men who are really ill bother coming.'

Ruso was conscious of the patients' eyes on him as he led his little troop across the end of the hall and into his surgery.

Ruso's working space contained three shelves, a collection of unmatched stools and chairs, an examination table by the window and a desk whose migratory tendencies had been curbed by a previous incumbent with a hammer and several large nails. One wall held a scatter of faded notices and a collection of coloured diagrams showing muscles and bones. The students looked uncertain whether to stand to attention or demonstrate their keenness by trying to memorize the diagrams.

'Stand where you can see,' he instructed them, laying his case on the desk and unfastening the clasps, 'and don't get in my light.' As they shuffled awkwardly around the stools he lifted the lid of the case and repositioned the bronze probe, which always slipped out of its place as soon as the case was vertical. He glanced up at them. 'Ready?'

The nods were a little too eager.

The feverish man was summoned, swiftly examined and sent down to an isolation ward with a prescription. The moment the man had been escorted out of the room, there was another knock on the door. Instead of the next patient, it turned out to be the porter who was part-owner of the invisible dog.

'Could I just have a quick word, sir?'

'Can't it wait, Decimus?'

'Very quick, sir.'

'Go ahead.'

'Sir, I thought you might like to know, Officer Priscus was seen arriving at the Street of the Weavers this morning. He's back at his lodgings, sir.'

Ruso stared at him. 'That's it?'

The man glanced at the students. 'We wondered if you wanted anything shifted, sir. Being as he might be here any minute.'

Ruso frowned. 'Why would I want anything shifted?'

'We're having a bit of a tidy-up, sir. So if you've got anything cluttering up any of the rooms, we could move it for you. Sir. If you tell us where to put it.'

Ruso scratched his ear. 'If Officer Priscus finds anything cluttering up any of the rooms, you can tell him I put it there.'

'Yes, sir.' The man hesitated.

'Well?'

'Sir, we think Officer Priscus might ask who helped you put it there in the first place. If there was anything. And then some people who were just trying to be helpful might be in hot water, sir.'

Ruso glanced around at his students to make sure they were at least pretending not to listen. 'I'll deal with it in a moment,' he said. 'Send in the next man.'

Next in was the optio with the bloodstained rag clutched to one eye. Ruso looked at his students and grinned. This would take their minds off any speculation about things cluttering rooms. This, he knew, was the patient they had all been dreading.

The optio did not disappoint. By the time Ruso sent him off on a stretcher to be prepared for surgery one of the students had fainted and the other two were looking as though they wished they could join him on the floor. Ruso supervised the revival of their fallen comrade and gave them all a brief lecture on the importance of not frightening the patient.

Next in was a pale standard-bearer with a recurrence of

acute abdominal pain on the right-hand side. He left clutching a prescription for a more powerful medicine. Privately, Ruso hoped that it wasn't gall-stones. They were the devil to treat and he dreaded elective surgery almost as much as his patients did. Recovery was at the whim of the gods, but no matter how careful he had been, the blame for failure always lay with the doctor.

The rest of the 'urgent' bench consisted of a man who had trodden on a nail and an unremarkable collection of conditions painful to the owner but mercifully palatable to the medical student.

'Finish writing your notes up,' he ordered the observers. 'I'll be back in a minute.'

The imminent arrival of Officer Priscus seemed to have had the same effect on the staff as a heatwave on a nest of ants. They had all emerged from wherever they hid during the day and were scurrying about, clutching blankets and bandages and bedpans and brooms.

The girl's room was quiet. She was sitting on the bed with her knees drawn up under her chin, apparently listening to the sounds of activity around her. Ruso glanced out into the courtyard garden. One man was busy scything the grass and another was on his knees ripping weeds out of the herb bed.

'I need to move you,' he said, automatically glancing around the room to see what possessions needed to be gathered up before realizing that she had none. Even the rags she came in with had been burned. He retrieved his comb from beneath the window and wondered if she had been trying to throw it out. Glancing at her hair, he concluded that it had sacrificed several teeth in vain.

He leaned down and placed one arm around her shoulders, the other beneath her knees. He was acutely aware that, underneath the rough wool of the old tunic, she was naked. He was going to have to face the business of finding more clothes for her very soon.

'Up!'

She seemed no heavier than when he had carried her in here. The matted hair rested against his cheek. He hoped he had been wrong about the head lice. He hooked one toe around the door and pulled it open, stepping out into the side corridor and pausing to crane round the corner and make sure no one was approaching.

The hospital formed a large square around the courtyard garden, with the long admissions hall and the operating rooms forming one side and the wards and other rooms around the remaining three. The quickest way out was to turn right and carry the girl up towards the hall. They could then escape through the side door beside the baths, which would surely be unlocked for the maintenance staff to get in and out during the day.

He had made it about twenty feet along the corridor when an unfamiliar voice sounded in the distance. The tone sounded authoritative and it was growing louder as the owner rounded the corner behind him.

Ruso dodged into another side corridor like the one he had just left. On either side of him were doors to isolation rooms. The voice was growing louder: '. . . and have it all scrubbed through immediately,' it was saying.

'Yes, sir!'

'Isolation rooms,' announced the voice, almost upon him now. 'Your responsibility, Festus Junius.'

Moments later Ruso emerged from one of the rooms, alone. At the sight of him, a tall, thin officer whose face was ten years older than his hair, paused in the doorway of the room opposite.

Pulling the door closed behind him, Ruso said, 'Optio Priscus, I presume?'

'Indeed,' replied the man, inclining the hair slightly towards him. The orderlies with him were stony-faced.

Ruso introduced himself. 'New surgeon.'

'Ah, good morning, Doctor. Welcome to the hospital. I am your administrator. We conduct a daily ward inspection, so if there is anything you require . . .'

Ruso jerked a thumb back towards the door he had just closed. 'Leave this one till later, will you? The old boy's only just got off to sleep.'

A flicker of something that might have been displeasure moved the muscles of the administrator's face. Then the hair inclined towards Ruso again and the man murmured, 'Of course.'

Back in the isolation room, Ruso gathered up the girl from where he had dumped her on the end of the bed. The old centurion had woken up. His eyes were wide and his chest was heaving with the effort of drawing breath to speak.

'Wrong room,' said Ruso swiftly. 'Sorry.'

The man's mouth opened.

'Don't try to talk.' Ruso gestured towards the bedside. 'Do you need me to ring the bell?'

The man shook his head.

'I'll be in later.' The old boy had deteriorated since earlier this morning. Ruso left the door ajar so the staff would hear the bell and, as he left, heard a wheezy voice suggest, 'You can – leave her behind – if you like.'

Priscus had turned right. As soon as the corridor was empty Ruso turned left and hurried back past the girl's former room, narrowly missing a big basket of dirty linen which someone had abandoned just around the corner and promising a voice which called, 'Doctor!' that he would be back later.

The girl seemed to have drifted off to sleep as he strode down the corridors. He took a short cut across the garden. A man who was standing in a lavender bed and scrubbing the wall beneath what had been the girl's window glanced up, but said nothing. Finally he reached the hospital kitchens. Ignoring the stares of the staff, he marched through the steamy atmosphere, wrenched open the back door and stepped out into the street.

Valens had gone out but fortunately forgotten to lock the house door. Welcomed by enthusiastic puppies, Ruso carried the girl over the threshold – a feat that required much less effort than it had with Claudia in his arms – and dumped her on his bed. The house smelled abominably of dogs and mould. He forced open his ill-fitting bedroom shutters and wondered how he could have failed to notice how bad it was before.

In the kitchen he poured a cup of water and hacked a lump of cheese from the end without small teethmarks.

He left the food with the girl and added a scrawled note on the slate which was supposed to be the house message system, 'Slave in my room temporary arrangement.'

He sprinted most of the way back to the hospital, entered through the front door, nodded to Aesculapius and made a determined effort to silence his breathing as he strolled across the admissions hall towards the surgery, where his students were waiting. Pausing by the door, he turned and saw two benches full of men, all watching him.

'Right!' he said. 'Who's next?'

16

The wolf was very large and very dead. Its skin was splayed against the white wall. Its fangs were bared in a snarl and the lively glint in its glass eyes suggested that it was about to leap up and attack the damp patch on the hospital administrator's ceiling. Priscus, presumably used to the sight, snapped open a folding chair for Ruso. He slid himself into position behind his desk as neatly as if he had been one of his own files on the shelves.

'Ah,' he said, smiling in a manner that made Ruso glance back at the wolf for comparison. 'I see you've noticed my little trophy, Doctor.'

'Is it local?'

'Oh yes. I ran into it a couple of years ago on my way to Eboracum. Quite a fine specimen, don't you think?'

'Very impressive,' agreed Ruso, wondering why the administrator had a better room than any of the medical staff.

'You'll find there is excellent hunting in Britannia,' said Priscus, running a hand lightly over the top of his head, as if to check that the hair was still there. 'Although personally I find it rather difficult to set aside the time.'

'I imagine you find plenty to do here,' suggested Ruso, not adding *especially if you don't give anyone else the keys.*

Priscus smiled again. 'Organization,' he said, indicating a large board nailed up above the shelves. Each notice on it was spaced an exact inch from its neighbour. 'Organization and teamwork,' he continued, 'the key to a pleasant and successful hospital, don't you agree, Ruso?'

'I find a steady hand with a scalpel quite useful, myself.'

'Precisely!' Priscus spread his fingers to grasp an invisible quantity of precision that he seemed to think was hovering just above his desk. 'Efficiency stems from a clear understanding of our various roles and responsibilities. So perhaps you will allow me to give a brief outline of the administrative arrangements.'

The administrative arrangements were impressive in their complexity: so impressive that once Ruso had spotted the underlying theme – that every decision was referred back to the hospital administrator – he stopped listening. He was wondering whether Priscus knew who was responsible for breaking into the linen cupboard when something caught his attention.

'I'm sorry, what did you just say?'

'As I was saying, a scribe could be extraordinarily useful. I think we can find a suitable man.'

Ruso frowned. 'A scribe?'

'My men aren't used to African writing, I'm afraid.'

The man had only been back for a day, and already he had found time to scrutinize the patient records. 'It's the same as any other writing,' said Ruso. 'The dispensary's never complained.'

Priscus' head inclined in agreement. 'No, they are very professional. But I took the liberty of discussing the matter with them just now and they agree that a scribe would be the best way forward. And of course, so much more convenient for you. Many of the medical staff with whom I have had the honour of serving have found it very useful. No need to keep stopping to take notes. Nothing to carry. Both hands free.'

Ruso scratched his ear. 'I suppose I could give it a try.'

'That's the spirit, Doctor.' As Priscus moved to indicate

a stack of writing-tablets on one side of his desk, a reflection of his hand glided across the polished surface. 'I'm sure it won't take long to copy these up.'

'You're intending to rewrite all my notes?'

'It will give your man a chance to learn what's required. He won't bother you unless there's something he can't make out.'

'Is this really necessary?'

'It would be extremely useful for the hospital. There must be a great deal of valuable information in there.'

'I suppose so,' said Ruso, realizing how neatly he had been outmanoeuvred.

'Excellent! Now . . .' Priscus leaned across the desk and lowered his voice. 'Let me tell you, in confidence of course, something I heard in Viroconium. I was told on good authority that not only do the Procurator's office have orders from Rome to prepare for a major audit, but it is quite possible that our new Emperor may inspect the Province in person.'

Ruso said, 'I see,' since the man was clearly waiting for him to express amazement before carrying on.

'In the meantime,' continued Priscus, 'every unit is to be scrutinized. Any waste and inefficiency is to be rooted out.'

This was hardly a surprise. Hadrian was reputed to be the sort of officer much approved by poets and taxpayers: a man who marched bare-headed with his troops, wearing the same clothes and eating the same food, perpetually inspecting and commenting and suggesting improvements. The sort of leader who was either an inspiration or a pain in the backside, depending upon your point of view.

'So naturally, Doctor,' the administrator concluded, 'we

will need to reconcile any irregularities in the hospital books before they are opened for scrutiny.'

'Naturally,' Ruso agreed. As he was wondering whether Priscus really expected the Emperor to read his medical records, the administrator reached down beside his desk and brought up a file. Ruso recognized the admissions log from the porter's desk.

'On the subject of efficiency, Doctor, perhaps you could help me with this? We seem to have a duplicate entry. Back on . . .'

Ruso gazed at the top of the administrator's head as his finger traced down the columns. As if he could read Ruso's thoughts, Priscus lifted his hand from the records and ran it lightly over his hair again as he said, 'Five days before the Ides of September . . .' He glanced up.

Ruso tried to pretend he hadn't been staring. Priscus returned his attention to the admissions log.

'This entry says quite clearly, *Female, early twenties*. Then a word that perhaps you could help me with, then further down the list on the same day, *Female early twenties* again – and this time the entry states, *to set broken arm.*'

He's painted his head. That's it. It's not only the hair that's dyed, it's . . .

'Shall I delete the first as a clerical error?'

'No,' said Ruso, 'there were two of them.'

The eyebrows rose towards the hair. 'I see.'

Ruso reached for the log. 'Dead,' he read. 'The first one was dead when we got her.'

'I see.' Priscus sat back in his chair. 'I shall have a word. Someone should have explained that we never accept civilian patients here unless we have a reasonable prospect of treating them.'

'I've been through this with the Second Spear. We didn't know who it was. By the time we got her she'd obviously been in the river for some time. Plus, she was stark naked and practically bald.'

Priscus glanced up sharply. 'I beg your pardon?'

'Bald. No hair.' Ruso paused to savour his own tactlessness before adding, 'She'd had it all cut off.'

The administrator's hand stopped halfway to his head and returned to rest on the desk. He stared at it for a moment, then said, 'I shall have to look into this. We can't have unidentified –'

'We know who she was. She turned out to be one of the local barmaids. Somebody had murdered her.'

Priscus' hand rose to smooth his hair. 'I see. How very, ah . . .' He seemed to be searching for a word. Finally he settled on 'unpleasant'.

'Yes.'

'I should have been made aware of any inquiry.'

Ruso shook his head. 'It's over. The Second Spear dealt with it. Apparently the girl was a runaway and the owner isn't in the mood to make a fuss, so since they aren't blaming the Army, that's probably the end of it.'

Priscus' gaze met his own. 'You sound a little dissatisfied, Doctor.'

'It's none of my business.'

'But are you suggesting the officer in charge could have done more?'

Ruso was not going to be led into criticizing the Second Spear. 'He couldn't find any witnesses,' he said. 'What more could he do?'

'What indeed?' Priscus made a note. 'So, the name will appear in the mortuary list instead of the discharge log.'

'Exactly,' said Ruso, with more confidence than he felt.

'Excellent. So there only remains the female with the broken arm. I am sorry to trouble you with all this, Doctor, but the discharge log has no record of her either, and without the proper records for civilians we are unable to bill the correct fees.'

'Are you?' Ruso scratched his ear and wondered whether that should be *aren't you?*

He looked the man in the eye. 'All this will be very much easier when I have a scribe who knows how the system works, Priscus.'

The smile reappeared. 'I'm sure it will, Doctor. I'm sure it will.'

On his way back to the surgery Ruso walked past the entrance to the linen store. A carpenter was sweeping up wood-shavings. The door had been mended.

17

The lamplight picked out the white sling resting on top of the grey Army blanket. Beneath it, the girl lay asleep on Ruso's borrowed bed. He watched the sling lift softly with each breath. Four days ago, this sight had been cause for celebration. Now it was cause for concern. By now she should either have died or perked up. Instead, apart from the brief revival sparked by his attempt to chop her hair off and the smile wheedled out of her by Valens' creeping bedside charm, the girl had shown little interest in anything. Not even her own recovery.

He had not been entirely sorry to see Valens proved wrong about the comb ('Ruso, *all* women are interested in their hair!'), but his own tactics had been no more successful. His inquiries about native cuisine had reassured him that she would be no stranger to gruel. Yet despite his carefully prescribed convalescent diet – following which his notes recorded disappointingly scant use of the bedside bucket – the girl was recovering neither strength nor spirit. Nor was she putting on weight. Ruso frowned. Tomorrow, he would repeat the worm treatment. Tonight, he had other things to think about.

He leaned back, relishing the familiar creak of his favourite chair as the front two legs lifted off the ground. He banished a fleeting regret. Claudia would never find out that he had now been sitting on this chair exactly how he liked for the last two years and he still hadn't broken it.

He stared at the box he had just collected from the porter's desk at the hospital, trying to guess what might be inside. Figs? Olives? Not peaches. Peaches would still be in season, but they wouldn't travel. If he'd had any money, he would have paid well for the simple pleasure of a tray of peaches. To feel the flesh pop between his teeth . . . the rich flavour flood onto his tongue . . . the sticky juice run down his chin . . .

He cleared his throat and reminded himself that if he had been born this far north he would never have tasted a peach. A peach was one of those things he didn't need.

What else would he find? A letter. There would definitely be a letter. And some gloves. His sister-in-law had promised gloves for the British winter, and his nieces a picture for him to hang on his wall. Since his nieces were only four and five, that should be interesting.

He expected nothing from his stepmother, a woman whose interests were restricted to personal grooming and home improvements, about which she knew everything except how they were paid for. *Publius dealt with all that, dear.* Nor was he expecting a greeting from either of his half-sisters, since he was not in a position to lend anything they were likely to want.

Ruso had already missed his father's funeral when the news of the death came. The sea passage from Africa was a tricky one and it had taken him almost a month by ship via Athens, Syracuse, Ostia . . . Under different circumstances, it would have been an interesting sight-seeing cruise. As it was, by the time he reached Gaul, Lucius had started to unravel their father's affairs — or more accurately, their father's affairs had begun to unravel around him.

According to their stepmother, Publius had 'investments'. The family had always assumed these investments were funding the very grand — and currently half-built — shrine to Diana the Huntress which Publius had commissioned for the centre of the town. 'Investments', however, turned out to mean 'loans'. Examining the documents stored in the trunk to which he had kept the only key, Publius Petreius' sons soon discovered that everything their father did had been done on an elaborate system of credit.

Initially the brothers tried to keep their dreadful discovery secret while they quietly shored up the loans. But they found themselves in the position of the children Ruso had seen playing on a British beach on the day he arrived, building dams against the incoming tide. Every time they secured one area, chaos broke through in another.

Valens' letter telling him about the vacancy with the Twentieth at Deva had come as a gift from the gods. It was all arranged by post with surprising speed. Using the excuse of the move, Ruso sent instructions to have all his surplus belongings sold. A suitable buyer was found for both his housekeeper and his valet. When the deals were complete Ruso withdrew as much from his account as the Army would allow (they insisted on keeping enough to bury him, just in case) and used it to pay off one of the few creditors who genuinely needed the money.

While he was making these arrangements, Lucius paid all the small-but-irritating debts. Then the brothers visited each of the large creditors individually, pointing out that slow payment was better than no payment, that the farm would produce a steady income and that Ruso was earning a good salary. If they wanted their money back they must keep quiet, keep faith and keep funding the building of the shrine to Diana which the brothers were obliged to finish, as it was their father's dying wish.

This last was a lie. The truth was that six different lenders thought they were funding the building of a shrine, when in fact most of them had been funding personal grooming and home improvements. No wonder Publius Petreius' heart had given out under the strain. Within days of his return home, Ruso was glad he had missed the funeral. His grief was frozen beneath a hard layer of anger.

He clunked the chair back on to all four legs, cracked the seal on the box and prised it open with his pocket-knife.

Over on the bed, the girl shuffled, sighed and settled back into sleep.

Ruso groped in the rustling straw. His fingers closed over a jar. He drew it out. 'OUR OLIVES' was chalked on the side in Lucius' hand.

The next find was a rolled piece of white fabric showing a smeared charcoal sketch. It was a wobbly oval topped with a pile of sticks – or perhaps a range of mountains, or a storm at sea. The centre of the oval contained an arrangement of blobs and in one corner of the fabric were two outlines of small hands. Ruso turned the picture to several different angles and could make no sense of any of them.

Next out: a pair of thick brown lambskin gloves. He brushed the straw off them and slid his right hand into the soft embrace of the fleece. Cassia had measured well.

Finally, the expected letter. Despite being sealed into the box the writing-tablet had also been closed and sealed individually.

'Greetings, brother,' announced black letters so closely crammed on to the thin wood that Ruso had to lean towards the lamp to make them out. 'I hope this finds you well. Cassia and the children send their good wishes and our step-mother . . .' Ruso ran his forefinger hastily along the formalities and slowed down for: 'On the subject which concerns us all, you will be pleased to hear that there are no further adverse developments.' So, no more debts had come crawling out from dark corners. 'The girls have drawn a picture of you, which I trust you will enjoy.' That was him? Heavens. He must get his hair cut. 'The harvest has been as good as we hoped,' continued the letter, 'and you will be as delighted as I am to know that Cassia is expecting another child in the spring.'

As delighted as I am, indeed. A neatly ambiguous statement from the man who had earnestly requested the latest advice on contraception after the birth of the last baby.

'I pray that you remain in good health despite the climate in Britannia,' continued Lucius, 'and hope you will write soon, Brother!' The final sentiments, having reached the bottom right-hand corner too early, performed a sharp turn and twisted up a narrow column of space between the ends of the previous lines and the edge of the letter. 'Do not forget our arrangement,' Ruso deciphered, turning the page sideways. The way the pen had skidded and fallen off the cut edge of the wood while forming the tails of the longer letters somehow added to the urgency of 'We all depend upon you. Farewell.'

Ruso glanced around the shadowy walls of his small but relatively private bedroom and knew he was lucky. *Do not forget our arrangement*. Lucius was in charge of four children, a wife, a farm, a stepmother and two goose-brained half-sisters, and now there was another baby on the way. All Ruso had to do was carry out his work and send home all the money he could muster every quarter to help keep a roof over his family's head.

Outside, the trumpet sounded the change of watch. It was getting late. Ruso stood to put the box away. Then he lifted the unconscious slave girl and carried her to the kitchen, where he laid her on a rug beside the warm embers in the hearth. She hardly stirred as he slid a cushion under her head and put his own cloak over her for a blanket.

He leaned against the wall with his arms folded and gazed

down at her. The surgery had been the easy part. If she perked up, she would have to be fed and sheltered through a long – and possibly unsuccessful – recuperation.

It was not difficult to see why some people threw out useless slaves. He had wondered briefly whether that was what Merula had done with Saufeia, the girl who 'wasn't really suitable for this kind of work', but that would not have made sense. Merula had not suggested that the girl was physically incapable of working, just that her attitude was poor. There were all sorts of jobs that a fit slave could be coerced to do, whatever her attitude. The girl would have been saleable to somebody, and her flight and subsequent death must have meant a financial loss to the business. Merula had received the news calmly not because she was indifferent but because she had expected the worst and prepared herself.

Merula had made one effort to claim compensation – the complaint about the hair – but when that had failed, it seemed she had given up. Since the Army provided most of her custom, he supposed it was a wise decision. In fact the only person who had shown any interest at all in the question of who had murdered Saufeia was the girl with the ankle-chain, the one they called Chloe. He had wished he could promise her that the Army would find the culprit and punish him. But if Merula was not going to make a fuss, it was unlikely anyone else would make any effort to narrow down the suspect list from the several thousand men currently in Deva. Besides, now he thought about it, the murderer might have been a woman.

The girl shifted and murmured something in her sleep.

Ruso's collecting women.

He was glad he didn't have to explain any of it to Lucius.

18

The grey light of dawn was making its way around the shutters of a house that contained three people. Two were asleep. The third was grappling with the problem of women's underwear. Where could a man get hold of some? Discreetly? As if that were not bad enough, there would be the monthly business to deal with at any moment.

Ruso wished, not for the first time, that he had been blessed with a useful sort of sister. According to Claudia, a man's only role in the mystery of feminine hygiene was to purchase a capable maid and then stay out of the way. So, although his training had covered the theory, in three years of marriage Ruso had evaded the practice so diligently that he had never really been sure what arrangements were necessary. Valens, of course, was bound to know, but he was not going to ask Valens.

Ruso stared at a cobweb that was trembling in the draught from his bedroom window and thought: *landlady*. The girl couldn't stay where she was much longer anyway. The obvious answer was to find a room in a house with a sympathetic landlady. A dispenser of nourishing meals and womanly advice who didn't charge too much. A landlady was the thing. He would go out this morning and find one. In the meantime, he would wander into the kitchen and see if his property had woken up yet.

He had grasped his overtunic between finger and thumb and was about to give it a good shake when he remembered again that this was Britain, where there were no scorpions to creep into dark crevices overnight. Buckling his belt and wondering if he would ever entirely break the wary habits of Africa, he made his way towards the kitchen. The couch, which would have been the obvious place for the girl to sleep, was still being shared between one of Valens' cronies and the dog.

He opened the kitchen door quietly. Something ran across his foot and shot away into the corner. He sighed, then started as his eyes adjusted to the shuttered gloom and he realized the hearth was empty. Instead, there was a figure curled up on the table.

'Good morning.'

The girl stirred. A tangle of hair slid across her cheek. She blinked sleepily and stretched her good arm above her head. Ruso had a sudden urge to seize her and take her to his own bed, where she would be warm and sleepy and – since he owned her – obedient. He swallowed hard and pushed the thought aside, not wishing to ponder the level of desperation it revealed.

He said, 'Why are you on the table?'

She stared at him for a moment, as if trying to remember who he was, and then gave a heavy sigh of recognition. She slid her good hand forward to grasp the edge of the table and leaned forward, surveying the floor.

Ruso followed her gaze. 'Are you afraid of the mice?'

He saw her fist tighten. She looked up at him. 'Mice do not hurt.'

'No,' he agreed, 'but falling off the table will.'

It was a question of simple economics. The longer her recovery took, the longer it would be before he saw his money. 'You won't spend the night here again,' he promised. 'I'll find a proper room.'

It was a promise he would regret by the end of the morning.

*

Several would-be landlords had chalked up advertisements on the amphitheatre walls.

The smell of urine and old cabbage stew which hit Ruso as soon as the first door opened failed to mask the personal odour of the toothless crone who announced, 'He an't here, I dunno where he is and he an't done nothing.'

'I'll keep looking,' said Ruso.

'Did have,' said the next one. 'We did have a room. Somebody should have rubbed the notice off.'

The third room was still having its walls plastered, but the owner's wife promised it would be ready by nightfall.

'How much?'

She told him. Ruso laughed and walked away, and she let him go.

As the morning wore on and his boot-studs wore down, it became clear to Ruso that he had a problem. He was here because Rome had decided that Britannia was worth the trouble of holding on to, and had stationed just about enough troops here to crack together the skulls of any Britons who refused to cooperate. Side by side with the stick, however, went the carrot. Civilization. Not only the fort, but Deva itself was undergoing a massive modernization project. Every man not currently engaged in keeping an eye on the hill tribes had a trowel in his hand or a hod over his shoulder. It seemed the legion's orders were to hack out all the available stone, saw up all the local trees and pipe water to every conceivable outlet. Until the last dog-kennel had underfloor heating or the new Emperor came up with a new plan, the Twentieth Valeria Victrix was to keep on building.

It was not the soldiers themselves who were causing Ruso's difficulties: they were either off skull-cracking or living in the barracks that they were slowly working their way round to modernizing. It was the unofficial wives and children, widowed mothers and spinster aunts the men collected around them. The wives and children and mothers and aunts – not to mention the veterans with nowhere else to retire to, who had wives and children of their own – all needed beds to sleep in. Then there were all the hangers-on who congregated wherever there were soldiers to be separated from their wages. Hangers-on needed beds, too.

The wail of a trumpet from the other side of the fort wall announced that the morning was almost at an end. Ruso was on duty in an hour and he was still no nearer keeping his promise to the girl. He was going to have to try Valens' suggestion after all.

Earlier that morning, he had pointed out that he had no intention of lodging his slave in a bar that was effectively a brothel.

'Ah, but it isn't,' Valens had explained. 'Not technically. We had a tax-collector in here the other day. Broken wrist: fell off his horse. Anyway, he said lots of those sort of places don't register their girls so they don't have to pay the tax on their earnings, and when anybody official asks why there's so many bedrooms, then, they say that it's because they take in lodgers. It's worth a try. Just don't let her eat the oysters.'

'A tax-dodging brothel. Marvellous.'

'You could always have a nice chat with Priscus. I hear his new place is rather spacious. Perhaps he'll find you a spare room.'

'Maybe I will,' agreed Ruso, just to see the expression on Valens' face.

As Merula swayed across the empty bar room in another stylish silky creation, Ruso mused that this was not the sort of landlady he had envisaged.

The elegantly plucked eyebrows rose at his question. Evidently he was not the sort of tenant she was used to, either.

'It's not for me,' he explained.

'For a friend?'

'Not exactly.' He was aware that he was scratching his ear again. He really must try to stop that. Claudia used to say she knew it meant he was lying, which showed how little they understood each other. He lowered his fist onto the bar-room table just below the initials of one CLM, who had felt it necessary to carve not only the first letters of his name but a majestic phallus as well, and said, 'I have a female slave whom I can't use at home and who is in need of lodgings. One of my colleagues suggested you might be able to find somewhere for her.'

'Ah. An officer at the hospital?'

'Yes,' said Ruso, suddenly seeing a way forward. 'I believe you know him. He was here a short while ago and he had to have some time off work as a result.'

Merula managed to look surprised, as if virulent food poisoning were something she could have hoped to keep secret. 'So you know about, ah . . . ?'

'I suggest we say no more about it.'

Ruso was satisfied to see relief on the woman's face. He was right: they had been afraid Valens would sue. When she said, 'I think we can find a place for her,' his problem appeared to be solved.

His problem appeared to be solved until Merula asked, 'Is the girl experienced in this kind of work?'

Ruso shook his head. 'She can't work. She's sick.'

'She can't work?' The painted eyes met his. 'So why did your friend tell you to send her to me?'

'I can't have her at my place, she needs to recuperate and I can hardly billet her in a barrack room.'

Merula pursed her lips. 'This sickness. Is it fever?'

'She's recovering from surgery on an injured arm.'

'And before long you expect her to be fit to work.'

'I see no reason why not. In the meantime all she needs is a quiet room and regular meals. You do rent out rooms?'

'Oh, yes!' After this confident assertion she paused. 'We don't have anything very comfortable just at the moment . . .'

'But you do have a private room?'

'We do, but –'

He followed her up the open staircase and along the creaking wooden landing that looked down over the bar. Several of the upstairs doors were ajar, revealing small cubicles with beds covered in bright blankets and cushions. It all looked reasonably clean. Ruso consoled himself with the thought that at least he was doing business with the best possible class of tax-dodging brothel.

In the gloom at the end of the corridor was a closed door. Merula scraped a key into the lock.

The room was bare except for a bench against one wall and a mattress in the corner. Merula glided forward and unlatched the shutters.

Before he could remark on the bars across an upstairs window, she said, 'We sometimes use this room for secure storage.' The light revealed the rings of old drinks and drips of candle-wax on the surface of the bench. Underneath, one leg had been replaced with a new chunk of yellow wood that was much too heavy, and the whole thing had been clumsily nailed to the floorboards. Ruso crouched and turned over the stained mattress. The straw was even lumpier than the one he was borrowing from Valens and it didn't smell good.

Merula started to explain that the room had not been used for a while. He interrupted her.

'Do you have mice?'

She frowned. 'The girl is on a special diet?'

'I don't mean on the menu. I mean running around. Wild mice.'

As soon as she told him they didn't, he said, 'Put in a clean bed and I'll take it.'

19

She was pretty. Old women said so to her mother, and her mother always laughed and replied, 'And she knows it.' Her brothers knew it too, although they would die before they said so. Sometimes her father came into the house smelling of beer, roared, 'Where's my beautiful girl?' and lifted her on to his shoulders while her mother shouted at him to *mind that child's head on the door*. And for a few moments she would be a giant, lurching around the houses, reaching for the edges of the thatch, taller than the horses and seeing right over the tops of people's fences until he put her down and ignored her pleas for more because parents had things to do and because being pretty did not make you important.

When her mother muttered and sighed and tugged at the tangles with the comb, it was because shiny golden curls needed a lot of looking after. She tried not to smile. Her mother would want to know what she was smiling about, and she already knew it wasn't her cousins' faults that they were ordinary little girls whose hair fell down in straight brown lines and she had to remember to be nice to them and . . .

And the smell was wrong.

Somewhere outside, a man's voice was making ugly, solid sounds that fell like rough logs.

Someone was trying not to pull her hair. Someone was –

She remembered the stink of the bath-house. The glint of metal blades.

'*NO!*'

Her eyes snapped open as her free hand lashed out and clouted a crouching girl across the face. A jolt of pain shot through her injured arm as the girl squealed and over-balanced in a flurry of brown skirt and dirty bare feet.

She had managed to pull herself up and lean against the wall by the time the other girl, who was dark and heavily pregnant, had managed to manoeuvre herself on to all fours and then haul herself up to sit on the wooden bench.

She remembered the bench. She remembered the room. She remembered what her name was supposed to be. She looked at the girl's hands, which were empty, rough and red with work. Then she looked around the floor. There was no sign of any shears. She said, 'Who are you?'

The girl shook her head and pointed to her mouth.

The question in Latin produced exactly the same gesture.

In Latin again: 'Are you dumb?'

The girl nodded, raised her eyebrows in a question and pointed at her, but she did not answer. A name, even one you had only acquired yesterday, should not be so easily given.

'Did they tell you to cut my hair?'

The girl shook her head with a look of alarm. The hand pointed again, this time at a section of hair that had now been untangled. At the far end dangled a comb, trapped in a knot. The girl had been trying to help.

'My name,' she said in Latin, 'is Tilla.' This produced a welcoming smile, but the traditional request for help in her own language, 'I am a stranger here,' was either not understood or ignored.

The girl heaved herself up from the bench, took the one pace necessary to cross the room and lowered herself to sit next to the mattress. She had begun to attack the tangle again when the door burst open and two men walked into the room.

One had grey eyes and cropped iron-grey hair above a thick neck. The thinner one's hair had once been ginger. The deep brown of his eyes added to the impression that the rest of him was fading into middle age. Tilla had time to observe this while both men stood calmly examining what they could see of her. She also observed that the dumb girl had stopped work and shrunk back to sit beside her with her back to the wall. Instead of staring back at these men who had not had the manners to knock (and whose muscle, Tilla noted, was running to fat around the belly) the girl had her eyes firmly fixed on the grey one's heavy Army sandals.

'Stand up,' ordered the grey one.

When Tilla failed to move, the girl tapped her arm and translated the order into a hasty scoop of one hand towards the ceiling, at the same time nodding encouragement.

'You want to listen to Daphne,' suggested the grey one. 'She don't say a lot but she knows what's good for her.'

Tilla, noting the girl's anxiety, pulled her knees up and managed to get to her feet on the mattress. Slowly, she forced her trembling legs to push her upwards. Her head felt as if it were full of dry sand that was draining away down her body as she stood. Fighting to stay upright, she slumped against the wall. With her eyes closed, she did not see him approach. She was only aware of the sudden cold as the hem of the tunic was lifted, the struggle to keep her balance as the hands groped and probed, and the urge to vomit as the hands withdrew and a voice whispered in her ear, 'Show us your smile.'

Clenching her teeth, she managed to open her eyes.

'Smile,' repeated the grey man, who was not smiling.

The other girl was on her feet now, moving round to where Tilla could see her, nodding eagerly and grinning, making upwards gestures at the corners of her mouth.

As Tilla's eyes drifted shut she thought, *Whatever you do to me here will speed me on my way to the next world*, and it was this thought which made her beam with pleasure.

By the time she was alone again the light through the barred window was fading. Food had been brought, but no one had offered a light. The rattle of the lock had confirmed that she could not leave this darkening room until someone came to let her out.

Tilla fingered the long braids that now held her hair under control and listened to the many voices downstairs. She heard the tramp of feet on stairs. The creak of the floor-boards. The false laughter. She understood what sort of place the Roman healer had brought her to. She understood too that none of this mattered, because she had lost all sense of hunger now, surely a sign that she would be in the next world very soon. But she had matters to attend to here first. The grey one had said he would come back.

She reached for the bowl and balanced it against the bandaged arm. Then she picked up the spoon. The lukewarm soup slipped down her throat, sending the strength of the slaughtered ox into her body. She closed her eyes and promised her mother and brothers that she would see them in the next world very soon. In the meantime she would not be shamed in this one. It seemed she was, after all, destined to die in a fight.

20

The kitchen boy took Ruso's message to Merula, who paused with the kitchen door half-open, reached up to a shelf inside and handed over a heavy iron key.

Ruso frowned. 'My girl is locked in?'

The painted eyes widened. 'You don't want her locked in?'

'I appreciate your caution,' he said, understanding that a business which had lost two girls in a few months would be nervous, 'but she's not in a fit state to run away.'

'It's for her own protection,' said Merula. 'Some of the customers like to go exploring.'

Ruso clattered briskly up the wooden stairs with a lamp in one hand and a medical case in the other, trusting it would be apparent to the idlers lolling at the tables beneath that he was not a customer going exploring, but a doctor come to treat a patient. He strode along the landing, passing two cubicles with their doors closed. From behind one came a male voice and a female giggle that sounded like the girl Chloe.

He had to probe with the key before it engaged and he could push the bolt out of place, swing the door open, retrieve his case and enter the room.

His greeting died as something hard smacked against his head. The case fell from his hand. His foot exploded in pain. He was staggering sideways, trying to keep his grip on the lamp, when something shoved him off balance and he crashed on to the floorboards.

For a moment he lay stunned, blinking at the wavering flame of the lamp, which had somehow remained upright. Cutting through the reverberations inside his skull was a pulsing agony in his foot. He managed to lift his head. The girl was squatting behind the door, wide-eyed, hands to her mouth.

He rolled over. The big toe of his right foot, which should surely have been a bloody pulp, looked pale but otherwise surprisingly intact. He rubbed the back of his head. A lump was developing already, and blood was making a sticky mess of his hair. Ruso brought his hand forward and squinted at the damp fingers. The blood seemed an odd colour.

The girl was still in the corner, apparently too frightened to move. Ruso sniffed at the blood, diagnosed soup, rubbed his head again, curled forward and sat up to clutch his injured foot. His case lay on the floor, undamaged after his toe had broken its fall. Scattered across the floor were the shards of what appeared to be a bowl. It occurred to him that the bowl must have been what she had used to hit him. It also occurred to him to ask himself whether he was seeing double, whether any dancing lights were appearing in front of him, or whether he felt sick. He was disappointed to note that despite deserving all these symptoms, he did not seem to have any of them.

He heaved himself up on one leg and hopped to the doorway. No one seemed to have noticed that he had been attacked. He closed the door and leaned against it, keeping one eye on the girl as he unlaced his sandal and made a closer assessment of the damage. The toe was turning crimson now. When he put the foot back on the floor it felt as though someone was boring into the toe with a hot fire-iron.

He sensed a movement and glanced across to see the girl crawling towards him. He made a grab for her wrist just as she pulled the medical case away out of his reach. The lid fell back. The pain banged at the back of his skull. He watched the girl's hand hovering above the neat rows of sharpened instruments. It occurred to him that perhaps she was mad. The unlovely Claudius Innocens might, after all, have been sorely provoked.

He was tensed ready to kick the scalpel out of her hand when he saw that what she had picked up was a white roll of wadding.

The girl dipped the wadding into a cup beside the bed. Then she reached up and stroked it across the back of his head, exclaiming as she felt the lump.

Ruso snatched the wadding from her. 'I'll do that.'

The girl retreated to sit on her bed. He pressed the cool, damp wadding against the back of his head and rested his head on his knees. There was some water left in the cup. He splashed some of it across his toes. It made cold trails inside his sandal but no difference to the pain.

He could make no sense of it. He had done everything in his power to help this girl.

He sat up straight. The girl shrank further back into the corner, eyes darting between his face and his hands, evidently waiting for the beating to start. He noted for the first time that her hair now hung in two long braids that left wispy curls around her temples.

'Well?' he demanded.

'Master?' she whispered, twisting the end of one of the braids around her finger.

'Are you insane, or do you have a good reason for wanting to murder me?'

'No, master.' Her Latin, he noted, seemed to have undergone a sudden improvement. He wondered in what other ways she had tried to deceive him.

'Do you know what happens to slaves who attack their masters, Tilla?'

The braid twisted tighter. Her lower lip began to tremble. 'No, master.'

He hoped she wasn't about to cry. 'Well let me tell you,' he growled, his head and his toe throbbing in grim unison. 'First every slave in the household is arrested. Then the questioners are sent for. It is the questioners' job to extract the truth, and they will carry on their work for several hours, whether their victim talks or not' – in fact it felt as if they were currently in action in the area of his big toe – 'because nobody believes that a slave will tell the truth without torture. And because it is not enough to punish the guilty. A message must be sent to all the other slaves who might be thinking of knocking their masters and mistresses on the head. An example must be set.' He glared at her. 'Is that what you want? To be an example? Or can you explain yourself?'

He removed the wadding and cooled it again in the cup. The pain was clanging about inside his skull like a clapper in a bell.

The girl swallowed. 'I am going to the next world.'

'If I call the questioners, young woman, you will go very, very slowly. And be hard to recognize by the time you get there.'

She seemed to be giving this careful thought. Finally, she said, 'I do not think it is you who comes.'

'You thought I was somebody else? I suppose it didn't occur to you to find out first?'

She lifted her good hand to touch one ear. 'Soldier boots,' she said, pointing to his feet. 'Bad man.'

Ruso stared at the pale figure with sudden comprehension. He said, 'You were going to fight off one of Merula's customers with a soup-bowl?'

She nodded.

He cleared his throat. 'You are completely wrong,' he informed her, arranging his words carefully because the ringing in his head was growing louder and threatening to jumble them. 'You are my patient, under my protection. I apologize if that was not explained to you. Clear up the mess and get back into bed. You will not be punished – this time.'

The girl crawled across the floor, gathering the broken shards of the bowl. Then she eased herself on to the mattress and pulled up the cover. Ruso noted that the bright blankets seemed to be reserved for the public rooms: this one was ordinary sheep-brown.

'You are here to rest until you get better,' he said. 'The door is locked to keep you safe.'

The girl glanced at the bars on the window, then closed her eyes, as if she was tired of trying to understand.

'Is your arm painful?'

She nodded.

He crouched beside her and checked the bandages. She was lucky: the splint had held. There was no sign of movement. He placed his fingers and thumb around her upper arm. No swelling or heat. He laid her hand between his.

'Move your fingers.' He felt the ends of the fingers twitch between his palms. 'Good. Are you eating the food?'

She nodded again.

'Light diet, no flesh, no strong drink, no seafood, and you must drink plenty.'

'Beer,' she ventured.

'Beer?' He cleared his throat, aware that a professional should not allow wispy curls and a borrowed tunic slipping down over one shoulder to distract him from his work. He recalled his mind to his duty. 'Absolutely no beer, nor anything like it.' He gestured towards the lidded bucket in the corner, glad that she had not had the strength to use it as a weapon. 'Are you passing water?'

She nodded.

'Good.'

He reached into the open case. 'I'll give you something for the pain, then you can sleep.' He measured a few drops into the empty cup and handed it to her.

She took a sip and wrinkled her nose.

'Drink,' he ordered, miming the gesture.

She tipped her head back. He retrieved the cup and measured himself a potent dose of the same painkiller, then stood up and closed the shutters. The room was chilly. She had only one blanket.

Downstairs, a lyre-player was competing with the din of voices, the to-and-fro slap of the kitchen door and the clatter and scrape of crockery. From the balcony Ruso could see only two serving-girls for all the tables. Both looked harassed. There was a shout of laughter from the far side of the room, where Merula was pouring drinks for a group of officers.

Ruso turned away. The noise was making his head worse. There was still one cubicle with an open door. He limped in and whipped a rich blue blanket off the bed. He picked up a cushion as well. In the doorway he paused, and skimmed the cushion back on to the bed. There was no point in making her too comfortable.

When he returned the girl was lying flat on the bed with her eyes closed. He laid the blanket over her and tapped her shoulder. 'Before you go to sleep,' he said, sliding the key into her hand, 'make sure you use this.'

21

Ruso was trying to make his way down Merula's stairs without it being obvious that he had acquired a limp during his visit, when he recognized Decimus, the hospital porter. The man was slumped over the crowded bar, wiping his eyes with a grimy fist. He also recognized the signals the barmaid was making to the doormen over the man's head. Ruso sighed. His head hurt. His foot hurt. His dignity was injured. He would not normally have interfered with an off-duty soldier's right to make a fool of himself in a public bar. But it was Decimus who had warned him about Priscus' imminent return yesterday morning, and he supposed he owed the man some sort of favour.

Hoping nobody would tread on his toe, he threaded his way between the tables. Finally close enough not to be overheard, he said, 'Time to go, soldier.'

The man looked at him wetly, sniffed and informed him that he wouldn't understand.

'You're drunk.'

'You don't know what it's like, sir.'

'Go now, Decimus, before you get into trouble.'

'You never liked him anyway. You always said get rid of him.'

'Ah.' Ruso rubbed the back of his head where what remained of the soup was setting his hair into stiff clumps. 'The invisible dog.'

'Bastard.' The porter twisted on his stool and spat noisily on to the floor.

'Oi!' A bald man whose toes he had just missed spun round and glared at him.

'Bastard made us knock him on his head. He was a good dog. He was my best friend. He was faithful, that's what he was.' The orderly waved an arm in the air. 'He was faithful! None of you lot, you don't know what faithful means!'

'Get a grip, man!' urged Ruso, feeling pain dance around his skull as he grabbed the man's arm and hauled him towards the door. Unfortunately for them both, Decimus' feet did not follow. Instead, with another shout of 'Bastard!' he toppled sideways on to Daphne, who screamed as her tray of drinks slid into the bald man's lap.

The bald man leaped up and shoved her aside, roaring, 'I warned you, sunshine!' at the porter.

'He was the best dog in the Legion!' yelled the porter. 'He was – ow!'

'Out!' ordered the ginger-headed doorman, ramming the porter's arm up behind his back while his colleague clamped a forearm around the bald man's throat and offered him the chance to be next if he wanted.

The man struggled to turn. 'You! Where's Asellina? You let somebody steal my Asellina! You let all the girls run away!'

'Out, pal,' repeated Stichus. 'You're banned.'

'All gone. All run away. She was the best girl in the – agh!'

The porter, assisted by Stichus, made an impressive exit. As the man floundered and grumbled in the street, Ruso paused in the entrance.

'We've had trouble with him before,' said Stichus, settling back on to his stool. 'Me, I wouldn't have let him in.'

'I need to leave a message for your mistress.'

Stichus gave him a look that said he was too busy to run

messages. Ruso ignored it. 'I've given my patient the key to her room,' he said.

'You what?'

'So she can choose who to let in.'

Stichus shrugged. 'Please yourself. But we can't be watching her day and night. If she's a runner, it's your problem.'

'She's not in a fit state to run anywhere,' Ruso insisted, although it had crossed his mind that if the girl managed an escape like Asellina's rather than Saufeia's, it might be better for both of them. 'And ask your mistress to keep a note of any refusal to eat and drink.'

'Starving herself, is she? Don't worry, we've seen it all before. Merula'll soon sort that out.'

'Good,' said Ruso, trusting the landlady's attempts to stimulate the girl's appetite would not stray too far from the diet.

His business here now at an end, he gathered up his case and limped out into the street. He had barely taken a step when a voice called, 'Sir!'

Ruso watched an unsteady salute being performed from a sitting position against the closed shutters of the bakery.

'Man in need of assistance, sir!'

Sir closed his eyes to the sight of the porter. He prayed for patience, and for the poppy-juice to work quickly.

Despite Ruso's efforts at guidance, the porter's progress was as much sideways as forwards. Not five paces down the street he stopped to deposit much of what he had drunk in the gutter. Ruso sighed, leaned back against the bakery wall with the weight on his good foot and observed that some wit had added the words 'Same old poison' to the words 'New Cook!' beneath the torch illuminating Merula's doorway.

Finally they swayed back up the dark street and in through the south gates of the fort. Ruso gave the password for both of them, and they were almost through the passageway when the porter seemed to realize where he was. He hauled himself to attention and shouted, 'Request to report a murdering bastard, sir!'

'He's drunk,' explained Ruso, as if the grinning guards were not able to see this for themselves.

'I'm drunk!' agreed the man. 'I'm drunk, sir, but at least I'm not a murdering bastard with a painted head and a –'

'Shut up!' snarled Ruso. 'That's an order.'

The man swung round to inspect Ruso's face in the light of the gatehouse torches. After a moment he announced with apparent surprise, 'I know who you are! You're the new doctor, Doctor. You bring dogs in but they aren't as lovely as my Asellina.'

Ruso glanced across at the gate guards. 'One of you take his other arm, will you?'

Between them they dragged the man forward into the middle of the perimeter road. To Ruso's relief, the painkiller was beginning to take effect. He dismissed the guard, assuring him that he could cope, although the man plainly seemed to doubt him. 'I'm perfectly sober,' he explained, steadying himself as he shifted to take the weight off his sore foot. 'I've just had a bit of a bang on the head.'

'Are you sure you don't need some help, sir?'

'No, I'm fine,' Ruso assured him, leaning closer to explain, 'I'm the doctor. I've prescribed myself something.'

He was starting to feel far more relaxed now. Confident that his command of the situation was secure, he began to half-drag and half-carry the man along the road, taking the shortest route up by the deserted scaffolding of the baths and round the corner past the streaks of light that marked the shutters of the senior officers' houses.

A couple of passers-by offered to help, but he dismissed them with a cheery smile and a wave. There was no problem. He was enjoying himself. He really ought to learn to relax more. See the funny side of things.

When he finally let go the orderly slumped against a post at one end of the dark lane between two barrack blocks.

'You're a good man, sir.'

'Go and lie down, Decimus,' said Ruso.

'You don't know nothing about dogs but you're a good man.'

The man staggered away into the gloom, leaning on the uprights of the portico for support. Finally he paused outside a door and fumbled with the latch. 'Drink plenty of water before you go to sleep,' called Ruso, feeling a rush of kind-ness towards the whole of humankind, encapsulated in this one drunken hospital porter, but the man was too busy falling through the doorway to hear him.

Ruso was still smiling when he climbed into his own bed, and so relaxed he decided not to bother taking his boots off.

22

Ruso shambled along to the kitchen, wondering which was more painful: his sore head or his sore foot. Wretched woman. He needed a long cool drink of –

Damn. The jug was empty. Valens had thoughtfully moved it to weigh down the lid of the breadbin against invading mice, but hadn't bothered to nip out and fill it first. Inside the bin was a chunk of bread so hard that the mice could have sharpened their teeth on it. There seemed to be nothing else edible in the kitchen. He chose the least dirty of the cups on the shelf and limped down to the dining room. Beer would be better than nothing.

A gang of puppies bounced around his feet as he dipped the cup into the barrel. He was replacing the lid when there was a knock at the door. Still clutching the cup and with puppies licking up the drips in his wake, he went to explain to whoever it was that Valens was out.

The moment the door opened, the arm of the young soldier outside shot up in a salute.

Ruso transferred the beer to his other hand, put out his good foot to prevent a puppy escape and lost his balance slightly before returning an untidy salute and asking, 'What do you want?'

'Albanus, sir, reporting for duty.'

Ruso frowned, trying to imagine what the man's duty might be. 'Have you come to help out?'

'Yes sir.'

'Oh. Good. Well, you can start by getting some water.

I've got a mouth like a sand dune and there's nothing to drink.'

The man looked puzzled. 'Water, sir?'

Ruso jerked a thumb over his shoulder. 'Jug's in the kitchen.'

He stepped aside, but the man did not move.

'Come in,' ordered Ruso. 'Shut the door before the dogs get out.'

'Sir?'

'What?'

'I'm your scribe, sir.'

Ruso stared at him, and noticed the clues for the first time. The ink-stained fingers. The slight bulge to the eyes caused by peering at documents by lamplight. 'Oh.'

The man held up a satchel. 'I've brought my equipment, sir.'

'Well you can take it away again,' said Ruso. 'I'm not on duty till this afternoon.' He paused. 'Report to me at the hospital at the seventh hour.'

'Yes, sir.' There was a pause. 'What would you like me to do until then, sir?'

Gods above, Priscus had sent him an enthusiast. 'Haven't you got some old records to copy up?'

Yes, sir, he had.

'Then you can get on with that. Anything you can't read, ask me this afternoon. Don't make it up.'

'Yes, sir.'

The wretched man was still standing there.

'Anything else?'

'No, sir.'

There was a silence, then Ruso remembered to say, 'Dismissed.'

After another snappy salute Albanus spun round, sending

his satchel swinging outwards and crashing back against his side, and marched off in the direction of the hospital. Ruso shut the door, sniffed the beer and decided it wasn't better than nothing after all. He limped back into the kitchen to fetch the jug. He had the feeling Albanus would have copied all the records in triplicate by lunchtime and be pestering him for more work. He could have given him the *Concise Guide* to copy. It was a pity that most of it wasn't written yet.

Ruso was carrying the jug out of the door when there was a crash and a skitter of paws across floorboards. He turned. Several puppies were running for cover. One was perched on a side table, peering over the edge at fragments of cup lying in a spreading pool of beer.

Ruso shut the door quietly, limped down the street to the water fountain and stuck his head under it.

23

Tilla could smell fresh bread. She pulled the blanket tighter around her shoulders and peered out between the window bars. Across the street, a pigeon was perched on the roof of the bakery. Beneath it, someone swung back the first panel of the door shutters. A plump woman appeared in the gap, bending to apply her bottom to the rest of the shuttering. The panels shifted on their hinges and the pigeon swooped away as the whole apparatus began to screech back along its groove.

Tilla watched the pigeon until the frame of the window blocked her view. Then she returned to her bed, slid her hand underneath and pulled out the iron key the healer had given her last night. She had felt sorry for the healer, who had done nothing to deserve being smacked on the head and who should have had her beaten – since it seemed she did, after all, still belong to him. Evidently she was not yet the property of the ill-mannered bullies who had sauntered in yesterday with the clear intention of sizing her up for their own use.

The question was, what should she do now? She had the key. If she could find clothes, if she ate and built up her strength, if she could judge the right moment, she could escape. Or, she could choose not to eat, to cheat the work of the healer and step forward towards her death. What honour, though, would she have in the next world if she had been offered a chance of freedom in this one and refused to take the risk?

A clunk from the loose board in the corridor warned her that someone was about. Moments later there was a soft knock at the door. Tilla pressed her face against the doorframe and squinted through the crack. She could just about make out a shape that was not tall enough to be either of the men.

'Daphne?'

The form moved and the hand knocked again.

Tilla slid the key into the lock, positioned one foot an inch away to hold the door while she assured herself it was only the girl and then let her in.

'Daphne,' she said, locking the door again. 'Thank you.'

The girl put the tray down on the bench.

'Did you sleep well?'

Daphne shrugged and indicated her belly in a way that suggested her expectations of sleep were limited.

'When is your baby due?'

A second shrug indicated that this was not a subject of great interest.

'My master has given me the key,' explained Tilla, 'so I can decide who comes in. I do not want those men in here. If you come alone, knock like this.' She demonstrated three short taps on the windowsill. 'Understand?'

Daphne reached out a hand and gave three short taps on the door.

'Only if you are alone, yes?'

Daphne nodded and pointed to herself. For a moment Tilla thought she was about to smile, but a yell of, 'Daphne!' from downstairs reminded her of her duties. Tilla let her out, locked the door and retreated to see what they had given her for breakfast.

24

The outside door to the hospital kitchen was propped open to let out the heat as usual. Ruso nodded a greeting to the cooks as he passed, pausing long enough to light a taper on the grilling-coals but not long enough to answer any questions, either about why he was limping horribly or why he didn't use the front door like everyone else.

He waited until the corridor was empty before making his way down to the courtyard door. Clutching his case in one hand and the taper in the other, he managed to hobble across the courtyard garden and enter by the consulting rooms without being accosted by either patients or staff.

Ruso leaned back on the closed door of the consulting room and contemplated his toe. Such a small part of the body. Such disproportionate agony.

He lit a stub of candle. Then he unlatched his case and retrieved the thinnest of the bronze probes, which had, as usual, fallen out of its place. He propped the thicker end of the probe on the top of an inkpot and moved the candle so the tip of the probe was being lapped by the flame.

While he waited for the instrument to heat, he unlaced his sandal, glanced around the room and then moved a chair away from the wall under the window. This was a quick and straightforward procedure. There was no need for painkillers or restraints. There was also no need for furniture for him to fall off if things didn't turn out to be quite as straightforward and quick as when he did this to other people.

Shielding his fingers from the heat with a cloth, Ruso

picked up the cooler end of the probe. He sat himself on the floor below the window and braced his back against the wall. He took a deep breath. Then he placed the tip of the probe against his toenail.

The door burst open. His hand jolted. The probe slipped out of his grasp and rolled across the floor.

'Ruso!' exclaimed Valens. 'They told me you were in here. What are you doing down there?'

He explained.

Valens examined the toe. His face brightened in a manner which Ruso found faintly unsettling. 'Shall I do it?'

'No thank you.'

'Well can I bring a couple of chaps in to watch?'

It was an unwelcome, but not an unreasonable, request. 'If you must,' said Ruso. He got to his feet with some difficulty and repositioned the probe over the flame.

Moments later Valens returned with the couple of chaps. Either he had lost the ability to count, or each of the chaps had invited a couple more chaps of his own.

'See how the blood's built up under the nail,' explained Valens as his audience shuffled about to get a better view of Ruso's blackened toenail. 'How does it feel?'

'Painful,' grunted Ruso. He could feel himself starting to sweat.

'It's the pressure that's causing the pain,' explained Valens. 'You'll see this a lot on fingers, too. Carpenter's thumb. You, pass that probe over, will you?'

There was movement in the corner. A voice said, 'Shall I put the candle out, sir?'

'Not yet,' ordered Valens cheerfully, 'he might want to have several stabs at it.'

Ruso, who hoped fervently that he would not need more than one stab at it, told himself this was only a very small

136

amount of additional pain. It would, as he assured his patients, bring instant relief. Suddenly, however, this logic did not seem to offer a great deal of comfort. But he could not change his mind now. Nor could he postpone the moment any longer. The probe was being held out for him to take between finger and thumb.

He adjusted his grip, positioned the tip of the probe over the dark blister that had formed under his toenail during the night and pressed.

He gasped as an excruciating wave of pain shot up his foot. Sweating, he forced himself to hold the probe steady and keep pressing as he smelled the nail burning. He closed his eyes, clenched his teeth and pushed harder.

Suddenly the resistance to the probe gave way. He withdrew it and gave an involuntary sigh of relief as the blood welled out of the burned hole, and the pain began to subside.

He looked up, surveyed the silent faces and grinned. 'Thank you, gentlemen. Any questions?'

After the students had been shooed out Valens said, 'Before you distracted me, I came to tell you I've been invited out to dinner tonight.'

'Really?' Ruso wiped his toe with a damp cloth and wondered if dinner invitations were so rare in Britannia that guests felt the need to boast about them.

'And,' Valens continued, 'it's a pity you've already performed your party trick, because so have you.'

25

A small informal dinner, as arranged by the wife of Centurion Rutilius, was one where Ruso was required to make conversation with seven people he didn't know plus one he'd seen too much of, while eating a selection of elaborate dishes that bore little or no resemblance to their stated ingredients.

He had been introduced to his fellow guests and promptly forgotten most of their names. This was a situation he was hoping to salvage by not speaking unless spoken to. He would ask Valens afterwards. Valens would know what everyone was called, particularly the two daughters of their host. Obviously they were both Rutilia something, but Ruso was damned if he could remember what. The younger one wasn't supposed to be there anyway: she had been summoned at the last minute when the Second Spear, who turned out to be her uncle, arrived alone. Apparently his daughter had a bad head cold and wouldn't be coming after all.

Valens, who might conceivably have been disappointed at this news, seemed to accept it stoically enough when etiquette now demanded a rearrangement of the seating plan and he found himself lounging between the plump and giggly wife of another centurion and the elder Rutilia, who must have been of marriageable age.

Ruso took another spoonful of something soft and eggy and wondered how long it would be before Valens offered the Second Spear's daughter a house call. Around him, his fellow diners were finding ways of informing each other that they thought Hadrian would make a fine Emperor, largely because nobody was yet drunk enough to dare say anything else. It was an example of the meaningless conversation which, as Ruso had once tried to explain to Claudia, was one of the reasons he could not see the point of dinner parties.

'What's wrong with people being nice? I suppose you'd rather stay at home and be grumpy?'

'I'm not grumpy. I'm busy.'

'Well just because you're busy, why do I have to stay at home by myself and be miserable?'

Claudia's parents, Ruso felt, had done their daughter a serious disservice. It was clear that they had never introduced her, either by education or example, to the words 'obedience' and 'duty'.

His hosts were going to have similar problems with the other Rutilia, who was not much younger than her sister, if they were not careful. While the plump wife moved on from praising the Emperor to admiring the catering and the décor of the dining room, Rutilia the younger was beckoning the wine-jug over for the third time. The slave, who should have had the sense to refuse, didn't.

Ruso licked meat sauce off his fingers and realized his hostess was speaking to him. 'I'm sorry, you said . . . ?'

'I said, are you enjoying our venison sauce, Doctor?'

He nodded. 'Excellent.' (So that was what it was.)

'I'll have the recipe sent over.'

He thanked her, wondering what sort of sauce would be produced by two medics who between them could barely boil an egg. Across the table, Valens caught his eye and grinned.

The plump woman, casually propping one hand under

her jaw to disguise her chins, leaned forward and peered at Ruso. He was diagnosing short sight as she said, 'So how long have you been in Britannia, Doctor?'

'Two weeks,' replied Ruso.

The woman appeared to be waiting for more. He felt there was something else he should add to this reply to pad it out a little, but since he had fully answered the question he could not think what the something might be. This was another reason why he disliked dinner parties. Claudia would insist that attending them was for his own benefit ('You must put yourself forward, Gaius! How will you advance if you never meet the right people?') but afterwards she would complain about his refusal to chatter mindlessly to the right people when he met them. It had just struck him that he could pass the baton by asking this woman the same question back when she gave up waiting and said, 'And what do you think of it?'

He hesitated. Britannia was dilapidated, primitive and damp, but some of these men might have chosen to serve here. 'It's interesting,' he said.

'Our mother doesn't think it's interesting,' piped up a young voice from across the table. 'Our mother says it's the back of beyond.'

'Rutilia Paula!' The woman frowned at her daughter across the top of the tureen. Her earrings glittered in the lamplight as she turned to Ruso. 'And what do you make of the natives, Doctor?'

'I haven't met many yet,' said Ruso, omitting the fact that he owned one of them.

'Are you married?' enquired Rutilia Paula.

'Divorced,' replied Ruso as one of Rutilia the elder's blue sandals gave her little sister a hefty kick, and her mother reinforced the message with, 'Paula dear, really!'

The mother turned back to Ruso. 'I'm so sorry, Doctor. You were saying?'

Ruso shook his head. 'I'd finished.'

Rutilia Paula, evidently encouraged by this response, said, 'Is it true you came from Africa and all your things were eaten by ants and now you're very poor?'

Her mother said loudly, 'They're not very interesting, I'm afraid.'

'Terribly primitive and superstitious,' put in the woman with the chins. 'They put their enemies inside great big men made of sticks and burn them alive, you know.'

'Not now they don't,' pointed out her husband. 'We've put a stop to all that sort of carry-on.'

'I certainly hope so,' replied the wife.

'Now they're just bloody argumentative,' put in her husband. 'Half the trouble we get is trying to stop them fighting each other.'

'They don't want to pay the taxes,' put in Rutilius, 'but they expect us to turn out when there's trouble.'

Ruso deduced that they were talking about the natives. 'Is there much trouble?' he asked.

'The lowland tribes don't give us much bother these days,' said the Second Spear. 'But the higher the mountains, the worse they get.'

'And they are so terribly *dirty*.'

To Ruso's relief the mention of dirt turned the conversation to the vexed question of who was responsible for the slow completion of the work on the fort bath-house. As the finger of blame moved around the fort and beyond, Valens remarked to their hostess how nice it was to meet someone socially who wasn't in the medical profession. 'Most people think we're either going to poison them or slice them up,' he explained, 'so we end up just socializing with each other.'

He glanced at Ruso. 'Except those of us who don't socialize with anybody, of course.'

'You're another of these medical fellers, then?' inquired the Second Spear, eyeing Valens through the steam rising from a roast bird (duck? large hen? small goose? It had been announced on arrival, but Ruso had been distracted by the sight of Rutilia the elder clamping her hand across the top of her sister's wine-glass until the water-jug appeared.).

'I am,' Valens was agreeing. 'I was wondering –'

'Never believed in doctors, myself,' said the Second Spear. 'Bunch of squabbling buffoons.'

Valens shook his head sadly as if in total agreement. 'It's not a well-regulated profession, I'm afraid.'

'Bloody right,' agreed the Second Spear. 'Killed my father. Only had a bit of a cough. Could have lived to be eighty. That lot started at him with the blood-cupping and the silly diets and shoving stuff up his backside, and he was dead within the week.'

The younger Rutilia started to giggle.

'Very unfortunate,' said Valens.

'That's what they said, too.'

Their hostess stepped in. 'Marcus, Doctor Valens was marvellous to Aulus when he was ill. Wasn't he, Aulus?'

Aulus Rutilius grunted assent.

'We were lucky to get him and Doctor Ruso here tonight. They work very hard at that hospital.'

'It'll be easier when we get the CMO back,' said Ruso.

The plump woman looked puzzled. 'The Chief Medical Officer,' Valens explained. 'He's on long-term sick leave.'

There was a 'Hmph' from the Second Spear as Valens added, 'Frankly, he's not likely to come back,' and Rutilia Paula could be heard whispering to her sister, 'Was that the hairy old man with cold hands?'

142

'Shut up!' hissed the sister.

As Rutilius beckoned a sharp-faced slave and murmured something in her ear, the plump woman said, 'I'm sure one of you doctors would make a lovely Chief Medical Officer.'

Valens grinned at Ruso. 'One of us would,' he agreed. He gestured towards the bird. 'This duck is excellent,' he said. 'Which reminds me, does anyone know somebody wanting to hire out a good cook?'

Neither of the ladies could suggest anyone. 'It is terribly hard to get good staff here,' sympathized the wife with the chins.

'This is the best meal we've had in ages,' said Valens. 'When we're off duty we tend to eat out, but you never know what you're getting when you eat in public bars. The other day I was nearly murdered by a dish of oysters.'

Encouraged by the interest this aroused, Valens went on to explain the effect of the oysters in the sort of detail that demonstrated another reason why people didn't socialize with doctors. Ruso took a long draught of well-watered wine. He was praying for a medical emergency that would require his immediate presence when he heard Paula suggest, 'Perhaps they used poisoned oysters to murder that girl in the river.'

Rutilius shot his wife a look as the sister retorted, 'Don't be silly. She was strangled.'

Before anyone could reply, the wife said brightly, 'Girls! It has been lovely to have you dining with us but unfortunately —'

'Is it true she was bald?'

'— it's time for bed,' continued her mother, gesturing towards the slave. 'Atia will take you to your room.'

The sharp-faced woman stepped forward, and Ruso heard the elder girl hiss to her sister, 'Now look what you've done!'

'Lovely girls!' enthused the woman with the chins after they had been ushered out of the room.

'Huh,' grunted their father. 'Need some discipline.' He turned to Ruso. 'Sorry about Rutilia Paula. I'll be having words.'

There was a pause, and Ruso realized he should say something. 'Your daughter is . . .' he began, 'she's, ah – very, ah . . .' The woman with the chins emitted a burp. A servant reached forward and removed an empty dish. 'She's actually quite funny,' he said.

The man scowled. 'I'm not raising a comedian: she needs to learn to behave herself.' He turned to his wife. 'How did she get hold of that business about the murder?'

The earrings swayed and sparkled as she shook her head. 'This is a very small place, dear. People talk.'

'It's nothing for you ladies to go worrying about,' put in the Second Spear. 'Just a runaway barmaid.'

'I wouldn't be surprised if it was her own people,' said the woman with the chins. 'They have some very odd ideas here, you know.' She leaned closer to Ruso and her voice dropped to a loud whisper. 'I didn't like to mention it with the girls here, but some of them *share their wives.*'

'Really?' said Ruso. 'Who with?'

The woman gave an alarming giggle that suggested she thought he was flirting with her. 'Each other, of course.'

Ruso, sensing that some reaction was needed, said, 'Glad I'm not a native.'

'Some of them,' she continued, 'don't like the girls mixing with our men. You see, the truth is, Doctor, our men are a much better prospect than theirs.' She turned to her husband. 'Aren't they, dear?'

'Much.'

'Our men have education and training and discipline, you

144

see. Not that theirs couldn't join the Auxiliaries if they wanted to, but most of them are too lazy to work their way up. I expect she was strangled by a jealous native.'

Ruso scratched his ear. The idea that Saufeia had been killed because the locals were jealous of the Army's suave sophistication was something he had not considered.

Their hostess leaned forward. 'Wasn't there another girl from a bar who went missing?'

'It was the same bar,' put in Valens.

'Really?' demanded the woman with the chins. 'The same bar? Perhaps there's a madman lurking there, pretending to be a customer!'

'Must be mad if he goes to the bother of getting them out past the doormen,' put in her husband.

'Perhaps he *is* one of the doormen. You never can tell with these types.'

The man ignored her. 'If he wants to murder women why doesn't he just snatch 'em off the street?'

Their hostess looked alarmed. 'We make sure our girls never, ever go out without a chaperone.'

'We're not talking about daughters of decent families,' pointed out the Second Spear. 'And the bar's just having a run of bad luck. The owner reckons the first one eloped with a sailor.'

The woman with the chins assured the Second Spear that he was bound to catch the murderer soon.

He took a draught of wine and said, 'We'll see. Trouble is, nobody's got time to turn the place upside down looking for him. It's not as if the girl was anybody important.'

'Not to us, perhaps.' The words were out before Ruso thought about them. Suddenly he was aware of a silence and the eyes of everyone round the table turned towards him. 'What I mean is,' he continued, realizing this apparent questioning of the Second Spear's judgement was just the sort of thing that would have annoyed Claudia, 'she must have been important to somebody, once. She had some education.'

Valens grinned. 'Ruso's been making inquiries.'

'Really?' The eyes above the chins were wide.

'No,' he said, glaring at Valens, who had now managed to imply that he didn't trust the Second Spear to investigate properly. 'I just happened to pick it up in conversation.'

'Well, you have to expect these things from time to time,' observed the husband of the woman with the chins. 'We've got over three thousand men stationed here at the moment. We don't pick them to be country gentlemen.'

'What a very sad end,' murmured their hostess. 'The Doctor's right. Somebody must have cared about her.'

'Somebody ought to ask the servants what happened to her,' ventured the plump woman, dabbling her fingers in the bowl held by a patient slave and drying them on the towel over his arm. 'Servants always know everything, you know. It's amazing.'

As Ruso dipped his hands into the warm water, he glanced at the face of the slave holding the bowl. The man's expression gave nothing away.

26

Ruso had just persuaded his stomach to calm down after the unaccustomed riches of a good dinner when the answer to his prayers arrived, much too late. He was woken with the message that he was needed at the hospital. The unlucky patient had been on the way back to barracks from guard duty. In the dark he had tripped, landed badly and dislocated his shoulder. He was finally drugged into semi-consciousness, then painfully and forcefully reshaped and strapped up. Ruso trod the couple of hundred paces back to his bed with more care than usual, only to be summoned an hour later to prescribe for a man having a seizure. On his return he left the message slate propped against his bedroom door with 'Sleeping in, do not disturb' scrawled across it.

Thus it was with neither joy nor enthusiasm that he opened the front door to urgent knocking shortly after dawn and found his clerk was calling to ask whether there was anything he wanted done.

'What I want done,' explained Ruso, summoning all the patience he could muster and wondering what sort of a clerk could fail to understand a staff rota, 'is for you to push off and not bother me until I tell you to. Is that clear?'

'Yes, sir.'

'Dismissed.'

'Yes, sir,' replied the man, saluting, but instead of pushing off as ordered he remained on the doorstep.

'I said, *dismissed*.'

'Yes, sir.'

'So?'

'Are you ordering me not to come, sir?'

'Of course I'm ordering you not to come! Is there something the matter with your hearing?'

'No, sir.'

Ruso leaned against the door-frame and yawned. 'Albanus,' he said, 'are you deliberately trying to annoy me?'

The man looked shocked. 'Oh no, sir.'

'Do you want to be put on a charge for insubordination?'

'Oh no, sir!'

'Then what is the matter with you?'

Albanus' shoulders seemed to shrink as he glanced round to make sure there was no one listening in the street. 'Officer Priscus' orders, sir.'

'Officer Priscus,' explained Ruso, 'has seconded you to me. So you do what I tell you.'

'Yes, sir.'

'So what's the problem?'

'Sir, he's my superior. So when he tells me to report to you in the morning, I have to do it.'

Ruso sighed. 'He only meant the first morning.'

Albanus shook his head. 'No, sir. He told me again yesterday.'

Ruso ran a hand through his hair. 'I'll talk to him. Now get lost.'

Albanus nodded eagerly. 'Shall I get lost anywhere in particular, sir?'

27

Priscus snapped open one of the folding chairs and held it out to Ruso before inserting himself behind the polished desk. As he sat down, Ruso noticed two things: that the glass eyes of the wolf-pelt were now glaring up at a coat of fresh limewash instead of a damp patch, and that the chair he had been given had surprisingly short legs. He was obliged to look up at Priscus in order to speak to him, although, since the administrator was busy aligning his bronze inkstand against the edge of the desk, there did not seem much point in starting yet.

Priscus lifted his hands and held them just above the inkstand, as if poised to catch it should it try to jump back to its original position. Finally satisfied, he smoothed his hair, which did not seem quite as black today. 'Really,' he remarked, 'one would think most men capable of obeying a simple order to leave things where they find them.' Finally he looked at Ruso. 'Oh dear. I seem to have given you the wrong chair. Would you like to . . . ?'

Ruso lounged back in the chair, tipping it on to two legs. 'This is fine,' he assured Priscus, enjoying the look of disapproval.

'I'm glad you've come to see me,' said Priscus. 'I need a word.'

'*Albanus,*' suggested Ruso.

Priscus' eyebrows rose in surprise that might have been genuine. 'Are you dissatisfied with his work?'

'His work is fine. He's keen, he knows Latin and Greek

and he's the only clerk I've ever met who could spell *phthisis* right without asking.'

'Excellent. I thought you would find him useful.'

'He's too useful. He follows me round like a shadow. I can hardly take a pee without he's there to record the event.'

'Ah.' Priscus inclined his head slowly as if he were afraid any sudden movement might dislodge the hair. 'This will be the result of my reassigning his other duties so he can concentrate on helping you settle in.'

'Fine. He's assigned to me. Agreed?'

'Indeed.'

'So I should be giving him his orders.'

Priscus entwined his fingers and leaned forward across the desk. 'Is there some difficulty of which I'm not aware?'

'I think we've just sorted it out.'

'Excellent. We try and run a tidy administration here, Ruso, but I do appreciate that the complexities are a little hard to grasp. So if there are any difficulties with which Albanus can't help you, I hope you won't hesitate to come straight to me.'

Ruso saw the man watch as he lowered the chair back on to all four legs 'There is one thing,' he said.

'How can I help?'

'We'd be able to use the supplies much more efficiently if the staff didn't have to keep finding you to ask for keys.'

Priscus placed both hands on the edge of the desk. 'The men are not permitted to help themselves to supplies,' he said. 'If I expect to be away for any length of time I arrange for adequate stocks to be available.'

'But . . .'

'Sadly, Ruso, this is a policy we have been forced to adopt. There are people in and out of the building at all hours, and even the staff are not always above reproach, so I find it wisest not to tempt them. Lock it or lose it, I'm afraid.'

'I've never had this problem before.'

'No. But there was an unfortunate incident with an inventory check some time ago, and the Chief Medical Officer was . . .' He hesitated, appearing to grope for a word. 'Most dissatisfied. My predecessor was given a dishonourable discharge. Not wishing to follow him, I instigated a policy of supervised access to storage areas.'

As he spoke there was a knock on the door. Having nothing further to say, Ruso made to get up. Priscus motioned him to sit. 'If you wouldn't mind waiting, Ruso? Just a couple more things . . .'

Ruso contemplated the wolf as its killer countersigned dockets for orders to the pharmacy and questioned the need for a new set of scales.

When the pharmacist had gone – leaving behind his request for the scales on a substantial pile labelled 'further consideration' – Priscus turned back to Ruso.

'I do apologize for the interruption,' he said. 'I'm sure you must be rather busy at the moment.'

'I'm told it will improve when we have a CMO.'

Priscus raised one eyebrow. 'Someone in this room, perhaps?'

'I'm the Second Medicus,' Ruso pointed out.

'But only in terms of date of arrival, surely?' Priscus attempted a smile. 'I hear you have combat experience. I would imagine that would stand you in good stead.'

Ruso, wishing to discuss neither the ghastly mess of the Jewish rebellions in Cyrenaica nor his own job prospects, said, 'What was the other thing you wanted to see me about?'

The administrator turned to one side and brought a file down from the shelf. 'Just a couple more small matters which need to be straightened out in time for the auditors . . .' He flipped open the file and ran his finger down the columns. 'Yes, here we are. Charge for private use of isolation room and facilities, five days, immediate payment requested. Perhaps the bill has been mislaid?'

'I don't think I've ever had one.'

'Really? I shall have to look into it. This is exactly the sort of slackness the auditors will pick up.'

'Let me have the bill and I'll see to it.'

'Thank you. I am sorry to have to mention it, but we must tighten up on waste. Otherwise we may be forced to cut back on the services the hospital offers.'

'Ah,' said Ruso, wondering which service Priscus would be proposing – reluctantly, of course – to cut.

'In fact, I was hoping to have a word with you and Doctor Valens about some suggestions for cost-savings.'

'Well, here I am.'

'Simple economies, Doctor. Matters which I assure you will add no burden at all to the medical staff.' Priscus spoke with an intensity that reminded Ruso of the gleam in the glass eyes of the wolf. 'For example, by insisting that most of the hospital business is conducted during the hours of daylight, we should save a considerable amount on candles and lamp-oil over a year.'

'So I imagine,' said Ruso, who had often wished he could find a way to stop men inconveniently falling ill during the night.

'Small savings soon add up, provided one makes a thorough costing first,' continued Priscus, moving his hands in parallel, as if caressing a small saving in the air above his desk. 'Let me give you a simple example. Boiling dressings in larger quantities gives an economy of scale, but we need to invest more in stock in order to keep the supply up. Short-term expense against long-term gain. Which is why . . .'

Ruso braced himself.

'We are instigating a system that will account for the resources each individual uses.'

'How many man-hours will it take to add that lot up?'

'That's the beauty of it, Ruso.' Priscus seemed genuinely enthusiastic. 'The men are here anyway. It's simply a matter of putting them to the best possible use. A short-term concentrated expenditure analysis will allow us to set consistent spending policies, which will in turn make it possible to exercise some form of budgetary control.'

'Are you telling me the Army's running out of money?'

'Oh dear me, no! But we should be making the best use of available resources, don't you agree?'

'I suppose so.'

'And these days the idea that everyone has the authority to order whatever takes his fancy just won't do. If everyone "just" orders in one thing extra, the budgets are out of control. Let me give you an example. Only yesterday I caught one of the orderlies changing pillows between patients.'

'Aren't they supposed to?'

Priscus positively beamed at him. 'The stock of pillows and covers,' he explained, 'is calculated to balance with the timing of the laundry. Unless they are noticeably soiled, pillows are changed on Fridays. Yesterday was Tuesday.'

'I ordered the change.'

Priscus looked surprised. 'Desirable, no doubt, but surely not medically necessary?'

Ruso frowned. It probably hadn't been necessary, but he was not prepared to concede that to Priscus. 'Fresh beds cheer people up. People get better quicker when they aren't miserable. It's a medical decision.'

'But one that has an effect on the laundry bills,' sighed Priscus. 'I appreciate your point, but next time there is a major call on our resources – an epidemic, or a serious accident, or more trouble with the locals – if the budget has been frittered away on inessentials, we have no contingency funds to deal with the crisis.'

Ruso scratched his ear. 'Well if a plague or a war breaks out won't someone in Rome notice and send us some more cash?'

Priscus shook his head sadly. 'Unfortunately, things are never quite that simple. But of course, nobody takes the trouble to discover the real reasons for difficulties: instead everybody blames the administrators. The fundamental problem we have, you see, is that the people who do the spending are not the ones who have to explain it to the Camp Prefect. I have to do that. And very shortly the Camp Prefect will have to explain it to the Imperial Audit Inspectors, and believe me, Ruso, no one wants to fall foul of the Imperial Audit Inspectors. They go through the books like terriers hunting a rat.'

'Hospital administrators hunting a wolf,' suggested Ruso.

'You may have heard that the hospital administrator of the Second Augusta fell on his sword after one of their visits.'

'Wasn't he the one who was selling the medicines and keeping the cash?'

Priscus looked offended. 'All I ask, Ruso, is that if you take decisions affecting my budgets, you clear it with me first.'

'You want me to prescribe whatever's cheapest?'

'The medical decisions are yours,' Priscus assured him. 'But I would be grateful if you would keep me informed. Perhaps we could ask Albanus to copy across any relevant items from your notes.'

Gods above, the man had been planning this ever since

his return! Ruso frowned. 'I can't have patient records put in the hands of the requisitions clerk.'

'Simply the treatments.'

'No. You could track them back. If you want to know how medicine stocks are going, ask the pharmacy. If you want to know how many pillows are being used, get someone to check your cupboards. That's your job. My job is to get the men here back on their feet as quickly as possible.'

Priscus drew a long breath in through his nose and said nothing.

Ruso suppressed a smile. He had never before seen himself as an irresponsible spendthrift. He was quite enjoying the notion.

His enjoyment was short-lived. Priscus reached for another file. Apparently in future the administration would be obliged if he would sign for meals taken when on duty.

'I shouldn't have to pay for them. They deduct enough for food as it is.'

'Precisely. Which is why I have seen to it that Albanus has spent the morning going through the rosters to give the pay office separate lists of meals the kitchen has served you when on and off duty. Because payday, as we are all aware, is almost upon us. And otherwise they would have charged you for all of them.'

Ruso stared at him for a moment and then said, 'Oh,' and forced himself to follow it with 'Thank you.'

Priscus inclined his head slightly. 'A pleasure to be of service,' he said.

28

Tilla was pondering the question of food – how much she could save and hide without arousing anyone's suspicions – when there was a thump low down on the door as if someone had kicked it, and a small voice announced in Latin, 'It's Lucco, missus. I can't knock, I'll drop your tray.'

The ginger-haired kitchen boy had brought a steaming bowl of broth, half a loaf and a cup of water. He placed the tray on the bench and watched as she tore a chunk of bread away with her teeth. She placed it on the windowsill before breaking it awkwardly into crumbs with one hand and pushing it out between the bars.

Finally he said, 'What do you do that for?'

'I have guests.'

The boy looked anxious. 'Cook didn't say nothing about guests.'

'You can wait and see them if you like,' she offered, moving the stool to use it as a table and seating herself on the bench. She gestured towards the tray and offered him some bread.

He shook his head. 'Mistress says you're too skinny and you got to eat it all.'

She tore off another chunk of bread and watched the glistening brown of the broth soak up and darken the bread. By the time she had eaten it the first sparrow had arrived. Lucco said, 'I could get Stichus to find a trap,' and at the sound of his voice the sparrow flew away.

Tilla frowned. 'I do not trap my guests. Sit still and say nothing.'

Moments later several sparrows returned, and there was frantic action on the windowsill until a male blackbird brought order by frightening the others away and helping himself to the last remaining crumbs. When he had gone, Lucco said, 'We could have had sparrow pie.'

'Is it good?'

'We'd find out.'

Tilla fished out a dripping chunk of bread with her spoon.

'I had dormouse once,' Lucco announced. 'And swan. Stichus brought me some back from a dinner party.'

Romans, Tilla reflected, would eat anything that moved. She could almost believe the rumour that they fattened snails in milk and ate them.

'How long have you worked here, Lucco?'

'I was born here,' he told her.

'In this place?'

'In this room.'

She glanced around at the bare walls and felt sorry for a child who had been given such a poor welcome into the world. 'How old are you?'

'Eight winters.'

She dipped the spoon to capture more bread. 'You have the same name as one of my uncles, Lucco, you measure your age in winters like me, and yet you speak in the tongue of the Army.' She switched to her own language. 'Who are your people?'

The boy shook his head. 'We talk Latin here. We honour the Emperor.'

'But amongst ourselves?' she persisted.

Still clinging to the Latin, the boy answered that the

mistress did not like them to 'talk like natives', adding, 'The customers don't like it neither.'

Convinced that he understood, she continued, 'Where can I find people around here who are not ashamed of their own tongue, Lucco?'

The boy looked at her for a moment, then stepped across to pick up the bucket in the corner. 'I forgot,' he said, 'Mistress says I got to empty you out.' Moments later he was gone.

She had not been alone for long when there were three short raps on the door. Instead of Daphne, the ample young woman with the silver ankle-chain was lolling against the door-post. 'Tilla,' she said. 'Is that your real name?'

'Is Chloe yours?'

'Of course not. Let me in.'

As soon as she was inside she closed the door. 'I hear you've been asking questions.'

'I like to learn.' So Lucco had talked. And Daphne had not kept the signal a secret. She would have to be more careful.

Chloe said, 'Leave the boy alone. If you must ask questions, ask me. And if you're thinking of running away, my advice is, don't bother.'

'I did not say what I was thinking.'

'They all think about it. I suppose you've heard the tale about Asellina and her sailor.'

'There is a girl who ran away with a sailor?'

Chloe shrugged. 'So they say. You did well to get hold of the key. Nobody's done that before. But if you think it'll be easy . . .' She opened the door a fraction and checked the landing before closing and locking it. 'It's time somebody told you what happened to Saufeia.'

It seemed that the ill-fated Saufeia had thought she was clever. Clearly she had not realized the dangers that lurked beyond the doors of Merula's.

Tilla said, 'Does no one know who killed her?'

Chloe shrugged. 'They had an investigation. Lined us all up and asked if anybody saw anything. Of course nobody was stupid enough to say yes. So the soldiers helped themselves to whatever they fancied, pushed off back to the fort, and we've never heard a word.'

'Surely it does not end there?'

'Where's it going to go?'

'To find out the truth.'

Chloe gave a bitter laugh. 'The truth isn't going to bring her back, is it? Round here you learn to keep your mouth shut.'

Tilla shook her head. 'Poor Saufeia, with no one to avenge her.'

Chloe looked at her strangely. 'They couldn't. They don't know who did it.'

'And no family to mourn her passing.'

'Look, we did our best. Merula paid for the funeral. Nobody knew what gods she served so we said prayers to all the ones we could think of while Stichus dug the hole, then we threw flowers in and poured a cup of wine over the urn. We even planted violets on top of the grave. Anybody would think we liked her.'

29

Moments after Ruso had emerged from Priscus' office, he spotted Albanus at the far end of a corridor. The clerk dodged back around the corner as if he was attempting to stay out of sight. Puzzled, Ruso continued down the corridor until he reached the corner, then turned to find the man pressed flat against the wall.

'Albanus, are you avoiding me?'

The clerk swallowed. 'You're not supposed to be here yet, sir.'

'Perhaps you'd like me to go away again?'

'Oh no, sir! But you told me to stay out of your way.'

Ruso sighed. 'I didn't mean you have to run off every time you see me.'

'No, sir. Sorry, sir. I could fetch my things and start now if you like, sir.'

'Please do.'

Albanus brightened. 'I'll fetch your post as well, sir, shall I?'

'Post?'

Ruso had been known to ignore his pigeon-hole for weeks and then find something important and out of date in there. Watching Albanus bustle off in the direction of the records office, it occurred to him that having a personal clerk might even turn out to be useful. Although he hoped he would not have to admit as much to Priscus. In fact he was intending to keep well clear of Priscus in future. Merely thinking about the administrator gave him an urge to beat the man over the head with his bronze inkstand. Which, for a professional healer attempting to follow the dictates of reason, logic and philosophy, was more than a little disappointing.

The first letter was from a seller of medical texts advertising his latest stock, none of which Ruso could afford. The second was from one of his former trainees in Antioch, asking for a letter of recommendation. The third was a fresh and unexpected letter from home.

He settled on a stool in the corner of his surgery and read them all. Then, with a calm he did not feel, he dictated a letter of recommendation. He left Albanus to copy it up and to tell anyone who asked that he would be back in time for afternoon clinic.

When he reached the cashier's office, the length of the queue suggested to Ruso that he would, after all, have to keep his patients waiting. At the counter, the duty clerk and a dim but determined soldier were locked in an argument about receipts. Ruso leaned against the wall and reread the letter which was the cause of his being here.

'Greetings, brother,' he deciphered mostly from memory, since as usual Lucius had crammed the lines together to fit everything on the page.

I trust you have sent us the package we are expecting. I thank you and eagerly await its arrival. Unfortunately I am now wondering whether our present course of action remains appropriate. Perhaps the full burden of responsibility for the farm is too much for the pair of us to sustain. As you are our father's heir I am writing to ask your permission to seek a buyer. I will endeavour to find someone who requires a sitting tenant and thus save the family any unnecessary upheaval.

You will be interested to hear that the oldest daughter of

Germanicus Fuscus is to be married in the spring. Naturally Fuscus will be providing his daughter with a suitable wedding celebration and will wish to make a generous gift to the happy couple, as will we.

We are all in good health, Brother, and hope you are the same. Write soon, I beg you.

Fuscus! Ruso certainly was interested to hear, although not about the marriage. Not two months ago, he and Lucius had shaken Fuscus' hand over an agreement to extend the terms of the loan. Now the man had changed his mind, and clearly Lucius had failed to persuade him to hold off.

'Sir?'

A second clerk had appeared at the counter and was beckoning him forward. Ruso did not look at the faces of the men he bypassed. One day, when they were officers, they would jump the queue too.

'I'd like a word with the cashier,' he said. 'In private.'

Afternoon clinic was busy, evening ward round was even busier and, although Lucius' letter was on his mind, Ruso was unable to find the privacy to reply to it. It was several hours after dark when he finally escaped from the hospital – and from Albanus – and made his way back to the house accompanied only by the smell of someone else's fried bacon.

Still pondering his brother's hint about the generous gift, he reflected that he did not have to stay in this inhospitable corner of the Empire. As a surgeon, he was not committed to serve out the twenty-five years of a career soldier. He could try to resign. Make the crossing to Gaul before the winter storms set in. There, he could exploit the tax-free status of a civilian doctor, take on his full responsibilities as paterfamilias and support the family on the ailments of neighbours rich enough to pay him.

The trouble was, would it be enough? What if Fuscus' failure to honour his agreement signified a general loss of faith? If all the debts were called in, there would be no farm to go home to. He would have given up a job he enjoyed, with a regular and very reasonable salary, for nothing. Maybe he should tell Lucius to sell up, and invite them all to join him in Britannia. It was no worse than his stepmother deserved.

What he needed, of course, was the salary of the Chief Medical Officer. Valens was shamelessly putting himself forward for the job on the flimsy basis of having been here first, but Ruso's experience was far wider, and Claudia had always insisted he could do better for himself if he just made more effort to be polite to people. He had taken little notice of her complaints. A man's work should speak louder than his words. The trouble was, hardly anyone here knew much about his work.

He had been wasting too much time messing about with injured and deceased slave-girls. For the sake of his family, he was going to have to find ways to impress the right people. He needed to make useful contacts. Get his face known. Gods above, if he was CMO he could even hunt down a rich widow and persuade her to marry him. He could be the sort of man who gave – the words rang through his head like the blast of a warning trumpet – *dinner parties*.

In the meantime, Lucius was waiting for an answer.

Safely shut away in his bedroom, Ruso opened one of the blank writing-tablets he had persuaded a dubious Albanus to part with (*I have to sign for them, sir*) and scrawled,

Greetings, Brother. Thank you for your suggestion, but I am not prepared to relinquish the burden just yet. Interested to hear about the wedding plans. Are there any more on the horizon? Keep me informed. I am eager to hear all the latest news from home. In the meantime, I am arranging to send three thousand denarii, which I trust will fund a suitably substantial gift.

30

When someone thumped on the door early the next morning, Ruso rolled over in bed, groaned and pulled the covers over his head. Surely he had made himself quite clear yesterday? His bed was warm, it was almost comfortable and he was not going to get out of it. Sooner or later, even Albanus would give up. If he tried the door, the dogs would frighten him off.

Instead of being frightened off, the man let himself in past the excited dogs and made his way into the kitchen. Moments later he was crashing about with the fire-irons. Worse, he was whistling.

Ruso wrenched open the door of his bedroom and roared, 'Albanus!'

The whistling stopped. A rotund stranger appeared in the kitchen doorway. 'Morning, sir. Beautiful morning!'

'Who the hell are you?'

'Justinus, sir. Officer Valens said would I drop by and lend a hand, sir. Get the fire lit, fetch the water, let the dogs out, that sort of thing, sir.'

'Did he tell you to make as much noise as possible?'

'Sorry, sir. Didn't know you were in.'

Ruso, who felt he had earned a lie-in, went back to bed. He had barely drifted back to sleep when he was woken by a knock on his bedroom door. The rotund man handed him a closed writing-tablet. 'From one of the centurions, sir. Thought it might be urgent.'

Ruso undid the tie and squinted at the letters scraped in the wax. 'Marvellous,' he said. 'Thank you.'

'You're welcome, sir. Mind if I ask how you're getting on with the inquiries, sir?'

Ruso frowned. 'What inquiries?'

'I heard you were looking into the murder of that girl, sir. Or is it supposed to be a secret?'

'No,' growled Ruso, 'because I'm not. I'm going back to sleep.'

The man failed to secure the door properly. Moments later it swung open, and a puppy bounded in. It disappeared under the bed and rushed out again with one of Ruso's sandals in its mouth. Ruso leaned over the side of the bed and flung the writing-tablet after it. So he did, after all, have a use for the recipe for venison sauce.

31

The woman at the bakery handed Ruso his breakfast roll without being asked and remarked that it was a good day for a celebration.

'Is it?' inquired Ruso, still resentful at being woken to see it.

The woman looked surprised. 'It's the birthday of the noble Emperor Trajan, sir, may he walk with the gods. We're closing early today.'

'So it is,' said Ruso, who now vaguely recalled some notice to that effect and, feeling some other comment was needed, added, 'Very good.'

'And the gods have blessed us with good weather.'

It struck Ruso that if the gods kept this up, he might not have to buy Tilla any winter clothes. 'When do you think it'll start getting cold?'

The woman assured him there would be no frost for a couple of months. She then contradicted herself by adding that you could never really tell, could you? And if he didn't mind her saying so, it was nice to hear that somebody was still taking an interest in the business of that girl who was murdered, and had he caught anybody yet?

'No,' said Ruso, wondering who had started this rumour and how he could stop it before it reached the ears of the Second Spear.

'We'd help you if we could, but she was hardly here more than a few days, and we don't pay much attention to what goes on over there. It's not very nice sometimes, you know. Especially when it gets late.'

'I can imagine.'

'Shouting and swearing and banging on the shutters.'

'Mm,' said Ruso, groping in his purse for his money so he could escape.

'Those doormen do their best to keep order, but really, it's terribly noisy. We keep ourselves to ourselves. All we knew about that one was that she had a pretty face and a foul mouth.'

Ruso looked up. 'Really?'

'Oh, yes!' The woman looked pleased at his interest. 'She came across the street one day wanting to say something to us. So the doorman, the ginger one – Stichus, is it? – he called her straight back. Which was quite right. We've told that Merula woman we can't have them hanging around here, you see, it puts the customers off, so he was quite within his rights. And when she didn't take any notice he came over and got her, and to be honest, Doctor, she seemed quite a nicely spoken girl up till then – but you should have heard what she said to him! Well, I expect you hear it every day in the barracks, but we don't expect it in the street. And from a young woman. We were quite shocked.'

'And then what happened?'

'What happened?' Evidently the woman had already reached the climax of the story, and Ruso was supposed to be impressed. 'Well, nothing. He took hold of her and got her in and straight up those stairs, and we didn't hear any more of it. The Merula woman did have the decency to come over later to apologize. I will say that for them, they do realize it's not good enough.'

'Tell me about the girl's hair,' said Ruso, suddenly curious.

'Her hair?'

'Was it . . .' Ruso tried to think what questions he could ask, and resorted to 'Could you describe it for me?'

'It was red. Very red, not ginger. Natural, I think. But of course you can never tell.'

'It was natural,' said Ruso, without thinking. Luckily the woman did not pause to wonder how he knew.

'I don't know about the curls,' she said. 'They could have been done with tongs. And I think it was probably quite long, but it was all pinned up, so I couldn't really see.'

'And it was definitely her own hair? Not a wig?'

'Oh yes, I think so. People say you can always tell, don't they, but of course if you couldn't tell you wouldn't know you couldn't, if you see what I mean, would you?'

'Right.'

'To tell you the truth, I wasn't surprised when I heard what happened to her.'

'No?'

'But I was sorry. Nobody deserves to die like that, do they?'

'No,' agreed Ruso, handing over his money, 'they don't.'

'I wish I could be more help to you.'

To his relief another customer arrived at the counter. 'You're not alone,' Ruso assured the woman. 'Nobody else saw anything either.'

She pressed the change into his hand and leaned closer to him. 'Never mind, Doctor,' she said. 'I'm sure you'll catch him in the end.'

Ruso sat on the sunlit bench outside the bakery to finish his breakfast and wondered what Saufeia had been so eager to say to the bakery staff. Probably nothing of any consequence. He decided he had been wrong about Saufeia. She was not a girl with education who had fallen on hard times, but a creature from the gutter who was sharp enough to pick up a cultivated accent and a few letters. He was aware that this should not have made a difference to his attitude:

that the bakery woman was right, and nobody deserved to die like that. But there were many worse ways. He had seen several of them. Perhaps everyone else had been right too. Saufeia had been offered protection. She should have had the sense to take it.

In the meantime, he had more pressing things to think about. He needed to decide whether to order some winter clothes now or wait until payday, when the legion would be besieged by travelling merchants eager to relieve it not only of its quarterly wages but also of any advance on Hadrian's promised bonus. When could a buyer secure the best deal? Claudia would have known. His former valet would have known. Until now, Ruso had never needed to know. Now that he had made the grand economy of selling his staff, he was finding day-to-day penny-pinching not only aggravating but quite baffling.

Reminding himself that Lucius had far worse difficulties to contend with, he brushed the crumbs off his tunic and crossed over into the shadow cast by Merula's bar. The shutters were half opened but there seemed to be no one about.

'They're out,' called Bassus from somewhere in the gloom at the back of the bar. Everyone seemed to be up early this morning.

'I've come to see my patient.' Ruso strode past the tables and started up the stairs.

'You won't find her up there, mate. Try the baths.'

Ruso paused. Perhaps he had been too impulsive when he handed over the key. 'I didn't say she could go out.'

Bassus emerged from the kitchen door, polishing an apple on the front of his tunic. 'You didn't say she couldn't.'

'Did anybody go with her?'

The doorman took a bite out of the apple and stopped

chewing long enough to say, 'You don't want to worry about her, mate. We got the best-kept girls in town here.' He paused to swallow. 'Bathed three times a week, chaperoned everywhere they go . . . Anybody out there messes with our girls, they've got me and Stich to answer to.'

'I see,' said Ruso, politely refraining from observing that two of the best-kept girls in town had chosen to run away.

Bassus grinned. 'If they want to mess with our girls, they got to come over here and show us the money first. Got to build up a retirement fund somehow, haven't I?'

'How's it going?'

The man shook his head. 'Born too soon, mate.' He slid a heavy knife out of the sheath at his belt and began to dig at a brown patch in the apple. 'Born too soon. Me and Stich, we do twenty-five years in the Legion, spend another five years scratching our arses in the reserves, and all we get is the discharge grant.' He flicked the rotten section of the apple out into the street. 'Now we got pimply kids been in the army a week coming in here telling us how they're going to spend the Emperor's bonus.'

'That's very bad luck,' agreed Ruso.

Bassus squinted at the remainder of the apple and, apparently satisfied, wiped the knife on his tunic and slid it back into the sheath. 'Tell you what, though. You and me might be able to do a bit of business.'

'We might?'

'That girl. You don't want to let her go to Merula. Feed her up a bit, she'd be worth something.'

'The thought had crossed my mind.'

'Let me know when you're thinking of cashing in.' He took another bite out of the apple. 'I'll put the word out for you.'

'You know a good dealer?'

171

The man shook his head. 'The dealers round here, they'll rob you blind. I know some people.'

Ruso said, 'I'm waiting till she's fit before I make any decisions.'

The man shrugged. 'Whenever you're ready. Let Merula get her smartened up and see how she turns out.'

'Right.' Ruso paused. 'You're not going to ask me about the investigation?'

'What investigation?'

'There's a rumour going round that I'm investigating the death of your Saufeia.'

'And?'

'And it's not true. So if you come across anything, you need to talk to the Second Spear or one of his people in Regional Control. Not me.'

'And what are they doing?'

Ruso scratched his ear. 'They're ah – as far as I can tell, they've completed the first stage of investigation and now they're waiting for developments.'

'Huh. I won't hold me breath, then.'

'So, when will the girls be back?'

'Shouldn't be long.'

Ruso nodded. 'I'll wait.'

The girl's room was much the same as before except that a stool had been brought in and set by the window. On the seat was a faded red cushion with a patched cover. Ruso wondered if Merula had supplied this comfort so his patient could sit and gaze out between the window-bars, or whether the girl had slipped out and helped herself.

Ruso glanced out at the street. The only people around were the woman at the counter of the bakery, a girl carrying a basket of eggs nested in bracken and a small boy leading a goat. There was no sign of Merula's staff returning from their escorted bathing trip.

Ruso settled himself on the rough bench and took out the *Concise Guide*. He persisted in carrying this one writing-tablet, despite having his own clerk following him around like a lost dog.

It had been a pity about that dog at the hospital, he thought. He should have been firmer in the first place. Made them give it away. Instead, it had fallen victim to the tidying urges of a man who seemed to have everything under control except his own bald patch. To be fair, the place was a lot cleaner since Priscus had returned. The hospital baths were neat, tidy and hot. The wards were swept every morning. Buckets were filled, candles replaced, shelves stocked and spillages instantly swooped upon by men clutching mops. In the drive to root out inefficiency, two more clerks had taken up residence in the records room and now the medical staff had to ask to see patients' files and wait to have them fetched. It was all very impressive, and Ruso supposed he ought to be pleased about it.

He opened the tablet, slid the stylus out of its holder and yawned. Glancing round at the bare walls, he wondered what the girl did in here all day. She did not seem to know anyone who would visit, which was unfortunate but not surprising. The ill-named Innocens must have travelled long distances with his trade. He could have picked her up anywhere in the province. Gazing out of the window was all very well, but if she became idle and dispirited, it would slow her recovery. Fresh air and a short stroll to the baths three times a week would do her good, but in between times, he needed to find something useful to occupy her.

What did women do?

Claudia, as far as he knew, spent a few minutes each day

giving orders to the servants and then went shopping, or sat exchanging mindless gossip with other wives, or tried a new hairstyle. When this became too tiring she retired to a couch with a selection of honey cakes and a scroll of trashy poetry. Since this girl had no servants, no money and no friends, Claudia's example was not much help. With only one arm working she would not be able to fiddle with her hair, and the only use she would have for a scroll would be to light the fire with it.

The little he knew about useful but sedentary tasks like spinning and darning suggested that they too needed both hands. After a moment of staring at the cracks in the plaster, Ruso realized that he did not have a clue what a servant would do all day if she were unable to work.

He glanced back down at the blank sheet of wax. It was surprisingly quiet in here. Bassus, whilst he might have other unappealing habits, was not a whistler, and the crashing din of the construction sites had barely started. Most of the builders would still be at daily training with their units.

Ruso yawned again and tried to remember what should come next in the *Guide*. It was difficult to think concisely when one had not had more than three hours' uninterrupted sleep in the last three days. He put the stylus and the tablet down on the bench. He would just have a quick doze to refresh his mind before pressing on with his work.

The blankets were folded neatly on the mattress. When he pulled them back, two apples tumbled out and rolled across the floor.

The mattress was no less comfortable than his own, which was scant recommendation. He pulled a blanket up over his shoulders and closed his eyes.

He was just drifting into a blessed sleep when he was

pulled back into the room by the sound of something scuffling close by. He resolved to have a good look at the floor later. If he found any mouse droppings, he would demand a discount.

A flurry of wings and frantic cheeping told him the noise was not mice. He opened his eyes. Small birds were squabbling outside the window. When he sat up they flew away. Rising to close the shutters, he noticed a torn scrap of crust and a scatter of breadcrumbs on the wooden sill. He reached through the bars and flicked the crust down into the street, then bent to blow the crumbs away before pulling the shutters across and latching them firmly against the bright morning.

Before long he felt the peaceful floating sensation of a man vaguely and happily aware that he is falling asleep.

He was dreaming in a world suffused with a gentle scent. In the dim light of the dream he could make out a woman sitting in front of him. She was wrapped in a dark blue shawl and holding a splash of bright yellow flowers against a long blue tunic. She had blonde wispy curls pinned back to frame a pretty face, and her eyes were closed. She seemed familiar, as strangers often do in dreams. Then he noticed that, under the shawl, the hand holding the flowers was in a white sling.

Ruso flung back the blanket, sprang to his feet and clapped the shutters apart. The girl's eyes opened.

'I was just waiting for you,' he told her. 'I need to check the dressings.'

In the improved light he observed that her colour seemed better than yesterday. When she removed the shawl he also noted with approval that the tunic – which he supposed he would have to pay for – was not new but patched at the elbows.

175

She reached through the bars to place the flowers on the empty windowsill before seating herself.

The splints seemed to be undisturbed, and the sling was providing even support all along the length of the lower arm and not cutting in at the wrist. Whoever had retied it for her at the baths had evidently used some common sense. He said, 'Where did you get the clothes?'

She pointed at the floorboards.

'Merula?'

The curls bounced as she nodded.

'I expect you to speak when I ask you a question, Tilla.'

She cleared her throat. 'Yes.'

'Yes, sir, or yes, my lord, or yes, master.'

'Yes.'

Ruso sighed. He knew she knew better, but he could not be bothered to argue. Standing beside her, he began the list of daily observations. Hands and feet: cold – and the feet were far from clean. 'Did you wear shoes to go to the baths?'

The curls swayed sideways this time. 'No.'

He would definitely need to explain some rules to Merula. He didn't need her decorated until she was fit. The money wasted on perfume and hair-pins could have been usefully put towards a pair of winter boots, and the draught from the window suggested that she would need a cloak before long. Would he be expected to pay extra for a brazier in the room? He didn't know. What he did know was that owning a sick slave was just one expense after another.

'Eating well?'

'Yes.'

The colour of the hand was normal. He took it between his palms.

'Move your fingers for me.'

He felt them twitch more strongly than before and would

have returned her flicker of a smile had it not been inappropriate. Instead, he said, 'Very good,' made a mental note to point out his patient's progress to Valens and put her through the usual questions about bowels and urine and sleep and pain. Finally he said, 'Right, let's take a look,' and reached behind her neck to untie the sling.

She began to roll back the sleeve of the tunic with her good hand.

The woollen sleeve of the tunic was clinging to the surface of the bandaging. He moved closer to help. 'If it's all doing well under here,' he said, concentrating on unwinding the grubby outer bandage and careful not to be distracted when he accidentally brushed his arm against her breast, 'we should be able to take the splints off in about twenty days.'

The outer bandage was removed. There was still no sign of infection. The smell was only of the cerate he had used in the dressing. The alignment of the splints was good. 'So,' he said, reaching into his case for a fresh bandage, 'before your arm was broken, what work could you do?'

Again there was the flicker of a smile. 'I grow wheat and beans,' she replied with surprising eagerness. 'I milk cows and goats. I make butter and cheese. I spin wool. I help when my mother bring out babies.'

'Anything else?'

She hesitated. 'I make blessings.'

He said, 'Claudius Innocens . . .' and saw her eyes widen at the mention of her former owner, 'said you were an excellent cook.'

The eyes met his. 'Yes, my lord.'

'Good!' he said, because he did not know anyone who wanted their garden tended or their cows and goats blessed, but an attractive and respectful girl with midwifery skills who was a good cook . . . He was glad, after all, that she had not seized her chance to run away. If he could get that arm fully functional, and if Bassus' judgement was sound, maybe Innocens' claim of four thousand denarii would not sound so ridiculous after all.

32

He was on the way to frighten Albanus again by arriving earlier than expected at the hospital when a voice called across the street, 'Ruso! Just the man!' One of Valens' friends emerged from a side street, hurried up to him and seized him by the arm. 'You've got to help me, Ruso. We've got a bit of a problem.'

Ruso, who had already done this officer's job for him once by breaking bad news to Merula, offered only a cautious 'What sort of problem?'

The man moved closer and breathed in his ear. 'You know that derelict building over where they're putting the new shops up – the one that had the fire?'

Ruso nodded. He had just left his purchase from that particular row of shops sitting in the drab little room at Merula's.

'Well. A demolition gang went in yesterday and started pulling it down. When they were packing up to go home for the day one of them was looking around what's left of the back room and noticed an odd shape in the corner.'

'I see.'

'It's not an odd shape when you know what it is. It's a body.'

Ruso remained carefully impassive. To his relief, the man let go of his arm.

'I don't know why this sort of thing always happens when it's me on duty,' the man grumbled. 'Now they want me to find some way of getting rid of it.'

'Why didn't someone deal with it last night?'

The officer scowled. 'Because the idiots wanted to get back for their dinner instead of hanging about answering questions. So they decided not to report it till this morning.' He glanced towards the street opening behind him. 'I hope they had nightmares.'

'Well, it's a nuisance, but I don't see what it's got to do with me. Or you, in fact.'

'Ruso, it's the noble Trajan's birthday. The town council are organizing some sort of do this afternoon. Priests in fancy dress parading about. Expensive sacrifices. The Legate's inviting important people to dinner. This isn't the day to announce that there's an unburied body lurking in the back streets, is it?'

Ruso scratched his ear. The man was right. The news that a departed spirit was wandering loose about the town would cause an upset: the fact that its corpse had turned up during the honouring of a recently deceased Emperor would be seen as a terrible omen. 'Can't they wait a day and find it tomorrow?'

The man shifted uneasily. 'How much do you know about ghosts?'

'Nothing.'

'But would you want to annoy one?'

'I wouldn't want to annoy whatever's left of the noble Trajan, either.'

'Exactly. We need to get out of this without upsetting anybody – or the ghost, if there is one – and the only way I can see is to give the body a decent send-off straight away.'

'Fine.'

'Only we can't get anyone to do it because no one's allowed to know it's there.'

'What about the builders? They should be good at digging.'

'They're refusing to go near the place. They think it's bad luck.'

'The mortuary's no use,' put in Ruso swiftly before the man could suggest it. 'It's not private enough.' Besides, admitting another unknown corpse would mean a fresh encounter with Priscus.

'I thought if we could find out who it was,' continued the officer, 'we could ask a couple of its family or friends to come and shift it on the quiet and then get the priests to purify the place first thing tomorrow morning so the builders can go back in. We just need to find out who it is without telling anyone it's there.'

'We?'

'I've made a start. The family who used to rent the place are all alive and well and HQ's got nobody reported missing.'

'I don't see what else you can do.'

'It doesn't narrow it down much, I know. You see my problem.'

'Yes, but I don't see how I can help you with it.'

The Regional Officer cleared his throat. 'Neither do I,' he admitted, 'but you're the one who knows about this sort of thing. Even the builders told me to fetch the doctor from the hospital who investigates suspicious deaths.'

'I don't! And I'm supposed to be at the hospital by the seventh hour.'

'Oh come on, Ruso – don't be modest!'

'Really. I'm not the least bit interested in investigating suspicious deaths.'

'But everyone thinks you are. Come on, man. Don't leave me on my own with this. We've all got to do our best for Trajan's birthday, haven't we?'

*

Any faint hopes of being able to identify the body were dispelled as soon as Ruso's boots crunched across the debris-strewn site of the burned building. At first glance it was difficult to distinguish the human form, which was the same colour as the blackened timbers in which it lay curled. He glanced back through the gap that had once been a doorway to see the Regional Officer standing at a safe distance. 'You didn't tell me it died in the fire!'

The Regional Officer winced. 'Keep your voice down!'

'How long ago was that?'

'Sometime in late spring. The place was already boarded up ready for demolition, so they didn't bother trying to save it. Just pulled down the one next door to stop the fire spreading and left it to burn.'

Ruso glanced around him. The undemolished remains formed a chaotic jumble that reminded him of the collapsed houses of Antioch. This would have been one of the old single-storey buildings: mostly wood with rough plaster, probably straw or dried bracken on the floor and a thatched roof. It would have gone up like a torch. Anyone caught inside would have had to move fast, and whoever this was hadn't moved fast enough.

He picked his way across the wreckage, testing the charred timbers to check they would take his weight, and crouched to take a closer look from a different angle. He was not sure what he was supposed to be looking for. Yes, it was a body. Yes, it was dead. No, there was no way even its own mother would recognize it. Ruso murmured a quiet assurance to its spirit that he came as a friend. Just in case.

The Regional Officer had untied his neckerchief to hold over his nose. He was making no effort to approach. Ruso scrutinized him for a moment, thinking. Then he unsheathed his knife and dug away a loose flake of charcoal. The fire had been fiercely destructive of human flesh but surely something must have survived that would give a clue to the identity of the body. A knife, a belt-buckle, a cloak-pin . . . maybe nails from the boots . . . All these were things that could have been found by anybody prepared to make the effort. All were things that Ruso should be finding and wasn't.

'Any ideas?'

Ruso shook his head. 'I really haven't got much to go on here.' He straightened. 'And I haven't the faintest idea whether it's suspicious. You'll have to . . .' His voice trailed into silence. He bent down again and poked at something with the point of his knife, then reached forward and pinched it between his thumb and forefinger. Then he dropped it into his palm, spat on it and tried to rub away the soot.

'What have you got?'

Ruso sheathed his knife and made his way back to the Regional Officer. 'I can't tell you who it is,' he said, glancing around to make sure no one in the street could hear him, 'but I think it's female.'

'Another one? Gods, that's the second one this month. And you've no idea at all who it is?'

'I'm a doctor, not a fortune-teller,' said Ruso, skirting the question rather than admit a tentative thought which would be best investigated tomorrow. 'Whatever they tell you, I don't investigate deaths, suspicious or otherwise. You'll have to start asking around in the morning.'

'Damn. It's going to have to stay here till then, isn't it?'

'Unless you have a better idea,' agreed Ruso. Unable to resist, he added, 'Good luck finding somebody to guard it.'

33

Ruso nodded to Aesculapius and then to Decimus the porter on his way into the hospital. He was going to have to talk to Decimus, but not now.

Albanus seemed relieved to see him. It was now well past the seventh hour, and the clerk seemed to think the patients queuing along the benches were blaming him for the delay.

Ruso had strapped a broken finger and dismissed its owner with instructions to send in the next patient when an expensive smell wafted into the surgery. He looked up. 'Priscus! Are you ill?'

'Fortunately, no,' was the reply. 'But I do need to see you.'

'I'm busy.'

'Of course. Perhaps you would be good enough to drop into my office when it's convenient?'

'Later,' agreed Ruso, not specifying a time.

Priscus closed the door. Ruso pictured him gliding away down the corridor, perfuming the rest of the hospital.

He was occupied with patients for most of the afternoon, but a discreet inquiry as he slipped out of the fort – avoiding Priscus – suggested that the public celebration of Trajan's birthday had passed off successfully. No rumours of ill omens seemed to have reached the men on duty at the East Gatehouse. If the Regional Officer had bothered to mount a guard, it must be very discreet.

Relieved that he would not have to face questions about

a cover-up, he hurried down the street towards Merula's. It occurred to him as he strode through the scatter of bruised petals, fallen leaves and animal droppings which marked the course of Trajan's birthday parade that he would not normally visit a broken arm twice in one day. On the other hand, neither would he normally lodge a female convalescent above a disreputable bar guarded by two ex-legionaries intent on a quick profit.

He was almost there when a female voice shouted, 'Doctor!'

He looked up. A pregnant belly, followed by its owner, also clad in vibrant yellow and blue check, was lurching across the street towards him.

'Doctor!'

The woman, who was wearing only one shoe, halted and glanced down at his case again. 'Doctor?'

Ruso closed his eyes briefly and dreamed of a world where women stayed quietly at home and sewed things and understood the value of modesty and obedience – not to mention not turning up dead in suspicious circumstances. When he opened them again, he was still in Britannia. He said, 'Do you need help?'

'Doctor!'

'Midwife?' he suggested. Perhaps he had an immediate use for Tilla after all.

A vigorous shake of the head suggested exasperation as well as denial. She stabbed a forefinger into his chest, then waved her arm back in the direction he had just come. 'Hospital.'

'From the hospital, yes.'

'Hospital!' She turned her head aside and spat in disgust.

'Ah,' said Ruso, feigning understanding and wondering whether her guardians knew she had escaped.

'Soldier!' The arm waved back towards the fort and then indicated her own large form. 'Soldier!' she repeated.

Ruso shook his head in a manner which he hoped looked suitably regretful and lied. 'I'm afraid I have no idea what you're talking about.'

'Tell her he'll marry her,' prompted a voice from across the street. Ruso looked up to see a veteran seated behind a work bench. 'She'll only have to wait twenty-five years.'

'Eyes!' declared the woman, ignoring him.

It was not the word, but the gesture, that sparked Ruso's sudden attention. 'Eyes?' he queried, repeating the gesture so that both hands gradually shaded his vision. He wished he could remember the man's name. 'The signaller? You're the signaller's girlfriend?'

She nodded. 'Signaller! Hospital! Pah!'

Another blob of saliva spattered on to the stones. He turned to the man, who he now realized was mending the woman's other shoe. 'Can you speak British?'

'Not me,' replied the man, not looking up from his work. 'Time they all learned a civilized language. We've been round here since Nero was in nappies.'

Ruso glanced in both directions, but the only people around seemed to be off-duty soldiers and a slave who was discovering that the street was too narrow for the ox-cart he was attempting to lead down it.

'How near are you to finishing that shoe?'

The man lifted the shoe to his face, bit through a thread and held it out. 'Done.'

Ruso turned to the woman. 'Come with me.'

He knew where to find a translator.

'Tilla!' Ruso called up to the barred window with the little pot of yellow flowers on the sill.

186

Stichus, lounging by the entrance with his arms folded, eyed the large form in vivid check before wrinkling his nose and turning to Ruso. 'Merula won't want that one, Doc. We got one that shape already.'

'I need to see Tilla,' said Ruso, just as her face appeared behind the bars. 'Tilla? Come down here.'

Moments later she had threaded her way between the tables, ignoring the attentions of several occupants who seemed keen to engage her in conversation and one who offered to kiss her arm better.

Not wishing to entertain Stichus any further, he led both women away from the bar. By the time they reached the fountain a rapid and energetic exchange in British had made his first question redundant.

'Stop!' he ordered. 'Now we know you understand each other, I want to know who she is and what she wants.'

'She is woman of the Cornovii,' replied Tilla, seating herself on a bench without asking his permission. Ruso placed himself at a suitable distance and the woman settled on the other side of Tilla and peered round at him.

'A woman of the who?'

Tilla reached out her good arm and swept it in an arc to indicate their surroundings. 'All around here is Cornovii land. Until the Army take it away.'

'I take it that's not what she's come to complain about?'

'Her man is Catuvellauni. They are a tribe who try to take over —'

'I know who they are,' said Ruso, who had ridden through the pleasantly civilized lands of the Catuvellauni tribe on the way north from Londinium, but was no nearer to understanding what this woman wanted.

'Her man is here in the Legion,' continued Tilla, in a tone that suggested this was nothing to be proud of, and added, 'he is soldier whose eyes are fading. She says, are you the doctor who say he can go to have his eyes mended?'

'I said we could try. It's a risky procedure. He understood that.'

'She wants to know,' said Tilla, 'why you change your mind.'

'I haven't changed my mind.'

Tilla conveyed this to the woman, who had plenty to say in response. 'She says,' was the translation, 'that her man tells her the new doctor sends him to Londinium to mend his eyes and he shows her the letter –'

Ruso had given the signaller a copy of the referral letter, not because he needed one but because it gave Albanus something else to do.

'And she has packed all the bags and taken her son to her sister's house and borrowed money to go with him and more money for lodgings and today he goes to collect his . . .' Tilla frowned. 'Something to say he can go on the road?'

'Travel warrant.'

'He goes to collect the travel warrant, but the officer will not sign because he is not going. So now he is in trouble with his centurion for not saying his eyes are fading and she has two children and a blind man to care for and everything is worse than –' she broke off, interrupted by the woman. For a moment the two of them were trying to talk over each other. Finally Tilla swivelled round to turn her back on the woman. Her mouth was clamped shut. She folded her good arm over the sling.

'Perhaps,' suggested Ruso, 'you would be good enough to translate?'

'She is a very rude person.'

'That is for me to judge.'

'She says things about you. I say you are a good doctor.'

The signaller's girlfriend splayed her knees to accommodate her belly and leaned further out from her seat. Ruso found himself being glared at by two women. He got to his feet. 'Tell her,' he said, 'that I am going back to the fort and I will have her man report to me immediately.'

Tilla stood and relayed this message with an impressive air of hauteur, then reported, 'She says he did not send her and she wants to know what you will say to him.'

'Tell her,' replied Ruso, 'that what I say to my patients is confidential. And that insulting a Roman officer is a very serious matter. She should learn to curb her tongue.'

The signaller looked pale when he turned up at the hospital. His tone veered between respectful and aggrieved as he explained the mysterious reversal of fortune that had fallen upon him. His centurion was now issuing a request for a medical discharge, but not before he and the comrades who had covered up for him had completed a month of ditch-clearing fuelled by nothing but barley bread and water as punishment. Possibly in an attempt to avert further disaster, he apologized on behalf of his girl. She might, he said, have been 'a bit overexcited' due to the circumstances and her condition.

It was dusk by the time the signaller had gone. Albanus offered to fetch a light, but Ruso told him not to bother and dismissed him for the day. Gathering up his medical case, he wondered what the signaller's girl had actually said, and whether he should insist on a translation, but then dismissed the thought from his mind. He was responsible for a mass of family debt, a sick slave, a list of hopeful patients he often didn't know how to help, and now word had got round that he had insulted the Second Spear by undermining his investigation into the suspicious death of the barmaid. In a moment he was going to have to sort out this business about the travel warrant, and tomorrow he would have to have a quiet word with Decimus. That was not going to be a pleasure for either of them. He had enough to worry about without wasting time on the opinions of hysterical women.

34

Contrary to Priscus' own policy, there was a yellow glow from beneath the administrator's door. Ruso, hoping the man's expensive smell had faded during the afternoon, took a deep breath of fresh air before knocking and entering. 'Priscus,' he said, relieved that the smell was not as bad as he had feared, 'I don't know what you want, but I want to talk about cataract surgery.'

Priscus indicated the folding chairs. 'Do please sit down, Doctor. I was wondering at what time I might have the pleasure of your company.'

'I recommended a patient for examination by a specialist,' said Ruso, snapping open the taller of the two chairs and ignoring the hint that it was his own fault Priscus was being forced to use artificial lighting. 'Now I'm told his travel warrant has been refused. Perhaps you could explain.'

'Ah.'

'That was a medical decision.'

'Indeed.'

'We've had this discussion before.'

'Indeed we have, but —'

'I believe I made my position quite clear.'

'Perfectly. And I made clear to you that I would appreciate being consulted before costly decisions are taken.'

'If you had been here,' pointed out Ruso, 'I would have mentioned it. As it was, nobody could tell me when you'd be back, and the surgeon's heading off to Rome at the end of the month. If the auditors don't like it, you can blame me. Now can we stop playing games and get this travel warrant signed?'

Priscus leaned his elbows on the desk and placed his fingers together at the tips. 'I'm afraid this is a rather delicate matter.'

'We can sort the delicacies out after he's gone.'

Priscus sighed. 'I realize that the decision was taken in my absence, before we had our little talk. I was only made aware of it yesterday when the man's centurion referred the sick-leave request back here to confirm your signature. Evidently he had not realized we had a new doctor. In the circumstances, I would not normally have intervened. Especially since you are particularly sensitive about this sort of thing. However, as you may be aware, I have the honour of supervising the Aesculapian Thanksgiving Fund.'

Ruso grunted. This was no surprise. Priscus seemed to have the honour of supervising everything remotely connected with the hospital.

'The Fund,' Priscus continued, 'is used to pay for items or services of benefit to the patients which it is not possible to cover within the normal hospital budget.'

'Of course. Is this relevant?'

'I believe loaning out amounts which are currently surplus to the needs of the Fund represents good stewardship.'

'So do I. I borrowed some of them.'

'I was delighted to note,' continued Priscus, as if his speech had been prepared in advance, 'that in my absence you took advantage of the very favourable terms we can arrange.'

'Is that some sort of a problem?'

'No. No indeed. Although of course we do have to make sure that, should the funds be required for an emergency, they can be swiftly replenished.'

Ruso leaned back in the chair. 'Are you telling me,' he said, 'that you've managed to lend out so much money we can't pay for one man to visit an eye surgeon?'

'No, no! Of course not. Although if I had not been away on business, I would have made sure the present level of the fund was checked before the loan was agreed.'

Ruso shrugged. 'If the auditors pick it up, I'll tell them it wasn't you who handed out the cash. And by the time the bill comes in from the surgeon, we'll be past payday and you'll have your money back.'

'Thank you.' Priscus reached for a writing-tablet. 'I'm afraid I must ask you to sign another chit. Just a formality, of course, but we do have to show that we have some sort of guarantee.'

'What for? The pay clerks can stop the money out of my bonus.'

Priscus' lips twitched. 'Of course,' he said. His teeth appeared in a smile. 'But in view of the second loan you arranged yesterday, based also on the Emperor's bonus, I think it would be wise.'

Ruso blinked. How in the name of all the gods did Priscus know what he had been doing at Headquarters yesterday?

'Rest assured that this is entirely confidential, Ruso.'

Was that smile supposed to be reassuring?

'But you understand, with such a substantial loan, certain inquiries have to be made. Normally the inquiries would stay within the Cashier's office, but since we have now won our battle to keep the Aesculapian Fund largely under hospital control –'

'Priscus, if this is some sort of turf war between the hospital and HQ . . .'

'Of course, as your colleague on the hospital staff, I said nothing to the Cashier's office that might cause you any difficulty. I thought you might prefer to settle this matter between ourselves. But as you see, that then leaves me in an awkward position. If we are to retain control of the Aesculapian Fund for the benefit of the patients, the auditors will want to see that correct procedures are followed and some form of security is agreed for the loans.'

'I see.' He saw only too clearly. He saw that Priscus was wondering why he was borrowing large sums of money. He saw that he did not have his father's cunning, and, if he was not careful, his attempts to save the family from the legacy of that cunning would quickly prove disastrous.

'Of course, if you would prefer,' Priscus was saying, 'we could ask the Camp Prefect to authorize a suspension of the normal conditions.'

Ruso had to admire the way the threat had been made to sound like an offer of assistance. 'As you've no doubt been told,' he said, 'I'm in the process of replacing my household effects.' It struck him that he was starting to talk like Priscus. 'But I do have an excellent library of medical texts,' he said, 'which I think you'll find more than outweigh the value of the loan.'

Priscus hesitated. 'There would be a slight difficulty there.'

'Really?'

'The market for medical texts is a little – restricted. Valuable, of course, but not instantly saleable. I'm afraid the auditors would be looking for something which could be turned into ready cash should the need arise.'

'It won't.'

'Of course not. As I said, this is just a formality.' Priscus' lips drew back to show his teeth again. 'I'm sure we can think of something suitable.'

Ruso could, but he was not going to admit to owning the title to the farm. If he did that, it would only be a matter of time before someone – and Priscus was bright enough, and nosey enough – would put everything together and realize how many layers of loans rested on that one small patch of land in southern Gaul.

Priscus moved a candle closer and made a show of rereading the loan docket. 'We really don't want to trouble the Camp Prefect if we don't have to, do we?' Still reading, he ran one hand lightly over the top of his head, as if to make sure all was firmly in place, and then glanced up. 'I believe you do own a girl?'

'She's a liability.'

'But rather attractive, I hear.'

There seemed to be very little Priscus had not heard.

'She would fetch a good price.'

'Not immediately.'

'No matter. As you say, the need will not arise.' The teeth reappeared. 'Shall we say the girl, then, Doctor?'

Ruso gave Aesculapius an especially careful nod on the way out and hoped, as he often did, that the god did not have the power to see into his thoughts. Was using the girl as a loan guarantee any way to repay the divine being who had kept her alive at his request? On the other hand, perhaps Aesculapius was in charge of the whole business. The god of healing was working beyond his usual field: he had looked ahead and saved the girl for the very purpose of helping Ruso solve his family's cash problems.

Ruso made sure he was well clear of the hospital before he allowed himself to admit a suspicion that the figure in the hall did not care one way or the other.

35

Ruso yawned and put the *Concise Guide* – which had advanced precisely three lines this evening – away in the trunk. As he turned he caught sight of his purse on the bedside table. It occurred to him that the blue glass bead he had removed from that body was still inside. He had meant to leave the bead in the mortuary for the night, but this evening's clash with Priscus had driven the plan from his mind. He was too tired to tramp over there now. The thought that it could bring bad luck had been a superstitious whim, and one of which he was faintly ashamed. Fear, he mused, was definitely contagious. And sometimes convenient. He had no doubt that the builders were frightened of the corpse, but they had probably enjoyed the day off work.

As he rolled on to his side he felt a series of small movements around him. The puppy that had scrambled on to his bed while he was writing must have sneaked under the cover. He stretched one arm out and felt for the latch on the door. The puppy could make its way out later if it wanted. Finally settled, he yawned again and pulled the blankets up over his shoulders. Valens was on call tonight. What a lot of things a man didn't need when he could feel delight at the simple prospect of an uninterrupted night's sleep.

Ruso had no idea how much time had passed when he found his mind being dragged to a place it didn't want to go by something bouncing about on the bed. He wriggled in annoyance. There was a yelp and a skitter of movement across the floor. Reluctantly his mind registered that whatever it was had gone away. The word *puppy* drifted past him. Wretched dogs. Moments later he thought: *this is one of those dreams where you think you are awake.* He must make some notes on it in the morning. Dreams were interesting. There were many claims for healing in dreams.

This dream was not about healing. It was full of barking dogs. In it he reached up and pulled the pillow around his ears. Dream or no, Valens would deal with it. It was Valens' job to get up, silence the dogs and put out the – great Jupiter!

Ruso opened his eyes and scrambled out from under the covers. 'Fire!' he bellowed, grabbing his pillow and beating at the flames that were shooting up from the foot of his straw mattress. 'FIRE! Valens! WAKE UP!'

36

The tunic was a pleasing colour. Blue suited her. Rianorix from the next valley had told her so. Of course she had ignored him and walked on, because she could do better for herself than an apprentice basket-maker and because the last time she had smiled at a compliment, the giver had burst out laughing and demanded payment from his friends. Her response had won him his bet. But Rianorix's words had stayed with her. 'Blue is a good colour for you, daughter of Lugh.'

So when the woman they called Merula had held up three colours against her this morning and chosen the blue one, she was not surprised. The fabric was a coarser weave than anything she would have worn at home, and it had reached the patched stage at which she would normally have handed it on to one of the servants. But it was infinitely better than the scratchy rust-red Army tunic that was wide in all the wrong places and much too short, and in which she had always felt like a curious exhibit in a cage.

Tilla blew out the candle and lay down on the bed. She closed her eyes. It was the will of the goddess that she should escape: she saw that now. Her prayer was answered. People were being sent to help her. Merula had provided clothes. And now the Medicus had told her the splints could come off in twenty days. In her own mind, in the plan he knew nothing about, that gave her eighteen days to find a good pair of shoes and a cloak with a hood to cover her hair. On the nineteenth day she would slip out, release her arm from the bandages and walk away, just another pedestrian in the street, while the man who thought he owned her would be searching for a woman wearing a sling.

She had wondered where she would go, but today the outraged girl in the awful yellow and blue check had provided her answer.

Before the Medicus had interrupted and insisted on asking his own questions, Tilla had learned with very little prompting that not everyone around here was as progressive as this girl with her soldier boyfriend. Even some of the girl's own family were still trying to pretend the Legion would go away if they ignored it. Although her man was a Briton by birth, he had chosen to join up and make something of himself. No man born a Roman citizen could have served the Emperor with more dedication – and now the Army had betrayed him.

Privately Tilla thought the girl should have known better than to involve herself with anyone from the Catuvellauni, a tribe who would sell their own grandmothers if the price was right. Nor was she interested in the woes of the boyfriend, who had probably done something he should be ashamed of to become a Roman citizen in the first place. What interested her was that the girl's family lived less than half a day's walk from here, and apparently they were not sympathetic to the Army. She had her first destination.

She would have to be careful, though. There were few people in these streets who would recognize her, but she must make sure she did not run into the Medicus who thought he owned her, or the good-looking friend who was in love with himself or, worst of all, the hideous Claudius Innocens. In the meantime, she must use her time here to watch and learn. She must find out how Asellina and Saufeia had managed to elude the men who guarded the doors.

After that, she would be on her own. And in order to give herself the best possible chance, she needed to find out whether anyone here really did know what had happened to Saufeia.

37

Ruso's soot-smirched hand was shaking only a little as he placed the little ointment pot on the ledge of the mortuary window. 'Rest in peace,' he murmured, then backed out swiftly and closed the door behind him. As he strode away down the hospital corridor, the blue glass bead remained in the pot, safely inside the mortuary. As – he hoped – did any spirit who might be feeling attached to it.

He took another long drink of water before washing off the worst of the soot in the bath-house, wondering what Priscus would have to say in the morning about the blackened state of the towels and the feathers floating about in the cold plunge. But minutes later, surveying the little hospital room that was his for the remainder of the night, he felt almost grateful for the administrator's insistence on cleanliness, tidiness and the readiness of all beds at all times.

Ruso placed the candle on the table next to the cup of water and made sure it was steady. He sniffed at the trunk he had brought across with him from the house and wiped at a couple of feathers stuck to its wet surface. Apart from the odd dark trickle, the water did not seem to have penetrated inside. His books were safe, thank the gods. He left the lid open. He would have to put everything out to air tomorrow. It would all dry sooner or later, but he would be living with the smell of smoke for weeks.

He delved into the trunk and took out one of his father's old letters. He placed it on the table beside the candle and thought how narrowly he had escaped joining him tonight.

Then, finding the scroll he sought, he climbed into bed and pulled up the white hospital blankets. If anything could lull a man back to sleep, Hippocrates' musings *On Airs, Waters and Places* was it.

The problem with Hippocrates, as Ruso realized some minutes later, was that he was not interesting enough to distract his reader from mulling over an eventful night.

After the scorched pillow had exploded in a snowstorm of feathers, Ruso had abandoned fire-fighting and dragged his burning mattress into the street. Yelling for help, he then rushed back into the house. Dogs raced about, barking and yelping, as he stamped out the wisps of burning straw the mattress had scattered in his wake. He wrenched open Valens' door, shouting into the darkness for him to get up and finally thumping him only to find his fist landing on an empty bed. As he ran back into the hall there was a commotion outside. Relieved, he hurried to greet the night watch and was hit in the face by a shock of cold water. Six men clutching buckets then stampeded past him into the house and proceeded to fling water about his bedroom in a manner that suggested they were enjoying themselves while he fought his way around them, desperate to save his books. Despite turning his bedroom into a swamp, the watch captain then insisted the house was abandoned for the night lest the fire should break out again.

'Well,' said Valens as he and Ruso made their way across to the hospital later, lugging as many of their valuables as they could carry, 'it's a shame about the stink, but at least you managed to save most of the stuff. And your very fine self, of course.'

'I can't understand it,' confessed Ruso. 'I went to bed as usual —'

'Ah well, it's easily done. And you have been rather busy lately, what with all your women.'

'But I didn't leave anything burning!'

They stepped inside the hospital entrance hall, returned the greeting of the surprised night porter and paused to nod to Aesculapius. Over the sound of their boots in the empty corridor Valens said, 'You'll have to take back everything you said about dogs, you know.'

'I've got nothing against dogs!' Unlike the captain of the watch, who had found plenty to say after the terrier bitch had bitten him in the excitement.

'Where did they go, by the way?'

Ruso shifted his grip on the trunk. 'The watch knocked up one of the vets to take them in and check them over. Listen, I'm sure I didn't –'

'Ruso, it doesn't matter. Really. They're sending a gang to help clean up in the morning, and I expect the stores will lend you some bedding until you can replace mine. Frankly, for a chap who's just nearly had his house burned down – and I could have been in it, did you think of that? – I'm really extremely calm.' He paused in the doorway of an empty room. 'I'll take this one. You can have the one round the corner. Don't snore too loudly or Priscus will complain.'

'Priscus?'

'He's around somewhere. Monitoring levels of after-hours activity.'

Ruso glanced round to make sure Priscus was not lurking in the corridor and cleared his throat. 'Valens?'

Valens flung his armful of possessions on to the floor. 'Gods, those feathers have got everywhere. What now?'

'What if it wasn't me?'

'Ruso, you're getting overwrought. What do you mean,

what if it wasn't you? Next you'll be blaming the dogs. Just try and be more careful in future, will you?'

Ruso put down *On Airs, Waters and Places*, rubbed his eyes and squinted into the candle flame. Perhaps he really had forgotten to pinch out his light. Perhaps the puppy had grabbed it, carried it down to the end of the bed and . . . and Valens was right, he was overwrought. He turned back to Hippocrates. Moments later he found himself mulling over the conversation with the officer from Regional Control.

How much do you know about ghosts?

Nothing.

But would you want to annoy one?

He did not believe in ghosts, but neither did he believe in mattresses that set themselves on fire. That was why he had deposited the bead in the mortuary. And why, although he could scarcely believe he was doing it, he now stepped out of bed and gazed around the little room, wondering what he could find that had a connection with the Emperor Trajan.

Eventually he delved into his purse and picked out a bronze coin. He placed it on the trunk that had been with him in Antioch. Trajan gazed sideways from the surface of the coin while Ruso stood facing him with his arms outstretched.

'Noble Trajan,' he said to the trunk, keeping his voice down in case anyone should overhear, 'Noble Trajan, this is Gaius Petreius Ruso. We met in Antioch. I was there when you –' He paused.

You must put yourself forward, Gaius!

'I saved your life in the earthquake,' he said. Just in case there was any doubt, he added, 'We got out through the window. Now, my lord, they tell me you may be with the gods, and I am in need of your help. I pray you will keep me safe through this night from any spirits who wish me harm, and I ask you to grant peace –' how very, very much he hoped Priscus was not lurking outside the door '– I ask you to grant peace to the spirit of the woman who died wearing the blue glass – oh, this is ridiculous!' He flung himself back on the bed. There was no sense in being logical about the gods in daylight, only to abandon oneself to superstition and trembling during the hours of the night. A man did not become a god just by dying, no matter what his successor might decree.

Ruso perched himself on the bed with the blanket around his shoulders, splashed cold water across his eyes and settled down to spend the rest of the night with Hippocrates.

38

The man who came to crash open Ruso's shutters and wish him a hearty good morning found him propped against the wall with his head lolled to one side. An abandoned scroll lay beside him on the bed, and a solid pool of wax marked the site of a dead candle.

'How are you today, sir?'

Ruso rubbed his neck and tried to manoeuvre his head back to an upright position. As he did so he suddenly realized why he was here. 'I'm still alive!' he announced to the surprised orderly.

The pleasure was short-lived. He had just remembered his first job this morning: to go and retrieve the contents of that pot from the mortuary and find Decimus.

How quickly a man's hopes could crumble. The porter clutched the little bead in his heavy fist as he tried to rub away the tears spilling over into the creases between his fingers.

'I'm sorry,' said Ruso.

The porter nodded and managed, 'Thank you, sir.' He sniffed. 'How did you know it was her?'

'I didn't. But I knew your girl had disappeared some time ago and I thought you'd be able to identify her jewellery.'

'I wish I hadn't said them things about her.'

'You were the only one who kept looking for her.'

The porter sniffed again. 'Did she suffer, sir?'

'I'm told there were people on the scene very quickly, but

nobody heard any cries for help. It's quite possible she lit a fire to keep warm, fell asleep and knew nothing about it.' Had it not been for the dogs, would he have woken last night? Would he have realized what was happening? He didn't know.

The man had opened his fist and was rolling the bead around his palm with the tip of a finger. 'I bought this for her in Virconium when I was on leave, sir. It was a necklace. Just a cheap thing.'

'She must have valued it to wear it.'

'She told me not to waste a lot of money on presents. I was saving up. I was going to get her out of there. She promised me she'd wait.'

Ruso said nothing.

'Why didn't she tell me she was going to run away?'

'Perhaps she went on the spur of the moment,' suggested Ruso. 'She didn't have time to send a message.'

The porter sighed. 'She was a good girl, my Asellina. I know what people said. But it wasn't her fault she had to work in that place. I was going to buy her out. We had plans.' The man looked up suddenly. 'All that about the sailor. I knew it wasn't true. First they tried to blame me for stealing her, then they just made up that sailor to shut me up. What do you think made her run away, sir?'

'I don't suppose we'll ever know,' said Ruso, not voicing the thought that finding the girl's remains proved nothing: she could have been hiding while waiting for any number of sailors. Or soldiers. Or even a well-heeled local. He put his hand on the man's shoulder. 'I'm very sorry, Decimus.'

The man picked up the bead between his finger and thumb. 'Can I keep this, sir?'

'Of course.' Ruso coughed, and wondered how much

smoke he had inhaled last night. 'Tell me some more about her,' he suggested.

'Oh, you should have seen her dance, sir! Chloe's good, but Asellina . . .' The man paused, savouring the memory.

It was not her dancing abilities that Ruso was interested in. 'She sounds . . .' He paused, not sure how to phrase it. 'She sounds a kind-hearted sort of girl.'

'Wouldn't hurt a fly, sir. She never had no enemies, Asellina. Got on with everybody.' The man paused. 'Except – well, you know. But she never meant no harm.'

'There were people she didn't like?'

'Oh, no, sir. She liked everybody. Well, near enough. They have customers down at the bar that nobody likes. But they have to be nice to them, it's their job. The thing was, sir, she used to see the funny side of things. She used to make me laugh. But not everybody knows how to have a good laugh, do they, sir?'

'No,' agreed Ruso, relieved. Clearly Asellina had not been vindictive in life: even if there were such things as ghosts, there was no reason to suppose that in death she would be any different.

Decimus wiped his nose on his fingers and got to his feet. 'She deserves a decent funeral, sir.'

'Now we know who she is, I'll get someone from Regional Control to go and see Merula. Then you'll have to talk to her about funerals.'

Decimus nodded and squared his shoulders. 'I'll see to it. Are you all right yourself now, sir?'

'Fine, thank you.'

'I was sorry to hear about your troubles last night. And now they go and find my Asellina this morning. What do you make of that, sir?'

'Nothing,' said Ruso, to whom daylight had brought the

conclusion that he must have left the candle burning. 'It's just a coincidence.' The puppy must have then knocked it over and rolled it along the floor, where the flame had caught a trailing edge of blanket. 'One last thing, Decimus.'

'Sir?'

'If you're going to drown your sorrows, don't do it at Merula's. And don't go alone.'

The porter managed a weak smile. 'Yes, sir. Thank you, sir.'

After Decimus had left, Ruso thought about the girl who had always seen the funny side of things, who had lain cold and unburied for all those months while the rest of Deva carried on its business around her. The second girl from Merula's bar whom he had met only in death. Now, surely, there would be a proper investigation. In the meantime, he had to go and see what was being done about making his lodgings fit to live in.

39

It was early evening by the time Ruso found time to check on his slave. He found men crowded around the bar entrance, blocking the pavement. As he approached, he heard the twitter of flutes. Evidently the bad news about Asellina had not been allowed to disrupt business. Finding a place in the crowd, he was in time to see the object of everyone's interest display a length of shapely leg through a slit in a silky outfit that left just enough to be imagined. The dancer arched her back and slid one hand slowly up her thigh. Ruso felt the surge of a desire too long denied.

A voice said, 'Good, ain't she, our Chloe?'

He had not noticed Bassus moving over to stand next to him.

'Very,' agreed Ruso, hoping he had not been watching with his mouth open.

'I'll get her to give your girl some lessons.'

Chloe was swaying across the room towards them. Ruso, making an effort to concentrate, said, 'I don't want her working here.'

''Course not,' agreed Bassus as Chloe entwined one braceleted arm around Ruso's neck. 'But a bit of private dancing, that's an extra skill, see?'

Ruso felt the flicker of Chloe's tongue against the lobe of his ear.

Bassus was saying something about it all being money in his purse.

'Yes,' said Ruso thickly, his mind not on his purse at all.

Suddenly he was deserted: Chloe had moved on to work the tables. A legionary was grinning with embarrassment as she ran her hand down his chest. His companions jeered and whooped as the hand slid lower.

Ruso tightened his grip on his medical case. He was making his way across to the stairs – ignoring complaints from customers whose view he was blocking – when Bassus' 'Not that way, Doc!' registered. He turned to find the man pointing him to the kitchen door.

Ruso retraced his steps to loud suggestions that he should make his mind up.

'She didn't have nothing to do up there,' explained Bassus. 'She's helping the cook out instead.'

'I said she wasn't to –'

The doorman's hand was heavy on his shoulder. 'Don't you worry, Doc, I'm protecting our little investment. She's well out of sight.' He winked. 'I told Merula we got to keep her as a surprise.'

Ruso wondered which was worse: having Bassus as an enemy or having him as a friend. 'And untouched,' he insisted.

'You leave it to me, Doc.' Bassus' words would have been more reassuring if he had not added, 'She'll be as untouched as the day she come in here.'

As Ruso entered the kitchen a cloud of smoke and steam that reminded him uncomfortably of last night billowed from the griddle. A stocky figure swung away with one arm raised to protect her eyes. Lucco swerved to avoid a collision. The dishes piled against his small chest swayed and rattled, but he managed to keep them balanced. Across the kitchen, Daphne laid down her rolling pin beside an expanse of flattened pastry and paused to massage the small of her back with floury hands. Both she and Lucco looked as though they had been crying. The cook, who would not have known Asellina, seemed only to be squinting because of the smoke. When it cleared she turned back towards the spitting griddle with a look of determination and a spatula, while Lucco resumed his journey to the crockery shelves. No one seemed interested in Ruso's arrival, and the figure seated at the table with her fair hair in two long plaits did not look up.

Tilla had steadied the bowl on her lap by trapping it between her knees and the tabletop. In front of her on the scrubbed wooden surface was a heap of untouched bean-pods, by her feet a bucket of hollow green halves. Ruso, feeling his tunic beginning to stick to him in the heat, watched unnoticed as she reached for a fresh pod. She pinched one end until it burst open, then widened the gap with her thumb and finally twisted her wrist so the pod was upside down before manoeuvring the thumb back down the inside of the pod to send the beans bouncing into the bowl. A couple shot over the rim. Tilla dropped the empty pod into the bucket and picked up another.

Ruso retrieved a bean that had rolled towards his feet. So, this was what a servant with one hand could do. He hoped the cook was not in a hurry for the vegetables. He stepped forward and dropped the escaped bean into the bowl. Tilla looked up at him in surprise just as the back door opened, sending in a waft of welcome cool air, and with it Merula's voice. 'Doctor! Just the man we need!'

'Give me something, Doctor.'

The hand that grabbed at Ruso's was cold.

Ruso, who had never expected to see its owner again, disentangled himself from the feeble grasp. The two men stood eyeing each other in the middle of Merula's back yard. The sweaty strands of hair that were usually combed flat across Claudius Innocens' head were dangling around his nose. His skin had a greenish tinge which Ruso found both professionally interesting and, on a personal level, deeply satisfying. The silence was interrupted by Innocens' need to bend over the bucket again.

Ruso commended Merula for keeping the patient away from anyone else. It could be contagious.

Merula turned. 'Phryne!'

A blonde girl who was barely more than a child appeared from the open doorway of an outhouse and sidled into the yard. A nervous smile flitted across her features. One hand instinctively rose to cover crooked teeth.

'Get a bed made up in there.'

'Yes, mistress.'

'Well, what are you waiting for?'

'Please, mistress, I don't know where –'

'Then ask someone!'

The girl fled.

Merula turned back to the merchant. 'I hope she isn't going to be another disappointment, Innocens.'

'She's just a little nervous, madam,' he assured her. 'She'll settle down – ah!' He bent over, clutching at his stomach.

Merula asked Ruso what he thought the problem was, adding, 'He hasn't eaten here,' before he could speculate.

Ruso scratched his ear. 'It's hard to say,' he said. 'It could be anything, really.' He turned to the patient, who was now slumped against the wall. 'It might just pass by itself. You really want me to prescribe you something?'

'Anything, Doctor, sir. I'm in your hands.' Innocens' head drooped, swayed towards Merula and lifted again. 'Excellent doctor. Business acquaintance of mine.'

'He sold me a half-dead slave,' explained Ruso.

Innocens made an attempt to plaster the strands of hair

back in place. 'And you got a bargain, sir. She's turned into a fine-looking girl.'

'No thanks to you.' Ruso had a sudden thought. 'Innocens, do you come to Deva regularly?'

'I pass through, sir. From time to time.'

'Were you here in late spring?'

'Ah – possibly, sir. Possibly.'

Ruso wished he had bothered to find out the specific date of the fire. 'How long had you been here before you sold me that slave?'

'Oh, dear . . .' The strands of hair fell down again and dangled while their owner struggled to form an answer. Finally he said, 'About two or three days, I suppose, sir. I really don't feel very –'

'Did you ever know a girl called Saufeia?'

Merula turned to stare at Ruso.

'Me, sir? Saufeia? I don't think so, sir. But these girls' names change like the wind, sir. If you're after something special I could –'

What Claudius Innocens could do was never made clear: he was too busy lunging for the bucket.

Ruso had to hurry back to his hastily cleaned but still smelly lodgings to fetch one of the ingredients for Innocens' medicine. By the time the ailing man had swallowed it, a bowl of pale, damp beans was resting on the table where Tilla had sat. Ruso knocked on her door without success and then, hearing her weeping, hurried downstairs to see if there was a spare key. That was when he learned that Tilla was no longer occupying the shabby little upstairs room. Merula had moved her in to sleep with the other girls.

'That isn't what we agreed.'

'I'll give you a discount,' conceded Merula, placing a jug

of wine and four cups on to a tray. 'We needed the room.' She glanced around the bar area and shouted, 'Daphne? Table four!'

'Whoever's in there now doesn't sound very happy.'

Merula handed the tray across the bar to Daphne, who had changed from her kitchen clothes and tied a green ribbon in her hair. 'I don't buy girls to make them happy,' said Merula. 'I buy them to work. Yours is in with the others. Through the kitchen and turn left.'

On a lone chair festooned with discarded clothes sat Chloe, now huddled in a brown blanket, her feet soaking in a bowl of water. Tilla, who had been lying on one of the lower bunks, swung her legs off the bed and stood up. Chloe stayed where she was.

Ruso had never considered where bar staff might live when they were off duty, but if he had, he would have expected something better than this. The room was dingy and cramped. What little floor was visible between the three sets of bunk beds was presumably mud beneath the covering of dried bracken. The walls had once been cream but were badly stained with soot. Limp feminine laundry had been draped over a length of twine tied between the bunks. The girls had made attempts to brighten things up: two cheerful red bows adorned the latches of the shutters and a familiar-looking cup filled with yellow flowers sat on the one shelf. Around the flowers lay a scattering that reminded him of Claudia: combs, mirrors, hairpins, pots of make-up.

He had the feeling of being too big for the room; as if any misjudged movement would knock over something precious and break it.

The girls, as was proper, were waiting for him to speak first. Trying not to think about Chloe's tongue exploring his ear, he cleared his throat and said, 'Good evening.'

Tilla bowed her head and murmured with a pleasing – and surprising – display of respect, 'My lord.'

Chloe reached for a towel. She looked tired. The black around her eyes was smudged. It was hard to imagine her as the seductress he had seen writhing in the bar.

Ruso coughed again. 'I hear there was a funeral today.'

Chloe lifted one foot out of the water. 'Some of us are starting to wonder who's next.'

'I am sorry for the loss of your colleague.'

'That's more than the management were. And I wouldn't call it much of a funeral. If it hadn't been for Decimus I bet they'd have dumped her in a ditch.'

Not sure how to reply, Ruso turned to his slave. 'Show me where you are sleeping now.'

Tilla indicated a rolled-up mattress stashed between two bunks. As Ruso checked to make sure it was the clean one, she said, 'A new girl is here.'

'Asellina's been replaced,' put in Chloe. 'They were starting to run out of staff.'

'The new girl is locked in the room,' Tilla continued.

It was not an unreasonable precaution. 'You should stay away from her for a day or two,' suggested Ruso. 'If she came here with Innocens she may have the same illness.'

'I hope he is very ill and then he dies,' said Tilla.

Ruso, who could not be heard to agree with this sentiment even though he might share it, instructed her to sit down. He knelt awkwardly in front of her to check the alignment of the splints. Chloe did not offer him the chair.

As he felt along the length of the lower splint, he said, 'I gather Innocens did not eat here?'

'If that's what Merula said,' put in Chloe before Tilla could answer, 'Then he didn't.'

Ruso glanced across at her. 'I'm not trying to catch anyone out. Nothing you say will leave this room, but it will help me do my job.'

He saw the two girls look at each other. Chloe shrugged, tossed the towel aside and reached for her sandals.

'He takes from the kitchen,' explained Tilla. 'When the mistress is not there.'

'What did he take?'

'Wine, apple pie and Mariamne,' said Chloe.

'Mariamne?'

'He might have made *her* feel sick,' continued Chloe, winding the thongs of a sandal up her calf, 'but not the other way round. There's nothing wrong with the wine, and other people have had the apple pie.'

Ruso pondered the possibilities as he checked the limited movement of the bandaged hand. He was paying no attention to Chloe grovelling about for something under one of the bunks, which was why, when he turned to find her hidden behind a golden cavalry mask and brandishing a sword, it was a shock.

Chloe raised the mask. 'It's blunt,' she assured him, lifting the sword towards the fading light from the window before sliding it back into its scabbard. 'You wouldn't believe what rubbish you have to put on here just so the customers can look at you taking it off again. Want to come and see the show?'

'I'm sure it'll be very, ah . . .' Ruso paused, looking for a word, 'artistic.'

''Course it will,' said Chloe. 'That's why they come to watch.'

When she had gone, he turned to his patient. 'Tilla, tell me what you know about Claudius Innocens.'

'He is a patch of slime.'

'Yes, but do you know what he was doing in Deva before I met him?'

Tilla shrugged. 'He stays at an inn. He leaves me locked up there when he goes to do business. He tells me he will fetch a healer, but I never see one.'

'And some of his business was here with Merula?'

'I do not know, my lord. If you ask him, he will lie to you.'

'Did he ever mention any other girls?'

'He says I am the most ungrateful girl he has ever met.'

'Hm. So he doesn't lie all the time, then. Tell me one more thing. Do you know why he is ill?'

The eyes that reminded him of the sea were wide with innocence. 'Perhaps he is cursed, my lord.'

'What would make you think that?'

'Perhaps your medicine will make him better.'

'Perhaps.'

There was a pause, then she said, 'What medicine do you give?'

Ruso looked at the door to the kitchen, which was closed. He looked at Tilla, and at the complex bandaging which covered the very best work he had been able to do, but which even now would probably not return her the full use of her arm. He said, 'I gave him medicines which are recommended by several authorities.'

She raised her eyebrows, waiting.

He took a deep breath and said, 'Some of my colleagues recommend chewing several cloves of raw garlic.' Although not necessarily to cure vomiting. 'And then to sweeten the breath, the patient should take honey containing ashes of mouse-droppings.'

Her eyes widened. 'And this is what you give for sickness of the stomach?'

'There are men who recommend these things,' he insisted, wondering what had possessed him to administer this ludicrous and disgusting treatment in which he had no faith at all, and scarcely able to believe that he had just admitted this weak – but oh, so enjoyable! – moment to a slave.

From somewhere in the yard outside the window came the sound of retching. Tilla said, 'I think it did not work.'

'No,' agreed Ruso solemnly. 'Perhaps he is cursed.'

40

Ruso's thoughts as he lined up with the First Century on the damp parade ground were a mixture of apprehension and annoyance. The apprehension was such as any man who has not recently undertaken serious physical training might feel at the prospect of a ten-mile run. The annoyance was partly with Valens, who could surely have found a more sensible way to impress the Second Spear. It was also with himself for rising to the challenge of Valens' 'I would have signed you up too, but after a summer off I don't suppose you'd be up to it.'

Pride had prevented him from asking exactly what he would be signed up for. Valens was obviously out to create an impression of being enthusiastic and committed, and it would not do to be seen as less enthusiastic or less committed than his rival in the race for promotion. So when Valens had asked him which of them should go first while the other remained on duty, he had volunteered. Now, standing on the parade ground surrounded by the fittest, fastest, fiercest and best-trained unit in the Legion, he knew he should have listened to his common sense rather than his vanity.

A centurion was bawling orders. The Second Spear was nowhere to be seen. It occurred to Ruso that a more suspicious mind might have described his friend and colleague as a devious bastard. It also occurred to him that there had been no need for him to do this run, but now he was here he had to finish it or risk public humiliation and serious damage to his hopes of promotion.

When the men first set off the shock to his system was as bad as he had feared, but once he had forced his thoughts away from the prospect of the next ten miles, his body settled back surprisingly quickly into the familiar anonymity of the training run. He was no longer an individual. He was part of a many-legged creature moving forward over the relentless crunch of boots on gravel. His lungs shared the heavy breathing of men keeping step. His own sweat mingled with the smell of others wafting through the after-noon drizzle as they passed the competing stinks of laundry and tannery. As they followed the East Road out between the green fields that were the territory of the Cornovii, his mind was free to wander.

It wandered back to the cheering sight of the signaller wav-ing at him from the departing wagon to Londinium this morn-ing. Tonight, if his legs were still capable of holding him up, Ruso would stand before the healing God and offer up a prayer for courage for the signaller, steady hands for the sur-geon and the large measure of luck that was needed for suc-cessful cataract surgery. And a prayer that, for all their sakes, the girlfriend would not deliver while they were on the road.

The thought of the woman led his mind down darker paths: back to the moment when he had realized that Claudius Innocens was supplying slaves to Merula's and might have been around when both of the dead girls dis-appeared. The thought that his own Tilla had narrowly escaped being offloaded to the highest-bidding bar owner had filled him with fury. That fury had led him over a boundary he had never imagined he would cross. Until yesterday, he had honestly been able to claim that, no matter how unlovely or annoying they were, he had always done his best to help his patients. Now he felt, not shame exactly, but a sense of being stained by the dirt of others.

He had not harmed Innocens. To his relief and Tilla's probable disappointment, the man had recovered overnight and had sent a message of thanks to the hospital this morning. Perhaps the purveyors of mouse-droppings had a point after all.

Mouse-droppings? There was another boundary he had never imagined he would cross. Not to mention his new-found doubts about ghosts, and his sudden rush of faith in Trajan. Ruso wiped a drip of drizzle off the end of his nose. Perhaps the damp climate was sending him soft in the head.

He must concentrate on what was important. His duty to his family was no less just because they were far away, but with all the distractions here – slave-girls, house fires, arguments with Priscus – he had given them scant thought recently. He must organize himself. He must adopt a logical approach. Observation, diagnosis, treatment.

Observations:
No cash.
Short-term extra costs of long-term investment (Tilla).
Large debts in Gaul.
Small debts in Britannia.
Grim (and dangerous?) living quarters.
No housekeeper.
Increasingly distracted, impulsive and unprofessional behaviour.

He was constantly finding his mind wandering away from whatever he was supposed to be doing. As if Tilla were not enough of a diversion, this morning he had found himself wondering if the two girls' deaths were not connected at all, and whether Decimus had lied to him. He only had the man's word for it that there had been no contact from

Asellina. What if the porter really had received a message that his girlfriend had run away to join him? Would it have been welcome? His dreams of a future with her would not have included harbouring and supporting her as a fugitive slave, or having to desert from the Legion to flee prosecution from her owners. What if he hadn't been prepared to take the risk? What if he had been afraid of being punished for encouraging her? What if . . .

Gods above, he was doing it again!

Diagnosis:
   A man burdened with too many responsibilities.

Treatment:
   Long term, concentrate on getting the family out of debt.
   In the meantime, stay calm.
   Hold out for eleven days until payday.
   Use Hadrian's bonus to clear all of the loan from the
   Aesculapian Fund and most of the one from HQ.

Find:
   private patients,
   ways to campaign for promotion,
   somewhere cheap and civilized to live (the CMO's quarters
   will do nicely).

Avoid:
   hospital administrators,
   rogue slave-traders,
   destitute or deceased females, and any temptation to find out
   what happened to them,
   Regional Control Officers,
   any more bright ideas from Valens.

Eventually, he would be able to realize his investment in Tilla. He would do it without the help of Bassus, whose bar-trade contacts would probably all be as seedy as Claudius Innocens. He had noticed an advertisement for a travelling slave-trader chalked up on a couple of walls on the way out of town, but he did not want to take that route either. Bassus' claim that the local dealers would rob him blind was not the only reason for his reluctance. Having kept her alive, he felt some responsibility towards the girl. He wanted to have some control over where she ended up. If there really was a shortage of good staff in Britannia then some respectable household would have a suitable vacancy. By the time the arm was healing — say in six or eight weeks — that officer would have turned up.

Ruso, counting three steps to a breath now instead of four, sniffed at the fresh drop of drizzle collecting on the end of his nose and glanced at the men slogging forward around him, who had now summoned enough breath to join in the indecent lyrics of marching songs. They would be earning a fraction of his salary, and many of them were supporting families. How did they do it? Were a poor family's needs less than those of the comfortably off? Were they all closet philosophers, assuring their women that there were lots of things they didn't need? Or was Priscus right: they simply stole whatever they wanted?

Underlying all these was a deeper question: how could one be an educated and intelligent man and not know this sort of thing?

On the first day of Ruso's apprenticeship, his uncle had warned him that a little knowledge would unlock the gates to vast and unsuspected deserts of ignorance. No matter how diligent he was in study, how careful in observation and how keen to learn from others, the causes of most diseases and the reasons why some patients recovered and some didn't would remain a mystery. The difference between a real doctor and the latest quack who shambled into town offering miracle cures in a bottle was that a real doctor knew his limitations. This speech the fourteen-year-old Ruso had regarded with a level of scorn that he was later glad he had kept to himself.

A true philosopher, he mused now, would be delighted instead of taken aback at every new revelation of his ignorance. A true philosopher would realize that the path to knowledge lay first with the discovery of new questions.

Did continuous rasping of short breaths signify swelling lower down the throat, and was it possible to kill oneself by running until one's airways closed up?

Ridiculous. Of course not. It just felt as though it was.

What caused the head to pound during exercise, and why, despite careful strapping to ward off blisters, did old boots always rub in new places?

You can do this, he told himself. *You have done it many times before. Count.* Each step a bonus. Each step an achievement. Set small targets. One and two and three and four and . . .

'Out of practice, Doc?' Ruso glanced at the fresh-faced young optio who had fallen in step beside him.

'Good to get –' he tried not to sound out of breath '– out again. Haven't had much – time lately.'

'Busy over at the hospital?'

'Short-staffed.' He must get the optio to do the talking. 'Been with the – Legion long?'

'Ten years this winter. My people are from Baetica, but my father was a centurion in the Twentieth.'

'Born in Deva?'

'No, no. My father got married after he retired back home.'

'Like it here?'

'You get used to it. Here, are you the doctor that's investigating the murder?'

'No,' said Ruso. He had neither the breath nor the desire to elaborate.

They were passing some native houses now. These were set well back from the road, beyond the wide verge where brown sheep lifted their heads as the soldiers approached, then bounded away to graze at a safer distance. Smoke curled from thick cones of thatch squatting on round, stumpy houses. Several small children of indeterminate sex were fighting over a rope swing dangling from the branch of a tree. Chickens wandered about in the mud, and a boy was leading a reluctant goat past an untidy stack of hay with a pole sticking out of the top. Ruso saw all this but heard none of it. The sounds of these other lives were muffled beneath singing accompanied by the thump of legionary boots and the jingle of buckles.

Aware that his 'no' had sounded abrupt, Ruso said, 'What are the locals like?'

'We've got both sorts round here,' explained the optio. 'One or two who know what a bath-house is for.'

'And?'

'And a bunch of thieving sheep-shaggers.'

'Ah.'

'You'll find some of the girls being friendly, but you want to watch your step.'

'Really?'

'Half of them have a string of brothers who want to knife you to restore the family honour. The other half are sent by those honourable families to latch on to an Army pay packet, so they can move out of the mud hut. Not much of a choice, is it?'

Ruso smiled. 'I hear the Second Spear has a daughter.'

The optio laughed aloud. 'You won't get near that one.'

'Not me. A friend.'

'Not a chance, Doc. Not a chance.'

Ruso glanced across at the native huts just as a shapely girl emerged from a gateway carrying two buckets. Moments later, he was aware of confusion ahead of him: the sort of confusion caused by someone tripping and the men behind not being able to stop in time. The singing gave way to shouting and swearing. Later runners saw what was happening and parted to flow round the sprawled bodies. Ruso sidestepped to the left, glancing across to where the playing children had stopped to stare. The girl had vanished. The optio stayed behind, yelling abuse at the tangle for watching the bloody natives instead of where they were going.

Minutes later a breathless man caught up with Ruso and conveyed the optio's message that one of the fallen men had a suspected broken ankle. Ruso muttered a silent prayer of respect to whichever fate had cursed the unfortunate legionary and hurried back to help. He no longer had to pretend now. He really was both enthusiastic and committed.

41

'You're doing *what?*'

Valens' hand, clutching his spare underpants, paused above his kit-bag. 'Seems they're paying a visit to some hairy mountain chieftain whose resolve needs stiffening.'

'And they want you to go along?'

Valens resumed his efforts to stuff underwear into the few remaining crevices in his kit-bag. 'I can do a quick tour of the outpost units while I'm there. It's time somebody checked them over.'

'That's going to leave the hospital a bit short, isn't it?'

'I did think about that,' agreed Valens, ramming the last sock down and hauling on the drawstring to close the bag, 'but then I thought it would give you a chance to shine, so you probably wouldn't mind.'

Ruso's weary mind groped towards a suitable reply and failed to find it. In the end he said, 'Very decent of you.'

'You're welcome!' It was not clear whether Valens was ignoring the sarcasm or had simply failed to notice it. 'I know you want the CMO post, so it's only fair to let you have a crack at getting yourself noticed.'

Ruso yawned. This afternoon, having rendered first aid and organized a party to carry the injured man, he had rejoined the returning runners of the First and just about kept pace with them for the four miles back to barracks. His legs were stiff. His feet were blistered. He could not be bothered to point out that his efforts to sustain three men's work single-handed at the hospital would only be noticed if something went wrong.

'Well,' continued Valens, 'I can't stay up talking, I've got an early start. They're leaving at sunrise, but I want to get down there early and bag a decent horse.'

Ruso said, 'You'll be missing your turn with the training run, then?'

'But I'll be with them,' pointed out Valens, as if he were intending to march with the First instead of ride past them on a borrowed horse. 'Now. Do you want me to wake you when I go, or will you be enjoying a lie-in in your lovely new redecorated bedroom?'

42

In the absence of Valens, it was Ruso who hurried across to HQ just after dawn for the morning briefing. He was not overjoyed to find Priscus already standing at the back of the hall. Each acknowledged the other with a curt nod.

Ruso frowned. He was unwilling to leave a man who would not know a plague from a pimple as the official representative of the medical service, but it was ridiculous for the hospital to be left to manage itself while both of them stood around listening to notices. He was about to give Priscus a departing raise of the hand — that surely would help to mend relations between them, as well as giving him a chance to snatch breakfast — when there was an untidy shuffle of men standing to attention, followed by silence. The Camp Prefect's voice echoed around the rafters, bidding the assembled officers good morning and announcing that he was in charge for four days while the Legate was away.

Ruso struggled to concentrate on the notices and ignore the gurgling of empty stomachs and the stifled heavings of a man in front of him who was trying not to cough. Finally the Prefect announced his chosen password for the day (*Tiger stripes*) and paused to take questions. Only as the briefing was declared closed did it strike Ruso that he should have raised his hand. It was what Valens would have done. It was the sort of thing Claudia would have encouraged. The Camp Prefect was directly responsible for the hospital, and asking questions was a way of getting yourself noticed.

The trouble was, there was nothing he actually wanted to know. No, that was not true. There was something he wanted to know, but he couldn't ask it in public.

He asked it later of Albanus, who looked uncomfortable. 'I'm not sure I can tell you, sir.'

'Why not?'

Albanus coughed and glanced across to make sure the surgery door was shut. 'Well they gave us a talk about security the other day. All about not telling anyone anything they don't need to know, and how the officers might test us, and . . .'

'Do you actually know the answer?'

Albanus looked even more miserable. 'Yes, sir.'

'Well if somebody's already blabbed it to you, it can't be that secure, can it?'

The scribe's face brightened. 'Is this a test, sir?'

'Yes. Well done, Albanus. You've passed.'

'Thank you, sir.'

'Now can you tell me whether the Legate has gone off on the same tour as Officer Valens?'

'Yes, sir.'

'Yes he has, or yes you can tell me?'

'Both, sir.'

'Thank you.' Ruso paused. 'I suppose you'll be wondering why I wanted to know that.'

'Oh no, sir.'

'No? Good!' Ruso put his hand on the door-latch. 'Right. Ready for ward round?'

By the end of the morning Ruso realized he was starting to like Albanus. The man made himself genuinely useful during a full ward round and busy clinic, taking a pride in the swift production of whatever information was needed and apparently enjoying his chance to boss the other clerks about.

Ruso made a point of thanking him and was amused to see Albanus blush. 'Go and get something to eat,' he told him. 'We'll start again at the seventh hour.'

The scribe hesitated. 'Will you be here, sir?'

'At the seventh hour.'

'But between now and then, sir . . .'

'I shall be somewhere else.'

'Yes, sir. Sorry, sir. Only Officer Priscus said I was to know where you were at all times. In case there's an emergency.'

'If the bandagers can't deal with it,' explained Ruso, 'get the watch to sound a call for me. I won't be far away.'

Ruso lingered only to leave brief instructions with the guards and then hurried out under the East Gatehouse, long strides taking him swiftly down the busy lunchtime street and away from the sound of all but the most energetic of trumpeters.

Moments later he heard a familiar voice calling his name. He kept walking. He had done his very last favour for the Regional Control people. If they had a problem, he didn't want to know about it. He had enough problems of his own.

'Ruso, wait!'

He turned. 'I'm in a hurry.'

'Oh, I don't want you to do anything!' promised the man from Regional Control, falling into step with him. 'I just want a quick word.'

'Very quick, then.'

The man broke into a jog to keep up. 'I just wanted to say I was sorry to hear about your fire. And to thank you for your help with naming that body the other day.'

'Oh,' said Ruso, slowing down to negotiate the ladder of

an off-duty soldier painting the front of a house. 'Right. It was just good luck that I'd spoken to the porter.'

'They've finished clearing the site now. There aren't any more bodies.'

'Well, I suppose that's good news.'

'I went down to the bar to tell them myself,' continued the man, as if liaising with civilians were not his job but someone else's.

'How did they take it?'

'The owner wasn't too happy about paying for another funeral.'

'No, so I hear.'

'I told her she ought to keep a better eye on her girls.'

'Maybe we need to keep a better eye on our men. This is the second runaway who's been found dead.'

'We are aware of that, Ruso. We aren't quite asleep over in HQ, you know.'

'You might also want to look at a part-time slave-trader who supplies girls to bars. He's called Claudius Innocens.'

'Really? What do you know about him?'

'Not much,' said Ruso. 'I just don't like him, that's all.'

'I'll mention it,' said the officer. 'If there's an investigation.'

'You mean there isn't?'

'It's not up to me,' said the officer. 'I just write reports. But thanks for the tip.'

As they parted company it struck Ruso that it was no wonder the men of the Twentieth needed to be given talks about security. They had been stationed here far too long. The staff weren't quite asleep in HQ, but there were certainly corners over there where a man with limited ambition could lie down and snooze undisturbed, except when he roused himself to pass on a piece of interesting gossip. He supposed it was the Regional Officer who had told Valens that the Legate would be leading the First's mission in person. No wonder Valens had wormed his way on to the list. Valens, not Ruso, was seizing the chance to shine. Valens, the Army doctor with no combat experience.

Not, by all accounts, that there was much chance of any combat on this trip. If the local chief were minded to have a change of heart about his loyalty to Rome, he would hardly be likely to have it during a visit from the Legate and the First Century. Which, of course, was the point of the trip. Anyone who really wanted to see some action, Ruso had been assured, would seek a posting up north to join in the fun the Army were having with the Brigantes.

Ruso had long ago lost any illusions about combat being fun, but it occurred to him that it would do no harm to check out the state of the medical service in the north. If he could cook up some excuse for a few days away, he could return Valens' favour by leaving him to manage all the medical work on his own. In the meantime, Ruso was going to take advantage of his housemate's absence to save himself some cash.

43

Tilla was shredding cabbage. She was doing it carefully, slowly and badly. No matter how hard she tried to hold the knife steady with her left hand, it wandered. Before they toppled on to the scored wood of the kitchen table and broke into untidy shreds, the slices of cabbage were tapered like door-wedges. This mattered to no one else – the cabbage was to be stewed anyway – but Tilla's mind was travelling far ahead of tonight's supper.

She put down the knife, grasped at the air to flex her stiff fingers and picked it up again. Her work was slow, but it pleased her. She needed to train her left hand into some sort of dexterity if she were to escape and survive. Even if the Roman healer had rebuilt her shattered arm perfectly – which seemed unlikely – her right hand would be feeble after being strapped up for so long. Besides, with every rasp of the knife through the crisp green flesh she could imagine it was not a cabbage she was slicing up, but a man.

To her relief Innocens had gone, leaving the girl Phryne locked in the upstairs room. Phryne, pale but apparently not ill, had been let out to join the other girls on the morning trip to the baths. Tilla had held a brief conversation with her on the way, but Merula had moved close enough to overhear, and they had fallen silent.

Inside the baths, Phryne was the last to take her clothes off. For a moment Tilla wondered if she was going to refuse, but Chloe stepped across and murmured something in her ear that persuaded her to cooperate. Finally undressed, Phryne sat in the corner of the hot room with her child's body huddled in a towel, watching the other girls as they strolled about in the steam, chatting and laughing, their naked flesh glistening with sweat. Her eyes kept returning to Daphne's blue-veined breasts and enormous rounded belly, taking in the dark line that ran down from the protruding navel and the silver streaks that showed where the skin was stretching and splitting. The girl brought one hand to her mouth as Daphne flopped down splay-legged on the bench, poured oil into one palm, rubbed her hands together and began to massage the surface of the bulge.

Two girls she did not recognize wandered into the hot room. As soon as they saw who was in there, they retreated. A few moments later some older women wrapped in towels paused in the doorway, looked round, glanced at each other and then ventured in. They clopped past Merula's girls in wooden bath shoes – they had brought their own, Tilla noticed – and seated themselves in the furthest corner, turning very straight backs towards the rest of the room.

Not long ago, Tilla would have shared these women's contempt for Merula and her girls. Yet now she lived amongst them, she had begun to realize things were not as simple as she had supposed. The girls were kept to serve the same army that had built this bath-house, which the respectable women were now enjoying. This morning, when a man in the street had shouted an insult at them, the same Bassus who had grabbed Tilla as if she were an animal went across to him, spoke to him and then with one swift movement smacked the flat of his hand against the man's ear. Several passers-by hurried on while Bassus stood over the fallen man with his arms folded, looking around as if he were daring anyone else to insult his girls. When Merula thanked him he shook his head sadly. 'People round here,' he said, 'they don't know nothing about respect.'

The hairdressers were plying their trade at the baths as usual. To Tilla's relief nobody showed much interest in her. Her hair was left in anonymous plaits.

Phryne had to sit on the stool while her flat, blonde locks were sprung into curls with the hot tongs and pinned behind her head in a complicated knot. She managed something like a smile when she was shown the results in the mirror, pursing her lips quickly to hide her teeth. The effect was soon over because Merula told them to take it all down again. 'That's not what we want,' she said. 'You've made her look older.'

Merula had gone shopping while Bassus escorted the girls back to the bar and ordered Daphne and Chloe to open up. As he took up a position by the door, Stichus emerged from the kitchen and looked Phryne up and down. He glanced across at Bassus, who shrugged indifference. Stichus seized Phryne by the wrist and dragged her towards the stairs.

Before she could consider the wisdom of it, Tilla had shouted, 'Leave her alone!'

The room fell silent. For a moment the only sound was the crackling of the fire under the hot drinks counter. Stichus, still keeping a grip on Phryne's wrist, looked at Bassus as if waiting for guidance. Everyone had stopped what they were doing to watch.

Tilla squared her shoulders. Still addressing Stichus, she said, 'She is only a child.'

Bassus' stool scraped back across the tiles. He made his way across the room, a slow smile spreading across his face. Tilla took a deep breath and stood her ground.

Bassus reached out a forefinger and lifted her chin. 'And

you,' he said quietly, 'are only a slave. Who won't always have that nice doctor around to look after her.' He withdrew the finger. 'Remember that.'

Stichus jerked Phryne towards the stairs. Tilla felt an arm around her shoulders. 'Into the kitchen,' urged Chloe. 'Cook needs you.'

Tilla plunged the knife into another cabbage and tried not to think about Phryne, or how easily the girl's fate might have been her own. She would not wait to find out what might happen when she did not have the doctor to look after her. In fifteen days, she would be gone.

Since the few windows that opened on to the street were barred against burglars, there were only two ways out of Merula's. The main entrance was shuttered and locked at night and guarded by Bassus or Stichus – or both – during the day. The kitchen door led to a gloomy yard from which a door in a high wall opened on to a side street. The door was barred except when kitchen deliveries came in, and the bar secured with a padlock whose key swung from Merula's belt. Even if she managed to steal the key, she would have to fiddle with the padlock in full view of the kitchen window, the upstairs cubicles (not that much window-gazing went on up there) and the row of private rooms occupied by Merula and the doormen, which ran all along the opposite side of the yard to join on to the building behind. The front entrance was the only realistic way out. She would have to find an excuse to go out into the bar in the evening, wait until the doorman was distracted and slip away into the night. Most people seemed to think this was the route Asellina and Saufeia had taken, although no one had actually seen them leave.

Strangely enough, it might be easier to escape now that Asellina had been found. The other girls had said little about the circumstances of her death, but they were clearly shocked and frightened by it. And, though only Chloe had dared to say so, upset to realize how little they would be mourned if the same fate befell them. The doormen would not be expecting anyone to venture out alone now.

A door opened behind her. She did not look up.

'Tilla!'

She twisted round, looked up into Merula's painted eyes for a moment, then put down the knife and scrambled to her feet. There was no one else in the kitchen.

'Tilla,' said Merula, folding her arms. 'I don't suppose for a moment that's your real name, is it?'

'My master says I am Tilla.'

'Don't stare at me like that, girl! Haven't you learned anything?'

Tilla lowered her eyes and gazed at the rings that looked too heavy for Merula's thin fingers.

'You look well, Tilla.'

'I am well, mistress.'

'Many people have helped you to recover. You should be grateful to them.'

'Yes, mistress.'

Merula reached forward and raised a tangle of untidily shredded cabbage between finger and thumb. 'Is that the best you can do?'

'Yes, mistress.'

'If you were one of my girls, you would be better trained.'

Tilla resisted the urge to look her in the eye. 'I am not one of your girls, mistress.'

The cabbage fell back on to the table. 'No,' agreed Merula. 'None of my girls would dare to question the actions of her superiors, or to speak of what did not concern her.'

'No, mistress.'

'Learn this for your own good, Tilla. Slaves who cannot control their tongues may lose them.'

'Yes, mistress.'

'Remember my advice. Now go and collect your things. Your master has come to fetch you.'

44

Ruso glanced round to make sure the girl was keeping up. He was glad to get her away from that place. He had explained that he was in a hurry, and since they had not yet added up the bill for Tilla's lodgings, Merula had agreed to have it sent over to the hospital. On the way out Bassus had given Tilla a smile that she did not return, said he was sure that they would meet again and said, 'You won't forget us, will you?'

Tilla looked him in the eye and said, 'I will not.'

Bassus turned his attention to Ruso. 'When d'you think she'll be fit?'

'Not for some time.'

Bassus' grin reappeared. 'You doctors. Never commit yourself, do you?'

'Not if we can help it,' said Ruso.

He was swerving out into the street to avoid the painter's ladder when he heard the approaching rhythm of boots on gravel.

He looked up to see a unit of infantry whose front men had now begun to clatter along the flagstoned street behind him. Ruso turned and called, 'Step back!' to Tilla. She might not know that a tired column within sniffing distance of its barrack rooms had all the braking ability of a boulder rolling down a mountain. The painter, seeing their approach, wisely scrambled down his ladder and moved its base closer to the house. A wandering hen jerked its head up, glared at the disturbance and scuttled out of the way.

Tilla stood with her back to the wall as the column began to pass. Judging from the mud, the sweat-streaked hair and the volume at which the centurion and his optio were berating the stragglers, these men were returning from the regulation twenty-mile full-kit training march.

Several men were looking across at Tilla and grinning. One or two winked at her. Instead of lowering her head like a modest woman, Tilla folded her good arm over her bandaged one and stared back boldly. Ruso moved to stand next to her just as the centurion spotted what was happening and bellowed, 'Eyes front!'

'Look away!' Ruso ordered her.

He surveyed the grimy faces of the legionaries trudging past. Any of them could have squeezed the life out of the unlucky Saufeia.

'Tiger stripes,' said Ruso to the gate guard without being asked, swiftly followed by 'So, have there been any calls for the doctor?'

'Not a thing, sir.'

Ruso handed the man a coin. He beckoned the girl in past the heavy, studded gates and led her under the arch. 'I'll organize a gate pass for you so you can fetch the shopping,' he said. 'Do you understand what your duties are?'

She nodded. 'I cook and clean and mind the dogs.'

'Good.' He unhooked the front door key from his belt and handed it to her. 'What can you cook?'

She looked at him. 'Soup?'

'Fine,' he agreed.

'What in soup?'

Ruso thought about that for a moment. There was unlikely to be much in the kitchen, and if there was, the mice would have found it by now.

'Something tasty,' he said, untying his purse. He picked out three coins and put them into her hand. 'Buy something for breakfast as well.'

Tilla picked up the coins and examined them on both sides as if she was not sure they were genuine. 'Soup should start in the morning,' she remarked.

'Well do your best,' he said. 'I won't be back before dark anyway.'

They passed into the main street of the fort. 'This is the sort of route you are to take back and forth,' he instructed her, sweeping one arm in the general direction of the Legate's residence. 'No exploring, you understand? Deva is not the place for a young woman to wander around on her own.'

Tilla's head rose. 'If a soldier touch me, my lord, he will be punished.'

'Perhaps,' said Ruso, without a great deal of confidence, 'but by then it will be too late. Listen to me. Both inside and outside the fort, you are to stick to busy streets where there are plenty of people. If a man pays you attention, walk away. Don't try to put him in his place. You may get away with boldness wherever you come from, but it won't do around here.'

Tilla said, 'I pray to the goddess to protect me.'

'Well, help her by using a little common sense. Two lone girls have died and I assume you know that at least one of them was murdered?'

'The goddess will punish that man, my lord. I have put a curse on him.'

'I see.'

'Also I will put a blessing on my master.'

'Let's hope your goddess is listening, then.'

The girl smiled. 'She is listening, my lord. You see already what she do to Claudius Innocens.'

45

The heavy door of the hospital swung shut and the latch dropped with a clank. The skies had cleared into a chilly night. Ruso nodded to the guards as he passed the Legate's house. The great man himself was away, but his family would be asleep beyond those grand studded doors. In moments of weakness, Ruso envied men who lived in married quarters: men who went home every night to a home-cooked meal and the pleasure of a woman to warm the bed. In such moments he usually took a firm hold of his imagination and brought it to heel by picturing the woman to be Claudia. Tonight, he had no cause for envy. He was going back to warm lodgings and hot food. There would be no one in his bed – he had told the girl to use Valens' room – but there would be no one nagging him in the morning, either.

What a lot of things a man doesn't need.

He shivered and turned to head towards his supper.

The house was pleasantly cosy, but only the dogs came to greet him. Evidently his servant had gone to bed. He lifted the lamp that had been left burning by the door and sniffed. Leeks? Onions? It was hard to say. He carried the lamp into the kitchen. Then he cleared a space on the table, laid out the wooden bowl, the spoon and some bread which had been placed in the box with the lid weighted down and settled down to enjoy his first home-cooked meal in Britannia.

The soup was lukewarm.

It was watery.

It was bland.

He took a mouthful of bread and then tried again.

This time the spoon brought out something rounded and hard. Exploring it with his tongue, he found peculiar soft strings attached to it. He returned the object to the spoon and held it towards the candle to examine it. In the yellow light he saw the top of a carrot with most of the leaves still attached.

Gaius Petreius Ruso sighed deeply and pushed the bowl away. Truly, he was alone in a barbarian land.

46

The bedroom door was wide open, but she sidled in, singing softly to keep her courage up. Her eyes scanned the floor as she moved forward with the broom held out in front of her. Satisfied that the floor was clear, she ran clumsily in the Medicus' big boots, twisted round and landed on the bed with her feet in the air and the boots sliding about on them. Then she laid the boots and the broom on the bed and crawled round the mattress on her knees, bending to check that none of the covers was hanging down. Finally safe, she turned to the dog standing in the doorway and said, 'Are you ready?'

The Medicus had told her to sleep in this room last night. It was the room of the other doctor, the friendly one, who had gone away. She had not slept well. To begin with she had lain rigid in the dark, listening for the sound of the Medicus coming home and wondering if he would bed her, because he was a man, or beat her, because she was not a cook, or both.

Instead of the Medicus' footsteps she had heard a faint pattering that she tried to tell herself was the sound of her own fear. As soon as she moved, it stopped. As she was drifting off to sleep, it began again. Then it squeaked. Fear might patter, but it did not squeak. So she had to keep listening, moving at short intervals, rolling over, kicking her legs or sighing, hearing the trumpet blowing the watches just as she had on bad nights in the hospital and trying to reason with herself that all houses had mice. No one died of mice. She had grown up in a house where mice crept through crevices in the walls and nested in the thatch. At night she had heard them rustling the bracken on the floor, and she had gone to sleep with the blanket over her head, knowing that Bran would protect her. But Bran was dead, and the dog in this house was not as fast. Even the Romans, with all their organization, could not control mice.

It was past the middle hour of the night when the Medicus came home. She watched a bright line appear and fade around the door as he carried the lamp into the kitchen. He did not spend long there. As soon as she heard his bedroom door scrape across the floor, she counted to ten, flapped the blankets to frighten the mice into their holes and fled on tiptoe to the dining room, where the dog – after some shoving on both sides – had finally assented to sharing the couch. She had lain beside it, pondering the strangeness of Romans.

When she had first been carried into this house – before he had taken her to Merula's – she had been too weak to observe much beyond that the place smelled bad and looked cluttered. She had assumed that the servant was lazy, or away, or perhaps ill. It had come as a surprise to find that there was no servant except herself. It seemed that, despite being surrounded by all this wealth, Roman doctors lived in poverty.

A healer amongst her own people would be better treated. Her mother was given gifts. Eggs, or a hen. A pot of honey. A shawl. A goat. A mirror and comb set. Beer. Once, when she had safely delivered a son to an elder whose wife had been in labour for three days, a cow in calf. They had lived well. They had a cook and a herdsman. Even when the harvests had failed, she could count on one hand the number of times the family had gone hungry, whereas this Medicus, with all his skill and authority, lived in a vermin-infested ruin and was reduced to bargaining for an injured slave in a back street. Small wonder that Romans had no respect for different tribes. They had still to learn respect for each other.

She must have fallen asleep on the couch, because the next thing she could remember was the sound of someone moving about in the kitchen. She rose to find the Medicus helping himself to the bread rolls she had bought for breakfast.

'That soup,' he said, without looking up.

She swallowed. 'Is – good?'

'Is that the sort of thing you eat over here?'

'Britannia cooking, master,' she ventured.

'Gods above. With that and the weather, I wonder you people have the will to live.' He had given her more coins and said, 'I haven't got time to go into it now. Get a couple of pies from a shop for supper. Not a British shop. Understood?' When he left he was clutching his case in one hand and an apple in the other.

Now she was back in the bedroom, determined not to pass another night like the last one. She had already used the broom handle to pull out the clothes that had been thrown under the bed. She had found amongst them a dish with greasy remains bearing small teethmarks and two cups with fluffy green pillows growing inside them. Now, from the safety of the bed, she bent and jabbed the broom at what looked like an old linen saddlecloth stored underneath the cupboard in the corner. Nothing happened. She pushed the broom further in and began to slide the saddlecloth sideways out from between the legs of the cupboard. The dog moved forward to sniff at it. A couple of puppies wandered in to see what was happening. The linen, once

248

red and now faded at the folds to orange, was gathering a rising tide of grey fluff and little black mouse-droppings around its leading edge as it moved.

How could anyone live like this? Once she had cleared this last corner, she would give everywhere a good sweep and block up all the holes where the boards had warped or knots had fallen out or the mice had gnawed their way in.

She pulled the broom out from under the cupboard, repositioned it on the folded fabric that had emerged and began to push sideways again. The fabric strained but did not move. It was snagged on the base of the cupboard. She crawled further up the bed and poked at it from a better angle, putting more of her weight behind the stick. Soon there would be no hiding places left in here. Tonight, if she brought the dog in and sealed the gap under the door, she might be able to get a better night's –

It was so fast she barely saw it. As the dog shot under the bed in pursuit the broom jerked in her hand and the fabric pulled clear. Tiny grey shapes leaped out of a tangled nest and scattered in all directions. The broom clattered to the floor. Puppies yelped and skidded. Tilla clapped a hand over her mouth to stifle the screams.

The narrow lane was empty. Tilla twisted the key in the lock and tested the door. Shut. She was safe now. Out of that horrible house. Before long, her heart would stop pounding and her breath would calm down. Out here, the sun was shining, and a fresh breeze brought the smell of the tide over the wall of the fort. A gull wheeled overhead, screaming. Somewhere in the distance was the clang of a blacksmith at work. She tied the key on to her belt like a proper housekeeper, picked up the empty shopping basket and hooked it over her injured arm. Then she slid the loop of the dog lead down from where she had secured it in the crook of her elbow. Grasping the lead firmly in her hand, she drew in a deep breath of the clean air and looked around her.

The house was set on its own at the end of a long, open space that separated the hospital and the next barrack-block. In the space, nettles had sprouted through what looked like the angular footprints of vanished buildings. The nettles might be useful, although it was late in the season now. Thistles, groundsel, dandelions and scattered tufts of broad-bladed grass had poked through the black of an old bonfire patch. In the middle of the gravelled alley that led past the front door was another scorched area. It seemed an odd place for a bonfire. She supposed it had something to do with the smoke stains and the burned smell in the Medicus' house.

The lead pulled against her hand. The dog strained towards the open area and promptly squatted to add its own contribution to the collection of droppings dotting the ground. Tilla wrinkled her nose and decided not to bother gathering the nettles.

To her right, at the end of the alleyway, a wide street paved in stone ran parallel to the high outer wall of the fort. A crow, suddenly alarmed, opened its wings and flapped away from the top of the wall. Two sentries appeared, walking along a high path set behind the top rows of stones. They passed without showing any sign of noticing her.

It struck her that she was the only person in her family who had ever been welcomed behind the walls of a Roman fort. The thought of the gate pass in the leather purse strung on her belt made her feel uneasy. It was not an honourable thing to be trusted by the Legions. Throats had been cut for less. And yet, the Medicus had made it so easy for her to escape! It must be the work of the goddess, who was more powerful than the gods of the Romans, even though she had hidden her face from her people for such a long time. The goddess was helping her to escape. Chloe had finally told her what little the girls knew about the loss of Saufeia. Tilla had not made the same mistakes. As for what had happened to Asellina, that was a mystery. But the goddess must know. The goddess would protect her.

Tilla pursed her lips and allowed herself a moment of pity for the Medicus, powerless before the will of the one who had chosen to answer her prayers. The Medicus had treated her well. She would serve him as best she could in the few days she had left here. She would do what she could to cheer up that dreadful house. In the meantime, she would find out how to cook something.

47

The third morning of Valens' absence dawned to the sound of musical weather. Walking through the fort, a listener could enjoy the sound of water drumming on roofs and splashing from the eaves, streams tinkling down gutters, drains gurgling and backing up. Inside the hospital were the complex rhythms of leaks dripping at different speeds, punctuated with the occasional *ping* where the staff had placed metal basins because they had run out of buckets. It had been raining since before dawn, as Ruso well knew, since he had been called out while it was still dark. Everywhere with a working brazier now smelled of wet wool hung up to dry. Adding to the cheerless mood of the staff was the knowledge that the planned modernization of the hospital building had receded by another day as the weather held up the work over at the bath-house. Even Priscus' powers, it seemed, had not extended beyond getting his own office ceiling dried out.

Ruso was dictating notes to Albanus in a mood of grim determination when the morning porter interrupted to announce a visitor. Ruso's temper did not improve when the visitor turned out to be the officer from Regional Control, come to ask if he could borrow Valens' hunting-net.

'On a day like this?'

'We're making an early start in the morning. Just me and a few friends. Why don't you join us?'

'I'm busy,' explained Ruso. 'Valens is away.'

'Oh, sorry. I suppose you are. We're busy too, you know.

Not like you, of course. Our work isn't life or death. Well, not usually.'

'No.'

'And frankly, if we do anything too fast, it just encourages them. They're supposed to take responsibility for themselves, you know.'

'Yes.'

'But of course they don't. Sometimes I wonder what they have a town council for. Anything that isn't keeping the drains clean and organizing jolly festivals gets sent to us. Widows who've had their prize goat stolen. Shopkeepers who've been punched on the nose by a soldier they can't quite identify. Natives who –'

His flow was interrupted by a knock on the door. 'What do you want?' he demanded of the orderly whose head appeared around the door.

The orderly glanced at Ruso and then back at the Regional Officer as if not sure which of them he was supposed to be addressing. 'Another visitor for the doctor, sir.'

'They all want an immediate investigation, you know,' concluded the Regional Officer, lifting his wet cloak from his arm and slinging it round his shoulders. 'And it's always when I'm on duty. Oh, by the way, I put your Claudius Innocens on the Second Spear's list for a little chat.'

'He'll have to move fast. Innocens travels around.'

'Really? Well if we don't catch him this time, we'll nab him when he comes back.'

Ruso turned his attention to the orderly. 'Who wants me now? I'm trying to get some work done.'

'It seems to be a native girl, sir. We would have sent her away, but she's insisting on seeing you.'

Ruso sighed. 'Send her in.'

Tilla appeared, busy rubbing her hair with a towel. Her

253

shawl had done little to prevent the rain soaking into the blue tunic that was now clinging to her with an appealing precision which Ruso did his best to ignore. Her feet were muddy up to the ankles.

The Regional Officer looked her up and down as they passed in the doorway, then paused to address Ruso from the corridor. 'I meant to say earlier,' he said, 'glad to hear you found your cook. Very nice. I'll look forward to the invitation.'

'Do,' said Ruso, calling after him. 'Wait till you try her soup!' He turned his attention to Tilla. 'Who gave you a towel?'

She frowned. 'Tall, thin, old. His hair . . .' She paused, then raised her hand in a gesture Ruso recognized.

'Officer Priscus, sir,' put in Albanus.

'I see,' said Ruso, not altogether pleased at the thought of Priscus sniffing round Tilla. 'Is there a problem?'

'I need money, master.'

He saw that she was trying not to shiver. 'I gave you money the other day.'

'Is spent.'

'What – all of it?'

She nodded, slung the towel over her shoulder and began to count on her fingers. 'Bread, pies, apples, onions, carrots, eggs, milk –'

'All right,' he interrupted. 'I haven't got time for a shopping list.' He loosened the strings of his purse and tipped a quantity of pitifully small coins into his hand. 'Take this,' he said, adding something he remembered Claudia saying: 'I shall expect an account at the end of the week.' As she bent to pick the coins out of his palm, he realized that the tails of her plaits were dripping. He could not imagine how long it would take to dry that much hair in a climate like this, and so far she had only walked the short distance from the house.

Moments later he watched his own cloak walk out of the surgery with Tilla underneath it. At least part of her would stay dry. He hoped she would not catch a serious chill before he could afford to buy her some footwear.

'Her name is Tilla,' he said, turning to his clerk. 'If I'm out I may leave the key at the desk for her to collect.'

'Yes, sir.'

'And wipe that silly grin off your face, Albanus. Anybody'd think you'd never seen a housekeeper before.'

48

By the fourth morning of her stay with the Medicus, Tilla had begun to wonder if he lived this way by choice. She had the floors of the usable rooms clear, the mess stacked up in the driest part of the empty room and the mice in retreat. She had found the best pie shop in Deva and slipped into Merula's for a quick lesson with the cook while both door-men were out escorting girls to the baths. Her repertoire was not extensive, but it was edible. Omelette. Poached salmon. Sausages. Boiled cabbage. Porridge. Stewed pears. Baked apples with honey drizzled into the space where the core had been. Yesterday, after the rain had stopped, she had shoved all the dirty clothes in the house into a bag and lugged them out along the Eboracum Road to the laundry. Then, feeling she deserved a rest, she and the dog had finished off the beer stored in the dining room. It had been kept too long anyway – but even this the Medicus did not appear to notice. He seemed to have no interest in anything beyond eating, working and sleeping.

Asked what the names of the dogs were, he looked as if he had never thought of that before. They had no names, he said. The bitch belonged to the man who had lived in the house before his colleague. She said, 'The pups are old enough to leave,' but all he said was, 'Good,' as if he hoped they would go off and find new homes by themselves.

When he was at home – which was not often – he ate, and then retreated to his room, or sat hunched on the couch scraping rows of figures into a writing-tablet, pausing to add the numbers up with a frown that deepened the crease between his eyebrows. Last night he had fallen asleep at the kitchen table. His chin was growing darker each day. It was another thing he did not appear to notice.

As far as Tilla could tell the Medicus did not have a woman, but her fears that she would be expected to fill the space had been unfounded. He had made no approach. Maybe he did not like women. Maybe, like many doctors, he was Greek. Everyone knew about the Greeks. But in the past she had caught him looking at her in a way that was not at all Greek. Perhaps he was just too busy. Whatever the reason, she was glad of it. The goddess was watching over her.

She finished laying the kindling in the kitchen hearth. She dampened the grubby bandage around her right hand – she had no wish to set herself alight – unwrapped the fire-steel and prayed for success before settling the dry fragments of scorched lint in the middle of the tinder and bringing the steel down on to the flint. For the first time since she had been forced to do this left-handed, one of the sparks caught straight away. Breathing gently on the glowing edges of the lint, she prayed again for what she was about to do.

She had wondered many times why she had been saved. Visiting Merula's this morning, she had found out. There were now eleven days before her arm would be freed from the splints, so ten days more in the service of the Medicus. Ten days in which to perform the new task the goddess had given her.

Tilla fed the tiny fire with dried grass and watched the smoke curl towards the ceiling.

49

'Jupiter optimus maximus!' muttered Ruso blasphemously, pausing in the doorway of the house and wondering whether to walk away again. It had been one of those days when Aesculapius had not been on his side. A bad day for the doctor and a worse one for his patients, whose sufferings had included emergency abdominal surgery that was unlikely to succeed, the extraction of a glass splinter from an eye and the amputation of an infected foot. He was supervising the cautery of the stump by a nervous junior medic when an orderly interrupted to tell him there were five stretchers in the hall, bearing the victims of a loading crane that had broken loose down at the docks. In the midst of this no one thought to mention the retired trumpeter who had come in complaining of chest pains and who was only brought to Ruso's attention after he had dropped dead on the floor of the admissions hall. As soon as the man's distraught wife had stopped shrieking at Ruso and been escorted away in tears, someone tapped him on the shoulder and whispered that the surgical patient had died, and Officer Priscus was conducting an urgent review of admissions procedures.

Ruso spoke to the comrades of the abdomen patient, saw to it that he was properly laid out and went home for dinner.

He took a deep breath and entered the house. The sound of a meandering melody came from the kitchen. Exactly what his servant was doing in there – other than singing – was a mystery to Ruso, who flung open the door and demanded, 'What on earth is that stink?'

The singing faltered to a halt. Tilla, flushed from leaning over whatever was boiling in the blackened pan above the coals, observed, 'My lord is home early.'

He said, 'Is that my dinner?'

By way of answer she pointed towards a shelf beyond the reach of the dogs. A coiled string of pink, glistening sausages were an unwelcome reminder of today's abdominal surgery.

'Dinner,' she explained. 'Soon.' There were damp wisps of hair stuck to her forehead.

Ruso returned his gaze to the coals. An unpleasant suspicion began to grow. 'Tilla, are you boiling socks in the same pan that you cook in?'

She shook her head vigorously. 'I do not boil socks.'

'It had better not be another of your British recipes.'

She glanced back at the pan as if she were wondering whether to lie to him, then drew herself up to her full height, looked him in the eye and said, 'Is medicine, master.'

Medicine? Ruso sighed. He was tired of medicine. He was not interested in medicine. He had come here seeking respite from other people's troubles and the last thing he wanted was a sick person in his own house. Mustering his sense of duty, he said, 'Do you need something else for your arm?'

'No, master.'

'Is there another problem I should know about?'

'No, master. I make dinner now.'

'Good. Give that pot a thorough scrub before you use it again.'

Those eyes were looking straight at him. The expression in them was not one of cooperation.

'Medicine is a tricky business, Tilla,' he told her. 'It isn't a case of boiling up a few weeds. You could end up poisoning yourself. I work with pharmacists who have trained for years, and even they don't get it right all the time.'

She turned away from him, gave the pan a vigorous stir and banged the spoon on the rim.

Ruso rubbed his hand over his tired eyes. He was being defied. He needed to do something about it. The something was probably not picking his servant up, shaking her and roaring, 'I want my dinner!' So instead he said with all the calm he could muster, 'If you are ill, you must tell me about it. I am your doctor.'

'Yes, master.'

'Are you ill?' *Please, almighty Gods, let it not be something female and complicated . . .*

'No, master.'

'Good.' He reached for the cloth that was lying on the table and wound the ends around his hands. 'Open the door,' he ordered, gripping the hot metal handles through the cloth and lifting the pan carefully off the coals. Beneath the steam was a greenish-black goo that heaved and spat as a final bubble came to the surface.

She followed him outside and stood on the gravel of the alley in her bare feet as he tipped the pot over the bonfire patch. The pan clanged as he scraped out the last vestiges of goo with the wooden spoon. Seeing her standing there with her good arm folded over her bad one – he must change that bandage, it was filthy – he wondered whether she had been conducting some bizarre magic ritual in his kitchen. Best not to inquire. He said, 'You have done good work tidying the house, Tilla.'

'Yes, master.'

'But I don't want to catch you making medicine again, do you understand?'

'You will not, master.'

It only dawned on him later, as he sat down in front of a dish of sausages shortly to be followed by a bowl of boiled cabbage and an apple (a three-course dinner!) that this was not an entirely satisfactory reply.

50

Valens returned full of tales of wild and wily tribesmen and how he had impressed both the locals and the officers by curing a fever in the hairy chieftain's youngest son. The next morning Ruso gave him a swift summary of the current hospital cases, told him to ask his friend at HQ if he wanted to know anything about the latest body, then escaped to enjoy some time off and catch up on some of the things he had been meaning to do for days. He did not want to waste most of the rare sunny weather standing in the queue at the barber's, so while he waited for a shave he strolled down the street and dropped in to a tailor's shop to inquire about the cost of woollen trousers.

He pushed his foot down inside the hole for the second leg, distentangled his boot at the far end and tugged the rough wool up around his waist. Holding everything in place with the spare fabric bunched in his fist, he tried a few experimental steps across the shop floor.

They seemed ludicrously baggy compared to riding breeches. 'Are they supposed to be like this?'

'If you just fasten your belt round the top, sir . . .'

'I look like a bloody native.'

'A lot of gentlemen lace their boots up around the legs and pop in a bit of sheepskin, sir. You'll find them very comfortable in the cold weather. Much warmer than leather.'

Ruso rubbed his growth of beard and looked down at his toes. His ankles were hidden under the rust-coloured wool that was already beginning to irritate his skin in unaccustomed places. He felt ridiculous dressed like this, but Valens had recommended this tailor, and Valens, he had to admit, usually looked surprisingly well turned out for one so disorganized. Presumably when the cold set in, the two of them would look no more outlandish than anyone else.

He glanced out of the doorway in the vague hope of seeing someone dressed like himself. Instead, he saw a young woman walking past, carrying a faded blue military cloak draped over a loaded shopping-basket. A young woman with curly fair hair, a bandaged arm and bare feet. A young woman for whom he had only this morning asked the cobbler to set aside a pair of second-hand boots, and who needed to try them on. She was heading out of town, and he guessed she was on the way to the laundry.

'I'll take them,' announced Ruso.

'I can show you some other fabrics,' offered the tailor, with the sudden anxiety of a man who suspects he could have sold something more expensive.

'They're fine. You can send me the bill care of the hospital.' Payday was in less than a week, which was why Ruso now felt it was safe to buy a few small necessities.

'If you'd just like to slip them off –'

'I'll wear them,' declared Ruso, pausing only to scribble his signature on the chit before snatching up his belt and hurrying out of the shop.

When he reached the street Tilla was already too far ahead for him to attract her attention without bellowing down the street like a drill sergeant. Acutely aware of the trousers flapping round his ankles with every step, Ruso decided to catch up with her when she stopped at the laundry, which was the only possible place where she could have any business out here. He passed the clanging din of a metalworker's shop, where a display of pots and pans swinging

263

in the breeze sounded a chaotic chorus over the steady rhythm of the hammer. Beyond it were a few tumbledown houses which might have been pleasantly positioned on the edge of town were it not for the stench that was already hinting at the nearness of his destination. He stepped aside for an ancient veteran shuffling along on two sticks, then looked up and realized she must have crossed over to walk in the sunshine. She was hidden by a heavy cart rumbling past in the middle of the street.

The owner of the laundry was taking advantage of the sunshine too. The yard was criss-crossed with loaded washing lines. Navigating by smell, he ducked to avoid being slapped in the face by a sheet and turned left to make the customary contribution in the Vespasianus. Gazing down into the yellow depths, he reflected that the greatest of men could be brought low by one simple act of stupidity. The general who had conquered much of Britannia, stifled a Jewish revolt and risen to the rank of Emperor was chiefly remembered for his attempt to put a tax on public pisspots. His musings were interrupted by a more practical thought. He had not checked for any exit arrangements in the trousers. Perhaps he had better practise in private first. Turning on his heel, he ducked back around the flapping sheets and into the steamy atmosphere of the laundry to meet his slave.

The counter clerk shook his head and managed to look even more vacant than he had before Ruso spoke to him.

'She must be here somewhere,' Ruso insisted. 'I just saw her. Fair hair. Broken arm.'

The youth scratched his head and then examined his fingernails, as if the information were hiding somewhere under his hair and he might have dislodged it.

'She's collecting my laundry,' prompted Ruso, glancing round. The only other people he could see were laundry workers: a couple of well-muscled women wringing out towels and child slaves trampling the urine vats.

The clerk had picked up a ledger. 'Name?'

Ruso told him. 'Or it might be under hers. Tilla. Or Doctor. It's not the laundry I'm after, it's the girl.'

The clerk ran a finger down the ledger, paused, squinted and walked across to check the labels dangling from the necks of linen sacks lined up on the rack behind him. Then he went back along the rack and read them all again. Finally he returned to the ledger and said, 'Medicus. Here, are you the doctor that's –'

'No. You're quite sure you haven't seen her?'

'It's still wet. Only came in yesterday. You have to give us –' But Ruso was already out of the door.

Back on the street, he saw her straight away. Although she had been expressly forbidden to wander, Tilla had passed the laundry and kept walking. She was now a distant figure, moving briskly along the side of the road in the manner of a woman who knew exactly where she was going and was anxious to get there.

Ruso was conscious of the fact that there were plenty of things he should be doing this morning, most of which began with a shave and a haircut and none of which included trotting along the Eboracum Road in a pair of ridiculous trousers, following a disobedient slave. Common sense dictated that he should shout to call her back now. Curiosity tempted him to continue just a little further and find out where she was going.

She was approaching the cemetery. He was catching up with her. He wondered whether he had time to duck behind one of the grander gravestones and slip off the trousers. He had fixed on a six-foot monument complete with decorative urn when the sound of wailing alerted him to a group of mourners approaching beyond a clump of trees, close enough to be offended.

Tilla was clearly in a hurry. She hardly bothered to step aside for a couple of cavalrymen trotting past: one of the horses, obedient to instinct rather than its rider, shied to avoid her at the last minute. The rider twisted in the saddle and appeared to shout something at her back. She took no notice. She bustled past a row of carts trundling into town under a weight of timber and mercifully had the sense to cross to the opposite verge while a military road gang downed their picks to watch her pass. A voice bellowed at them to get back to work. Ruso was relieved. It meant they were too busy to gawp at his clothing.

Even if he had managed to put them on properly, it was entirely the wrong weather for trousers. He was beginning to understand why people said the climate here was as unpredictable as the natives. Yesterday the rain had been torrential. Today, sunlight flashed on the metal heads of the picks as the road gang swung back into action. The feathery seed-heads of the grasses on the verge waved gently in a light breeze. His encumbered legs carried him along behind Tilla, feeling hotter with each movement.

He tried to imagine what his servant could be doing out here. Several possibilities came to mind, none of them reassuring. Despite the fate of Saufeia and now apparently Asellina, she could have taken it into her head to run away. But in that case surely she would have spent his grocery money on shoes. Whereas she seemed to be carrying a full basket of shopping – which was puzzling in itself. If she was intending to return, why shop first and haul it all the way out of town? Unless, of course, she had used his money to stock up for her journey.

On the other hand, she could be on a repeat expedition

to gather whatever she had found yesterday to put in that stinking medicine. In which case he would be faced with the uncomfortable task of punishing her.

He tried to remember what he had seen out here on the training run. Beyond the stubbled fields where a couple of plough teams were now plodding muddily along behind their oxen lay an area where the road and its wide verge had been cut through thick woods. Beyond the woods he could remember very little. Pasture? Scrub? He knew there was a native settlement about four miles from the fort, because they had passed the milestone just before the broken ankle incident. Could she be intending to carry the shopping all the way out there?

A worse possibility occurred to him: that she was on the way to some sort of rendezvous. Surely she would have more sense than that? But Tilla seemed to have more faith in her goddess than in any of the practical steps he had suggested to keep herself safe, and any number of unsavoury characters could have crawled into her confidence while she was at Merula's. If there really was a madman, he could have come back for a second – or was it a third – victim, this time choosing an isolated spot away from the danger of witnesses. Well, whoever he was, he would be getting a surprise visit from the medical service.

She was still about fifty paces ahead, showing no sign that she realized she was being followed. This, he told himself, is ridiculous. If he had never downed that cup of fake Falernian, if he had never decided to interfere at the fountain, if he had kept his mouth shut and let events take their course, he would not now be wasting his morning running around after his own slave.

He was glad Valens could not see him now. Valens already thought he was crazy. Valens had arrived home last night, tipped the contents of his kit-bag on to his bedroom floor and wanted to know where all his stuff had gone. Ruso had explained about Tilla moving in and he had grinned. 'I thought you'd never get round to it. So, tell me. What's it like with a one-armed woman?'

Ruso had given him the look he usually gave malingerers. 'She's a patient.'

Valens crouched down and let the dog lick his face. 'I suppose you could give her some interesting hand exercises.'

'I told you, she's a —'

'You smell better,' Valens informed the dog as he pushed her away so he could stand up. 'Has somebody bathed you?'

Ruso shrugged. 'I think Tilla took it for walks. Can you bathe a dog when you've only got one arm?'

'She seems to be able to do most things. You're a lucky man. She hasn't got a sister, has she?'

'I wouldn't introduce you if she had.'

'Dear me, you are grumpy.' Valens lifted the lid from the beer barrel. 'I see you've developed a taste for this stuff at last.'

Ruso peered into the empty barrel. 'Tilla must have thrown it out,' he said. 'She wasn't too impressed with our housekeeping arrangements.'

'I'll ask for wine next time.' Valens dropped the lid back down. 'Well done, Ruso. I knew I could rely on you to come up with a decent servant in the end.'

'I told you, we're not keeping her.'

'*We're* not keeping her,' Valens had repeated in triumph. 'There you are. She's become *our* housekeeper. Excellent! I'll chip in with the costs if you like. I promise not to bed her without asking first.'

'Nobody's going to bed her!'

Valens had eyed him curiously before shaking his head.

'Ruso, Ruso. You are a good chap and I love you dearly, but you really must learn to relax and enjoy yourself a little.'

Ruso scowled at the hems of his trousers. It was all very well for Valens to say he should relax. Valens didn't have the responsibility of shoring up a secretly bankrupt family in Gaul and finding a decent place for a slave over here. A slave who was, he now realized, too attractive for her own good.

Claudia had often complained that her maids were stupid and lazy but never once, as far as he could recall, that they were not pretty enough. He was beginning to realize that Bassus was right. There was a market for beautiful slave-girls. It was not in the homes of happy families. He was not proud of it, but the people who depended on him were going to need the kind of price that market would pay.

He glanced up. Apart from a group of cavalry horses approaching in the distance, the road ahead of him was empty. Tilla had turned left, crossed the ditch and was making her way over the open expanse of the verge towards a patch of woodland.

If she had turned to look, she would have seen him step on to the heavy tree-trunk that provided a dry foothold across the ditch, then scramble up on to the narrow, muddy path that led through the long grass. Instead she took not the slightest precaution, hurrying into the woods like a woman late for an appointment.

Anxious not to lose her amongst the trees, he lengthened his stride until there were only twenty or thirty paces between them. The path twisted and turned through the gloom of the woods. The road he had just left was out of sight. Moments later he could barely hear the shuffle of hoofbeats on gravel as the cavalry troop passed. His own boots padded along on mud made slippery by damp leaves.

Knotted roots had broken through the surface of the path. Brambles snatched at his trousers. More than once he had to adjust his stride suddenly to avoid snapping a dead branch. Several times he stopped to listen, and was reassured that Tilla was making no effort to be silent. Whoever she had come to meet would know she was approaching. As long as he was careful, Ruso would be able to take him by surprise.

The sunlight filtering through the branches caught the blue of the cloak moving ahead of him. Ruso hurried on, stepping over another dead branch while his right hand moved to unlatch the knife at his belt.

It wasn't there.

In place of the knife was an uncomfortable bundle of trouser-fabric. He was cursing himself for leaving the weapon on the counter back at the tailor's shop when he realized the path was leading into an empty clearing. Ahead of him lay open grass dappled with sunlight. The blue cloak was there, dangling from a branch. Tilla was nowhere to be seen.

Ruso stepped off the path and hid behind a broad tree-trunk which trembled with ivy. He held his breath, straining unsuccessfully to hear the sound of footsteps. Peering though the ivy, he surveyed the clearing.

Grass. Bushes. Bracken. The folds of the empty cloak shifting slightly in the breeze. There seemed to be at least two paths leading away, but he could not believe she had had time to take either of them unseen, and there was no sign of unnatural movement amongst the leaves. Nor was there any sign of anyone else. He would have heard if she had greeted a friend, and she could hardly have been attacked without him noticing. This was the woman who had planned to knock out a legionary with a soup-bowl. She must be hiding somewhere, waiting for whoever she had come to meet. Or perhaps she had seen Ruso after all, and was hoping if she kept out of sight for long enough, he would give up and go away.

Somewhere ahead of him, he could hear the trickle of a stream running through the woods. He hoped Tilla's patience would give out quickly. He was due on duty at the seventh hour, and it must be past noon by now.

A black bird with a yellow beak hopped across the clearing. Gently, slowly, Ruso shifted his weight into a more comfortable position. Undisturbed, the bird continued to stab at something in the grass. There was no other sign of movement.

As he hid behind a tree-trunk with his back exposed to the rustling undergrowth, it occurred to Ruso that following a native into the woods unarmed had not been a sensible thing to do. He was beyond shouting distance from the road. If there were more than one man to deal with, or if that man were carrying a weapon, he was in trouble.

That was probably why the voice terrified him. Only for a second, though, as he assured himself later. Of course he had not believed for more than a glancing moment that he was hearing the triumphant war-cry of a native about to hack him to pieces. Or that a vengeful ghost had come to steal his spirit away in the depths of the woods. He had realized, as soon as he had recovered from the surprise, that the sound was nothing to fear. Unfortunately his head did not communicate this knowledge to his heart, which continued to pound against the wall of his chest as if he were being pursued through the forest by a pack of howling wolves, instead of leaning against a tree-trunk listening to a woman singing.

Tilla's singing in the kitchen had never been like this. At first shrill and ululating and eerie, then gradually descending,

271

becoming breathy and resonant and peculiarly intimate. Ruso moved slowly forward to peer through the leaves again. He could see her now. She seemed to be alone. He frowned with confusion before realizing she must be standing down in a dip which was hidden by the bracken on the far side of the clearing. Her good arm was raised to the sky. Her face glistened with water. Darkened tails of wet hair stuck to her forehead. Her eyes were closed in concentration. The expression on her face was little short of ecstatic. He released a long breath. His servant had not ventured into the woods to meet a lover, but a god.

A thin trail of smoke rose into the air. The question of how Tilla had lit a fire in the middle of the damp woods merged in his mind with the question of what she had been carrying in the basket. He suspected he was now going to have to add 'theft of firewood' to her list of misdemeanours.

The song rolled on. It was, in a peculiar barbaric way, beautiful. Sometimes there were strains of a tune Ruso felt he should recognize, then the notes soared away in unexpected directions. Sometimes the same tune seemed to repeat and tangle round itself before giving way to a different one. Another high eerie section gave way to huskiness and a tune that meandered about in a sequence he thought he recognized from the kitchen.

Ruso retreated behind the tree and surveyed the damage to his new trousers. They were now snagged in several places. The bottoms hung limp and muddy around his feet. As he watched, a beetle scurried across the front of his boot. He shifted his foot. The beetle scuttled off and buried itself under a leaf.

The song, or collection of songs, was still going on. Ruso began to experience a familiar sensation. It was the feeling that usually crept over him during the first few verses of after-dinner poetry recitals: the sense that time was slowing down around him and that this damned performance was going to go on all night. Tilla, however, seemed to be enraptured.

Although he could not share it, there were times when Ruso was jealous of the comfort other people seemed to draw from their religion. Patients who retained a calm hope in the face of desperate and painful situations. One man had even offered to pray for Ruso's soul while Ruso amputated two of his toes. So although he had troubling doubts about Aesculapius, very little faith in Jupiter and his ilk and – usually – silent contempt for the so-called divinity of Emperors, Ruso had a solid belief in the value of religion. Leaving aside the water engineer who had to be tied to his bunk until he lost faith in his ability to fly from the top of his aqueduct, even the craziest of beliefs seemed to do less harm than any effort to dislodge them. So he would, if asked, have given Tilla permission for some sort of religious worship. But he had not been asked, and now he was witnessing blatant disobedience of a kind he had never encountered in a servant before. He had excused the attack with the soup-bowl as a mistake. The business of cooking up medicines in his kitchen had been more of a misunderstanding. This was nothing short of defiance. He was now obliged, for the first time in his life, to administer a serious beating.

He was not sure what to use. Claudia had usually marked her displeasure by snatching up whatever came to hand – a spoon, a hairbrush, a shoe. He would have to use his belt. To that end, and because he was uncomfortable in them anyway, he would let the singing warble on while he climbed out of the trousers.

He was out of one leg and easing the second boot through

273

the tube of fabric when he felt something drop into his hair. Logic vanished. Both hands shot up to sweep away the scorpion before it stabbed him in the scalp. The movement threw him off balance. He hopped sideways, grabbing at the tree-trunk to stop himself falling. A bird flew up, clacking in alarm, and as Ruso realized that the thing which had fallen on his head was an autumn leaf, the song stopped.

He flattened himself back against the trunk, scarcely breathing.

In place of the song came a peculiar chanting, as if she were repeating the words of a spell over and over again. The chanting grew nearer. She was walking towards him.

There was no point in trying to hide. He stepped out from behind the tree.

The chanting stopped. Tilla was staring at him. At his face. At his feet. At his trousers. Then at his face again.

'Tilla.'

'My lord.'

'You are supposed to be at work.'

'Yes, my lord.'

'Instead, you are here.'

'Yes, my lord.' She lowered her gaze again. For a moment neither of them spoke. Then she said quietly, 'My lord's trousers are fallen down.'

Ruso slowly unrolled the belt from his palm and buckled it around his tunic, trying not to speculate on his servant's perception of what he was up to behind the tree. The punishment would have to wait until he had recovered some dignity.

51

Ruso looked up from the whetstone and put the scalpel down. 'Come in, Albanus.'

The door opened. Albanus appeared. 'How did you know it was me, sir?'

'Magic,' said Ruso, who had recognized the knock. 'Any luck?'

Albanus advanced into the surgery. 'Sir, the pharmacist says he doesn't know anything that uses all those ingredients.'

'Did you ask if you could use them separately?'

'Yes, sir. Or in any combination. And he said yes, it was dog's mercury, and you could use it as a purgative but you'd be safer using hellebore because too much would cause severe gastric problems and coma. The wood sorrel – he said he didn't know any uses for it, but if you took lots of it you'd probably be ill, and he said the best thing to do with garlic mustard and nettles is to mix them with scrambled egg and eat it while it's still hot.'

'Good. Thank you.' Ruso retrieved the scalpel and began work on the other side of the blade.

A wax tablet and a collection of wilted leaves appeared by the whetstone. 'I wrote it down, sir.'

Ruso glanced across. The notes inscribed in the clerk's neat handwriting really did end with 'eat while still hot'.

'Very thorough as usual, thank you.'

'And there's somebody to see you, sir.'

'Right,' said Ruso, clearing the greenery to one side of his desk. 'Send him in. Have you got his notes?'

'It's a her, sir.' Albanus left a slight pause before adding, 'I think you've got the notes already.'

Albanus had gone, leaving Ruso alone with his slave.

'Close the door, Tilla.'

The latch clanked into position.

He carried on stroking the triangular blade across the stone, conscious that she was waiting for him to speak. Her feet were in his line of vision. She was wearing the boots.

He had asked her to report to him here as soon as she had finished the shopping. By this time, he felt, he would have worked out what disciplinary measures were appropriate. But despite mulling it over throughout their swift and silent walk back to town, and again in the few minutes since he had finished ward round, he had failed to make a decision.

He drizzled more oil on to the stone. As it soaked into the worn grey surface in the wake of the blade, he reflected that at least she had turned up as instructed. He had thought she might go gallivanting back to the woods in search of the plants he had confiscated from the basket. Garlic mustard and nettles. Edible and harmless, as the pharmacist had confirmed. Mix with scrambled egg. Eat while still hot. Perhaps he had done her an injustice. But dog's mercury? Severe gastric problems and coma? Surely it was a common enough plant around here for no one – especially the daughter of a midwife – to mistake it for something else?

He glanced up to find those eyes looking directly into his. Her mouth was set in the sort of line that suggested a direct approach would be a waste of time. Instead he said mildly, 'Are the boots a good fit?'

He could see he had taken her by surprise. She lifted her skirts to look at them. 'They are, my lord,' she said, and then added, 'I thank you.'

He nodded. 'Good.' She had tidied her hair. He noticed

276

for the first time that she had made beads from three acorns: one brown flanked by two green, threaded on a length of thin twine to form a necklace. As her doctor, he should have been pleased to note that she was starting to take an interest in her appearance. As her owner, he had more pressing concerns. He laid the scalpel on the whetstone and pushed it to one side. 'Now bring the basket over here and let's see what you've bought me.'

She had bought him bread, apples, five eggs, cheese, bacon and green beans. He glanced into the greased leather pouch that held his own flint and steel, and which she had no business bringing out of the house. He put it back without comment and said, 'Tell me, Tilla. What tribe do you come from?'

She laid the folded cloak back across the top of the basket and put them both on a stool. 'The Brigantes, my lord.'

The ones who were causing trouble. Somehow this was not a surprise. 'They are from the hills north and east of here?'

'Yes, my lord.'

'And are they a very religious people?'

She shook her head. 'Not all of them, my lord.'

'But you are faithful to your gods.'

'The goddess protects me.'

'And when you make medicine, is that something to do with your goddess?'

No reply.

'I'm interested in your medicine. Some of your plants here are new to me. Maybe I have something to learn.'

No reply.

He lifted up one of the wilted stalks. 'What is the use of wood sorrel?'

No reply. Her good hand was picking at a frayed strand of linen at the end of the bandage.

277

He put the first plant down and picked up the second. 'I'm told this is dog's mercury. What would you use that for?'

No reply.

'You were in the kitchen when Claudius Innocens was taken ill. You put a curse on him.'

'Yes, my lord.'

'Had you also made medicine for him?'

'No!'

'So if I ask the other people who were there, they'll confirm that you didn't go near Innocens or his food?'

Tilla pursed her lips as if she were about to spit, then cast a sideways glance at the floorboards and thought better of it. She said, 'I do not wish to go near Claudius Innocens.'

'No,' agreed Ruso, 'that's quite understandable.' He ran a forefinger through the stubble he still hadn't found time to have shaved. Perhaps he should give up and hope beards would come into fashion when Hadrian's famously hairy chin began to appear on the coinage. He said, 'Who were you making medicine for yesterday?'

No reply. The hand went back to the bandage.

Ruso sighed. 'This blessing and cursing business, Tilla. Cooking up potions. Chanting. Wandering off into the woods. It's got to stop. People will think I'm harbouring a Druid.'

No reply.

'Am I?'

'The Druids are all gone.'

'Am I, Tilla?'

'The Army kill them all.'

Ruso was quite well aware of the official line. The Druids, chased out of Gaul generations ago, had taken refuge in Britannia and made their last stand on a far Western island in the territory now covered by the Twentieth. It was rumoured that some had escaped, but Rome had taken comfort in the fact that Druid knowledge was not only secret and murderous, but complicated and coupled with a widespread refusal to write anything down. It took, they said, twenty years to train a Druid. So instead of hunting down hidden copies of documents, all the Army had to do was keep culling the Druids on a regular basis and they would finish them off, like chopping down weeds before they had a chance to seed.

'Those songs,' he said. 'What are they about?'

'They tell stories.'

'About Druids?'

'About my people. We sing of our ancestors. If we do not sing, our story is lost.'

Ruso pondered that for a moment. It was plausible. The locals seemed to have no proper statues or tombs. A people without that tradition would have to keep the memories alive in another way. 'Somebody should write it down,' he suggested.

She looked at him as if he had just said something very naive. 'My lord, the people could not read it.'

'They could learn.'

'But why would they want to when they can sing?'

'Refusing to learn to read and write,' said Ruso, determined to win at least one point, 'is a very short-sighted view.'

'Saufeia could read and write.'

'Indeed,' said Ruso. 'Even women can learn.'

'Saufeia is dead.'

He scratched his ear. This was the sort of illogical leap that made women so difficult to deal with. 'Saufeia wasn't murdered because she could read and write.'

279

'If you say, my lord.'

'She was murdered because she met a bad man.'

'She was stupid. I am not stupid like Saufeia.'

'Wandering off to the woods by yourself is hardly clever, Tilla. Especially at the moment. Did anyone else suggest you went there?'

'No, my lord.'

'You found the place by yourself? Nobody helpfully told you where to find a nice stream?'

'No, my lord.'

'Even so. If I could follow you, so could someone else. Now explain to me about the medicine.'

No reply.

'I have to know. I can't leave a servant I can't trust in charge of my house.'

The loose thread on the bandage began to unravel. She wound it round her forefinger.

'The medicine, Tilla.'

Finally she said, 'Is for someone else.'

'Who?'

The end of her forefinger was turning pink.

Ruso sighed. 'I don't want to have to punish you, Tilla,' he said, wondering what sort of doctor contemplated beating his patients. Besides, he was not sure where to hit her. On the back? On the legs? Across her one usable hand? 'I also assume,' he said, buying time, 'that you stole my firewood.'

'No, my lord. I took from a pile by the hospital.'

'Oh, marvellous. You stole the hospital's firewood.' Priscus had probably counted the logs and was in the process of billing him for them. 'Now. Tell me about the medicine.'

The finger tugged more thread loose and then jerked to

a stop as the unravelling reached the knot where the bandage was tied. 'Is the goddess!' she said suddenly. 'The goddess tell me to do it!'

'Who did the goddess tell you to give it to?'

'I cannot say.'

Slowly, Ruso pushed back his chair and stood up. He put both hands on the buckle of his belt. 'I don't want to do this, Tilla,' he said. 'Tell me.'

She shook her head. 'I cannot.'

He sighed again and unfastened the belt. He had spoken the truth: he did not want to do this. Discipline was like surgery: unpleasant but necessary. He wrapped the heavy buckle end around his right hand, making sure the studded straps were safely clutched in his palm and would not flail about. He did not want to injure her. But neither could he allow any suspicion that his servant might be poisoning people at the whim of some mad native god.

He grasped the loose end of the belt in his left hand and stretched it out so she could see it. The belt was supple with age. He knew, from years of polishing, every scar in the deep brown of the leather; every scratch on the silver of the trim. He had never before considered using it to inflict pain. Now he snapped it taut and stepped out from behind the desk. 'Tell me,' he said, seeing the colour fade from her cheeks. 'Now.'

She bowed her head.

Someone was knocking at the door.

Ruso felt his voice rise to a shout. 'Not now, Albanus!'

'Sir, a message from Officer Priscus!'

'In a minute!'

'Right-oh, sir! Sorry, sir!'

Ruso closed his eyes for a moment and attempted to compose himself. He heard the whisper of fabric. When he

281

opened his eyes she was kneeling at his feet with her head still bowed, as if pleading for mercy.

He was beginning to feel exasperated. He had put up with far more than most owners would tolerate. Now, because he had tried to treat her fairly, this wretched girl had assumed she could get away with whatever she liked, and he found himself having to fill a role he found deeply distasteful.

He took a long breath. 'You have been collecting poisonous plants,' he said. 'If there is an innocent explanation, you must give it to me. Otherwise, I will have to report you. I have already told you about the questioners. You will beg for mercy, and they will not listen.'

In the silence that followed, he prayed she was not going to tell him something he would have to report anyway. The cursing would not go down well if it were made public. If the questioners got hold of her, the best she could hope for was a swift end.

A dark tear-splash appeared on the floorboards in front of her. A second fell beside it. Ruso clenched his fists. This was not fair. She was doing it on purpose to avoid answering questions. Sooner or later, this was the trick they all resorted to. Gods, how he hated having to deal with women! It was as if they sensed that he wouldn't know what to do.

Tilla sniffed and lifted both fists, still held together by the thread of bandage, to wipe her eyes.

'Oh, for pity's sake!' He turned and flung the belt at the desk. It skidded across the top and sent the whetstone and the scalpel clattering onto the floor. 'Get up!' he snapped. 'Sit on a chair and stop fiddling about with that bandage.'

Tilla sniffed again and scrambled up on to the nearest stool.

Ruso retrieved the scalpel from under a chair, lifted her hands and stroked apart the thread that held them together.

The limp forefinger lifted as he unravelled the binding, then fell back into her lap. The white indentation that ran around it gradually turned pink.

Tilla said flatly, 'I have failed.'

This so accurately mirrored his own feeling that he paused before asking, 'At what?'

'If I speak,' she said, not looking up, 'I will be punished. If I do not speak I will be punished.'

Ruso sat on his desk and folded his arms. He was almost sure she was telling the truth about Innocens. She could not have picked anything more dangerous than a dandelion around Merula's, and anyway, the girls never went out without the protective supervision of one of the doormen. So what on earth could she have to confess? As gently as he could he said, 'Then you may as well tell me now.'

'If I tell,' she said, 'my tongue will be cut out.'

Ruso frowned. 'Is this some Druid nonsense? The Druids are finished, Tilla. We're in charge here now.'

'Is not Druids!' she blurted in exasperation. 'Is Merula!'

Ruso felt his shoulders drop. 'Merula?'

'You have seen Daphne!'

He stared at her. 'The pregnant one?' He tried to grasp the connection. 'Are you telling me Merula cut out her tongue?'

'Daphne asks a customer to help her run away. He says he will help, then he tells Merula. You see what happens to slaves who talk!'

He slid off the desk, crouched in front of her and gripped her by the shoulders. 'Tell me,' he insisted. 'Tell me exactly what's going on. I'm going to put a stop to this nonsense right –' There was another knock at the door. 'I said not now, Albanus! Is this life or death?'

'Yes, sir! No, sir!'

283

'Which?'

'Yes not now, sir, no it's not life or death, sir.' There was a pause, then the clerk's voice said uncertainly, 'Shall I come back in a minute, sir?'

'Don't bother,' said Ruso. 'I'll come and find you.'

He returned his attention to his servant. 'Quickly,' he urged.

52

'So,' said Ruso, scratching one ear and trying to make sense of what his servant had just told him. 'This new girl at Merula's, Phryne —'

'Is not her real name.'

'Well just pretend it is for the moment. This is a girl from your own tribe who accepted a lift from Innocens and then found herself kidnapped and sold to Merula.'

'She is not a slave. She is free born. Her father is carpenter.'

'These are serious allegations, Tilla.'

'Yes, my lord.'

'And are you saying that Merula knows her history?'

'She tell her.'

'These are *very* serious allegations, Tilla.'

'Yes, my lord. Merula —'

'Threatened to have your tongue cut out if you talked. I know. How was she going to explain that to me?'

She shrugged.

'Clearly she didn't expect to have to do it. So you're convinced that your goddess has given you the job of saving this girl, but rather than have your tongue cut out, you were encouraging her to run away and making magic potions and prayers to protect her from the same fate as the other girls.'

'And I put —'

'Don't say it!' he interrupted. 'If you've been putting curses on Merula or anyone else, I want you to keep quiet about it. I happen to think it's nonsense, but there are people who won't. You could get yourself into a lot of trouble.'

Suddenly she looked up as if a bright idea had occurred to her. 'My lord could buy Phryne!'

He frowned. 'Buy Phryne? What would I want to buy her for?'

'Or my lord's friend, the good-looking one, he could buy her!'

'Even if we wanted to,' Ruso pointed out, unable to imagine the good-looking one exerting himself for a slave he didn't want, 'neither of us can buy her if she's stolen, can we?'

'Then you send her home, and Merula does not know that I tell you!'

'And the lightness in my purse is counterbalanced by the weight of moral righteousness.'

She looked at him blankly. 'Is what?'

'Never mind.'

'You get your money back,' she said. 'I tell her family, they pay you.'

'Marvellous. I'll go into business with Claudius Innocens. He can be the muscle man, and I'll send you to do the extortion.'

She said, 'Oh.'

He was conscious of time moving on. He really should go and deal with whatever Priscus wanted. 'There's no need for all these complicated schemes, Tilla,' he told her. 'I know your people have trouble believing it, but this part of Britannia is under Roman protection. A man can't steal a free man's daughter and sell her into slavery, and an owner certainly can't buy a slave and put her to work knowing her to be stolen. You've acted correctly in reporting a crime. I'll pass on the report and it will be dealt with in the proper way.'

'But my lord, Merula –'

'Don't worry about Merula. The law says that slaves are the property of their owners. Merula might get away with bullying her own girls, but nobody's going to cut out the tongue of my property. I'll make it clear to the bar staff that they're to leave you alone in future. Understood?'

She nodded. 'Yes, my lord.'

'Now go over to the house and get on with dinner. And don't steal anybody else's firewood.'

'Yes, my lord.' She stood and gathered up the cloak and the basket. Her hand was on the door-latch when one last question occurred to him.

'Tilla?'

She turned. 'My lord?'

'You are legally a slave yourself, aren't you?'

She raised her hand to the place on her upper arm where the tunic hid the copper slave band. 'I am, my lord.'

'And Innocens didn't steal you?'

'He paid money, my lord.'

'Hm. Not as much as he told me he did, I'll bet.'

She smiled. 'No, my lord. I think not.'

53

To Ruso's surprise and mild embarrassment, the urgent message from Priscus had been a referral to a private patient with the toothache. By the time he arrived at the office the administrator had gone out, but Albanus introduced him to a small boy who had been waiting to take the first available doctor to his grandmother.

He followed the boy out of the fort gates and down a street behind the amphitheatre to a barber's shop. A veteran with a spectacular scar running down into a patch over one eye was perched on a stool by the entrance, steadily stropping a wicked-looking razor and ignoring the sound of raised female voices from somewhere in the depths of the building. He stood up as Ruso entered the shop.

'I was told you needed a doctor.'

The veteran's one good eye glanced down from Ruso's growing beard to his medical case, then across at the boy who had brought him. He said something to the boy in British. The boy's reply seemed to satisfy him.

'It's the mother-in-law.' The man jerked his head towards the back of the shop. 'Needs a tooth pulled. Good luck.'

The boy picked up a broom and began to sweep clumps of hair off the floor. Ruso made his own way past shelves stacked with towels and basins and stoppered jars. He rapped on the door.

The younger of the two voices in the back room launched into a fierce tirade of British that seemed to be aimed at someone else. The only word he understood was 'medicus'.

'I'm the doctor,' he announced, and pushed open the door in search of his patient.

The room smelled of smoke and boiled cabbage. It contained a table, two stools, an unmade bed and an exasperated woman. The woman was standing by another door that led towards the back of the house. This door was closed. From behind it came a speech in which he could again make out the word 'medicus'. This time it sounded like an accusation.

The woman pushed a strand of hair out of her eyes. 'Well, Doctor, you've worked a miracle already. My mother is out of bed.'

'I understand she wants a tooth pulled.'

'She doesn't. We do.'

Ruso said, 'Ah.'

'All week,' announced the woman, still in Latin but slowly, and loud enough to be understood from the other side of the closed door, 'all week she has been tormented with worms in her tooth. We have tried everything we can think of. We have bought medicines to drive the worms out. My husband offered to pull it. We have taken her to the healer. She is still in pain. Now my husband has called for a medicus . . .'

The stream of British from the other side of the door contained the words 'Roman' and 'medicus' in a tone that suggested they were interchangeable with 'bloodthirsty' and 'maniac'.

'My husband,' continued the woman, 'whose life was saved by a Roman medicus, has hired a surgeon for my mother at his own expense, and my mother shames us all by refusing to see him.'

'Sit down, Doctor,' offered the veteran's voice from behind him. 'The wife will pour you a beer.'

'I've told her he's here,' explained the woman, unnecessarily. 'She still won't open the door.'

'This often happens with toothache,' observed Ruso, suspecting he was only a transient player here in a long-running dispute. He offered to leave some paste to pack around the tooth. For answer, the woman placed one of the stools in front of him. Then she reached down a cup from the shelf and poured beer from the jug on the table.

'How do you usually get them out?' inquired the veteran.

'The worms?'

'The patients.'

Ruso took a sip of the beer and decided it would have been better used on the tooth-worms, which if they existed must be devious little beasts because neither he nor anyone he knew had ever seen one. 'I don't,' he said.

The woman banged a cup down in front of her husband and poured more beer. The husband peered at it with his one eye. 'Steady on, woman. You could drown a fly in that.'

The woman shrugged and returned to her station by the door. She seemed to be listening for movement. The veteran helped himself to more drink, evidently not troubled by the mysterious objects floating in it. 'Women, eh?'

Ruso braved another mouthful of the beer. 'Tell me something,' he said. 'You do women's hair as well as men's?'

The barber shook his head. 'Never had much chance to practise in the Army. I'll do a quick trim on the locals, but we don't go in for all that twiddling about with pins and curling tongs.'

'I just wondered if you'd had anyone in asking about selling hair.'

The barber hooked something out of the beer with his little finger and wiped it off on the edge of the table. 'I might look at something valuable. Blonde, or red. Mouse brown you might as well use for stuffing cushions.'

'Have you had anyone in asking about red?'

The one eye met his. 'Is this about that tart in the river? I heard some doctor was poking around.'

'This isn't official. I was the one who took the body in. I just wondered how far the inquiry had got.'

'Well nobody's come bothering me.'

'Right.' Ruso was beginning to wonder if the Second Spear was doing anything at all about the dead girls. At this rate Innocens would die of old age before anyone found the time to question him. 'Well, if you should happen to hear anything —'

'If we get anyone round here I'll tell them what I'm telling you. I don't want nothing to do with it.'

The woman began to pound the door with the heel of her hand.

The man leaned forward to be heard over the din and said, 'From what I heard, those girls were well looked after down Merula's. Compared to some of the places down the Dock Road, Merula's bar is a palace. They took it into their heads to run off —' He broke off. 'Will you stop that, woman? The old bat might be daft but she's not deaf!' He turned back to Ruso, leaving the wife to deliver another tirade in British. 'Don't take a genius to work out what happened to them, does it?'

'I know what happened to them, and at least one of them didn't die by accident. What nobody seems to be able to find out is who did it.'

'If I was you, Doctor, I'd stay out of it. You start asking too many questions, you upset people. I know who I buy from. I don't buy from murderers.'

'I wasn't suggesting —'

''Course you weren't. But you want to be careful who you ask. People who go round poking into other people's business can end up in a whole lot of trouble.'

'Why would anybody shelter a murderer?'

'I'm not saying they would. I'm just saying, you want to watch out. Me, I mind my own affairs and I don't let my woman wander round this place after dark.' The man rocked his stool back to lean against the wall and turned to the aforementioned woman. 'Did I just hear you tell her I'd take the door down?'

The woman stabbed a finger towards Ruso. 'Our money is sitting there, doing nothing!'

'Do you *know* how much it costs to fix a door, woman?'

Ruso rubbed his chin and decided to ask now before he or the barber drank any more of the beer. He gestured towards the shop, which, since it opened westwards on to the street, would still catch the best of the daylight. 'Any chance of a shave while I'm waiting?'

An hour or so later the patient lay on her bed in a drugged stupor, minus two disgusting black molars that had now vanished into the dusk along with her grandson. Ruso had a smooth chin, short hair, and he hadn't been bitten once.

As he closed his case he was still weighing up whether to knock the cost of the haircut off the fee. Charges tended to fluctuate depending upon the means of the patient, but asking too little was as bad as asking too much. Word got round. Precedents were hard to break.

'About the fee . . .'

The barber frowned. 'I know you had a bit of a wait, Doc. But you did have professional services during the waiting time.'

'Exactly.'

'The other officer told the lad it was a flat rate.'

Ruso's face must have betrayed his confusion. 'The other officer?'

'Old whatsisname – Priscus. Up at the hospital. Recommended you very highly.'

'I see.'

'He said you'd got an arrangement. We pay him and he passes it on to you.'

'Ah,' said Ruso, '*that* arrangement.'

Ruso strode across the paved area towards the fountain, the fall of each boot on the flagstones coinciding with the rhythm of the speech he was rehearsing for Priscus. 'And ex*actly* what *right* have *you* . . . ?' He was distracted by a gaggle of children gathered by the steps that ran up the outside of the amphitheatre. On the wall behind them he could just make out the white of a chalk scrawl announcing the forthcoming visit of L. Curtius Silvanus, Dealer in Slaves: Reliable Staff for the Discerning Employer. Below, half a dozen children were scrabbling to peer into the hand of a boy whom he recognized as the barber's son.

'Ugh, look, there's roots!'

'Look at the blood on them!'

'Did you see the worms wriggling?'

He was passing the entrance to the oil-merchant's when one of them shouted, 'Hey, mister! Got a penny, mister?'

Ruso ignored him. Others joined in the chorus. He could hear their footsteps running up behind him. 'Mister! Mister!'

Ruso spun on his heel and the gang stopped dead, a small and ragged bunch gathered just out of arm's reach. He pointed to the barber's son. 'Does your father know you beg in the street?'

The boy hesitated, then grinned. 'I know something you don't,' he said.

'No doubt.'

'I'll tell you, but you got to pay me first.'

'Why would I do that?'

The boy glanced round at his comrades, then sidled closer to Ruso. 'I know something about red hair.'

Ruso stared at him.

'I heard you ask. You want to know about somebody selling red hair.'

'Somebody sold red hair to your father?'

The boy held out one hand, and made a show of clamping the other over his mouth.

Ruso sighed, and filched out the one meagre coin inside his purse. The boy took it and removed his hand from his mouth to let out the words, 'It was a man.'

'Do you know his name?'

'No.'

'What sort of a man? What did he look like?'

The boy looked round at his friends for support. 'I don't know. He was just a man.'

'Old, young, fat, thin? It's no good holding out, I haven't got any more money.'

The boy frowned. 'He was old.'

'Was he a soldier?'

'I don't know,' said the boy, backing away.

'When was this?'

The boy's friends closed around him. 'He was just a man!' he called as they turned and fled.

A man. Ruso frowned at the backs of the retreating children. With a little effort Regional Control could have found that out – and probably more – days ago. In the morning HQ would be receiving another report and might even have to interrupt their hunting trips to go to question the barber. In the meantime, Ruso had told the boy the truth. Despite treating his second private patient in Deva, he had no cash in his purse.

Another thought struck him. Priscus' lodgings were somewhere on the east side of the town. He might well be at home. According to Decimus, who was not as discreet as Albanus, the miserable old weasel had gone home to keep an appointment with his decorator.

Ruso tightened his grip on the handle of his case. Why wait for morning? He spun round on his heel. He was going to straighten out this business of the fees right now.

'Ow!'

The girl he had collided with stumbled back against the wall. He made a grab to steady her and knocked something from her hand. It clanged as it hit the pavement. 'Sorry,' he said as the noise reverberated around the narrow street. 'I didn't see you.'

The girl shook off his hand and bent to retrieve the item she had dropped. 'If this bloody thing's broken again, you'll pay for it. It's only just been –'

'Chloe?'

'Oh! Hullo, Doctor.' Chloe held a large saucepan up for inspection. She wiggled the handle experimentally. 'Still attached. No harm done.'

Ruso frowned. 'Should you be wandering around out here? It's getting dark.'

He was conscious of an arm snaking round the back of his neck. 'Mm,' Chloe murmured, 'you never know who you might run into.' Cheap perfume wafted over him as a husky voice whispered in his ear, 'Fancy a little stroll?'

'No,' said Ruso's mouth before the rest of him had a chance to argue.

Chloe detached herself and shrugged. 'Oh well, it was worth a try. Sweet dreams, Doctor.' Swinging the pan by her side, she set off in the direction of Merula's.

She had not gone ten paces when Ruso caught up with her. 'Change your mind, then?'

'I need to know where the Street of the Weavers is.'

'Ask me nicely.'

'Tell me and I'll walk you back. Why didn't they send someone with you?'

'What for? I'm not going to run away, am I?'

'That wasn't what I meant,' he said, falling into step with her.

'I'm going straight back.' Chloe lifted the saucepan. 'And I'm armed.'

'I'm serious.'

'Asellina was unlucky,' she said. 'Saufeia was clueless.'

'I heard she was quite bright.'

'Not in any ways that were any use to her.'

'No, I gather she wasn't brought up for, ah . . . for your kind of life.'

'Not many people are, are they? Some of us just find we have a natural talent.'

Ruso smiled. 'Tilla seems to have convinced herself Saufeia was doomed by the curse of being able to read and write.'

For a moment Chloe did not answer, then she said quietly, 'No offence, Doctor, but if you want to do Tilla any favours, you tell her to keep out of what doesn't concern her.'

It was his second warning in one evening. 'Chloe,' he said, 'do you know something about what happened to Saufeia?'

'Me? I don't know a thing. And if anybody asks, you can tell them I said so.'

They walked on in silence. When they reached the bakery, Chloe paused and turned. The light from the torch outside Merula's was making a halo in her hair. 'Thanks for walking me back, Doc. I appreciate it.'

'Be careful,' he urged her.

'Do me one more favour, eh? Don't mention my little offer to the management.'

'I wouldn't dream of it,' said Ruso, who had already guessed that Chloe's efforts at private enterprise would be frowned upon by her owners.

Chloe laughed. 'Tilla said you were all right, and you are.'

'So, where do I find the Street of the Weavers?'

She took his arm and pointed down the alleyway that ran alongside the bar. 'Just down there.'

'You don't happen to know which house the hospital administrator lives in?'

'You ask a lot of questions, don't you?'

'Tall, thin, interesting hair,' prompted Ruso. 'I won't be mentioning anything to your management, remember?'

'Bad smell under his nose?'

'That's the one.'

'Sounds like our new neighbour,' said Chloe. 'Try the first house you come to on the right.'

54

Someone was in: there was a yellow streak of light where the door didn't fit the top of the frame. While he was waiting for Priscus to open up Ruso observed that the man had made a smart choice of neighbours. His house backed on to Merula's bar, but the noise which the woman at the bakery found so disturbing would all be out at the front, where the shutters opened on to the road. Priscus' house would back on to the kitchen yard and the private apartments occupied by Merula and her 'boys'. Beside Priscus' front door were shutters covering the shop-front of a basket-maker and on the opposite corner a weaver had gone home for the night. Even when the shops were busy, the hospital administrator's peace would hardly be disturbed by the sounds of weaving or fiddling about with willow-wands. Ruso pondered, not happily, the irony of Priscus enjoying peaceful and private lodgings while the men who actually dealt with the sick shared a vermin-infested dump awaiting demolition.

The administrator not only had peaceful and private lodgings, but a slave whose limbs were all in working order. Admittedly, a dumb slave. The man stood silhouetted in the doorway, communicating by the shaking of his head and the raising of one palm that his master was not at home to visitors.

'I'll wait,' said Ruso, putting one boot inside the door and indicating his medical case.

The slave made an effort to shut the door.

'It's business,' said Ruso, pushing in the opposite direction.

The slave looked thin and tired, as if the effort of communication was wearing him down. He glanced round, perhaps hoping someone was coming to back him up. Seeing the whitewashed corridor behind him empty, he stood back to let Ruso enter.

Ruso followed the slave into a spacious reception room which smelled of lavender and lamp-oil. To one side a chest of drawers held a lamp burning in front of the household gods. In the centre, two wicker chairs were set round a spindly-legged table bearing a fruit bowl, a jug and a cup. They were arranged as if someone was about to paint them. Priscus was nowhere to be seen.

The man motioned Ruso to a chair and indicated the cup. Ruso shook his head. The wicker chair creaked as the weave adjusted to his weight. He looked around him. This was one of the new houses, and far more spacious than the place where the barber's family lived. One door led off towards the back of the building, another to the side. From behind one of them there was a faint cry: too indistinct to tell whether it was male or female, pleasure, pain or surprise. The slave glanced at the doorway leading deeper into the house, then at Ruso. He stepped forward and offered the fruit bowl.

Ruso helped himself to a couple of grapes and wondered how far they had travelled. 'Will he be long?'

The man gave an expansive shrug and retreated to the side room, which Ruso guessed was a kitchen. Ruso had the feeling he had gone to hide from Priscus rather than fetch him.

Ruso put a grape into his mouth and burst it with his tongue. The juice flooded his mouth with memories. The grapes would be in at home now. Lucius, who wouldn't have received his letter yet, must be wondering whether this was the last batch of their own wine they would ever make.

He was just enjoying the second grape when there was a shrill and terrible scream from the rear door. A howl of rage cut across it, followed by Priscus yelling, 'You filthy little bed-bug!'

Ruso leaped out of his chair when the door burst open and Priscus emerged.

The administrator did not look happy. His hair was awry. His face, and most of the rest of him, seemed to have been splattered with something that might once have been edible, and which he was attempting to wipe off with a hospital blanket. He staggered as he trod on the untied thong of one of his own sandals and roared, 'Tadius!' at the closed door before turning and clutching the blanket to his chest at the sight of Ruso.

'What are you doing here?'

The slave emerged from the other room.

'Get a cloth and a bucket of water!' ordered Priscus. 'And find me a clean outfit.'

The slave hurried away. Priscus bent over, trying to wipe his face on a corner of blanket and adjust his hair at the same time. The smell of fish sauce was almost, but not quite, overpowering his bath-oil.

'I seem to have called at a bad time,' remarked Ruso, noting that Priscus' attempts to rearrange his hair had succeeded in leaving it resting in a clump above one ear. 'Have you had an accident?'

'It's nothing,' snapped Priscus, following Ruso's eyes to where a shadow was moving in the doorway behind him. He turned and slammed the door shut. The slave, who had been hurrying towards it clutching a bucket and cloth, retreated in confusion.

'Seems we've both had a busy evening,' said Ruso. 'You've been seeing your decorator and I've been pulling teeth.'

Priscus scowled. 'This is really not a convenient time –'

'I can see that. I just dropped by to collect my fee.'

'Your –?'

'Professional fee. Apparently we have an arrangement.'

The slave reappeared holding a folded tunic. Priscus turned to Ruso. 'We'll discuss this in the morning.'

'We'll discuss it when you've got clean clothes on.'

Priscus glanced at the slave as if he was wondering whether to ask him to throw his unwanted visitor out, then thought better of it and shuffled across to the kitchen in his unfastened sandals, beckoning the man to follow him.

Ruso helped himself to a couple more grapes and seated himself in the creaky chair. From behind the kitchen door came the sound of Priscus complaining and the sharp crack of a slap as Tadius evidently failed to please. From behind the other door, Ruso thought he could make out the sound of someone moving about. Whoever it was did not emerge.

'Disgraceful,' Priscus was saying as he emerged clean from the kitchen wearing a neatly pressed tunic and a realigned hairstyle. 'Utterly disgraceful. If the owner doesn't come up with some very acceptable compensation I shall cancel my order and have my meals delivered from somewhere else. Tadius? Make sure you give the floor a good scrub, put on a clean bolster-cover and have the other one laundered first thing in the morning.' He closed the kitchen door and turned back to Ruso. 'Now, what was it you wanted?'

'My fee,' said Ruso, getting to his feet. 'For the tooth extraction.'

'Ah. The tooth extraction. Yes.' Visibly making an effort

to take control of himself once more, Priscus indicated the table. 'Would you like a drink?'

'No, I would like my fee.'

Priscus sighed. 'We seem to have got off on the wrong foot, Ruso. Do sit down.'

Reluctantly, Ruso resumed his seat.

Priscus, who seemed to have made an impressively swift recovery of his composure, adjusted the position of the other chair and lowered himself into it. 'You are obviously most unhappy.'

'I was told by my patient that you and I have an arrangement. Apparently I go out on house calls and you pocket the fee.'

'Oh dear, no. I can see we've had a little misunderstanding.' Priscus smoothed the top of his hair with his hand and explained that it was hospital practice to make deductions at source for loan repayments. 'I would have spoken to you about it, but the boy said it was an emergency. I don't have the documents to hand, of course, but I can show you the account in the morning.'

'This was a private patient!'

'Ah, but the boy came to the hospital to ask for a doctor.'

'A couple of denarii is hardly going to make much of a dent in the loan, is it? Or are you expecting me to work it off?'

'No, no, of course not. But when it was sanctioned I was not aware that the Camp Prefect would be ordering an inspection of the hospital accounts prior to the arrival of the auditors.'

'We've been through this. I've already signed over a guarantee.'

'The loan is perfectly in order. But I do need to be able to show some repayments on the account, and this seemed the simplest way. Of course I would have asked for your approval, but the boy said it was an emergency and you were not available for discussion.'

Ruso sighed. He couldn't imagine the Camp Prefect having the slightest interest in a reduction of two denarii from the loan account of the Aesculapian Thanksgiving Fund, especially since he had already signed over his slave in the event of default. He could well believe, however, that Priscus was taking revenge for Ruso's persistent attempts to avoid him.

'All right,' Ruso conceded. 'We'll leave things as they are. But in future I'll negotiate and collect my own fees.'

'Of course.' Priscus paused. 'And perhaps we could agree to conduct hospital business within the confines of the hospital? This really was a most unfortunate time to call.'

55

Ruso had intended to dictate a note about the Brigantian girl, but the business of the red hair complicated matters. In the end he decided to request an appointment with the Second Spear to explain things in person. Granted a brief audience, he passed on his information about the barber — although not its source — and was acknowledged with a grunt that might have been encouragement but did not sound like it. He then went on to explain that a stolen girl, knowingly supplied by one Claudius Innocens, was in imminent danger. To his relief, this roused a better response. The Second Spear could not be expected to have much interest in the welfare of Brigantian carpenters' daughters, but he was shrewd enough to agree that action needed to be taken before some scruffy native with a grudge spotted the girl and used her as an excuse to stir up trouble. 'We've had enough bother with that bar,' he growled. 'We'd shut it down, but the others are worse. Just do me a favour and don't find any more bodies.'

The sun came out as Ruso strode back towards the hospital. He found himself feeling surprisingly cheerful and murmured a prayer of thanks for all that had happened to him in Britannia. There were only four more days to payday, and despite some worrying moments, he was going to reach it with his credit intact. He had been given the chance to run the hospital single-handed on two occasions, he was more or less in favour with the Regional Control people, and if there were any justice in the Army (which was doubtful) he would be well in line for the CMO's post. He had rescued one girl and saved her arm and now he had taken steps to retrieve another and put a stop to a filthy trade in stolen human flesh. This evening he would have the satisfaction of pointing out to Tilla that there was no need for all that cursing and howling and mumbo-jumbo over the cooking pot. He would not go into the details of why the Army were going to investigate Phryne's case even though they had not received an official complaint. He would simply explain that . . . In fact, he would not have to wait until this evening, because she was walking towards him.

'Tilla!' He was glad to see she had chosen this route. It was wide, it was busy, and the progress of any passing female would be closely supervised by numerous builders clambering about on the scaffolding of the bath-house.

'Tilla, good news!' He waited until she joined him before beginning his explanation of how, in a civilized society, criminals were dealt with by the law.

He was halfway through his first sentence when she flung herself at him. Off balance and bewildered, he staggered backwards and was thrust flat against the wall as something spattered up the gravel inches from his feet.

'Sorry!' shouted a voice from the scaffolding.

Ruso found himself gazing at a shuddering trowel, its point embedded deep in the road where he had just been walking. Moments later he realized that he was still clutching Tilla against his chest, almost as if he had saved her instead of the other way around. In fact, anyone walking around the corner now would get quite the wrong impression of what was going on. Unable to back away, he placed his hands on her shoulders and moved her to a more acceptable distance. 'Are you –' He glanced across at the trowel, paused to clear his throat and began again. 'Are you all right?'

'I am, my lord.'

He let go. 'Thank you.'

They stepped away from each other, both turning aside to brush down the creases in their clothing as footsteps clattered on the planking above them. Tilla glared at the builder who was making his way down the ladder. 'You are very careless!'

The builder glanced from one to the other of them, said, 'Sorry, sir,' then added, 'miss.'

'You could kill my master!' continued Tilla. 'Why do you throw this – this *thing*?' She flapped a hand at the trowel, evidently frustrated at not knowing enough Latin to give him a fluent scolding.

'I didn't throw it,' said the man, stepping across to retrieve it, 'it was an accident.' He wiped the gravel-spattered remnants of cement off the trowel on to a leg of the scaffold, and turned to Ruso. 'Sorry about that, sir. Slipped out of my hand. Lucky you got her out of the way.'

'I didn't,' said Ruso, squinting up at the high walls of the refurbished bath-house. 'What's your name, soldier?'

'Secundus, sir. From the century of Gallus.'

'Well, Secundus. You need to be more careful.'

'Yes, sir.'

'When's this work going to be finished?'

Ignoring Tilla's scowl, the man pointed out that it was only a month over schedule, as if this were something to be proud of. This week they had been held up because a batch of tiles had come in the wrong size. Once the roof was done, the plumbers and plasterers and painters would be finished in about ten days. They were working right up to dark to get finished.

'Good. Then perhaps somebody will fix our hospital roof.'

306

'You're next on the list, sir,' promised Secundus with an ease that suggested he had said it many times to many people.

After he had gone, Tilla said, 'That man is a liar.'

'I know,' agreed Ruso. 'But there's no point in arguing with them or they'll take even longer.'

Tilla frowned. 'I am not talking about the roof,' she said.

56

As Tilla left the room, carrying the cleared dishes, Valens pushed the nearest light away with his toe, put his feet up on the table and went back to his favourite topic of the evening. 'Are you sure there was somebody there?'

'Positive,' said Ruso. 'He was shouting at them.'

Valens chuckled. 'I don't know which is more amazing. Priscus and a secret assignation, or Priscus stealing the hospital bedclothes. Dear me. What a shame you couldn't see who it was. Male or female, do you think?'

'I couldn't tell. All I had was a glimpse of a shadow in the doorway.'

There was a crash from the kitchen. Ruso winced. Valens said, 'Don't be too hard on her, old man. It must be tricky washing up with one hand.'

'She's got some use in the right hand now,' pointed out Ruso.

'Which you *very* kindly saved for her,' agreed Valens. 'And I suppose she *has* got all evening to do the pots.' He leaned back on the couch, yawned and stretched his arms above his head as the dog scrambled out from behind him. 'Do you realize,' he observed to the ceiling, 'this is the first time we've both had dinner at home? You are a remarkable chap under that dour exterior, Gaius Petreius.'

Ruso poured himself more wine and maintained the silence of his dour exterior.

'First you wander down a back alley and find us a house-keeper, then you pay a visit to the hospital administrator and – gods, I wish I'd seen the expression on his face. Silly old fart!' Valens, who was on call this evening, bent forward and poured a generous amount of water into his own wine before raising it to his lips. 'So, he tried to pretend he was just having his dinner delivered?'

'Well, there was certainly food involved.'

'Dear me. He can't have imagined you'd believe him.'

Ruso swilled the wine around his cup. 'I don't want to guess what might be in Priscus' imagination,' he said. 'He's probably crouched in a corner of his web right now, plotting revenge.'

'Well. Old Priscus, eh?'

'I'd be grateful if you'd keep your mouth shut for a while. He's got it in for me already.'

'Me? Soul of discretion. But I must say, it's all quite wonderful. Priscus! The last man I would suspect of having a wild private life.'

'He does have that wolf on his wall.'

'I'd always assumed he bought that from a hunter. Well. Perhaps I'm wrong about that, too. Maybe there's more to our diligent pen-pusher than we all thought.' Valens took a long draught from his cup.

Ruso said, 'Do you know a roofer called Secundus? Centurion's called Gallus.'

Valens frowned. 'I can't recall him. Why?'

'He dropped a trowel on my head this afternoon. From the top of the scaffolding.'

'Why didn't you say so? Want me to take a look?'

'He missed,' explained Ruso. 'He said it was an accident. But I'm starting to wonder.'

'Really? You're usually such a sensible sort of chap.'

'After that business with the fire . . .'

'You've just had a run of bad luck, that's all. Go and offer a pigeon to Fortuna if you're that worried.'

'Do you really think that would help?'

Valens grinned. 'Of course not. But it might make you feel better. You're probably a bit out of balance. Have you tried a purge?'

'No.'

'Are you watching your diet?'

'No.'

'Getting enough sleep?'

'Not really.'

'There you are, then. I don't go around thinking somebody was trying to poison me with those oysters. It was just an accident. It doesn't do to brood on things, you know.'

There was another crash from the kitchen. This time it sounded as though something had smashed.

Ruso shouted, 'Be careful in there, Tilla!'

The only reply was the swish and tinkle of a broom chasing broken crockery across the floor.

'Never mind,' said Valens, indicating the wine-jug. 'We've got the important stuff in here. Drink up, you're not on duty.'

Ruso rocked the front legs of his favourite chair off the ground – he had moved it in here for dinner – and put his feet up opposite Valens'.

'I must say,' observed Valens, 'your Tilla may be a bit cack-handed but she's not making a bad fist of the cooking. For someone who hasn't done it before.'

'She has done it before,' Ruso corrected him. 'Just not our sort of food.'

'Really?' Valens' brows lowered with puzzlement. 'That's funny, because she told me –'

He was interrupted by the sound of someone banging on the front door. 'Damn,' he muttered, swinging his feet down from the table.

There was a brief and largely inaudible conversation at the door, then it closed, and Valens reappeared clutching his cloak. 'Got to go,' he said, 'Tribune with a tummy-ache. Tell the lovely Tilla she can warm my bed up if she wants.'

'What was it she told you?'

'What? Oh.' Valens flung his cloak over his shoulders. 'Before her home was raided by some rival tribe or other, she lived in a family that owned a cook.' His voice distorted as he squinted down to see where he was pushing the fastening-pin. 'So, she never bothered to learn. I thought you knew.'

After Valens had clattered the door shut, Ruso remained in his chair, gazing at the lamp. 'I thought I knew, too,' he informed it. Well. He hoped the Army would investigate Claudius Innocens very thoroughly. Preferably with a sharp implement. Innocens had promised him Tilla could cook.

Which reminded him. He needed to talk to her.

He paused in the doorway. Tilla carried on drying a spoon with a cloth and then flung it down with such force that it bounced.

'The chicken stew was very good, Tilla.'

'Thank you, my lord.' She snatched up another spoon and gave it a swift wipe.

'I have some news for you.'

The second spoon clattered down beside its mate.

Ruso cleared his throat. 'Is something the matter?'

She glanced at him. 'No, my lord. I am very lucky.'

'Indeed you are.'

She tossed the cloth over the hook by the hearth. 'I am very lucky not to be Phryne.'

'That's what I came to tell you about,' he said. 'When I saw you this afternoon I was on the way back from reporting the problem. I've been assured there will be some action very soon.'

She turned. 'Tonight?'

'Not that soon.' It was hardly the sort of emergency that would persuade the Second Spear to miss his dinner.

'So Phryne is still at Merula's tonight.'

Ruso had not expected thanks, but he had expected that his slave would be pleased. 'She will be a lot safer there than she would be out on the streets,' he said.

'With the men.'

'Yes,' said Ruso, exasperated. 'With the men. Who are unlikely to do her serious harm, because if she's laid up she can't earn any money for Merula. Now stop throwing our things about.' As Tilla opened her mouth to speak he said, 'And don't start wailing and cursing, either, because I have work to do.'

He snatched up his wine in one hand and his chair in the other. He was heading towards his room when he heard her say, 'I will be silent. I will control my tongue.'

'Good!' A leg of the chair banged into the wall and the wine lurched towards the side of the cup. 'Get on with your work, and don't break anything else.'

'I know what happens to slaves who talk too much!'

'Yes!' he shouted back. 'And I'm beginning to understand why!'

Ruso placed a lamp on his desk, kicked the bedroom door shut and blew the dust off the pile of writing-tablets. He flipped open the first one and sat down. 'Treatment for Eye Injuries'. Gods above, he had been on this section for months. Tonight he was going to finish it.

He moved the lamp to a better angle and began to read through what he had written so far. Halfway down the page he paused to note with satisfaction that Tilla had stopped crashing about in the kitchen. No doubt she was regretting her display of temper. He thought he had handled it rather well. Now he had the rest of the evening for 'Treatment for Eye Injuries'.

His finger had reached the bottom of the first page before it struck him that he could not remember what he had just read. This was not encouraging. If he found it boring, what about his readers? He picked up his stylus, tweaked the wick of the lamp with the sharp end and reassured himself that the author of a book whose content was worthwhile need not concern himself with elegant style. People who wanted to know something useful would not want to hunt through pages of authorial showing-off to find it. The task of a medical writer – particularly a concise one – was to offer immediate and practical help, not tell jokes. He took another gulp of wine and started to read again in the brighter light.

Perhaps he should leave the bedroom door open, just in case there was some very quiet wailing and cursing going on.

Perhaps not.

He had more important things to do than waste his evening wondering what his servant was up to.

The trouble with women was that, no matter what you did, they were never satisfied. Instead of being grateful for the efforts made on their behalf – sometimes quite considerable, and at no small inconvenience – they chose to pick on one small matter that had not been attended to and complain about it.

What else was he supposed to have done about that girl? Stride into the bar and demand that Merula hand her over? What Tilla did not seem to understand was that in the absence of an official complaint by someone willing to take

up her case — which Ruso certainly wasn't, since the girl was none of his business — no one was obliged to do anything at all about Phryne. Not tonight, not next week, not ever.

In the meantime, while the Medicus to the Twentieth sat in the wavering light, pondering the welfare of local barmaids over a cup of wine and a belly full of chicken stew, there could be a frightened legionary lying injured out in some dark and distant outpost, unable to summon even a bandager, wishing to the gods that either he or his companions knew something about first aid.

Ruso straightened his chair, cleared his throat and began to fill the central leaf with writing.

He wrote steadily to the foot of the wax, read it through and was correcting it when he heard the front door open. He and Valens grunted a mutual goodnight, and moments later he heard the other bedroom door shut. There was no sound from the kitchen.

Ruso flipped the wooden leaf over and began to fill the other side.

He was surprised when a distant trumpet sounded for the next watch and told him he had been writing for a couple of hours now.

The lamp was starting to sputter as he finished the last sentence. He pushed the wick down to conserve the oil, propped the tablet beside the lamp and reread his work. It was good. He slapped the tablet shut and put it back on the top of the pile. He would get Albanus to make a fair copy in the morning.

His thoughts returned to Tilla's concern for Phryne. She had a point. The girl's situation was not a happy one, and it would doubtless be getting worse with every hour she spent in that place. At least, though, she had the protection of being the daughter of a free man. The law would – eventually – help her in a way that it would never have helped Saufeia, or Asellina, or the unfortunate Daphne. Neither the law nor the Army offered any hope to slaves whose owners expected them to work as prostitutes. Their only choices were to cooperate, kill themselves or run away. And if the escape went disastrously wrong, there seemed to be few who would care. He hoped the business about the hair had whetted the Second Spear's appetite for investigation. And that Phryne would not take it into her head to run away tonight.

Ruso picked up his wine-cup. He blew out the struggling lamp before the flame scorched the dry wick and headed for the door.

He stood for a moment, breathing in the warm air of the dining room. As his eyes adjusted to the dark he could make out a bundle huddled on the couch, faintly outlined by the dull glow of the dying embers in the fire. He held his breath, but he already knew how quietly she slept. He could hear only a faint crackle of burning and the thud of his own heart. He took a step forward.

There was the rustle of fabric and the bundle moved. 'My lord?'

He groped for a taper and knelt to push the end into the embers. 'That business this afternoon, Tilla. The near miss.'

'Is not an accident, my lord.'

'Whatever it was, you did well. That's all. Go back to sleep now.'

'Goodnight, my lord.'

The end of the taper caught into a yellow flame. He lifted it out and set it to the candle on the table.

'My lord?'

'Yes?'

'I know you try to help Phryne.'

315

He paused, candle in hand, by the kitchen door. 'I am sorry if you were hoping for more.'

'I am not hoping for anything, my lord.'

Ruso poured himself a drink of water in the kitchen. *I am not hoping for anything, my lord.* Considering the fortunes of the slaves he had come to know since moving to Deva, that was hardly surprising.

He paused by the couch on his way back to the bedroom, setting the candle and the water on the table. 'Before you sleep, Tilla,' he said, 'I have something to ask you. No –' he held out a hand, 'don't stand up.'

She pulled the blankets around her shoulders, curled her feet in underneath her and stifled a yawn. The dog must be sleeping on Valens' bed: there was room beside her on the couch. Ruso chose the edge of the table instead. One of his feet brushed against something. He glanced down to see two small boots set in a neat pair. 'I have been told more than once,' he said, 'that Saufeia could read and write.'

'Yes, my lord.'

'There is something people are not telling me.'

She frowned. 'I am telling my lord everything he asks.'

'I want to know why it matters. Does it have something to do with what happened to her?'

From outside the house the sound of boots on gravel rose and rapidly faded as the guard relieved from the last watch took a shortcut on their way back to bed.

'What about the other girl? Do you know anything about that?'

'Asellina. She ran away.'

'Was she meeting someone?'

'Her man says it is not him. Nobody knows another man.'

'What do the girls think happened to her?'

'Nobody knows anything, my lord.'

'And what about Saufeia? Does anybody know anything about her?'

She did not answer.

'Merula isn't going to hurt you, Tilla. She's no fool. She wouldn't dare touch someone else's slave.'

Her hair was loose over her shoulders. She began to twirl a strand around her forefinger.

'You told me about Phryne, and something will be done about it. If someone would tell the truth about Saufeia, perhaps something can be done about that, too.'

'The truth will not bring her back.'

'The truth may save some other girl from the same fate.'

There was a crackle from the grate as the embers shifted and sent up an orange fountain of sparks. The finger stopped twirling. 'The truth I know, my lord,' she said, 'is not enough. You will ask more questions, and people will hear the questions and know I tell you, and the person who tell me will be very sorry.'

'The person who tell – who told you is Chloe, isn't it?'

'Whatever you say, my lord.'

'You are a very stubborn woman.'

'Yes, my lord. Whatever you say.'

He shrugged. 'I'm not staying up to argue. In the morning, I want you to tell me.'

He was almost at the door when he heard her voice, low and urgent. 'Nobody knows who Saufeia's letter is to, my lord. Nobody knows what it says. To ask questions is to dig in a wasps' nest where there is much danger and nothing to eat at the end of it. Saufeia is gone to the other world. Leave her in peace.'

As Ruso pulled up his blankets and pinched out the lamp it occurred to him that he was lucky to be blessed with a sensible friend like Valens. And a strong sense of logic.

Otherwise, he might be thinking that the fire had not been an accident or a haunting but the work of someone who did not like him asking questions. Someone who had forced open his ill-fitting shutters and tossed something burning on to his bed.

57

'No file copy, sir?' Albanus looked surprised.

'Just one for me. I'll have the notes back with it when you've finished.'

Albanus turned over the top leaf of the *Concise Guide*. 'There's quite a lot of work here, sir.'

'I'll see you're rewarded,' promised Ruso, reminding himself that it was only three days to payday.

'Oh, I didn't mean that, sir!' Albanus seemed genuinely shocked. 'Three pages is nothing. What I mean is, I wouldn't recommend keeping the only fair copy and the notes together in one place. If there's a fire, or the roof leaks over them, you could end up having to start all over again.'

'Are you telling me,' said Ruso, incredulous, 'that you keep file copies of everything?'

Albanus shook his head sadly. 'No, sir. There isn't room. We have a list of priority items to keep that end up in HQ – mens' records, that sort of thing – and the rest is stored for a time depending on what it is, and then burned.'

Something stirred at the back of Ruso's mind. 'And is that just the hospital, or the whole fort?'

Albanus blinked. 'I think that's what everyone does, sir. You simply can't keep everything, there wouldn't be space.'

'So a letter that came in would be kept for – how long?'

'I don't know, sir. I could find out. I suppose it depends on what it is. And obviously there's no control over personal letters to the men.'

'Ah.' Of course. Even if Saufeia had addressed her

mysterious letter to a legionary boyfriend, she was hardly likely to have been corresponding via the official post. He was not thinking clearly.

'They just go on the daily lists,' added Albanus.

Ruso stared at him. 'Daily lists?' he repeated. 'Are you telling me someone sits down with the post sacks and makes a list of every letter received into the fort?'

Albanus nodded. 'Ever since a letter got lost that told the Camp Prefect his mother had died, sir. There was a bit of a fuss. So now if it comes through the gate, it gets noted down – recipient and sender – and signed for.'

'And who has access to these lists?'

'The HQ clerks, I suppose, sir. To be honest I don't think anybody looks at them much. It's one of those things you don't need because you've got it.'

Ruso scratched his ear. 'And how easy would it be,' he asked, 'for someone to make a discreet inquiry?'

'For someone like you, sir? I think the clerks would want to know why you were looking. In case you were going to put in a complaint about them.'

'I see.'

'But you wouldn't need to do it, would you sir?' Albanus' face brightened. 'You've got me.'

58

Tilla had deliberately left the baker's till last and now, as she rounded the corner, there was Lucco sweeping the opposite pavement in front of the drawn shutters and the red writing on the wall. The boy sloshed a bucket of grey water across the stones, picked up the broom and chased trickles of bobbing dirt down crevices towards the street drain.

Tilla glanced up and down the street and checked that the upstairs window of Merula's was shuttered. 'Lucco!'

The boy gave the broom a final swish and looked up. 'You've missed them,' he said. 'They've gone to the baths.'

The goddess had granted her prayer: Bassus was safely out of the way. She moved closer to Lucco so she would not be overheard, 'Do you know if Phryne was with them?'

The boy shrugged. 'Dunno.'

'No,' said a voice. Strong fingers clamped around her bandaged arm and Bassus slid out from behind the shutters. He told Lucco to get lost. The boy scuttled back into the bar. 'Phryne's feeling a bit off colour this morning,' said Bassus.

Tilla felt a stab of pain as he squeezed her arm.

'Nice of you to ask, though.'

She dared not move. She had thought the goddess would keep her safe. Now it seemed she was expected to manage on her own.

'Surprised to see me, are you?' he asked. 'Stich took the girls out this morning.'

Two women with baskets were standing chatting at the

bakery counter across the street. Tilla announced loudly, 'You are hurting my arm!'

One of them turned.

'I am not afraid of you!' she added, ashamed that the words were not true.

Bassus followed her gaze across to where everyone had now stopped talking to watch what he was doing.

'If you hurt me,' added Tilla, struggling to keep her voice level, 'my master will have you punish with the law!'

There was a sharper stab as he pulled her against his chest. 'Round here, girl,' he hissed, 'I *am* the law.'

Before she could decide whether to scream, Bassus burst into laughter and released her. 'It's all right, ladies,' he called across to the audience, holding up both hands in mock surrender. 'Just a lovers' tiff.'

He turned back to Tilla. 'Cheer up, gorgeous. You're worth too much to damage. Me and your doctor friend done a deal, did you know that?'

'You are lying.'

'Am I? I'm going to introduce him to some people I know. We should get a good price for you.'

She stared at the man's heavy, seamed face. She took a deep breath. 'My master will never deal with a man like you!'

Bassus shrugged. 'Ask him yourself.' He cocked his head to one side and examined her face. 'What's the matter?' He smiled and shook his head. 'Oh dear, oh dear. Gone soft on him, eh? You thought he was going to *keep* you, didn't you?'

59

'Here you are!' declared Valens, settling himself on the wooden lid of the row opposite Ruso in the hospital latrine. 'I'll tell them I haven't seen you.'

'Who?'

'Apparently the Second Spear wants your balls roasted on a spit.'

Ruso washed the sponge out in the water-channel, shook it and tossed it back into the basket. 'Any particular reason?'

'Seems he spent a whole afternoon looking for a kid-napped girl.'

Ruso pulled his tunic straight and adjusted his belt. 'Good. So what's the problem?'

'The problem, Ruso, is that when they found her she insisted she wasn't kidnapped at all.'

Before he could reply, an orderly appeared in the door-way and exclaimed, 'There you are, sir!' as if he too thought Ruso had reason to hide.

Ruso sighed and waited for what he knew must be coming. But instead of an urgent summons to report to the Second Spear, he was told there was a veteran waiting to see him at the East Gate.

'Tell them to take a message,' said Ruso.

'They said he wants to see you personally, sir.'

'I'm busy. If he wants to see me he'll have to come back after the tenth hour.'

The orderly disappeared. Ruso dipped his hands in the bowl, shook off the water and headed for the surgery.

Albanus handed him the record for the first patient and returned to perch on his stool by the door. Ruso surveyed the notes from the recruiting panel. Under 'Lucius Eprius Saenus, age twenty, height five feet eight inches, medium build, distinguishing features, scar on left temple' the scribe of the recruiting panel had written 'general physique satisfactory, eyesight good, hearing good, teeth – three missing in upper jaw, two in lower, genitals normal, no sign of disease, feet not flat'. The examining doctors at the recruitment panel had already done most of the work. Ruso's job was merely to prod Lucius Eprius Saenus again in places he didn't wish to be prodded, look at places he still wouldn't want looked at and generally confirm that his health had not deteriorated since he had been confirmed fit to join the Army. This performance would have to be repeated for the other twenty-two stubble-headed recruits lined up on the benches in the hall, all of whom would resent him by the end of the afternoon, but not as much as they would loathe and dread their centurions by the end of the week. Almost as much, in fact, as Ruso was dreading his next encounter with the Second Spear.

'Right,' said Ruso, opening his case and extracting a tongue-depressor. 'Let's get started.'

Albanus leaned out of the door and said something to someone. An orderly who was evidently afraid the recruits had gone deaf bellowed, 'FIRST MAN TO SEE THE DOCTOR!'

A pale and skinny youth in a loincloth appeared in the doorway and stood to attention.

'Come in,' suggested Ruso. 'I can't see much of you out there.'

324

The youth entered and stood to attention before the desk, goosepimpled flesh motionless and eyes roving over the array of instruments in Ruso's case.

'Lucius Eprius Saenus,' said Ruso, closing the case. 'Strip off.'

The youth looked at him as if he didn't understand the instruction.

Ruso gestured towards the loincloth. 'The Army needs to see all of you, Saenus.'

'Yes, sir,' agreed the youth, not moving.

'That's an order.'

'Yes, sir.'

'Well what are you waiting for?'

The youth swallowed. 'I'm not Lucius Eprius Saenus, sir.'

Ruso glanced at Albanus. 'You're not?'

'No, sir.'

'Well why didn't you say that in the first place?'

'You didn't ask.'

Ruso got to his feet and walked slowly in a circle around the youth, who was clearly a couple of inches shorter than the description. There was no sign of a scar on the temple. 'Who are you, then?'

'Quintus Antonius Vindex, sir.'

Albanus bent down and began to scrabble through the records box.

'Quintus Antonius Vindex,' continued Ruso, 'have you ever heard the expression "rhetorical question"?'

'No, sir.'

'No. Well, the correct answer to "Why didn't you say so in the first place?" was "Sorry, sir".'

'Yes, sir. Sorry, sir.'

Albanus had given up scrabbling and was now kneeling

in front of the box, pulling the records out and heaping them up on the floor.

'Go and find Saenus,' Ruso suggested to the youth. 'I'll call you in when I'm ready.'

They must have realized the mistake outside, because Ruso was still returning to his seat when the next man entered.

'Lucius Eprius Saenus?' inquired Ruso, rereading the description carefully and taking no chances this time.

'Do I look like it?' demanded a familiar voice.

Albanus leapt to his feet with the eagerness of a man seeing a chance to redeem himself. 'You can't come in here!' he cried. 'The Doctor's busy!'

'I can go where I like round here, mate,' retorted Bassus. 'Know a lot of people, don't I?'

'It's all right,' Ruso reassured Albanus, who had sized up Bassus and was moving towards the door to call for reinforcements. 'Go and find Saenus, will you? I'll be back in a minute.'

Safely beyond the front door of the hospital and over-hearing ears, he turned to Bassus. 'What's going on?'

Bassus frowned. 'I come here to ask you that. We've had investigators crawling all over the bar like cockroaches and now I'm having to trail over to HQ with a bunch of slave documents. And what I'm wondering is, who was it told them they might find something?'

Ruso took a careful breath. He could feel his heart beating. 'Are you telling me,' he said, 'that you have the official ownership documents for that new girl?'

'I was right, then. I thought it was you. 'Course we have. Merula just couldn't find them this morning, what with the girls screaming and lads crashing about all over the place.'

Ruso got to his feet and said quietly, 'I owe Merula an apology.'

'I wouldn't go near her right now, mate. Keep your mouth shut and stay out of the way. That's what I come to tell you.'

'Thank you,' said Ruso, not entirely sure why Bassus seemed to be defending him. 'I shall.'

'Next time you got any problems, Doc, you talk to me first. We're business partners. Right?'

Ruso scratched his ear. 'I seem to have been misinformed.'

'That's what I thought,' said Bassus.

'I'll see to it that my informant is dealt with.'

'Bloody women,' sympathized Bassus. 'Always stirring things up. You can't believe a word they say. People think I'm hard on 'em, but they don't have to put up with it like I do.'

Ruso nodded. There seemed to be nothing he could add.

60

By the time Ruso had formed the opinion that all twenty-three recruits were fit enough to be driven to exhaustion, despair and finally to usefulness, the message he had been expecting had arrived. He was to report to the Second Spear.

One of the qualities needed for promotion through the Centurionate was the ability to single-handedly compel eighty trained killers to do things they didn't much want to do, and to do them instantly. In this respect, as in many others, the Second Spear was generally reputed to be heading for the very top. As Ruso entered the man's office, he was conscious of adopting the stance of legionaries he had seen being humiliated on the parade ground: shoulders square, head high, eyes straight ahead, focused on nothing.

'Doctor Gaius Petreius Ruso, sir,' announced the orderly.

The Second Spear ordered his man to wait outside. When the door was closed, he got to his feet. 'Well, Doctor? What have you got to say for yourself?'

'I'm sorry about what happened, sir. I was misinformed.'

'I'm not talking about that farce in the whorehouse, Ruso. All you've done there is upset a local trader, wasted my time and made the Army look ridiculous. The Camp Prefect will deal with all that. And if you're expecting me to go running around hunting down slave-traders and hair-dealers on your say-so, you're a bigger fool than you look.'

'Yes, sir,' said Ruso, wondering what else the Second Spear could want to talk about. He was staring at a point just to the right of the man's shoulder and silently bidding farewell to any hopes of the Chief Medical Officer post when he was conscious of a sudden movement. A hand grabbed his throat. He was knocked backwards. His head crashed against the wall. The Second Spear's face filled his vision. The mouth opened. 'Give me one reason,' it growled, 'why you aren't about to have a very nasty accident.'

Shocked, winded, struggling for air, Ruso attempted to croak, 'Don't know what you mean, sir.'

'Don't treat me like an idiot, son. You might be able to fool them down at that hospital but you're not fooling me.' Each sentence that followed was punctuated by a tightening of the grip around his throat. 'Thought you could get away with it, did you? Thought you'd try your luck? Thought she might talk me round?'

Realizing too late what this was about and that his rank was not going to protect him, Ruso mouthed, 'No.'

The Second Spear relaxed his grasp for a second, and Ruso was gulping in air, when the grip clamped back around his throat, and his bruised skull slammed back against the wall. Over the ringing in his ears, a voice roared, 'Don't lie to me! You were seen!'

61

Ruso stumbled in through the front door and across the room. He dragged a blanket off the couch and stretched out, laying his throbbing head on a cushion that smelled of dog and stale beer.

'Tilla!' he croaked. 'Get me some water.'

The sound of his head bouncing off the wall was still echoing around his skull. His throat felt as though the slightest twist would split his windpipe and crack his neckbones apart.

He had almost begged Tilla's goddess for help as the strength drained out of him like desert sand sifting between his fingers. A distant voice was shouting, 'Sir! Sir, you'll kill him!' and finally the vice around his throat had loosened and he collapsed to the floor.

She had not heard his request for water. He couldn't call any louder. He rolled on to his side and tried again, the word rasping in his throat and ringing through his aching skull.

'Tilla!'

Still no reply. Too tired to lift himself off the couch, he closed his eyes and waited for her to find him.

Something was jumping on his stomach. An African drummer was practising on the inside of his skull. Something was bouncing on his chest. A chisel was being scraped up the inside of his throat. A rough tongue was licking his face. He lifted an arm and batted away a small warm body. The licking stopped. The body yelped as it landed.

A voice called, 'Off, boys and girls! He doesn't want to play!' The bouncing ceased. The drumming and scraping didn't.

Ruso opened one eye to see Valens scoop up a whining puppy. 'You're not hurt,' Valens assured the puppy after a perfunctory check. He turned to the couch. 'Are you all right there, Ruso?'

The water helped. He was less sure about the liniment. 'I got it from one of the vets,' explained Valens. 'He says it's marvellous stuff. I've been waiting for a chance to try it out.'

Ruso grimaced.

'Don't worry about the smell, you won't notice it after a minute or two. So, what happened?'

Ruso pointed to his throat and moved his head carefully from side to side.

'Write it down,' suggested Valens. 'Hold on, I'll find something . . . if the lovely Tilla hasn't chucked it all out . . . where is she, by the way?'

Ruso lifted both palms in an exaggerated shrug. Valens disappeared into his room and began throwing things about in the hunt for writing materials. Ruso hauled himself to his feet and shuffled across the floor.

The kitchen fire was dead. There was no sign of any attempt to prepare supper. The water jar was almost empty, and there was no bread in the bin. The wretched girl must be up to her old tricks with the goddess. She could not possibly have the meal ready on time if the fire wasn't lit by now. He wondered whether she knew what had happened at Merula's and was hiding from him.

Ruso wandered into his bedroom. Rubbing the lump on the back of his head, he stood in the doorway and tried to remember whether he had put his best cloak away or whether it was missing from the hook on the wall.

Valens appeared, clutching a slate. 'So. Speak to me.'

There were many things he wished to say to Valens, but the slate was not big enough. Instead he scrawled, 'My throat hurts, my head hurts, I have no money, my servant has disappeared and I am about to do a ward round smelling like a sick horse.'

'Ah.' Valens reached for the slate. He licked his forefinger, rubbed out the word 'horse' and wrote 'donkey'.

Carefully, Ruso tipped his head back towards the pharmacy ceiling, gargled the last of the foul mixture and spat. Watching it slide down the side of the waste-bucket, he pondered the efficiency of military communications. It was a mystery why the Army bothered with a signal system when its men were so good at gossip. He had left the Second Spear's house barely an hour ago, and just now the pharmacist, after expressing sympathy for his sudden cold, waited until the last patient had left to murmur between gargles, 'Sorry to hear about the Second Spear's daughter, sir. That was bad luck.'

Ruso turned towards him and croaked, 'What about the Second Spear's daughter?'

'If it's any consolation, most of us think she wouldn't be your type, sir.'

'I'm not bloody interested in the . . .' Ruso paused and lowered his voice. 'Any rumours about myself and the Second Spear's daughter are groundless. I'm sure she's a lovely young lady, but I've never actually set eyes on her. So go back to whoever told you this nonsense and tell them if they spread any more lies I'll deal with them myself.'

Halfway through late ward round, he met Valens in a corridor. 'How's it going?' demanded Valens.

Ruso paused to insert another throat pastille before strong-arming him towards an empty isolation room and latching the door.

'Jupiter!' Valens wrinkled his nose. 'You'd think that pong would have worn off by now, wouldn't you?'

'I've been thinking,' said Ruso. 'Have you been smarming around the offspring of the Second Spear?'

'I did have a pleasant chat with her the other day. Nice girl.'

'Well don't. Her father thinks you're me, and he doesn't like it.'

'No? Well, I wouldn't either. Look at the state of you. Your eyes are bloodshot, your hair's sticking up and you smell like something they clean the drains with.'

'I know. And it's your fault!'

'She hasn't complained to him, has she?'

'*She* hasn't. You were seen.'

Valens smiled. 'I didn't think she would. I knew she'd be a sensible sort of girl. She's got a sensible sort of nose.'

Ruso opened his mouth to argue, then decided it would only make his throat worse.

'I'll tell you all about it later,' suggested Valens. 'Over tonight's supper served by the lovely Tilla.'

'I can't find Tilla.'

'Dear me. You are having a bad day.'

'I am,' growled Ruso. 'But it'll improve when I kill you.'

62

The house felt chilly as he entered. The dog offered him the briefest of greetings and then dodged past his legs and out of the door. Ruso sniffed and glanced round at the floor. The puppies must have been locked in for hours.

The kitchen hearth was a blackened void where the fire should have been. Ruso sniffed again and crouched to inspect the floor. Beneath the table was a small brown turd.

Outside, he heard Valens whistle for the dog. Moments later there were footsteps on the gravel. The main door slammed and Valens appeared in the kitchen, surveying the empty shelves and the dead fire. 'Where is she?'

'I don't know. The dogs haven't been let out.'

'So where's our dinner?'

Something in Ruso's expression must have told him this was the wrong question.

'She's probably gone shopping,' suggested Valens. 'Met up with a friend, or something. You know how women talk. Perhaps she's dropped round to Merula's.'

'I'd be amazed if she's gone there. Anyway, she'd know to come back by now.'

'Well, I can't wait till she turns up. If you get the fire going, I'll go and talk nicely to the kitchen staff. See if they can sneak something past Priscus.' Valens paused. 'I wouldn't worry, old man. She's bound to show up before long.'

'It's getting dark. Something's gone wrong.'

'Then she'll be back any minute, won't she?' Valens

grinned. 'Cheer up. You'll be able to give her a good spanking.'

'Thanks.'

'I'll do it if you like.'

Ruso scowled. 'Just bugger off, will you?'

By the time men and dogs had eaten Valens' gleanings from the hospital kitchen ('This is just like old times, isn't it?') it was time to light the lamps. Leaving Valens to cover his on-call duties, Ruso put a lead on the dog and went out to look for his servant.

It was not as dark outside as it had seemed in the house. As he waited for the dog to finish sniffing around the shadowy nettle-patch, Ruso's eyes adjusted to the gloom. He could pick out the rectangular shape of the next barrack-block, the roof of the hospital and, turning, the outline of the main wall at the end of the street across the perimeter road. As he watched, he heard the tramp of guards. Two shapes moved steadily towards each other along the top of the wall, crossed and continued in opposite directions.

A breeze plucked at the thin fabric of his spare cloak and suggested there was rain on the way. 'That's enough, dog,' urged Ruso, keen to move but not sure of his direction. He did not want to imagine what might have happened to Tilla, but imagination was his only tool in deciding a sensible pattern of search. If she had run into the wrong man – and the gods knew, he had tried many times to warn her – she could be anywhere. Alive or dead. Inside the fort or out. Inside, he felt, was less likely. The men's lack of privacy and propensity to gossip would serve as some protection.

He called at the hospital in case there was a message, but there were no notes at the desk. Decimus' assurance of 'I'm sure she'll turn up soon, sir!' was bright rather than confident, and Ruso wondered how many people had said the same thing to him about Asellina.

'Decimus, what do you know about a builder called Secundus – century of Gallus?'

Decimus frowned. 'Nothing, sir. Gallus' men haven't been back long.'

'Where from?'

'I don't know exactly, sir. Somewhere in the north.'

'When did they get back here?'

'Last week sometime, sir. They brought a couple of wounded in for treatment.'

'Oh.'

'I could find out which day if you like, sir.'

'No,' said Ruso, 'last week is good enough.'

In the end he headed towards the East Gate. A couple of times on the way he called her name experimentally into the night air, as if he were calling a lost pet. There was no reply.

There was a brief flash of hope at the gate when one of the guards said, 'Ah, you mean Tilla, sir!' He and his comrade had seen her leave clutching a shopping-basket at her usual time in the morning. He sounded as though they looked forward to it. Disappointingly, they had been elsewhere since then and had only just come back on duty.

'Have you lost her, sir?'

'No,' said Ruso. 'She's just very late. If you see her, tell her to report straight to my house.'

He passed through the gates and made his way across the open area that separated the fort from the civilian buildings. At this time of night the town was little more than a huddle of angular shapes picked out by the occasional glimmer of a torch. Somewhere amongst the buildings, a dog barked. There was the faint sound of a baby crying. He heard the approach of voices and stepped sideways on to the verge. Three men wandered past, too deep in a disagreement about horse-racing to notice him. When they had gone, the street was empty. Ruso stepped back on to the paved surface and tried not to imagine what might be happening to a girl who was wandering the streets on a night like this.

The entrance to Merula's was lit by the usual pair of torches. Someone was playing twittering flute music inside but a quick glance from the safety of the shadows across the street confirmed what Ruso suspected: there were few customers tonight. He wondered whether the security raid had frightened them off, and whether Merula had guessed as much as Bassus.

Stichus was leaning back against the bar with his arms folded, looking bored. Behind him, Daphne paused from pouring drinks to press her hands into the small of her back and stretch her expansive belly. A girl whom Ruso vaguely knew as Mariamne emerged from the kitchen with a loaded tray. She carried it across to the table in the corner, where Merula was mercifully busy with a couple of customers whom Ruso recognized from the early-morning officers' briefing. There was no sign of Tilla.

A pair of heavy boots appeared on the stairs. Bassus made his way down to the bar, ordered a drink from Daphne and emerged to drink it outside under the torch. Ruso crossed the street and stood beside him, out of sight of the bar.

Bassus frowned. 'I thought you weren't going to show your face round here?'

'I came to ask if you'd seen Tilla.'

Bassus slapped at something on his neck. 'Bloody gnats. You'd think they'd be gone by September. She's not run out on you, has she?'

'Is she here?'

Bassus took a draught of his drink. 'She *was* here,' he said. 'Dropped by this morning. Just before our visit from the lads. We had a nice little chat. You know what? I think she fancies me.'

'Did she say where she was going?'

'You haven't gone and lost her, have you? What about our agreement?'

'Not lost,' promised Ruso. 'Just — temporarily mislaid. Did she meet anyone here that she would have gone off with?'

'You told us to keep her away from the customers, remember?'

'Do you have men from the century of Gallus in here?'

'Not at the moment.'

'Recently?'

'Had a bunch of them in a few days ago. Just got back from the north. Celebrating.'

Ruso scratched his ear. Bassus had confirmed what he already suspected: Secundus could not have been involved with the death of Saufeia. Valens was right: he was out of balance. The accident with the trowel had been a simple coincidence. As for the fire — he did not have time to worry about the fire now. He said, 'Would any of the girls know where she was going?'

'The girls didn't see her. I did. And then she buggered off. And if you don't want to get me into trouble, you'll do the same.'

Tilla had still not returned when they went to bed. Ruso heard the third and fourth watch sounded. Once he got up to investigate a noise that might have been someone knocking, but when he opened the door there was nobody there. He called her name into the darkness. The only reply was a blustery spatter of rain.

He woke with an uneasy feeling that there was something he should remember. When he remembered it, the unease blossomed into an anxiety that lifted him out of bed before dawn to pace about in a house where her absence was almost tangible. He tried to silence his imagination by telling himself she had chosen to leave. Her arm was recovering: she did not need him any more.

Instead of being worried, he should be pleased. He owed it to his family to sell her, but he had not been looking forward to it. Now she had solved his dilemma by running away. The tale about Phryne had been a cover for some sort of primitive good-luck potion she was cooking up for herself. Tilla had fled from Deva and was safely on her way to the hilly lands of the Brigantes.

Valens came wandering into the kitchen, rubbing his eyes. 'No breakfast, then?'

Ruso shook his head. 'Can you manage without me this morning?'

Valens' eyes squeezed shut and his mouth widened in a lopsided and unstifled yawn that displayed a couple of missing teeth and distorted his agreement into something like 'Euhhhh.'

Ruso wished the girls who called him 'the good-looking doctor' could see him now.

'Wretched girl might have bothered to send a message,' remarked Valens.

'I think she might have run off,' confessed Ruso.

'Even so.'

Ruso nodded. His relationship with the girl had been awkward, hesitant and frequently bad-tempered, but he thought they had developed some level of mutual respect.

'You did fix her arm for her,' Valens continued, voicing Ruso's own thoughts.

'And paid money for the privilege,' he grumbled. Damn it, if he hadn't rescued her from Innocens there might well have been a third dead girl found in Deva.

Immediately he wished he had not brought to mind the image of those bodies: the one naked and bloated and the other barely recognizable as human. Why would Tilla have chosen to leave before her arm was healed? He had no evidence that she was on her way back to the Brigantes. Her soul could already have begun the journey to a darker place. If that was true, then he wanted to know. He wanted to bury her himself. And then he would not only hunt down whoever had killed her: he would seek out the people who should have investigated the previous deaths and hadn't. The trouble was, he was one of them.

He turned on his heel. 'I'm going out,' he announced.

In the gloom of his bedroom, he dragged on his overtunic without thinking once about scorpions. He flung his cloak around his shoulders and paused to run a finger over the smooth, cold hilt of his knife.

63

Once he had passed the cemetery, Ruso urged the borrowed horse into a canter. It was a broad-backed beast, recently retired as the mount of a tribune who, according to the groom, was not the steadiest of horsemen. It was mild-tempered, comfortable and too staid to be in great demand. It was the ideal horse for a man who needed an animal that could carry an extra rider.

He slowed it to a trot to pass a string of heavy carts, then wove round a road gang and a couple of mounted men leading a string of shaggy ponies. A local family were heading into town carrying baskets of vegetables. Half a dozen legionaries were heaving against the tilted side of a vehicle that had one wheel in the ditch, evidently determined to right it without unloading it first. A couple of them glanced hopefully up at him, realized he was an officer and bent back to their task.

Further out, the traffic grew lighter. Sheep were grazing beside the road, watched over by a small boy with a large stick. Ruso concentrated on the opposite verge, looking out for the path that led across to the woods.

The horse seemed surprised at being asked to jump the ditch – evidently the tribune had demanded very little of it – but it landed on the other side in a reasonably tidy fashion. A couple of birds flew up from the trees in alarm as it approached. Apart from birds, the woods appeared to be deserted. The horse slowly picked its way forward along the narrow path, apparently unperturbed by its rider's occasional lurch forward to lie along its neck as they passed under overhanging branches.

There was no smell of smoke amongst the trees: only that of damp earth and rotting leaves. A better tracker than Ruso would have known whether anyone had passed this way recently. Unable to read the signs, he concentrated on making his way safely through the undergrowth and strained to catch any sounds beyond the brush of leaves, the creak of the saddle and the warble of distant birdsong.

He emerged from the woods, picking twigs out of his hair, and circled the horse around the clearing, trying to look into the trees and over the bracken to the muddy patch where the spring rose. There was no sign of her.

'Tilla!'

His shout died away into silence. The birdsong had stopped.

'*Tilla!* Can you hear me?'

He tried several times, twisting in the saddle to call in different directions, waiting each time for a response that did not come.

He swung down off the horse and left it to graze while he pushed his way through the bracken to the spring. The remains of a small fire lay in the grass, sodden and cold. The fire could have been lit on her last visit or last night: he had no way of knowing. What was certain was that it had not been active this morning.

Ruso got to his feet, took a deep breath and shouted, 'Tilla! Where are you?' one last time.

He turned to face the spring. He raised one hand in the air as he had seen his servant do. Glad that no one but the horse could hear him, he offered a prayer to the goddess of the spring, asking her to keep safe her faithful servant whose name was . . . he pulled the document from his tunic and read out, 'Dar . . . lugh . . . dach . . . a,' and then added, 'but who is known to me as Tilla.'

His approach to the native houses was announced by several excited dogs. As he drew closer, chickens scuttled to safety under a gate on which a small boy sat staring with his mouth open. A couple of squawking geese made experimental runs at the horse. It flattened its ears but carried on plodding forward.

Ruso dismounted and led the horse towards the gate. The boy scrambled down the other side of the gate and fled toward the houses. Women appeared in the doorways. An old man emerged from behind a hay-rick and shouted an order. The dogs, which to Ruso's relief were tethered, fell silent.

When he turned round from fastening the gate, the occupants of the houses had all gathered in a silent line. Several women had their arms folded. One, white up to the elbows with flour, rested a reassuring hand on the head of the small boy, who was now hiding behind her skirts. To the right of the people, swinging gently in the morning breeze, Ruso saw the reason why the dogs were tethered. The carcass of a freshly slaughtered sheep dangled, still dripping, over a tub of thick blood. As the natives stared at him in silence it struck him that the outer skin of civilization was very thin here. He had no doubt that, not so very long ago, these people would have slaughtered him with as little compunction as they had killed the sheep and cheerfully nailed his severed head to the gatepost.

Surveying the eight pairs of eyes watching his every move, he wondered where the men and the rest of the children were. The girl whose appearance had distracted the First on its training run was nowhere to be seen. There must be

343

people still hiding in the houses. He wondered if he should have unlatched the safety strap on his knife. He wondered if he could vault on to the horse before they reached him. He wondered whether the horse could clear the gate. Then he began.

'My name,' he announced, 'is Gaius Petreius Ruso, Medicus with the Twentieth Legion. I have come here to look for a woman.' He stopped. It was, he realized, an unfortunate start. Worse, his audience showed no sign of understanding it. Faced with impassive stares, he asked, 'Does anyone here speak Latin?'

The small boy blinked. There was no other response.

'I am looking for the woman who is my servant,' he said, pulling out the sale document. 'Her name is . . .' He read out the complicated name again, suspecting that he was pronouncing it all wrong. 'She has gone missing. She has curly fair hair –' with a twirling motion he indicated his own, which was indeed hair, but entirely the wrong colour – 'and her arm is –' he made a chopping motion with his left hand on his lower right arm and then mimed winding a bandage around it. 'Her arm is broken.' Although by now they probably thought he was threatening to chop it off. 'I want her to know that if she comes home she will not be punished.' *Even though*, he wanted to add, *she very much deserves it.*

He cleared his throat. 'I am anxious to know that she is safe,' he said.

A cockerel strutted across the mud that separated him from his audience. The small boy tried to stuff a fistful of his mother's skirt into his mouth. Without taking her eyes off Ruso, the woman crouched and gathered the child into her floury arms.

'I want to know that she is safe,' Ruso repeated. He

glanced around at the blank faces. 'If I had any money,' he continued, 'I would be offering a reward. But I don't, so I can't. And if I thought any of you understood a word I was saying, I would tell you that even if I can't find Tilla, I'd like to find out what's underneath that splint. I'd like to find out because I want to know whether there's anything I've done since I came to your miserable country that has made it worth the bother of coming here. So. There you are. Well, thank you for all being so tremendously helpful.'

As he squelched out through the mud in the gateway – he was not going to pick his way around the edge as if a Roman officer were afraid of getting dirty – the dogs began to bark again. This time no one tried to stop them. A few paces beyond the gate he glanced over his shoulder.

They were still watching.

64

There was no sign of her at the house, where he only stopped long enough to clean off the rest of the mud before going to the hospital to find two messages. Albanus was trying to track him down, and Priscus wanted an urgent meeting. He managed to find Albanus first. As they entered the surgery the clerk asked, 'Any word on your housekeeper, sir?'

'Nothing. What did you want me for?'

'Officer Priscus says —'

'Yes, I know. Urgently. Was that it?'

'No, sir, not entirely.' Albanus glanced round to make sure the surgery door was closed. 'It's about that delicate matter, sir,' he began. 'I told them at HQ that I'd lost a document and it was all rather embarrassing, and they let me have a private hunt through the record store. You'd be amazed at the volume of correspondence, sir.'

'And?'

'I've been through every list for the last two months, but I can't find a letter from a Saufeia anywhere.'

'Damn,' muttered Ruso.

'Would you like me to go back any further, sir?'

Ruso shook his head. 'There's no point.'

'If there's anything I can do to help you find the house-keeper, sir . . .'

Ruso settled himself on the corner of his desk and folded his arms. There were things he needed to know, but he was more likely to acquire a broken jaw from the Second Spear than any information. Valens had offered to sound out his friend in Regional Control, but the only sounds forthcoming were negative ones. Ruso was going to have to consult a source he despised: Army gossip.

'Albanus,' he said, 'who or what do the men think was responsible for the deaths of those two girls?'

Albanus' eyes widened. 'Do you think the same person might have taken your housekeeper, sir?'

'I hope not. But I'm running out of other ideas.'

Albanus thought for a moment. 'To be honest, sir, nobody seems to know. Most people just think there's a madman around who likes killing women.'

'I've been through that. Why two from one bar?'

'It could be a very important customer. Somebody the management are scared of.'

'How important?'

Albanus scratched his head. 'I can't see the Legate or any of the tribunes down there, to be honest, sir, can you? It's more likely somebody with a grudge against the management.'

'Right. How many people would that include?'

'If you count all the men who've ever been thrown out of Merula's? Quite a lot, sir. That's before you look at the staff.'

Ruso decided not to mention doctors who had been poisoned by the food. Even if both the girls had been victims of one man with a grudge, that grievance must have been incurred long before his own arrival in Deva. His chances of discovering the right complainant – and quickly – were slim.

'Of course, there might be no connection at all, sir.'

'Do you think Asellina really did try to run off with a sailor?'

'To tell you the truth, sir, most people think she led poor old Decimus a bit of a dance. It would have taken him years to save up enough to buy her. And he's still got fifteen years to serve, so he couldn't run away with her instead – not unless he deserted, and then what would they have had to live on? So she decided to go with the sailor instead.'

'Does anyone know anything about this sailor? Nobody seems to have seen him.'

Albanus frowned. 'I don't know, sir. It was all looked into at the time. Then it all blew over and everybody forgot about it. Except Decimus, of course. And I suppose the people at the bar.' He glanced up. 'Perhaps that was why Saufeia thought she'd give it a try, sir. Because she thought Asellina had got away with it.'

It suddenly occurred to Ruso that he might have been looking in the wrong place for a letter. What if Saufeia had been trying to contact the last successful runaway? 'Do you happen to know,' he said, 'whether Asellina could read and write?'

Albanus shook his head. 'I shouldn't think so, sir. From what I hear, Saufeia was a bit unusual.'

'She certainly doesn't seem to have been as popular as Asellina.'

'No, sir. Of course there are the other theories about Saufeia.'

Ruso was beginning to suspect that the hospital staff had spent more time considering this case than the official investigators. 'Tell me.'

'Well, one is that her own people killed her because of the shame she'd brought on the family by working at Merula's, sir. Which does sort of make sense, because what was a girl who could read and write doing in a place like that?'

'I don't know. From what I hear, she'd probably

been hanging around with soldiers for years. Anything else?'

'I did hear a rumour that it was one of the married officers who'd had a fling with her and didn't want his wife to find out what he was up to.'

'No name, I suppose?'

'No, sir. But most people seem to think she wandered off, then had an argument with a client who didn't want to pay, and he turned nasty.'

'Hm,' said Ruso. 'Well, that seems to cover every possibility.'

'Cheer up, sir. If it was any of those, then your housekeeper's disappearance has nothing to do with the others, does it?'

'No,' agreed Ruso, scratching his ear. 'It doesn't.' The thought should have been reassuring, but it wasn't, because it left him with nowhere to look.

'Unless there really is a madman, of course.'

'Yes. Thank you, Albanus.'

'Sorry, sir. I didn't mean to –'

There was a rap on the door. Albanus opened it and a familiar voice said, 'Didn't you get my message, Ruso?'

'Ah.' said Ruso. 'Priscus. There you are.'

Glaring at Albanus, Priscus added, 'I specifically stressed that this was *most urgent*.'

'I was just sending him to find you,' said Ruso, noting inwardly that his ability – and readiness – to tell lies had improved no end since he had come to Britannia. He dismissed Albanus, then motioned the administrator to a stool while he himself remained seated on the corner of his desk, reversing their usual positions. 'How can I help?'

'I haven't come here to ask for help, Ruso. I have come here to tell you how I am going to help you out of a very awkward situation.'

Ruso, wondering which of his many awkward situations Priscus had found out about, raised his eyebrows and waited.

'Your missing servant,' Priscus continued, unaware of the relief these words offered to his listener. 'I take it she hasn't been found?'

'Not yet.'

'Very well. I have had notices drawn up. They are being distributed as we speak.'

Ruso found himself scratching his ear again. 'Notices?'

'Missing slave notices. The usual sort of thing. I'm surprised you hadn't done it yourself.'

'I was hoping she would turn up,' said Ruso, feeling he probably should have.

'Frankly, Ruso, I was also surprised not to be notified of her loss. As custodian of the Aesculapian Fund.'

Ruso looked him in the eye. 'The loan will be paid in full,' he insisted. 'On the due date.'

Priscus inclined his hair in his usual careful manner, and said, 'Of course.'

Ruso remembered that hair sticking out in a wild clump during his visit to Priscus' house, which it seemed the administrator was going to pretend had never happened. 'So, from your point of view,' he continued, forcing himself to concentrate, 'the girl is irrelevant.'

'Nevertheless, as a responsible custodian –'

'Priscus, the auditors can't hold you responsible for my slave running off.'

The hand that smoothed the hair trembled slightly, and for the first time Ruso wondered if the man was genuinely frightened of the imperial auditors. 'Nevertheless,' Priscus was repeating, 'as a responsible custodian I should be seen to be taking precautionary measures.'

'Very thorough of you,' said Ruso, wondering if the

administrator stuck his nose this far into everyone's affairs, or whether he was particularly unlucky. Surely this couldn't still be revenge for the linen cupboard? Standing up to terminate the interview, he said, 'I seem to be in your debt, Priscus. Let's hope your notices will do the trick, eh?'

65

Another night passed, and still there was no sign of Tilla's return. During a brief lull in morning surgery Albanus ventured to inquire whether his officer was feeling all right.

'Perfectly well, thank you,' replied Ruso crisply. 'Is there a problem?'

'No, sir,' said his clerk, too tactful to point out what Ruso already knew: that several times he had asked patients the same question twice. Sometimes it was because he had forgotten the answer. At other times it was because he had not only failed to register the answer but had forgotten that he had already asked the question.

By the end of surgery and ward round he had seen forty-two patients and had made at least three final and utterly contradictory decisions about where Tilla had gone and what he should do about it.

Midday saw him leave the fort by the West Gate, for no other reason than that he had not been that way recently. He had no real hope of catching sight of Tilla. She was either long gone or hiding or . . . he recalled this morning's vow not to speculate about worse fates. Whatever had happened to her, he was going to find her. He strode down towards the docks.

The elegant houses stared out through a thin drizzle at a view that held none of the charm it had offered on the morning that the *Sirius* had brought his belongings. The tide had pulled out to reveal a weed-strewn and smelly expanse of mud flats. The furthest legs of the jetty reached out into the river channel, where a couple of bulbous merchant ships were moored. The sound of hammering came from one of them, and a figure jolting one arm a heartbeat before each of the blows was dangling on a rope slung from the bows. A couple of figures sat on the jetty, swinging their feet in the air and their fishing lines into the water. Closer to shore, a man and a group of barefoot boys were plodding slowly across the mud, heads down, searching for whatever they were collecting in their buckets. A sail-mender was plying his trade, sheltered from the drizzle by one of his own creations stretched over a wooden frame. Ruso felt bizarrely disappointed, as if he had expected Tilla to be sitting down at the dockside like a parcel, waiting to be collected.

As he turned to make his way back up the hill, he scanned the many offerings scrawled on the wall of the warehouse on the corner. Amongst the advertisements for lodgings, hot food, the visiting slave-trader and 'Beautiful girls and boys! Dancing for you!' he read in the much clearer script of a clerk who was used to posting official notices,

RUNAWAY SLAVE
Attractive female aged about 20. Fair curly hair.
Slim. 5 feet 4 inches tall. Right arm injured, may be bandaged.
Missing since 3rd before Kalends of Oct.
REWARD for return or information leading to capture
Contact G. Pompeius Priscus, Administrator, Aesc. Thanksgiving Fund, Leg XX Hospital.

He scowled. The notice read as if Priscus owned her himself. Not even a mention of his own name. The man's presumption passed all bounds of decency. The notice was skilfully worded, though. The words 'Attractive female' would blind the eyes of many a potential searcher to the fact that the amount of the reward was not specified – which was just as well. He supposed he, as the owner, would end up having to pay it. He wouldn't put it past Priscus to send him a bill for the sign-writing as well.

He paused on the way up the hill to ask a fearsomely painted female lolling on a bench outside a whorehouse whether she had seen a woman answering Tilla's description. He had barely got half a sentence out when her owner appeared in the doorway behind her and assured him that yes, they had a girl just like that. If the gentleman would just step inside she would be very pleased to meet him.

'I don't want a girl like her,' explained Ruso, 'I want the girl herself.'

'She'll be whoever you want her to be,' promised the owner, leaning closer and leering. 'New to the business but keen as mustard – and fresh as a daisy.'

A hideous thought crossed Ruso's mind in the wake of this unlikely description. 'Let me have a look at her.'

The man's smile widened as he beckoned him forward. 'Right this way, sir. Satisfaction guaranteed.'

'I'm not coming *in*,' explained Ruso. 'You've just told me you've got a new girl who answers the description of my missing slave.' The man's smile dropped away. 'I want you to send her out here.'

The man frowned. Ruso heard a creak and a sigh as the painted female got up from the bench. A heavy hand landed on his shoulder and a husky voice said, 'Want me to get rid of him, boss?'

The man nodded in her direction and introduced her. 'Elegantina,' he said. 'Champion lady wrestler in three provinces. Recently retired.'

Ruso twisted round and nodded a greeting to a face held uncomfortably close to his own. 'Ruso,' he said. The woman

354

was as tall as he was, and probably heavier. He turned back to her owner. 'I heard Merula's got raided the other day,' he said.

'They didn't find nothing,' pointed out the owner.

'No, but they're obviously in the mood to look.'

'All my staff are registered.'

'I don't doubt your honesty, but you could have been deceived. Let me put your mind at rest.'

The man glared at him for a moment, then said, 'All right, Ellie.' The weight lifted off Ruso's shoulder as the owner turned into the doorway and yelled, 'Camilla! Here! Now!'

Moments later a small creature with badly bleached hair was blinking pink-rimmed eyes at the daylight.

Ruso shook his head. 'It isn't her.' He leaned forward and put a coin in the hand of the wretched girl, who promptly and automatically handed it to her owner. 'If you see or hear anything,' he added, wondering how many more miserable creatures were caged like animals in places like this, 'the details are written up on the wall down there. There's a reward.'

Four days' growth of stubble on his chin gave him a good excuse to visit the barber. Conversation during the shave was limited to the weather and inquiries after the mother-in-law, who was apparently still a mad old bitch but no longer a mad old bitch with toothache. Once the blade was put away Ruso ran a thumb along the newly smooth line of his jaw and said, 'Have you seen the notices about the missing slave-girl?'

The barber untied the towel and shook it. 'I heard another one ran off,' he said. 'Expect she'll bob up before long. If she hasn't cremated herself.'

Ruso rose from the stool. 'This one is my housekeeper.'

355

The man paused. 'Sorry, Doc. No offence meant.'

'I know what you think of people who ask questions, but this is important. If anyone knows anything at all about what happened to the other girls, it's his duty to say something. In confidence, of course.'

The man shrugged and looked away. 'Sorry, Doc. Wish I could help.'

Ruso fixed his gaze on the one eye. 'Try harder. I heard you bought some red hair not long ago.'

'Who told you that?'

'Never mind.'

'I buy and sell all the time. It's my business.'

'It was brought in by a man. I need to know who he was. My girl could be in danger.'

The man folded his arms. 'Like I said before. I don't buy from murderers. And like I told you, you're going to get yourself into trouble, going round accusing people.'

'I'm not saying he did it. I'm saying he could have information.'

'If you know so much, why isn't this an official investigation?'

This was getting nowhere. 'She's a Briton,' said Ruso, pulling open his purse to pay for the shave. 'She comes from somewhere up in the hills. I'm hoping she's just decided to head for home.'

'More than likely,' agreed the barber.

Ruso handed over the last of his cash and thanked the gods that tomorrow was payday. 'If your wife hears anything . . .' He hesitated, not wanting to say, *If anyone offers you any blonde curls that aren't their own* . . . 'Just ignore the official name on the notices,' he concluded. 'Send a message direct to me. There's a reward.'

*

She'll bob up before long. It was not a cheering thought with which to lean on the damp rail of the bridge and stare down at the water swirling along the channels in the mud flats. Ruso had not been gazing for long when he was aware of movement and saw a pair of long brown plaits dangling down over the rail to his left.

'My husband,' announced the stranger, 'is a good man.'

Not sure where this was leading, Ruso decided not to encourage the woman by replying. This was a ploy he regretted as soon as he risked a glance and recognized the barber's wife.

'He looks after his family,' she continued, evidently not put off by the silence. 'He keeps us all. Even my mother, who treats him like a bad smell. He has done nothing wrong.'

Ruso said carefully, 'I haven't accused him of anything.'

'It was nothing to do with him, you understand? He was not involved. People sell hair all the time. It is business.'

'I'm just trying to find my housekeeper,' said Ruso. 'I'm not interested in anything else.'

'They are very loyal to each other,' said the woman. 'You know what the men are like. Stupid, sometimes, but loyal.'

'I understand.'

'Would you betray a comrade?'

Ruso watched a dead branch drifting down one of the channels of the river. 'If I thought it would save a life, I might.'

The branch caught on a mud bank and swung round in the current. A spur caught in the opposite bank and the branch was stuck, straddling the flow.

He said, 'So, it was a soldier.'

'A veteran.'

'And this was shortly after the last girl disappeared?'

357

The woman nodded. 'My husband did not know the girl was dead, you understand? It was just business.'

Water was pouring over the branch in a long shimmering curl that crashed down into a line of foam.

Ruso said, 'I have no money with me, but I will see to it that you are —'

The bar of the bridge gave a sudden shudder as the woman's fist landed on it. 'I am not doing this for money! You Romans, you think everything is for money!'

'I need more help,' he explained. 'I need a description. A name, if you have one.'

'I came to speak with you,' said the woman, ignoring his words with a haughtiness that reminded him painfully of Tilla, 'because I think you are a good man.'

'I'll be grateful for anything you can tell me that might help my servant.'

'I do not know,' she said, 'how the man got the red hair. For all I know, the girl may have cut it off by herself and given it to him to sell. He is the only one who can tell you that; you must ask him.'

'How do I find this man?'

'I do not know his name,' she said, 'but he works at Merula's bar.'

66

At Merula's most of the lunchtime customers had gone, leaving only a few hangers-on who had nowhere better to go, or else no inclination to go there. Tomorrow would be different, insisted Stichus as he palmed the coins Ruso had just borrowed from Valens. Tomorrow was payday. Stichus indicated the girls seated around the bar. Today, a customer could take his pick.

Ruso was glad there were few witnesses to see Chloe rise from the table with a smile, slide her hand into his and lead him up the stairs.

The cubicle was, he knew, the best the place had to offer. The wide bed was strewn with plump blue cushions. Chloe pulled the door shut behind them and the yellow glow of a lamp rose to help the light that struggled in through a small pane of bubbly glass. Ruso found himself trying to work out a tangle of naked bodies painted on the walls in various uncomfortable-looking combinations as Chloe's arms slid around his waist. He felt her breath against his ear. 'I knew you'd change your mind,' she murmured.

Ruso grasped both her hands and held them still. He opened his mouth to speak and found himself suddenly hoarse. 'I just want to talk,' he croaked.

'You can talk to me,' whispered Chloe, nuzzling the back of his neck. 'I'm a good listener. It's nice and private here. You can tell me anything you want.' He felt a gentle push towards the bed. 'Let's get comfortable, shall we?'

As he felt himself sink into the cushions, he reasoned

that it would do no harm. Chloe was very attractive. She was warm. She was willing. She was a professional, and he had paid. He could always talk to her afterwards.

She was curled around him on the bed, pressing herself against him. He glanced down to watch her foot sliding up his thigh. The charms on her ankle-chain trembled with each movement. Her skin was smooth. Her toes were perfect. She was nibbling his ear.

Ruso closed his eyes. At last: a woman who understood what he needed. What he deserved. And the beauty of it was, there was no commitment. He could have this whenever he wanted. Because this was a professional service. A business transaction. Like the buying of someone's hair . . .

Restraining Chloe's exploring hand, he pulled himself up to sit with his back against the wall. 'When I said I wanted to talk,' he growled, hoping there was no one listening behind the door, 'that's what I meant.'

Chloe arched her back and stretched, draping herself across his lap and looking up at him 'But you're so *nice*,' she said, pursing her lips and miming a kiss.

'No,' he said, heaving at her shoulders to lift her away from him. 'I'm not nice. And I'm tired of being lied to.'

She swung her legs off the bed and sat up. 'Suit yourself.'

'Do you know where Tilla is?'

'No.' She bent to fiddle with one of the pins that held her curls in place. 'Is that it? Can I go now?'

'No. Is she here?'

Chloe pushed the pin back into place and sighed. 'You don't learn, do you?' She turned to face him. 'It was you who told them about Phryne, wasn't it?'

When Ruso said nothing, she continued, 'Well you were a big help to her. She'd tell you how much herself if she was well enough for visitors.'

'Is she all right?'

'Of course she's not all right.'

'I could –'

'You've caused enough trouble already. Lucky for her, it's payday coming up. They aren't stupid here. She'll be fit to work by tomorrow.'

Ruso found himself staring at the tangle of bodies on the wall. For a girl in a place like this, being fit to work was a dubious blessing. Perhaps the child had indeed pretended to be stolen in the vain hope of escape. Or perhaps he had been right the first time: the whole thing had been a story concocted by Tilla to cover her own escape. He no longer knew whom to believe. 'Chloe,' he said, 'do you think Tilla's run away?'

'I don't know.'

'The last person to see her was Bassus. He said she came here while you were out at the baths.'

'Well she's not here now. Ask him where she went.'

'Are you not telling me because you don't know, or because you're afraid?'

She gave a snort of derision. 'You know the first thing you learn in this place? Never show fear. Something Phryne needs to learn. And you know the second thing? Mind your own business.'

'If one of your management's done something to Tilla . . .'

Chloe shook her head. 'I can tell you one thing about Bassus, Doctor. He won't damage anything that might make him a profit.'

'I heard that somebody here hurt Daphne.'

'So? You don't have to be much of a talker to do this job. They'll have her back to work after they've sold the baby.'

Ruso took a deep breath. 'And what about Asellina? Or

Saufeia? Did they really run away, or were they allowed out like you are?' He paused. 'Do the girls do home visits? Private parties, that sort of thing?'

'What's that got to do with Tilla? It's you she's run away from, not us.'

'Because she's gone missing like the other two. And the only thing that links them all is this place. What's going on here, Chloe?'

Chloe stared at him for a moment, then got to her feet. 'I don't know what you think you're stirring up,' she said, 'but I don't want anything to do with it.' She stepped forward and lifted the latch on the door. 'Time's up.' She walked out on to the landing. 'Get out now, or I'll call the boys. And don't come here again.'

Chloe's sandals clattered away down the stairs. Ruso sighed, gave a parting glance at the tangled bodies – the participants looked depressingly bored – and followed her down to the bar.

'Bassus!'

The man turned. 'Back again, eh? Come to pay your bill?'

'Come for a chat,' said Ruso. 'Can we go somewhere private?'

'No thanks. You're not my type.'

Ruso shrugged. 'I can say it in front of everyone, if you like.'

Bassus glanced around. The bar held four members of staff, three customers and, in a cage beside one of them, a jackdaw. Bassus jerked a thumb towards the door. 'Outside.'

On the way out they passed Stichus. 'You're getting soft,' Bassus told him. 'Letting bloody cage birds in.'

'It talks,' retorted Stichus.

'Show me something round here that don't.'

'Daphne,' suggested Stichus, with what he clearly thought was wit.

'Take a walk a minute, Stich? Me and the Doc have got business.'

Stichus retreated into the bar. Bassus leaned against the painted wall, folded his arms and glowered at the woman behind the bakery counter as if he were daring her to eavesdrop. 'Make it quick,' he said. 'I'm a busy man.'

'So am I,' said Ruso. 'But you said next time I had a problem to come to you. So here I am.'

Bassus sighed. 'What is it now?'

'I still haven't found Tilla.'

'How many times have I got to say it? I don't know where she is! If I knew, I'd tell you. I got a couple of nice buyers lined up. If she don't turn up soon I'm going to have to let them down.'

'But in the course of looking for her, I've run across some troubling information.'

There was barely a hesitation before, 'And this information would be?'

'I'll get to that in a moment. I'm trying to stop Tilla meeting the same fate as the other two runaways. Tell me, is it true that Saufeia wasn't much good at her job?'

'What's that got to do with it? She was useless. Even when she was trying, which weren't often.'

'And what do you do with girls who don't please the customers?'

'Sell them, of course.'

Ruso nodded. 'That's what I thought.'

'Sounds to me like you thought we take them out the back and strangle them.'

'What I can't understand,' said Ruso, 'is why her hair was all shorn off. She wouldn't do it herself if she was planning

363

to work the streets or run away with a lover, and Merula certainly wouldn't do it if she was planning to sell her.'

Bassus shrugged. 'Sorry. Can't help you there.'

'What I'm thinking,' explained Ruso, watching him carefully, 'and correct me if I'm wrong, is that it must have been done after she was dead. Perhaps not by the murderer, but by someone else who knew him. Who might be able to point me in his direction.' He paused. 'Someone who then went and sold the hair.'

Bassus was staring at the pavement opposite, scratching his neck with one finger.

'If something's happened to Tilla,' said Ruso, 'I want to know about it.'

Bassus continued to ponder for a moment. Finally he gave a sigh. 'All right. This is it. I don't know nothing about Tilla but I know a bit about the other thing. You keep your mouth shut, agreed?'

'Agreed.'

'When Merula noticed Saufeia weren't around, me and Stich took a couple of torches and went to look. We found her in a back alley.'

'Which back alley?'

'Over by the amphitheatre. Propped sitting up in a corner like she was waiting for somebody. The bastard only just got away. I reckon he heard us coming. She was still warm.'

'You didn't call for help?'

Bassus looked him in the eye. 'I know dead when I see it, Doc. Besides . . . I'm not known for being a patient man. Twenty-five years in the Legion, I believe in discipline, see? People don't know what we have to put up with, with these girls. Murdered runaway, dark night, back alley – who'd have believed us?'

'But she was your own slave.' Executing one's own slaves

was officially frowned upon, but fellow slaves were not in a position to complain, and it was hard to see who else would bother.

'She weren't ours,' explained Bassus. 'She belonged to the business. And if Merula thought we'd done it she'd have gone mad.' He paused. 'I know what you're thinking. We should've just walked away. I wish I had. Only Stich, he decides to be clever.'

This seemed an unlikely proposition, but Ruso let it pass.

'He says, if we just leave her here, then some greedy bastard's going to find her and nick all her fancy clothes and everything. What all belong to the bar. That hair was worth something, too. So we took what was ours and we give her a decent send-off.'

'In the river?'

'We weren't to know she'd come back, were we? But we didn't kill her. I swear. And I don't know who did.'

Ruso nodded. 'And would you know anything about an accident happening to someone who asked too many questions?'

Bassus folded his arms. 'Could be arranged. Who you thinking of?'

'Never mind.' If the man had known anything about the fire or the incident with the trowel, he was a good actor. 'One last question. Do you know anything about a letter?'

There was a slight pause before, 'What letter?'

'There's a rumour that Saufeia wrote to somebody. I know she was telling everyone she wouldn't be here much longer. I assume she was arranging to meet someone.'

Bassus shook his head. 'I don't know nothing about no letter,' he said. 'And she wouldn't have been here much longer 'cause we'd have traded her on. But your Tilla couldn't be writing to nobody, that I do know. Look.

Asellina was unlucky. Saufeia run into a customer what didn't want to pay, and whoever he was he didn't bother taking her far to finish her. If he'd got your Tilla you'd have found her by now. I reckon she's run off, like it says in the notices. You ask me, you want to stop wasting time poking around with dead tarts and hire yourself a slave-hunter.'

67

Payday dawned at last. There was still no sign of Tilla. Ruso spent the morning trying to do justice to the needs of his patients, which were as pressing as ever. Outside, however, it was apparent that the Twentieth was working itself up to a level of excitement that heralded a busy night for the medical service. The enthusiasm raised by the quarterly arrival of cash had been swelled by the anticipation of at least the first instalment of Hadrian's bonus to his loyal troops. The bath-house scaffolding was abandoned, its occupants presumably waiting in other jostling queues like the one he was now passing outside a centurion's quarters. A neglected noticeboard at the head of a barrack-block announced an inter-unit sports event this afternoon in the amphitheatre – a gallant but probably doomed attempt to direct the Twentieth's payday energy into useful channels. If this unit was anything like any of the others Ruso had known, by evening the real entertainment would be in full swing. The bars would be overflowing with off-duty soldiers, and men who ought to know better would be doing things they would very much regret in the morning. If Tilla was still somewhere in the town, he hoped she would have the sense to stay behind closed doors.

Minutes later, he walked away from the Camp Prefect's office, still staring at the bottom figure on the copy of his account. *Perhaps you'd like to take some time to check the figures, sir.* This couldn't be right. There must be some mistake.

She had not miraculously returned to the house while he was out. He sat on his one chair and ignored the puppy that scrambled up his leg and circled round before settling on his lap. Outside, a shout of laughter echoed along the street from one of the barrack-blocks. Ruso dipped his hand into the jar Valens had been given by a grateful patient and groped around for the last of the olives.

The figure at the top of the sheet was fine. The 'Brought forward' figure was correct. Miraculously, the Army had managed to send his records across two seas and two continents in time for the clerks to do the arithmetic. The down payment on the gift to celebrate the accession of the Noble Emperor Hadrianus was most welcome, except that a large chunk of it had been compulsorily diverted into his savings account. 'Deductions', read the line underneath. That was where the trouble started.

Following all the usual deductions for his keep and the legionary knees-up at Saturnalia was a figure for 'loan repayment' – they'd taken the whole advance back at once, of course – and an item called 'expenditure'. The amount defied all his attempts to live frugally. The details were listed on a separate sheet and included 'Meals taken at hospital' and 'Private use of hospital facilities'.

Perhaps you'd like to take some time to check the figures, sir. Ruso licked the olive-brine off his fingers and began to count. Three attempts brought three confirmations of the impossible figure against 'Makes a total of'. Next he deducted the amount he owed the Aesculapian Fund. Then he took off the sum he had arranged to be sent to Lucius. Finally he subtracted enough to cover his bill at Merula's.

Ruso leaned back in his chair and stared gloomily at the empty olive-jar. What would remain in his purse was barely enough to see a civilized man through the next three weeks, let alone three months. No wonder men on basic pay resorted to thieving from Priscus' linen cupboards. He could not live for three months on this. He must take the time to find more private patients. He must get on with his writing. He must get promoted. He must find Tilla alive – and when he had, he must sell her.

As he framed this thought in his mind, two things occurred to him simultaneously. One was that he didn't want to sell her and he never had. The other was that today he had somewhere new to look.

Ruso had never bought a slave at a market. There had always been someone else – father, uncle, wife, other slaves – to deal with that sort of thing. The only time he had needed to buy his own staff was after his divorce, when he had taken the post in Africa. That had been a simple matter of moving into the house occupied by his predecessor and handing over a sum of cash to retain the slave couple who already worked there. He had, of course, bought Tilla, but that had not been a planned purchase. He had never been called upon to assess the suitability of strangers to join his household and he had never paid any attention to how it was done. Which was why, he supposed, he was surprised to see that the notice announcing the arrival of the slave-trader had now been amended to read 'VIEWING FROM 6th HR TODAY, AUCTION AT 9th HR'.

Deva, being less a town than a collection of houses outside a fort, did not have a forum. Instead, the action had been crammed into the space between the amphitheatre and the fountain. Peering above the heads of the shoppers, Ruso could make out stalls offering jewellery, efficient scribe services, hot pies, fortune-telling and portraits painted while you wait. A succession of bright balls rising and falling in the air marked the passage of a juggler, and the area by the oil-shop had been cordoned off to make a performance space for a dancing bear, currently sitting in its cage with its back to the crowds.

Ruso pushed his way towards the huge open-sided marquee which filled one side of the open space. From its roof swung a sign announcing 'L. Curtius Silvanus, Supplier of Staff for the Discerning Employer'. The people crowded into it fell into four categories. The merchandise were the cheerless ones with chains around their ankles and labels around their necks. The customers were the ones peering and poking at the merchandise and asking it to open its mouth, flex its arm muscles, or prove it could speak Latin. The security staff appeared to be doing nothing at all while a couple of clerks fluttered around a makeshift office formed by a row of folding desks.

Ruso shoved his way across to the desks and arrived just as an African with a lined face and a thick gold rope around his neck pushed his way in through a flap at the back of the marquee.

'Are you the owner?'

The man bowed. 'Lucius Curtius Silvanus, at your service.'

Ruso explained about Tilla.

'I assure you, sir, my staff take great care. We very rarely buy in the street and only then with full documentation and references.' He indicated the stock with a sweep of his arm. 'All purchases come with a money-back guarantee for a full six months. We certainly wouldn't take on anything with an obvious injury.'

Ruso nodded. 'And is this everyone? Or do you have a special collection?'

The man smiled, revealing a wide gap between his two front teeth. 'Ah, sir, I'm afraid they are for inspection by appointment only. But all our present collection have been with us for at least ten days.'

'Nevertheless –'

The man's expression hardened. He summoned a clerk and ordered him to show Ruso the list of the private collection. There were a couple of Greek tutors, a geometry teacher, a painter, a family physician (Ruso would have liked to meet that one), three 'beautiful young boys' whose talents were not listed and a set of fourteen-year-old twin girls, described as 'very beautiful, black hair, green eyes, good figure, softly spoken and eager to please.'

'How much are the girls?' he inquired, wondering what prices were like here.

'More than you can afford,' said the clerk, evidently a sharp judge of character.

Nothing here seemed likely to lead to Tilla. He was about to leave when a woman's voice said, 'Good afternoon, Doctor!' and he turned to find Rutilius' wife smiling at him.

'We heard about your housekeeper,' put in Rutilia the younger. 'Have you come to buy another one?'

'Such a shame,' sympathized her mother. 'It's so difficult to find good staff.'

The daughter said, 'I hope the madman hasn't got her. Have you looked in the river?'

'Really, dear!' chided the mother. She was apologizing for her daughter's tactlessness when Ruso heard a distinct cry of 'Doctor!' from somewhere across the marquee. 'I'm sorry,' he interrupted, relieved. 'I have to go. Someone's calling me.'

'Doctor!'

The boy was perhaps eight or nine years old. He had ginger hair and his face was blotched with pink, as if he had been crying. He was dressed in a plain brown tunic. Like all the other slaves, he was barefoot. The iron cuff looked as though it could snap his thin white ankle. He was chained to a massive bearded native on one side and an elderly man with a bent back on the other. Ruso stared at him, trying to remember where he had seen him before.

The boy sniffed, wiped his nose on the back of his hand and said, 'It's me, Doctor. Lucco.'

Ruso frowned. 'Lucco? From Merula's?'

The boy nodded. 'Yes, sir.'

'What are you doing here?'

The boy's eyes glistened with tears. 'I'm being sold, sir.' He swallowed hard and squared his shoulders. 'I'm a good worker, sir. And I'm quick to learn. Really I am.'

Ruso gazed at the skinny form with a mounting sense of dismay, knowing he could not say what the boy was hoping to hear. What could a man with no money possibly say or do to reassure a child who was chained like an animal, waiting to be auctioned to the highest bidder? He closed his eyes and fought the urge to utter a curse on the spirit of his weak-willed father, on his spendthrift stepmother, on his half-sisters who combined the worst qualities of both. He wanted to lay a hand on Lucco's shoulder and assure him that all would be well. Only it probably wouldn't.

At least he could save the boy from being poked and peered at for a few minutes. He said, 'Why are you being sold, Lucco?'

The boy eyed him for a moment, as if he was wondering what to answer. Ruso groaned inwardly as he realized his mistake. The child thought he was being interviewed for a job. 'Lucco,' he explained gently, crouching down to speak to him face to face, 'I can't buy you. I'm sorry. I may look rich to you but the truth is, I'm not.'

The boy sniffed again. 'Yes, sir.'

The old man burst into a fit of coughing. In his efforts to stifle the cough he staggered backwards, dragging the chain and jerking Lucco's ankle sideways. The boy winced and bent to rub his leg. The big native turned and growled something at the old man, who ignored him.

'Lucco,' said Ruso, wishing he did not have to ask this, 'you remember my slave, Tilla?'

'She used to feed her dinner to the birds.'

'Well now she's gone missing. I'm afraid that whoever hurt Saufeia might hurt her. If you know anything at all about what happened to Saufeia, or to Asellina, you must tell me. Nobody's going to punish you for talking now.'

The boy shook his head. 'I don't know nothing about Saufeia, sir. Everybody thought Asellina had gone to live somewhere nicer. All the girls cried when they found her.'

'I see.'

'I like it at Merula's,' said the boy. 'I don't want to go nowhere else.'

'You're a bright boy, Lucco,' said Ruso. 'You'll do well wherever you go.'

The boy replied politely, 'Yes, sir.'

Ruso stood up straight, glancing around him and wondering if it would be kinder to get out of the way and let potential buyers assess the boy's worth. The more the better. A slave for whom there were several bidders would fetch a higher price, and logic dictated that a valuable asset would be well treated. The trouble was, logic rarely dictated what people did in the privacy of their own homes.

'Sir?'

He turned.

'Sir, please could you give my mother a message?'

'Your mother?'

'Please could you tell her Bassus told Merula about the oysters?'

Ruso frowned. 'Bassus told Merula about the . . . ?'

'The oysters, sir. So Merula told him to take me to the trader.' An energetic sniff was followed by, 'Bassus said he was going to find a nice family for me but now he's gone and told Merula about the oysters. My mother doesn't know.'

Ruso was now thoroughly confused. 'Your mother doesn't know about the oysters?'

'She doesn't know I'm here.' The boy glanced over towards the clerks behind the desks. 'Do you think they'll let me go and say goodbye?'

Ruso doubted it very much. 'You are being sold because of oysters?'

The boy nodded. 'I didn't mean to do it, sir. I mean, I didn't mean . . .' His voice tailed into silence.

Ruso scratched his ear. This story was beginning to sound familiar. He lowered his voice so they could not be overheard. 'Wasn't Merula's last cook sold because of serving up bad oysters?'

Lucco nodded, dumb.

'And now Merula's found out you were involved?'

Something approaching panic entered the boy's eyes. 'Please, sir!' he muttered, barely audible above the hum of conversation in the marquee. 'I won't ever do it again!'

'I'm not going to tell anyone, Lucco.' If no one had seen to it that the damnation of 'attempted poisoner' was written on the child's label, he was certainly not going to do it himself.

'I didn't mean it, sir,' whispered Lucco. 'Somebody said the officer from the hospital was there. I thought they meant the nasty one.'

374

Ruso was having difficulty following him again. 'Tell me about these oysters,' he suggested.

'Cook had them on the side to throw away.'

'And you sent them out for a customer?'

He nodded. 'It was just a bit of a joke, sir.'

A bit of a joke that could have ended in a charge of attempted murder and a gruesome execution for its perpetrator. As it was, Valens had suffered acute food poisoning. Ruso had been obliged to do the work of three men and had ended up so far out of his senses that he had bought a girl on a building site.

He put his hand back on the boy's shoulder. 'I'll go and see your mother straight away. Where do I find her?'

'She'll be working, sir.'

'Yes, but where?'

The boy stared at him. 'Where she always works, sir. At Merula's.'

It was Ruso's turn to stare.

'You do know her, sir,' said the boy. 'They call her Chloe.'

68

Earlier that same morning, two young women in local dress were walking away from the huddle of native houses that Ruso had visited two days before. They were making their way down the track that led to the main Eboracum Road. The taller of them was carrying a small sack over her shoulder.

Her companion turned to glance at her. 'It's not too late. You could stay.'

'And repay kindness with trouble?'

'No one knows you're here.'

'Sabrann, sooner or later someone will talk. Now the worst they can say is that I came, and I went.'

They walked on in silence for a few steps, then the smaller girl frowned. 'Stop a moment.' She reached up and tugged at her companion's hood. There had not been enough plant dye – or time – to disguise the whole of the hair. Brown wisps curled around the temples, but beneath the hood was a long blonde plait. 'You must remember to keep this forward,' she warned. 'I can't pin it any tighter. I don't know how you're going to manage tomorrow'

The taller girl shrugged. 'Someone will be sent to help.'

'You'll have to keep moving. It's a good fifteen miles and the state of the tracks will slow you down.'

They reached the edge of the road. The only traveller they could see was leading an ox-cart back in the direction of the fort.

'Do you have all you need?'

The hooded girl lowered the sack to the ground. 'Bread, a comb, a blanket. Everything I asked, and your mother gave me cheese and bacon.'

Sabrann put a hand on her shoulder. 'May the goddess walk beside you.'

'And keep you ever in her gaze.'

Their embrace was awkward, the hooded girl careful to keep her right arm concealed beneath her inconspicuous grey cloak. 'I must go,' she said, fingering her acorn necklace before raising the sack to her shoulder. 'While the road is empty.'

'Don't forget!' Sabrann waved an arm in an easterly direction, raising it to indicate distance. 'Beyond the bridge, after the oak tree, take the track to the left. You must be careful not to stay on the road any longer than you have to.'

The hooded girl stepped up on to the gravel surface. When she turned, Sabrann was already on the way back to the houses. She was alone on the road once more.

Three days earlier, the walk to this place from Deva had tired her more than she had expected. She had been relieved to be offered water and, after the briefest of introductions, summoned to the big house to be inspected by the grandmother who was head of the family.

Led over to face a chair near the fire, she had knelt in the bracken that covered the floor. As her eyes adjusted to the familiar gloom of a house with no windows, she found herself being peered at by a wizened old woman with sparse white hair scraped back behind large ears.

'Darlughdacha,' said the old woman, repeating the name that had been shouted into one of the ears by her interpreter, the girl Sabrann. The grandmother shared the girl's strangled accent, and her speech was distorted by the absence of teeth to trim the ends of the syllables, but the name was clear enough. 'Daughter of Lugh,' continued the grandmother. 'Why have you come to us? Do we know you?'

'I spoke with a woman who was born near here, Grandmother!' shouted the young woman who had been Tilla for a few weeks, and before that had been nobody for so long that being addressed by her own name now made her feel that someone else must be kneeling beside her. 'Her name is Brica! She told me I could find people of honour here!' It was difficult to shout without sounding angry.

'It's no good,' said Sabrann. 'I have to shout everything right into her ear.'

The old woman, realizing she was missing something, turned to Sabrann, then squinted at her and frowned. 'Where is your hair, girl?'

Sabrann grinned. 'I put it up!' she shouted, twisting to show the back of her head and miming a stabbing action with her fingers, then turning back to shout, 'Hair-pins!'

The grandmother shook her head as if in disbelief. 'This will all come to an end when you have a husband and some proper work to do!' She aimed a forefinger at Tilla. 'What did she say?'

Sabrann leaned close to the old woman again and shouted, 'She has heard that we are people of honour!'

'Yes,' snapped the old woman, 'but who says so?'

Sabrann hesitated before shouting, 'Brica, Grandmother!'

'Aha!' The woman smacked one blue-veined hand on to the blanket that was tucked around her knees. 'So, my brother's family remember what honour is!' The chin rose and the creased lips clamped together. After a pause they opened again. 'I hear Brica's man is losing his sight,' she declared. 'The gods are just.'

Behind her back, Sabrann gave Tilla a look that was

378

somewhere between weariness and apology. Tilla prayed silently to the goddess that she would not be turned away from here because of someone else's quarrel. She had nowhere else to go.

Sabrann bent down again. 'She asks hospitality for nine nights!' she shouted. 'Until her arm is healed! Then she will leave!'

'Why does she not go to my brother's family?'

'Because she seeks people of honour!' yelled Sabrann, clearly embarrassed at her grandmother's rudeness. 'She does not want to stay with friends of the Romans!'

The grandmother plucked at the edge of the blanket, tugging it higher up her lap, then returned her attention to the figure kneeling in front of her. 'Tell me, daughter of Lugh,' she said, 'who are your family?'

Relieved, Tilla who was now Darlughdacha again had begun the business of naming her tribe, then her parents and her grandparents and her great-grandparents, while the old woman frowned and put in occasional questions about brothers and cousins and who was married to whom and who had fought beside which warriors and eventually they found the connection they were both seeking: an obscure second cousin who had once sold cows to the old woman's late husband's brother. 'Now we know who you are,' declared the woman, nodding with satisfaction. 'You are welcome to stay with us while your arm heals, Daughter of Lugh, child of the Brigantes. You may sleep with this one who stabs herself with hair-pins.'

Tilla inclined her head. 'It is an honour, Grandmother.'

'She says it's an honour!' yelled Sabrann.

Extra bracken had been hauled from the drying-racks and thrown down to make a bed on the floor of the small house where the unmarried girls slept. On that first night, comfortably fed, stretched out on a borrowed blanket, covered by the Medicus' cloak — she would have to get rid of that, a problem she would think about later — Tilla had lain listening to strangers chattering in her own tongue. She rolled over to watch the glow of the firelight. A hound had wandered in earlier and settled close to the warmth. One of its ears twitched and it gave a sudden shudder as it dreamed. It occurred to her that there must be mice, and to her surprise it also occurred to her that she did not care. She took a deep breath, savouring the familiar smells of wool and woodsmoke and muddy dog. As she thought, 'I am happy,' she was aware of a voice in the near-dark suggesting, 'Perhaps she is sleeping.'

'Are you sleeping, daughter of Lugh?' demanded a second voice.

'Shh, Sabrann!' urged a third girl. 'Don't wake her!'

She closed her eyes and said nothing. She did not want to answer questions about where she had come from. She did not want to think about where she was going, or what she might find when she finally reached home. She wanted to lie here, in this bed, and remind herself over and over again: *I am free.*

The questions had followed soon enough, though, as had the expressions of sympathy when they found out her family were dead and her arm had been broken when she tried to defend herself from a Roman merchant who had brought her down from the north to sell her.

It was as much of the truth as it was safe for them to know and it would have satisfied them, if only a Roman officer had not arrived that afternoon on an elderly horse and announced that he had come to look for a woman.

The blank expressions with which he was faced were a defence the family had used many times. In truth several of them understood what he was saying, and all grasped what he wanted, but none chose to reveal that the woman he sought was inside a house not ten paces from where he stood.

The Roman had finally given up and squelched back through the gateway. It was not until he was out of sight that the arguments started.

By this time the men had arrived, summoned from the fields by those nearest to home, who had heard the dogs.

Their guest, it seemed, had lied to them. (Her objection of 'I told no lies!' was ignored.) She was a runaway. It was against the law to harbour runaways. She must go.

No, insisted other voices, she must stay. She was a Brigante, true, but not a complete foreigner. She was nearly one of their own people. It was a matter of honour not to betray her.

Tilla, realizing she was not expected to be a part of this argument, slipped back inside the house and sat by the door, listening as indignation rose on both sides of the debate. A couple of the women tried to intervene. Nobody took any notice.

Someone cried that it was a disgrace to deny hospitality to an injured woman.

'Her master is a healer. Let him deal with it.'

'Her master is a Roman!'

'She has brought the Army to our doors!'

'One man on an old horse?'

'Romans are like rats. Where there is one there are more.'

'What if they decide to search the houses?'

'What, for one slave?'

'Enough!' It was the voice of the old woman, quavering

but loud enough to silence the debate. 'Enough,' she repeated. Tilla wondered who had gone to fetch her and how much they had managed to explain. 'The girl will stay here tonight. We will discuss this matter after dark. You all have work to do. Go.'

The arguers did not bother to mute their grumbling as they dispersed, and Tilla overheard someone say, 'She's not his slave, you fool.'

'He said *ancilla*. *Ancilla* means slave.'

'Never mind what *ancilla* means. She's not his slave. She's his woman.'

The evening meal was finished. The other girls had gone to mind younger brothers and sisters. The adults had carried lamps across to the big house and closed the door behind them. Tilla was squatting by the fire in the girls' house, busying herself grinding corn while she waited to be told her fate. It was a job that could be done, albeit slowly, with one hand.

As the stone scraped and rumbled round on its base she thought about the people she had left behind. She thought about the girls at Merula's, and the boy Lucco who did not know that it was forbidden to eat swan, and Bassus, and Stichus with the ginger hair, and the woman she had got to know at the bakery. She thought about the pregnant Brica, whose man might lose his sight, and the handsome doctor who always smiled at her, but mostly she thought about the Medicus, who hardly smiled at all. She supposed he was smiling even less now. It served him right. Behind her back he had made arrangements to have her sold. At first she had not believed Bassus, but later she had arrived back inside the fort with the shopping and there he was, standing in the street outside the hospital, chatting to the Medicus as if they were old friends. That was when she finally understood what the Medicus had meant when he had told her she would be useful to him. He had mended her arm not out of kindness, but out of greed. Instead of going to his house to prepare supper, she had turned round, made her way back out through the East Gate and kept walking.

The dog lying beside her suddenly lifted his head and turned it towards the door. Moments later, a hinge creaked, and a figure slipped in.

'My cousins are seeing to the little ones,' announced Sabrann, 'and my aunt is shouting for the grandmother.' She dropped the sack on the ground. 'I brought you some more corn, daughter of Lugh.'

'Thank you.'

It was the first time they had been able to speak privately since the argument erupted. Sabrann said, 'They are talking about you.'

'I know.'

'I would have you stay.'

'Others would have me leave.'

Sabrann reached a hand inside the sack and trickled a fistful of corn into the hole in the centre of the stone. 'He was quite good-looking,' she observed.

Tilla tightened her grip on the handle and carried on swivelling the top stone back and forth in a half-circle over the lower one. 'Who?'

'Your Roman. And not such a shortarse as most of them.'

'No,' Tilla agreed, stilling her arm as the girl reached a hand forward to scoop up the speckled flour that was trickling out from between the stones to form little mounds on the cloth.

Sabrann dropped the handful of flour into the bowl. '*Are you his slave?*'

383

The stone began to move again. 'He thinks so.'

'Did you go inside the fort?'

'Yes.'

'Is it true what they say about the granary?'

Tilla frowned. 'The granary?'

Sabrann nodded. 'Everyone says they have a great big building filled with enough corn to stuff themselves for a year.'

'It's possible. They like making great big buildings.'

'Can you imagine how many families that would feed? And still they take the taxes.'

'Is this why your grandmother is angry with Brica?'

'It was bad enough my great-uncle's family chose to trade with the Army. Now one of them allows a soldier to father her children.' Sabrann paused to watch the stone's movement round and back. 'They say,' she said, 'that most of them have to pay women to lie with them.'

'They speak the truth.'

'Why would any woman do that? I would never do it.'

'If you thought they would kill you,' said Tilla slowly, 'you might consider it.'

The stone ground away and back, away and back before the girl murmured, 'Forgive me. Everyone says I speak before I think.'

Tilla shook her head. 'No need. The goddess was protecting me. The Medicus is not like that.'

'People are saying you are his woman.'

There was a grating sound from the millstones. Tilla let go of the handle and flexed her stiff fingers. 'People are wrong.'

Sabrann reached into the sack and gave a sudden giggle. 'Can you keep a secret?'

'Always.'

'Before we sent the corn tax in, we all took turns to spit in it.'

Tilla smiled. 'This was to wish them luck?'

'Of course.' Sabrann cupped her hands to trickle more corn into the opening. 'The boys wanted to piss in it, but Da said they would notice the smell. And they'd see it was damp. Spit, you can stir in.'

Their eyes met, and both girls grinned.

'Your Medicus might be eating spit,' observed Sabrann.

'Good luck to him,' said Tilla, seizing the handle and scraping the millstone faster back and forth on its half-circle.

'My cousin could put a curse on him for you if you ask,' Sabrann offered.

'Your cousin has the power of words?' Tilla had no intention of enlisting the cousin's help. If there were any cursing to be done, she would do it herself. Fortunately Sabrann, who was nodding eagerly, did not seem to have noticed that she had dodged the question.

'Not ten days ago,' announced Sabrann, 'my own cousin made a whole squad of soldiers fall over.'

Tilla's hand paused. 'How did she do that?'

'She was carrying water up to the house when about a hundred and fifty of them came running past, all squashed up together like they do, and you know how they stare at you?'

Tilla nodded.

'My cousin was tired of being stared at so she spoke a curse. And the moment the words were ended one of the soldiers tripped over and all the ones behind him landed on top in a big heap. And when they got up one of them couldn't walk and had to be carried away with his leg strapped up. We were all laughing so much we had to run and hide behind the fence.'

'Daughter of Lugh!' It was a man's voice.

Enjoying the tale, they had noticed neither the dog nor the door announce his arrival.

Tilla got to her feet. 'I am here.'

'I am to take you to the grandmother.'

There must have been twenty people gathered round the fire in the big house. The grandmother sat straight-backed in her chair and motioned Tilla to kneel in front of her.

'Daughter of Lugh,' she said, 'everyone here has spoken about you. Now I wish to hear you speak for yourself.'

Tilla got to her feet, brushing the bracken off her knees. She looked round at all the faces turned towards her, silent in the flickering firelight. She took a deep breath, raised her hands, and began a song.

'She is singing!' shouted a woman in the grandmother's ear.

'I know!' snapped the grandmother. 'I can hear it!'

She sang some of the story of her ancestors. She sang a blessing on the grandmother and her family. And she sang a farewell.

69

Even at this distance, Ruso could hear the roar from the amphitheatre. The sports must be well under way – some of the Twentieth burning off energy and the others merely reaching a height of excitement that would wash over the town like a wave when the exit gates opened.

At Merula's, they were getting ready for a busy night. Bassus and Stichus were outside nailing the torches into their brackets ('Bastards pinch 'em else'). A few early customers were in, being served by Mariamne. Daphne was lumbering up the stairs with a pile of fresh sheets.

Behind the bar, Merula was tasting the offering from the hot drinks cauldron. She winced. 'Not enough cinnamon,' she snapped to a girl who was lining up jugs behind the bar.

Ruso reached for his purse as he approached. Merula saw the gesture, and her scowl gave way to a professional smile.

When he had settled his bill he said, 'I need a word with Chloe.'

The frown returned. 'She's not working at the moment.'

'I just need to give her a message.'

'She's ill.'

'I'm a doctor,' pointed out Ruso.

The lines around Merula's mouth deepened, but she waved a hand in the direction of the kitchen. 'If you can get her back to work,' she said, 'I'll be the one paying you.'

Unusually, both doors of the kitchen were propped open, but despite the passage of air the smoke and steam still made Ruso cough. One end of the table was covered in dirty bowls and discarded onion skins, and at the other a pale squad of uncooked pies was lined up ready to march into the oven. None of the staff who were attempting to work and argue at the same time took any notice of him. Ruso suspected that the decision to sell the kitchen slave on the eve of one of the busiest nights of the year had not been a popular one.

He rapped on the side door that led to the room where the girls slept, paused briefly and then strode into the room.

A figure in one of the lower bunks rolled over to face him. The face was red and wet. The eyes were swollen with weeping.

'Chloe?'

'Don't come near me!'

'Chloe, about Lucco —'

'He's gone! They took him away!'

'I know.'

'They promised I could keep him! They promised!' She sniffed violently. 'He's all I've got!'

'I've seen him.'

Chloe did not appear to have heard. With a sudden movement she swung her feet to the floor and leaped at him. 'You did this!' she shrieked, pounding at him with her fists. 'You did this!'

Ruso made a grab for both arms and held them still. Instead of pulling away, Chloe thrust her distorted face into his. 'You couldn't keep your nose out!' she wailed. 'You had to show off what you'd found out, didn't you?'

Ruso held her at arm's length, and looked her in the eye. 'Sit down, Chloe,' he ordered, 'and listen to me.'

'I won't sit down! Lucco is my life! It's your fault he's gone!'

'My fault?'

'Why did you have to interfere?' she shrieked. 'Look what happened to Phryne! Everything you do makes trouble!'

'SIT DOWN!' roared Ruso, pushing her roughly down on to the bed and narrowly missing banging her head on the top bunk.

She was silent now. Her hands were shaking as she lifted them to cover her face.

'He's gone,' she moaned, 'my little boy, my little boy, my baby . . .'

Ruso shifted a pile of clothes and a hairbrush, and seated himself on the only chair. 'I've seen him,' he said. 'He's with a visiting trader.'

Chloe shuddered, then managed to say, 'Is he all right? He'll be frightened.'

'He wanted me to –'

He was about to explain about the message when the door burst open and Stichus announced, 'I know where he is!'

'With the trader,' groaned Chloe.

'I'm going down there to get him.'

'I haven't got any money,' said Chloe, reaching down to unfasten her ankle-chain. 'I've got this, and a bit saved up, but it's nothing.'

'Don't matter,' announced Stichus, 'me and Merula have had words. I'm leaving. I get my share after closing time tonight. I'll go down there, put a bid on the boy and pay up in the morning.'

Chloe reached for his hand. 'You'd do that? Really?'

Stichus grinned. It was not a pretty sight, but Ruso guessed it was kindly meant. The man, whom he had always thought of as Bassus' shadow, was showing commendable initiative. There was only one problem.

'They may not give you credit,' he said. 'There's a sign saying cash only.'

Stichus stared at him as if only now noticing he was there. Finally he said, 'Right,' and turned on his heel. 'It's my money, I'll have it now.'

When he had gone Ruso said, 'Your son says to tell you that Bassus told Merula about the bad oysters.'

'I know that already, bless him,' said Chloe. She sniffed and groped around for something to wipe her nose on, finally settling on a soggy ball of rag that she shook open and applied to her blotched face. 'It's all my fault.'

Ruso, relieved that he was no longer being blamed, said nothing.

'I should never have said anything about Saufeia's stupid letter,' said Chloe, unexpectedly. 'Then you wouldn't be poking your nose in and asking questions . . .' she paused to sniff, '. . . and Bassus wouldn't know I'd talked. He told Merula about Lucco's silly trick with the oysters so she would sell him. And he did it to get back at me.'

Ruso let out a long sigh. It was his turn to lower his head into his hands. He should have more sense than to question Bassus about the letter. 'I'm sorry,' he said. 'I'm just trying to find out what's happened to Tilla.'

Chloe stretched herself out on the bunk and lay with her eyes open, gazing at the slats holding the mattress above. 'I knew it would all go wrong in the end,' she said.

From beyond the kitchen door there was a crash and a shout of exasperation. Ruso took a deep breath. He stared at his toes. He wished he were somewhere else. Another country. Another lifetime. Anywhere where he could never have met the girl he called Tilla. If he had ignored the fuss around the fountain, none of this would have happened. But Chloe was right: he *had* to interfere. And from that moment everything had gone wrong. It was as if he was cursed from the moment those beautiful eyes had . . . gods above! Now he was starting to believe all that rubbish himself.

Stichus reappeared, looking angry. 'I can't get the cash,' he said. 'Miserable cow says it's locked in a strongroom and she hasn't got the key. I'm going down there anyway.'

'Stop!' Ruso was reaching for his purse. 'How much are you expecting?'

Stichus waved a hand to indicate that anything Ruso could offer was nothing compared to his need. 'A bloody sight more than you've got.'

For answer, Ruso knelt on the floor and upended his purse. Chloe gasped.

Ruso glanced at Stichus. The man opened his mouth and closed it again as if he had lost the power of words.

'I'm about to repay a loan,' explained Ruso. 'But they can wait a day.' Since Tilla had vanished, Priscus could hardly seize her if the Aesculapian loan was not paid on time.

When Stichus had hurried out with the money, Chloe said, 'I am sorry for the things I said. I think you do try to do the right thing.'

'I'm beginning to wonder why I bother.'

He glanced across. Chloe had managed a weak smile.

'I examined Saufeia's body after they pulled her out of the river,' he told her. 'Someone said to me that no one should die like that. And it's true.'

Chloe sat up and put her bare feet on the floor. 'If I knew where Tilla was,' she said, 'I would tell you. I don't. But I can tell you some of what you want to know. If you promise, really really promise, to keep quiet about it now? You won't tell anyone or ask any more questions?'

'If it will help someone, I can't stay silent.'

'How can it? It's about Saufeia, and she's dead.'

'Very well.'

'I don't know who killed her in the end. But I do know the thing they're so frightened of everyone finding out. Saufeia was a Roman citizen.'

Ruso felt himself blink. 'A citizen?' he repeated. A citizen could not be a slave, let alone a slave forced to work as a prostitute. 'How could she be . . . ?'

'What she told us – what she started to tell everybody before Bassus gave her one of his little private training sessions – was, she was a centurion's daughter who'd run away with her boyfriend after a fight with her stepfather.'

A centurion's daughter. So that explained the smattering of education. And the knowledge of Army expletives.

'Then she fell out with the boyfriend – that was the one thing she was good at, falling out with people – and he dumped her on the road. She had no money, of course. So she went to an inn to ask for help and got picked up by some low-life who said he'd take her home. Well of course he didn't. So she ended up here.

'As soon as she got here she started whining about who she was, but Merula was short-staffed so she told her to shut up and they put her to work. They must have known they'd done a stupid thing but by then they were in serious trouble anyway, so they just kept on serving her up to the customers, and everybody was too scared to talk because Merula said we'd all be arrested and flogged. Of course, they couldn't ever let her out. She must have realized they were just going to work her to death. Or sell her on to somewhere worse.' Chloe gave a bitter laugh. 'Don't believe any of those stories about girls from places like this being rescued by men who fall in love with them. I've been here longer than all of them and I can tell you, it doesn't happen.'

'Tilla told me about Daphne's punishment.'

'Daphne should have had more sense. Most of the men we meet aren't as soft as poor old Decimus.'

'She was trying to copy Asellina?'

'I always thought it was odd that Asellina didn't get in touch,' said Chloe. 'The truth is, the only way you can go from here is down.'

Ruso wondered if the men who came to relax with these girls realized the true ghastliness they were paying to support. 'You've been fortunate.'

'I've been determined,' she said. 'I have a child to think of.' She dropped her head into her hands. 'What if someone outbids him?'

'He has plenty of money,' said Ruso, whose own unspoken question was, *What if he runs off with it?* 'Tell me some more about Saufeia.'

Chloe nodded. 'The cook took pity on her and got her some writing things. She wrote a letter to the Legate at the fort asking to be sent home. The cook was supposed to deliver it but Bassus saw it and said he'd take it instead. We all thought she'd get a beating when he read it, but it looked as though he'd just gone and delivered it, 'cause a couple of days later some official lackey arrived here with a letter for her. Said he wouldn't hand it over to anybody else. She burned it as soon as she'd read it and she wouldn't tell anybody what was in it, but I got the idea she thought somebody was coming to save her.'

Ruso scratched his head. 'But if someone was coming to get her, why did she run away? Surely if she'd waited they'd have sent an officer down with a whole squad, made arrests . . .'

'Like they tried with Phryne.'

Ruso scratched his ear. 'I truly meant well, Chloe. I was told the child was kidnapped.'

393

'You were told that by Tilla?'

He nodded.

'She should have known better.'

Ruso shrugged. 'She was convinced it was true. She was cooking up potions to help.'

'I meant, she should have known better than to tell you. Of course Phryne was kidnapped.'

'*What?*'

'I tell you, if they ever get their hands on that Claudius Innocens, he's a dead man. After Saufeia you'd think they'd learn, but he offered them Phryne cheap and they didn't ask too many questions. And nobody round here was going to say anything, not after everything that had happened.'

'But I was told the Second Spear questioned Phryne in private!'

Chloe pursed her lips. 'Your Second Spear's men aren't very bright. One of them told our lovely management why he was here before he sent them to fetch her. So they had time to have a word with her before they brought her downstairs. They told her a string of lies about how much trouble she'd be in if she didn't say what they wanted. She was too scared to know who to trust.'

'So where did Bassus get her documents?'

'Bassus and Innocens between them,' said Chloe, 'must know every forger in the province.'

Ruso shook his head slowly from side to side, as if trying to settle all this jumbled information in his brain. 'Tilla told me I was poking about in a wasps' nest,' he observed.

'We did try to warn you.'

Ruso frowned. 'Let me get this straight. You're telling me Saufeia knew help was coming but she still ran away?'

'No,' said Chloe, 'that's not what I'm saying.'

'It was staged!' said Ruso suddenly. 'They couldn't get ri

of her here without everyone knowing so they forged an official letter telling her someone would meet her outside.'

Chloe gave a weak smile. 'Does it take you this long to diagnose all your patients?'

'Without the letter or any witnesses to the murder, nobody can prove anything.'

'Of course,' Chloe agreed. 'Saufeia was stupid, but they aren't. The letter probably held instructions for her to burn it.'

'Which she did because she thought she was keeping it secret.' Ruso paused. 'This is only a theory. It could be wrong.'

'It isn't,' said Chloe. 'Listen. They've always let me out because they knew I'd come back for Lucco. But after Asellina went one or two girls started to get ideas, so they tightened up. I'm the only one who gets past them now. All that stuff about escorting girls for their own safety? It's rubbish. It's so nobody makes a run for it. Every slave here is in chains, Doctor. They just aren't the sort you can see. Saufeia wouldn't have got out of here unless they wanted her to.'

'The doormen let her out, followed her and then killed her.'

Chloe shrugged. 'I don't know. If they didn't, they know who did. It doesn't much matter, does it? Nobody knows who her family were or what her real name was, and it won't bring her –' She broke off to look up as the door opened. 'Lucco!' she shrieked, leaping to her feet and pulling the boy into her arms. 'Oh, Lucco, my baby!'

Stichus, standing in the doorway, caught Ruso's eye and grinned. 'Bet you thought I'd run off with the cash,' he said.

'It never crossed my –' Ruso's lie was stifled by an enthusiastic kiss from Chloe, who then flung herself at

Stichus in a similar fashion before seizing her son again and ordering him to say thank you.

'It was nothing,' said Ruso, finding his mouth stuck in a foolish grin and relieved that at last he seemed to have got something right. He was making for the door when Stichus said, 'Stay a minute, Doc, all right? I got something to say and I want a proper witness.' He stepped in and closed the door.

Chloe glanced at him, puzzled.

'I should have said this a long time ago,' announced Stichus. He placed a hand on Lucco's head. 'I don't know what your mother's told you but I know she knows. And she's never said nothing to me but I know she knows I know too.'

Lucco, Ruso felt, was making a good job of trying to look impressed without having the faintest idea what his rescuer was talking about.

Stichus cleared his throat. 'This here young man,' he said, addressing Chloe and Ruso, 'is my legal property as of today. But I don't think of him that way. You and I both know' (here he glanced at Chloe, who was looking apprehensive) 'that this here young man is my own flesh and blood.'

Lucco's eyes widened. He turned to his mother. 'Am I?'

Chloe reached up and tweaked Stichus' fading red hair, then grinned at Lucco. 'You never guessed?'

Lucco scratched his head, giving his father – who now seemed not to know what to do – a hint to remove the hand.

'That all right with you, then?' Stichus asked him.

'I *knew* there was something,' said Lucco. 'You were always nicer to me than the others were.'

Ruso, not needed here and due at the hospital, tried to sidle around Stichus towards the door. Stichus' hand landed on the latch before he got there. 'Right,' he announced, 'busy night ahead, got to get back to work. You coming, son?'

After they were gone Chloe took Ruso's hand. 'I'm grateful, Doctor. I know you won't let me show you how much, but I'll see he pays you back in the morning.'

'It was nothing,' Ruso repeated. 'I have to go now, there are patients . . .'

'If Tilla was here I'd ask her to put a blessing on you.'

'If Tilla were here I wouldn't have had the money,' he observed. 'The gods move in strange ways.'

'They do,' agreed Chloe. 'Who would have guessed that for all these years old Stichus has been thinking my boy was his son?'

Ruso paused with his hand on the door-latch. 'Isn't he?'

Chloe grinned. 'He is now,' she said.

70

Tilla was singing quietly to herself. The sack of provisions swung and bumped against the small of her back with each step. Its weight was a pleasure. It meant independence. There was no one out here to give her orders or ask where she was going.

She was not entirely sure where she was going herself. After two years she had little idea whether anything was left of her home. Whatever she found, though, would be better than the place she had left: a place built by foreign warriors who fought not for honour but for money and hid their shame by bullying everyone else. In the end even the Medicus had turned out to be little better than his companions. She had begun to think he could be trusted. She had even begun to grow fond of him. Now she realized what a fool she had been. The time she had spent with Sabrann had opened her eyes anew to the twisted thinking of the Emperor's men and all those who served them. She was lucky to have escaped before she had been hopelessly corrupted like Merula, a woman who survived by trampling on others. Or Chloe, who had no vision of anything beyond the walls of the bar.

She wished she had been able to bring the child with her: the one they had called Phryne. When she reached home she would spread the word of what had happened to her. Perhaps the child's people would send warriors. Perhaps not. There were cowards amongst the Brigantes, too. Elders who acted out of fear and called it being sensible, or abandoned their own ways and called it progress. The taint of Rome spread like rot through a crate of apples.

There was a dip in the road ahead. She could see the tops of wooden rails that must be the sides of a bridge. Beyond them, set well back – the Romans were afraid of ambushes and always chopped down everything close to the road – stood a massive tree that was the right shape for an oak. That must be the marker for the track Sabrann had told her to follow.

As she looked, two cavalry horses appeared over the brow of the next rise. Tilla tugged the sack into a new position on her shoulder and kept an eye on the riders, who were progressing towards her at a leisurely trot. She slowed, not wanting to meet them on the narrow bridge.

It occurred to her that if she had a horse, she could make the journey far more easily. The weak arm would make it hard to mount, but once she was up, she would manage one-handed. She was a good rider. She had been allowed to ride her father's horses as a child. Perhaps someone would lend her a pony. Perhaps, if they wouldn't, she would wait until no one was looking and help herself.

She heard the clump of hoofbeats on the wooden bridge. She kept walking, head down, close to the verge so the horses would have plenty of room to pass.

Something inside the sack was poking into her back. As she shifted the weight the sack pulled at the fabric on her shoulder. She felt the grey hood slip backwards. Quickly, she lifted her right hand to pull it forward again, but the cloth was caught under the weight of the sack and her weak arm did not have the strength to tug it free.

The horses were only about thirty paces away now. She turned to one side, swung the sack to the ground and bent over, busying herself with adjusting the hood and pinning it

399

back into place. She could hear the approaching crunch of hooves on the gravel. The men were talking to each other.

The hood was back in place. The horses were almost level with her now. She slid her right arm in under the cloak, realizing as she did so that two or three inches of grimy bandage had been poking out of the end of her sleeve.

The horses were next to her. The riders were still chatting as if they had noticed nothing. The bandage had probably looked like a glimpse of undertunic.

They had passed. She grabbed the neck of the sack and swung it back over her shoulder.

Behind her, the hoofbeats faltered and began to grow louder. The riders were coming back.

'Halt!'

Tilla froze.

'What's your name, girl?'

She turned, keeping her head bowed in a pretence of respect. 'Brica, sir.'

'Brica, eh? What are you doing all the way out here, Brica?'

Tilla stared at the polished hooves of the front horse. 'I go to visit my aunt, sir. She is sick.'

The second rider moved round to take up a position beside her.

'What do you think?' said the first rider to him. 'She look like a Brica to you?'

'Hm.' There was a creak of leather as the second rider bent down from his saddle to examine her. 'Chin up, girl.'

Tilla lifted her head a fraction.

'You know what she looks like to me?' offered the first rider, circling his horse behind her and nudging her forward into the middle of the road. 'She looks like Attractive female aged about twenty.'

'Slim, about five feet four inches,' continued his companion as if they were quoting from something. 'Hold out your arm, gorgeous.'

Tilla slid the sack off her shoulder and held out her left arm.

'The other one.'

Her left hand darted inside the cloak and tugged down the offending sleeve before she reached out her right arm. 'If you touch me,' she said, 'my master will have you punish.'

A sword swished out of its scabbard. A blade glinted in front of her. Its tip plucked back the fabric of her sleeve, revealing the dirty linen bandage.

'I think you're the one who gets to be punish, gorgeous.' Both horses were circling around her now. 'We're the ones who get the reward.'

Tilla let the sack fall, grabbed her skirts and dodged through the gap between one horse and the next. Leaping across the ditch, she scrambled up on to the rough grass and raced towards the woods. If she could just get between the trees, she stood a chance . . .

Over the rasp of her own breath she heard cheering. Then the approach of hoofbeats. There was a horse cantering either side of her now. She slowed: they slowed. She speeded up: they increased their pace. The men were laughing. Playing with her. She stopped dead, spun round and ran back the other way, but it was hopeless. There was no cover ahead of her now, only the open road. The thud of hooves on turf surrounded her once more. The horses were crowding her. Hands reached down and flung her cloak back over her shoulders. 'Now!' shouted one of the men. She ducked. Too late. They grabbed her under both arms and scooped her up with a swift, practised movement. Legs flailing helplessly, blue boots brushing the tips of the grasses, she dangled between the two horsemen as their mounts cantered back towards the road.

71

Ruso should have gone straight to the hospital, but instead he hurried back to the house and spent several minutes scratching notes on to a tablet which he then thrust into the trunk with all the versions of the *Concise Guide*.

Albanus was waiting for him with the look of anxiety that seemed to be his permanent expression lately. 'Lots of people have been asking for you, sir. There's a queue waiting in the hall.'

'Where's Valens?' Ruso was still breathless after sprinting across from the house.

'Officer Valens has been taking the urgent cases and telling the rest you'll be back any minute, sir. And Officer Priscus said you had an appointment with him – about the Aesculapian Thanksgiving Fund?'

'Yes, I know about that one. Anything else?'

'I need a word with you too, sir.'

'Is it urgent?'

'Not really, sir.'

'Good. Let's get this queue shifted.'

He had almost emptied the bench in the hall when there was a commotion in the corridor, and the door shuddered as if someone had fallen against it. Ruso glanced up. 'Put the bar across, Albanus, will you?'

The clerk leaped to secure the door, and Ruso carried on cleaning up a nastily torn ear as the shouting faded away down the corridor. 'How did you get this?' he inquired.

'Over at the wrestling,' explained its owner. 'We're cheering our lad on and there's a bit of an exchange, like, with some lads sitting behind, and next thing I know I'm upside down with somebody's boot sliding down the side of me head.'

'Ah,' said Ruso. 'Sport. Always brings out the best in a man. Albanus, just poke your head into the corridor and make sure there's nobody lying dead out there, will you?'

Moments later Albanus returned to report that some plasterers from the Twentieth had got into a dispute with a visiting crew of a warship. Knives were out before the centurial staff had been able to wade in and restore order. Now the wounded of both groups had been brought in for treatment and, having tried to carry on the fight in the corridor, had been sent to wait under guard in separate rooms.

'Idiots,' observed the man with the torn ear.

'What a joy payday is,' remarked Ruso. 'I'll just pop a few stitches in this ear, then you can go and have a nice lie-down while I have the pleasure of meeting the Navy.'

In fact it was Valens who dealt with the sailors while the plasterers were assigned to Ruso. Only one was seriously injured: a stab wound that had probably penetrated a lung. The man required some immediate and careful patching up before he was admitted for observation, nursing care and an outcome whose uncertainty would have frightened him if he had been sober. The others he released into the care of their centurion, who looked willing to inflict a few injuries himself if anyone showed any more signs of misbehaving.

'We'll be seeing that lot lined up outside HQ tomorrow,' observed Ruso as they left. 'What's next?'

'Evening, Ruso.' Valens appeared round the door in a gruesomely bloodstained tunic. 'Good of you to turn up.'

'Nice outfit,' Ruso observed.

'Don't insult me, I've taken time off from my onerous duties to bring you some news. They've found Tilla.'

'Where? Is she all right? Where is she?'

Valens shrugged. 'According to my sources, a road patrol found her taking a stroll eight or nine miles out of town.'

'Where is she? Is she all right?'

'I imagine they've taken her to Priscus in the hope of a reward. As advertised.'

A dreadful thought crossed Ruso's mind. 'To Priscus?'

'That is what it said on the advertisements, isn't it?'

Ruso turned to Albanus. 'What time is it?'

'I think I heard the eleventh hour just now, sir.'

'Is the pay office still open?'

Albanus frowned. 'I doubt it, sir. They'll have locked up some time ago and gone to the sports.'

'Tell the next patient to wait a minute. I need to go and see Priscus.'

Ruso sprinted along the corridor, narrowly missing a collision with a couple of orderlies carrying a man on a stretcher. When he reached the office, it was locked. One of the records-room clerks informed him that Officer Priscus had been called away. The clerk's tone suggested that it was very convenient for Officer Priscus to be called away early on payday while everyone else had to stay behind and work.

'Where are the records for the Aesculapian Fund?'

The clerk looked surprised. 'In Officer Priscus' room, sir.'

'And if someone wanted to make a payment while he was out?'

'We'd tell him to come back tomorrow, sir. We aren't allowed to handle cash. We don't have the facilities.'

Valens had gone by the time Ruso got back to his surgery. 'Albanus,' he said, 'I need to get at the records of the Aesculapian Fund. I need to, ah – find out how much I owe. I was supposed to pay it back today and I haven't had time.'

Albanus frowned. 'They'll be in the administrator's office, sir. Nobody can get in there.'

Ruso looked him in the eye. 'Is that definitely true, Albanus? Surely a man as thorough as Priscus would arrange for a spare key somewhere in case one goes missing?'

Albanus was chewing the end of his stylus. 'I really couldn't say, sir. Officer Priscus wouldn't tell the clerks anything like that.'

'No, because he's a secretive bastard. But you know where it is, don't you?'

'Sir, I really can't –'

'Albanus, I am your superior officer, and this is an order. Find a way to get me into that room.'

Albanus stood to attention. 'Yes, sir!'

'I'm sorry, sir. I don't think it's here.'

They had been through the whole of the Aesculapian Thanksgiving Fund file twice, the second time struggling to read by lamplight. Ruso sighed. 'It's no use. He's taken it with him.'

'Is there anything I can do, sir? Shall I keep looking?'

Ruso shook his head. 'Put all this stuff away and lock up. I've got to go out for a while. I'll go and warn Valens he's on his own.'

Valens was predictably annoyed, but unable to prevent his colleague from leaving.

Making his way down to the South Gate Ruso heard footsteps running along behind him in the darkness. 'Doctor, sir!' gasped a breathless Albanus.

'I'm in hurry, Albanus. Can't it wait?'

'No, sir, I don't think it can.'

'Walk with me.'

The clerk fell into step with him. 'Sir, you remember I said there was that one thing I needed to say to you?'

'What was it?'

'Well, sir, you know I went through all the incoming post logs looking for a letter from Saufeia and I didn't find one?'

'You've found one?'

'Not exactly, sir. But I thought, maybe it came in some other way and somebody replied to it. So I went back and looked through the outgoing logs instead.'

'And?'

'And I found it. A letter to Saufeia. Dated two days before she died.'

'Is there a file copy?'

'No sir, just a listing in the log. Date, who to, who from.'

'And are you going to tell me who it was from, or do I have to guess?'

'Yes, sir! No, sir! I'd be glad to tell you, sir. To tell you the truth I was a bit concerned.'

'Albanus, *who is it?*'

Albanus told him. Ruso turned to look at the shadowy figure of his clerk. 'Are you absolutely sure?'

'Yes, sir.'

'Who else knows about this?'

'I haven't said anything to anybody else, sir.'

'Don't. Don't say anything to anyone unless . . .' Ruso hesitated. They were approaching the torches of the main gate now. A couple of men passed them in the dark. 'Don' say anything unless I, ah — unless I appear to have got into difficulties tonight. If that happens, go to my house tomorrow morning and go through my documents very thoroughly. Then I want you to tell the whole bloody province.'

72

'Let the doctor through!' roared a guard as the gates swung open and an untidy jumble of men surged in under the torchlit archway, eager to be out of the rain that was now cooling the payday fervour of the Twentieth. Ruso shouldered his way forwards against the flow.

'Let the doctor through!' echoed a second guard, helpfully shoving the nearest man aside and dragging Ruso forward.

Once outside, he sprinted along the street, weaving in and out of groups of off-duty legionaries. Several were under escort and attempting to step smartly. A couple had abandoned their legs altogether and were being carried home by their comrades. The bars must be closing. So, this was civilized Britannia. A place where the Army felt it could trust the locals enough to relax in their presence. Ruso was willing to bet that these sort of antics were not going on in the hill country.

There was a rectangle of light around Priscus' front door but no one answered his knocking. He slammed the flat of his hand three times against the wooden panelling so the whole door shook. 'Priscus! It's Ruso!'

'Oi! You!' bellowed a voice from down the street. 'Get away from that door!'

Ruso slammed his hand against the panel again. 'Priscus! Open up!' He spun round to explain, 'Doctor. Medical emergency,' just as the pair of junior officers moved apart in the darkness to grab an arm each.

'Name?' demanded one of them.

408

He told them.

'Where's your bag of tricks?'

'I came straight here,' said Ruso, truthfully enough.

'Why aren't they letting you in, then?'

'I don't know. This is definitely the house.' He turned and hammered on the door again. 'Priscus!'

'There's someone in,' observed one of the men, bending to try and peer through the gap at the side of the door. 'There's a light. Perhaps he's too ill to get to the door.'

Ruso lifted one boot to crash it against the lock, but Priscus' house was made of stronger stuff than the linen cupboard. The door shuddered and held firm.

'Don't you worry, Doc,' one of the men assured him. 'We'll get you in. Ready?'

Moments later the three of them were picking themselves up from Priscus' front door, which was now detached from its splintered frame and lying flat on the corridor tiles.

Insisting that he didn't need a stretcher team, he dismissed his helpers and strode down the corridor to where a figure – not the one he had expected – was standing with folded arms in the doorway of Priscus' living room.

'Bassus! Where is she? What's he done with her?'

'He can't see you,' said Bassus, showing no sign of surprise at the unusual form of entry. 'He's talking to me. Put the door back on your way out.'

The veteran's silhouette filled the narrow corridor. He was a fraction shorter than Ruso but a lot heavier, and he was a professional doorman. Ruso wished he had not dismissed his eager comrades in arms. If it came to a struggle, he was not going to get in.

'The Army won't let you sell her,' he said. 'He's trying to take her for the hospital fund.'

'Who?'

'Tilla. He's found Tilla. Didn't he tell you?'

From somewhere behind Bassus came a cry of 'Doctor!' Surprisingly, Priscus sounded relieved that he had arrived.

'Miserable bastard's not telling me anything,' observed Bassus. 'Yet.'

'She was picked up earlier today,' said Ruso. 'He's got her somewhere. Let me talk to him.'

Bassus appeared to think about it for a moment, then said, 'Be my guest,' and stepped aside to allow Ruso past.

Priscus, hair awry, was huddled in one of the wicker chairs. He half-rose to exclaim, 'Doctor!' then shrank back into the chair as Bassus approached.

'Pull up a seat,' suggested Bassus, gesturing towards a stool in the corner.

'I haven't come here for a rest,' retorted Ruso. 'I've come to find my servant.'

'Suit yourself.' Bassus flung himself into the second wicker chair. Priscus closed his eyes to shut out the sight of the doorman's large boots being planted on the delicate table.

Underneath the table, the fruit bowl lay in pieces. Its contents rested where they had rolled across the floor. The servant was nowhere to be seen. Ruso, who had no idea what was going on and no time to find out, said, 'Priscus, where's Tilla?'

The administrator cleared his throat. 'As steward of the Aesculapian Fund –'

'Where is she?'

'As steward of the Aesculapian Fund, I have a duty to . . .'

Ruso's steps made a sharp sound on the tiled floor. Standing over Priscus, he emphasized each word. 'Where is Tilla?'

Priscus sat up in the chair and made an attempt to push his hair back into place. 'As I have just been telling this . . . man,' he said, glancing at Bassus, 'I will not be bullied. The girl is in a safe place and I must remind you that following default of a loan repayment I have a perfect right as steward of –'

'I want to see her. Now.'

The wicker creaked as Priscus squirmed in the chair and glanced across at Bassus. 'In the circumstances,' he said, 'I could perhaps arrange release of the girl on receipt of immediate cash payment. With an additional sum as penalty for a missed deadline plus the cost of recovery.'

It was Bassus who demanded, 'How much?' as Ruso said, 'The girl. Now. You'll get the money first thing in the morning.'

'Oh dear, no, I'm afraid not. It has to be a simultaneous –'

'Don't be ridiculous,' snapped Ruso, wishing he had not lent all of his spare money to Stichus. 'Nobody's going to walk around at night carrying that much cash. You've got my signature on the agreement. Just hand her over and you'll get your money in the morning.'

Bassus was shaking his head sadly. 'He needs the money tonight, Doc. He's got a few debts to pay himself.' He reached down into the chair and waved a writing-tablet at Priscus. 'Haven't you, sunshine?'

Priscus sighed and looked up at Ruso as if hoping for support. 'I have already explained,' he said, 'that the money is in long-term investments. I am not in a position to withdraw such investments without warning, and certainly not at this hour of the night.'

'Long-term investments, my arse! You've been feathering your nest!'

'Bassus,' said Ruso, feeling he should show more loyalty

than he felt, 'you're talking to an officer. Watch what you're saying.'

'I know what I'm saying.' Bassus lifted his legs and gave the table a swift kick. It toppled over. The crash as it landed on the tiles echoed round the room. 'Oops,' he said, 'there goes another long-term investment.'

Priscus sprang to his feet. 'Really! I must protest!'

Bassus moved surprisingly fast for such a heavy man. The chair skidded backwards on the tiles as Priscus landed in it, gasping for breath.

'Now listen to me, you scraggy-faced runt,' growled Bassus. 'Me and Stich, we work our balls off out there, and we don't get nothing from you except trouble and promises.'

Ruso looked from one to the other of them, baffled. He had assumed Bassus was collecting a debt. Why would Merula's doormen be expecting anything from Priscus?

Bassus was thrusting the writing-tablet forward so it was almost touching Priscus' nose. 'There it is, see? All written down. All agreed. My retirement fund. You told us it was there.'

'It is there.'

'Good. Because I want it now. And if you don't hand it over, I'll have the girl instead.'

'The girl is the property of the Aesculapian Fund!' insisted Priscus. 'She's legionary business.'

'Legionary business, eh? I'll bet the Legion don't know how much it's chipped in to the cost of this place. Where is she?'

'She's not here.'

Bassus leaned forward and hauled Priscus out of the chair. He was saying, 'Well tell me where she is and we'll go and get her, shall we?' but Ruso was not listening. He was moving towards the sound that had just turned his stomach. It was the muffled sound of a woman screaming.

It was the shrill, tormented shriek of a woman in terrible pain. By the time he burst into Priscus' bedroom it had stopped. There was nobody in the room. Just the empty bed, a few cupboards too small to hide a prisoner, and . . .

He stepped forward and tugged aside the curtain covering part of the back wall. This should surely have been the rear boundary of the property, but instead of blank plaster there was a door. It had already been forced: the lock was hanging loose. As he dragged it open, another scream filled his ears.

The dark space in front of him seemed to be a corridor. 'Tilla!' he yelled, heading towards faint streaks of light that marked a doorway. 'Tilla!' He collided with something that fell over with a crash of broken crockery. It barely masked the screaming. Holy gods, what were they doing to her?

'Leave her alone!' he roared.

All three occupants of the room looked up as he burst in: the naked, sweating and breathless woman squatting on the floor and the people either side of her, holding her by the arms.

'You'll be all right,' one of them assured her. 'The Doctor's here.'

In reply the naked woman grimaced, flung her head back, and gave a terrible groan of pain. It was the pain of a woman in labour. Instead of Tilla, Ruso had found Daphne. He glanced around the room, mystified.

'What are you doing here?'

'She can't give birth in the bar, can she?' retorted one of the girls supporting Daphne. 'So they've dumped us back here, out of the way. We don't know what to do.'

413

'It's stuck,' added Phryne, who was holding Daphne's other arm.

Ruso stared at Daphne. He was an Army surgeon. He was a medic. He was a man. A man who knew the limits of his knowledge, and a difficult delivery might well be beyond them, even if he had his case with him. 'Where's the midwife?'

'On another call,' explained the girl grimly.

Ruso lifted a candle from its stand and squatted in front of Daphne. 'I'm just going to take a quick look, see what's going on,' he explained.

It was worse than he had feared. It was not even a breech. What he could see of the child was not a head nor a pair of buttocks, but a tiny hand. The baby was wedged sideways. There was no way to bring it out at this angle. If it would not turn, he would have to improvise a scalpel with the knife slung at his belt. And someone would have to decide which should be allowed to live: the mother or the child.

Before he could say anything, the cords in Daphne's neck tightened, her mouth opened and she let out another long and piercing shriek, as if all the pain and horror of her mutilation were finally being released to reverberate around the room

There was a brief silence as Daphne paused for breath. He put his hand on her arm. 'Try not to push,' he urged. 'I'm going to get help.' He had no idea how much Till knew about delivering babies. He prayed that it was more than he did.

He realized where he was on the way back to find Priscus. The had put Daphne in one of the rooms that looked out on to Merula's narrow back yard: the private living quarters that joined on to the building behind. The bedrooms used by Merula and the doormen.

It was becoming clear to Ruso that he had underestimate

iscus. The man's tentacles stretched far beyond the hospi-
. It seemed that the administrator employed the doormen
Merula's. Quite possibly he controlled Merula herself.
hat had Valens' friend from Regional Control said? *Invest
a bar by all means, but don't get involved in running it. It won't
down too well higher up.* With the help of his builder, Priscus
d contrived a private entrance through which his every
petite could be indulged whilst his respectable front door
nained unsullied by the murk of the bar trade.

Ruso heard the administrator before he saw him. The
an was still protesting, the pitch of his voice rising with
r. Bassus, not distracted by Daphne's screams, had him
ined against the wall of the living room. Priscus peered
und as Ruso approached. 'Ruso! Help me, he's gone mad!
'll kill me!'

Ruso addressed himself to Bassus. 'If we don't get Tilla
there in the next few minutes,' he said, 'Daphne will be
ad and so will the baby. That's not going to help your
irement fund.'

'See?' grunted Bassus, making a sudden movement that
ulted in a howl of pain from the administrator. 'He's not
ing to help you. He's on my side. Where is she?'

With something like a sob, Priscus said, 'She's quite safe.
romise. Let me go.'

Bassus tightened his grip. Priscus gasped.

'Where?' demanded Bassus.

Priscus seemed to be having trouble getting the words
t. 'In the – in the store room. Behind the shop –' The
tence ended with a shriek.

'Which shop?'

'Next door!' screamed Priscus. 'The basket-maker's!' He
isted awkwardly to look across the room. 'That key on
hook.'

73

Tilla had sat exhausted on the floor of the little store room for some time, wondering what to do next. She did not understand why the officer with the many long words and the odd hair had ignored her requests to send a message to the Medicus. Nor did she understand why he had brought her to this place outside the fort. She knew where she was. Even if she had not recognized the route from the glimpses afforded by a badly tied blindfold, she would have guessed from the rattle of the brittle willow-wands that rolled away under her as she sat down.

It must be dark outside now. The shop had fallen silent. She had heard the shutters being dragged across, and the clank of the lock. It seemed no one would come for her until morning.

Then not long ago there had been shouting and banging near by. She thought she recognized the voice of the Medicus. She had leaped up and begun hammering on the door. 'My lord! It is Tilla! I am here, my lord! Help me!'

From somewhere outside there was a loud crash, and then the voices faded. No one came. Perhaps it was not him. Perhaps he would not have helped her anyway.

Not long after that came the sound of voices raised in anger. The words were muffled by the stone of the wall. She could not make out what was happening.

Her captors had left her necklace in place. She ran forefinger along the smooth curve of one of the acorns. She would not taste the poison yet. But if she could escape no other way, it was ready.

The willow-wands rattled as she stood up. The officer had ordered the man in the shop to help him drag something heavy across the door after she was shut in. Tilla felt around for the latch, running her fingers around the cold metal shapes and trying to understand how the mechanism worked. The latch was the kind that could be opened from both sides. It seemed the officer had not bothered to wedge it shut, relying on the weight of whatever they had put against the door to hold it closed. She bent down and snapped the end off a willow-wand, then poked it under the latch to hold it up. She cleared the rest of the wands back to make a space for her feet. Then she braced herself with her back against the door and the boots the Medicus had bought her planted firmly on the floor and pushed.

Nothing happened.

Tilla relaxed, took a deep breath and heaved again. Something behind her moved a fraction, then fell back into place as her strength gave out. She stood up, shrugged her bruised shoulders to loosen them, shook each leg in turn, then braced herself a third time, took a deep breath, pursed her lips and heaved. The door moved further, but not far enough. The fourth attempt was worse than the first. She was sliding down in despair when she heard someone jangling the lock on the shutters. A man was shouting her name. A man she had once hoped she could trust. She held her breath.

'Are you in there? Tilla, it's me! Ruso! Can you hear me?' And then, to someone else, 'Can you see how this damned thing works?'

The Medicus had planned to sell her. But he was a better

prospect than the one with the odd hair, who reminded her of a dead spider. 'I am here, my lord!' she cried, banging on the door again. 'Help me!'

Moments later she was almost knocked backwards by the enthusiasm of his embrace. 'Tilla! Thank the gods! Where have you been? Are you all right?' He drew back. 'What's the matter?'

She shook her head. She must remember why he was pleased to see her. It would be so easy to be deceived again. 'It is nothing, my lord.' If she explained how the cavalrymen had left her bruised and stiff, he would pretend to care.

'I was afraid you were dead.' The dark eyes were searching hers. 'Where have you been?'

She swallowed. 'You would sell me.'

'What? No, you don't understand – I never wanted to –'

From somewhere back in the shop, Bassus' voice cut him short. 'You never wanted to? Are you joking? We had a deal!'

'Nobody will be selling her,' put in another voice. 'That slave is the legal property of the Aesculapian Thanksgiving Fund.'

The Medicus turned and demanded to know how long she had been locked up there. 'Until the deadline ran out, I suppose?'

They both ignored the torrent of words that followed.

'So,' she said to him, 'it is true. You would sell me.'

She tried not to flinch as the Medicus took her by the shoulders. He looked as he must look when he was trying not to tell a patient bad news. 'No,' he said. 'I mean, didn't . . .'

She raised one hand to her throat.

'Well, yes . . .' the Medicus stumbled on, correcting himself. 'But I didn't – what are you doing?'

She put the acorn to her mouth. 'Why should I live as a slave in this world when I can be free in the next?'

His grip on her shoulders tightened. 'What are you talking about?'

Her lips brushed against the curve of the acorn as she made the words. 'Let me go, or I will take the poison.'

'Tilla, for pity's sake!' He was looking at the acorn, trying to decide whether he could grab it before she put it between her teeth. He would not be fast enough. They both knew it.

'You are as bad as the others,' she told him. 'You are worse. You pretend to have honour.'

For a moment he said nothing. Then he raised his head. 'Daphne needs you, Tilla. The baby is coming and she's in trouble. I think she's going to die.'

'Go and help her yourself,' she told him. 'You are the Medicus.'

'That's how I know,' he said.

'You lie to me. You are lying now about Daphne.'

'Daphne will die,' he urged. 'I'm begging you, Tilla. If you know how to help her, come now.'

She knew what he was thinking. He was wondering if she had lied about bringing out babies just as she had lied about being able to cook.

'Why do you care for Daphne? She is a slave. You are Medicus to the soldiers.'

'If you can't help,' he said, 'say so now and I'll go and do my best.'

He was afraid, but not for himself. He was afraid for Daphne.

'You will make it worse,' she told him. 'Let go of me and

show me where she is.' She raised her voice so the other men could hear. 'If anyone comes near, I will go to the next world.'

The Medicus turned to the men. 'Stand back,' he ordered. 'Let her pass.'

74

By the time they reached Daphne, she seemed barely conscious of what was going on. Her head was hung down,
her hair plastered flat with sweat. The girls holding her
looked weary and frightened. Merula was standing over
them, hands on hips. She looked relieved to see Ruso.
'Doctor! Do something, will you? The customers can hear
her through in the bar!'

Ruso knelt beside the pale form and put one hand over
hers. 'Daphne, it's the Medicus. Can you hear me?'

The girl's eyelids flickered and fell still again. 'Daphne,
Tilla's here. We're going to help you. Just hold on.'

Daphne's head lifted for a second. Her lips parted but
instead of a cry of pain a misshapen vowel sound emerged.

'That's the spirit!' urged the older girl.

Ruso glanced up. 'What did she say?'

The girl grinned. 'She says piss off.'

'Take no notice!' ordered Merula, turning to glare at Tilla.
'What's she doing here?'

Tilla stepped forward and knelt by Daphne, talking in
her own tongue as she examined her. Without looking
up, Daphne stretched a trembling hand forward and Tilla
reached to grasp it.

'You need to wait outside,' Ruso said to Merula.

Beyond folding her arms, Merula failed to move. 'Of all
the nights,' she remarked, eyeing the unfortunate Daphne.
'Three girls out of action back here while we're rushed off
our feet in the bar. And now the door staff are playing

up. We've even had to borrow a servant from one of the neighbours. Not that he's much help.'

This, Ruso supposed, explained why Priscus' man had not been at home. It was hard to imagine the timid house-slave being much use as a security guard. 'Go back to work,' he urged. 'We'll manage here.'

'It's too late now. Madam here's made so much fuss she's frightened all the customers away.'

Tilla turned. 'You must all get out.'

Ruso said, 'I'll stay in case you need any —'

'Out!'

'Who do you think you are?' demanded Merula. 'He is a doctor, and this is my room!'

Tilla put her hand to her throat. 'There is poison inside,' she explained, fingering the acorns as she glanced between Ruso and Merula. 'If anyone comes near, I will eat it. I will die. And her,' she pointed at Daphne, 'and the child. Understand?'

Ruso grasped Merula's arm and forced her back towards the corridor. 'We understand,' he said, and closed the door behind them.

'She's bluffing,' said Merula.

'No she isn't,' said Ruso. 'She knows about poisons.'

They heard the thud of the bar dropping on the other side of the door. 'Bitch!' muttered Bassus, who had apparently been lurking outside with Priscus. 'We'll sort her out later.' He glanced at Merula. 'Busy night, then, was it?'

'Yes. No thanks to you, or to madam back there. Stichus is closing up. You might think of helping him.'

'He can work for free if he wants,' retorted Bassus, heading off down the corridor. 'I'm going to pick up a bit of what's owing to me.'

'Don't you dare touch that money!' shouted Merula

running after him. 'It isn't yours. I have to take out costs, pay the bills . . . !'

Priscus turned to Ruso. 'I don't think we need you now.'

Ruso hesitated just long enough to bid his promotion a silent and sad goodbye, and to wonder how many night duties he would owe Valens because of this. Then he said, 'I'm not leaving here without Tilla.'

'The girl belongs to a legionary welfare fund. If you attempt to remove her, you will be put on a charge, and she will be taken from you.'

Ruso was about to argue when there was a roar of, 'Bastard!' from somewhere at the far end of the corridor.

He asked, 'What time did they find her?' but Priscus was already hurrying towards the sound, calling over his shoulder, 'I have the documents, Ruso!'

Ruso followed him along the corridor, through the empty kitchen and into the brighter light of the bar.

Bassus was still shouting. 'Bastard! Thieving snivelling ginger bastard!' The top of his head was visible as he rummaged about behind the counter. Everyone except he and Merula seemed to have gone.

Merula flung herself across the counter, elegant bottom in the air, arms flailing, reaching down for something. As Ruso watched she slid back to the floor. In her hand was the box in which the takings were kept secure behind the bar. She upended it above her head. A sprinkle of dust and a small brown feather drifted towards the floor. She gave a howl of despair. 'The whole payday takings!'

Priscus was saying, 'But who –?' when Bassus rose from behind the bar and hurled a jug across the room. 'Him and that cheap tart!' The jug hit the wall opposite with a dull crack and shattered on the floor.

A couple of late-night customers who had crept in round the unlocked shutters made a hasty retreat.

'But who –?'

'Stichus and Chloe, of course!' exclaimed Merula. 'I should never have trusted him once that little vixen got hold of him.'

Ruso closed his eyes and let out a long, slow breath. He had been relying on Stichus to give him back the money to pay the Aesculapian Fund. Instead, it was clear the man had stolen the bar takings and fled. Without the money to cover the loan, even if Tilla were released tonight, Ruso would have to hand her back to Priscus tomorrow.

There was a scrape of wood on tile and a clatter of tumbling cups as Priscus shoved a table aside. 'They won't get away with this!' he announced, peering round the shutters into the dark street. 'We'll have them followed.'

'In the middle of the night?' snapped Merula.

'This is your fault!' said Bassus to Priscus. 'If it weren't for you and your tight-arsed money-saving schemes, none of this would have happened.'

Priscus glared at him. 'You were supposed to be on the door!'

'And you're supposed to be the one with the brains!'

Priscus sighed and lowered himself on to a bench. 'Merula. Find me something to drink.'

'The good wine's in the kitchen,' said Merula, heading towards it.

'And two cups!' shouted Bassus after her. He seated himself beside Priscus. 'I've had enough of this. I want my money.' He slid along the bench until he was pressed against the administrator, who visibly braced himself to avoid being pushed off the end and on to the floor. 'So until you come up with it . . .' Bassus gave a smile that was truly frightening

'You got the pleasure of my company. Give me the girl and we'll call it even.'

'The girl isn't his to give,' put in Ruso, stepping forward.

The two men looked up at him. 'As I have explained, Ruso,' said Priscus, 'she is not yours either.'

Ruso, hoping neither of them knew that he had lent his money to the vanished Stichus, said, 'Give her back to me, Priscus. Women aren't safe with you. You don't want someone tracing Saufeia's family and telling them how she died, do you?'

'Saufeia?'

'You know what I'm talking about.'

'Nobody knows how that girl died!' snapped Priscus. 'She was just a slave who ran away. Tilla is a slave who is signed over as guarantee for a loan. The two are not connected.'

'Both were bought on the cheap without asking too many questions.'

Priscus shrugged. 'I have no idea what you mean, Ruso. Nor do I know how you can justify wasting time here when you should be on duty at the hospital.'

Ruso did not know the answer to that one himself. Instead he said, 'How much did you know about Saufeia when you bought her?'

Priscus frowned. 'Don't be ridiculous. I am not responsible for buying bar staff.'

'Of course you are. It's your bar.'

'Merely a business investment. I arrange the finances. I employ a manager to do everything else.'

'Including the deals with cockroaches like Claudius Innocens? Or do you do those yourself?'

'I have quite enough responsibilities at the hospital without taking on any more.'

'Where do you think those girls come from, Priscus? Don't you stop to wonder why the prices are so low?'

Bassus rammed an elbow into Priscus' ribs. 'See? What did I say to you?'

'Hold your tongue!' ordered Priscus, moving to another seat and bending to rub the bruised side of his chest. 'You should never listen to malicious gossip, Ruso. Merula's bar is a respectable business.'

'It's easy enough to buy a cheap girl, isn't it?' Ruso continued. 'I've done it myself. But I didn't force mine to work in a place like this. Whereas your people were stupid enough to do that even after Saufeia had told them she was a citizen and asked for help.'

There was only a slight pause before Priscus clasped his hands together in apparent dismay. 'Are you telling me,' he said, 'that poor Saufeia girl was a Roman citizen?'

Bassus snorted. 'Don't pretend you didn't know.' He turned to Ruso. 'He knew all right.'

'Don't be ridiculous!'

'I was there when Merula told him,' Bassus continued, ignoring the interruption. 'He said we'd got to shut the girl up.'

'What did he mean by that?'

'How should I know? I did what I always do when they play up. I explained a few things to her for her own good. In a way that would help her remember. Only instead of being sensible she went and wrote a letter asking for help and tried to send it to the Legate. What was I supposed to do then?'

'I don't know,' said Ruso. 'What did you do?'

'I went to the management,' said Bassus. 'I told them we ought to be careful. With her being a citizen.'

Unlike the unfortunate Daphne, thought Ruso, whose talkativeness had been cured with a sharp knife.

'I'm only the head doorman,' continued Bassus, nodding towards his employer. 'I give the letter to him. Then it all happened like I told you.'

'He's lying,' insisted Priscus. 'I never saw any letter. I had nothing to do with what happened to that girl. I told you, I leave all that to the manager.'

'But Merula couldn't deal with this, could she?' said Ruso. 'The girl wanted protection from a Legionary officer.'

'I don't know what she wanted!' snapped Priscus.

'And when an officer wrote back to her, offering to help, she didn't have the sense to realize it was a trap.' Ruso turned to Bassus. 'Did she really give you the slip, or were you told to let her out?'

'What do you think?' growled Bassus. 'You think I can't do my job? 'Course we were told.'

'Not by me!' insisted Priscus.

'No,' agreed Bassus. 'But I don't reckon Merula dreamed it up by herself. I reckon she thought you were letting the girl go.'

'Letting her go?' demanded Priscus. 'Merula would know better than that! The girl would have gone back to her family, raised a complaint, created a scandal – you would all have been in serious trouble!'

'So would you,' pointed out Bassus. 'You bought her.'

'Nonsense!' retorted Priscus. He turned to Ruso. 'You see the difficulty I'm in, Ruso. My staff made a terrible mistake and tried to cover it up. I only found out when it was over. It was too late to save that poor girl, and now they're trying to save themselves by blaming it on me.'

'It weren't me what killed her,' insisted Bassus. 'And it weren't Stich either.' He glowered at Priscus. 'We just got orders to go and clean up your mess. Again.'

The hand that rose to smooth Priscus' hair was shaking.

'I am not responsible for any of this,' he insisted. He turned to Bassus. 'If you try to claim I was involved, I shall tell the whole story, and you will be tried and executed. And as for you, Ruso – you've been trying to undermine me ever since you came here. If you attempt to pass this slander on to anyone else, I shall sue.'

'Fine,' agreed Ruso. 'And I'll produce the evidence of the letter, and we'll let the governor decide.'

'There was no letter!'

Ruso shook his head. 'The trouble with terrorizing your staff, Priscus, is that they're too scared to bend the rules. I don't know what you said to the clerks, but one of them was so thorough he made sure your reply to Saufeia was entered in the official record.'

'You're joking!' exclaimed Bassus. 'He used the official post?'

'Shut up!' Priscus scowled at Ruso. 'You're lying.'

'You said she wasn't going to bother us again!' shouted Bassus. 'You said you'd dealt with her and nobody would know!'

Priscus leaped to his feet. 'Keep your mouth shut, you fool! He's lying!'

They were both looking at Ruso now. He paused, savouring his sudden feeling of power and wishing he had the money to back it up. 'You know what I'm like with administration, Priscus,' he said. 'Not my strong point, is it? Do you really think I would have dreamed up a tale about post logs? And before you start to think about strangling me in a back alley . . .' he glanced at Bassus, 'or performing tongue surgery, or arranging any accidents, you should know that I've followed your example and made a file copy of all this.' He made his way towards the kitchen door. 'It's to be opened later this evening if I don't return

So,' he added, 'I'll be leaving with Tilla as soon as she's finished.'

He left them to argue. The last words he heard as the kitchen door swung shut were from Bassus. 'The official post? Are you really that stupid?'

The kitchen was still empty. The staff seemed to have abandoned the mess and retreated to bed. There was no sign of Merula, either, or the wine she had gone to fetch. Beyond it, the corridor that led to the back of the building was in darkness. Ruso paused, waiting for his eyes to adjust, listening for any sound from Daphne or the child. There was none. Suddenly he had the odd conviction that there was someone else there with him.

He held his breath. His right hand moved slowly and silently towards his knife. From behind him came the faintest rustle of fabric. He spun round, knife pointed at where someone's throat might be. 'Don't move!'

'Don't hurt me!' It was Merula's voice.

He said, 'Why are you hiding?'

'I thought you might be one of the others.'

Ruso lowered the knife. 'How's Daphne?'

'I don't know,' she said, 'and I don't care.' She bent down and heaved up some sort of bag. 'This place is finished. I'm not staying around to take the blame for what they did to that girl.'

Ruso said, 'Did they kill Asellina as well?'

'That was Priscus. The gods alone know why. That's what started all this. We had to find a replacement.'

'So you did a deal with Innocens?'

'It wasn't me. I'd have had more sense. I worked my way up here, Ruso. Seventeen years in the trade: I know what I'm doing. Then Priscus went and bought the place and started interfering. Never paying full price for anything. I told him, if you're going to run a business like this, you have to invest. But he wouldn't listen.'

Ruso slid the knife back into the sheath. 'Was it you who put Saufeia to work?'

'We all make mistakes, Doctor.'

'True.'

'I should have left when Priscus took over.'

'Yes,' agreed Ruso, 'I know exactly what you mean.'

He was on his way to the end room when he heard the squeal of a hinge out in the yard, and then the gate slam shut. Ahead of him was the angry, scratchy cry of a newborn child.

75

lla sat back against the wall, clutching her arm to try and
se the ache. Beside her, Daphne lay exhausted but alive
1 the bed, which was soaked with blood and the waters of
e birth. Phryne was kneeling by the bed, holding a blanket
ound the squalling and slimy child they had laid on its
other's belly. Now that the thick cord joining mother and
by was no longer blue, the other girl tied it as Tilla in-
ructed. They had not been able to find anything suitable
the room, so the cord was strangled with blue leather
ongs removed from her boots.

Tilla leaned forward and wiped her hands on the filthy
dspread. Her work was almost over. Soon the men would
me back for her, and she would have to decide what to do.

So many days had passed since she had met the Medicus,
d yet her choice was the same as before. She was not
raid of death. The poison had failed her today on the road.
artled by her capture, she had not thought to reach it
fore they tied her arms. Now, at last, she understood. The
ddess had kept her in this world not to save Phryne but
welcome Daphne's child. Praying now for Daphne, who
d been kind to her, she closed her eyes.

She was woken by the Medicus' voice outside the door.
artled, she rubbed her eyes. She must not sleep. They
ew now about the poison that was her freedom. As soon
she dropped her guard, they would take it away from her.
e had to leave for the next world tonight, or find a reason
linger in this one.

He was banging on the door now. Calling her. The girls were looking at her and at the bar across the door, not sure what to do.

She straightened her back. 'Are you alone?'

'Yes.'

She nodded to the girls. 'Let him in.'

Once inside he stood awkwardly, eyeing the figure on the bed. 'Is she –'

'She is alive.'

He said, 'You did well.'

'I need your knife,' she said.

Without question, he crouched down and slid it along the floorboards towards her. After she had severed the cord, Phryne swaddled the child in the shawl they had found in the trunk under the window and she settled it on its mother's breast, where it finally fell silent. 'Be proud of yourself,' she told Daphne in their own tongue. 'Be proud of your son.'

When she turned back she saw the Medicus was resheathing his knife. 'There's blood on that bandage,' he said frowning at her arm.

As she said, 'Not mine,' Daphne gave a soft moan. Tilla slid her hand under the blanket and felt the belly harden.

'Soon you can rest,' Tilla told her, lifting the blanket up to see if the afterbirth was coming yet. 'You are a strong girl. You have done well.'

They were waiting in silence when there were footsteps outside. The one with the odd hair appeared in the doorway, trembling and asking the Medicus to look at a wound on his head. As usual, he was full of words. This time he was talking about working out a plan.

'We can extend the terms of the loan,' he was saying as the Medicus lifted one of the lamps to get a better view of

432

the back of the head, from which a trickle of blood glittered black in the light. The wound had not stopped him talking. 'You can keep the girl,' he continued. 'She's too much trouble.' Tilla turned her head to listen. 'Too much trouble' surely meant they were talking about her.

He was sounding excited now. 'We can say Stichus killed Bassus in a fight over the takings –'

The Medicus interrupted to say the wound needed cleaning before he could examine it, and he would have no part of killing anyone.

'No, Ruso, no. You don't understand. It was self-defence. You saw him attack me earlier.'

The afterbirth was coming now. 'Good girl,' she urged, crouching to watch. It was important that it should be whole. Daphne should not be allowed to slip into the next world now. Not after such a struggle.

Daphne groaned.

'Good girl,' Tilla repeated, wishing the men would have the sense to leave them in peace. 'It is nearly done.'

'It was terrible,' the one with many words was insisting, as if anything could be terrible compared to what the girl on the bed had just been through. 'I was frightened for my life. He grabbed me round the throat and banged my head against the counter. A stone counter, Ruso. I could have died! I still feel giddy.'

She glanced round. The Medicus was scratching his ear in the way he did when he was uncertain. He said, 'Are you telling me –?'

'I was all on my own with him! You deserted me, you abandoned a fellow officer . . . I had to wait till he went to find a drink and get a knife from the kitchen. It was terrible!'

'You've just stabbed Bassus with a kitchen knife? Gods in heaven, Priscus! Let me past, I'll have to –'

But the talkative one was clutching his arm, still complaining.

It was whole. She tied the towels in place, tucked Daphne into the blanket and murmured a prayer of thanks to the goddess, with a final plea that the bleeding would stop soon. Behind her, the men were arguing in the doorway. The one called Priscus was promising the Medicus that the man was quite dead and would not be telling any more tales.

An evening of blood.

She stroked Daphne's forehead and tidied a strand of hair that had fallen over her eyes. 'The goddess has favoured you with courage, sister. You did well. He is a fine healthy baby.' It was not the time to be asking if there was a father to be told the news. Instead, she turned to the men in the doorway. 'We need help.'

The Medicus glanced round. 'We need help,' she repeated, raising her voice over that of the one with many words. 'She needs to be carried to a clean bed.'

She stepped aside. The Medicus eyed her for a moment as if he were not used to taking orders, then told Phryne to bring the child and said stiffly, 'Congratulations, Daphne,' before stooping to gather her up in his arms. She left the girls to guide the Medicus to a clean bed. The one called Priscus scuttled after them, talking faster and faster.

Alone, she took a long, cool draught of water from the jug. She had not eaten since breakfast. The soldiers had taken her food and eaten it while she walked behind them, tethered like a donkey, all the way back to Deva. She leaned back against the wall and slid down it until she was sitting on the floorboards with her legs stretched out in front of her. The blue boots were flapped open, thongless, useless for running even if she had the strength. She fingered the filthy bandage the Medicus had put on her arm – how many days ago now? So much trouble, and for what? To bring her here to save one unborn child?

She felt her eyes drift shut, and rubbed them hard. She must not sleep. Her hand moved to the twine fastened around her throat. She must decide tonight. She must ask a sign from the goddess. She must get up and bar the door. In a moment, she would do all these things. She would just sit here for a while first, surrounded by the mess that comes with the welcoming of a new life, and recover her strength.

76

Bassus was slumped over the counter, his head in a dark pool of red wine mingled with the blood that had welled through the fabric of his tunic. No breath stirred the surface of the pool. Ruso's fingers moved slowly around the warm flesh of the neck, pressing for the throb of a pulse. He shook his head. The doorman was, as Priscus had claimed, quite dead. He lifted the man's shoulders, then lowered him on to the counter again and stepped away. There appeared to be more than one wound, and all were in the back. It did not look like self-defence.

'It could have been Stichus,' Priscus was saying. 'It all fits, do you see? Stichus wanted to steal the takings and –'

Ruso turned on his heel and strode out of the bar.

Tilla was asleep. Priscus, who had followed him, was now talking about having the connecting door blocked up and selling the business. 'Frankly, it was always something of disappointment. Terribly difficult to find the right staff. As you know yourself, of course . . .'

Ruso knelt beside Tilla and ran a finger through the brown curls that she must have hoped would disguise her. Her eyelids flickered, then she settled back into sleep. Priscus was saying something about learning from one's mistake and putting this unfortunate affair behind them.

Ruso stood up and moved away. He would let her sleep a little longer. He was now so late that a few more minutes would make no difference. 'Accessory to kidnap and rape of a native girl, accessory to repeated rape of a citizen of

ome, strangling that citizen and now stabbing a veteran in
1e back,' he said. 'Plus I gather the other mess Bassus had
) clear up for you was Asellina.'

Priscus scowled. 'I really cannot be held responsible for
1ving to put an end to that girl. I warned her more than
1ce to pull herself together. She was quite mad.'

'Really? I heard she was a cheerful and popular member
f staff.'

Priscus tightened his lips. 'She was warned! She was
rdered to show appropriate respect!'

Ruso glanced at Priscus' hair and tried to imagine the
fect it would have on a girl who was prone to giggling.
'ou mean she wouldn't stop laughing?'

'I told you. She was quite mad.'

Not everyone likes a good laugh, do they, sir? Poor Decimus
1d been wiser than he realized. 'Did you invent the story
)out running off with the boyfriend,' Ruso asked, 'or was
1at someone else?'

'How was I supposed to know the wretched girl had an
1mirer? When Merula made a fuss I told her to make up
)me sort of reason why the girl had gone and I gave
:r an example. A better manager would have used some
1itiative. Instead she just repeated what I'd said.'

'So when her boyfriend turned up and demanded to
10w where she was, someone had to invent the mysterious
ilor.'

'That girl was the property of the business. My property.'

'And you didn't like your property laughing at you.'

Priscus glared at him for a moment, clenching and
1clenching his fists as if he were making a conscious effort
» rein in his temper. Finally he said, 'What does it matter?
'hat happened was a little unfortunate, but as her owner,
.e only loss was mine.'

437

'This whole business has been more than a little unfortunate, Priscus.'

Priscus took a deep breath and appeared to recover his composure. 'It has been an extremely difficult episode,' he agreed. 'But I think we can both feel relieved now.' The hand that smoothed his hair was hardly shaking at all now. 'We just need to tidy up a little. Then we can put everything behind us and make a fresh start. I'll confirm that you were called to an emergency here so your absence won't damage your promotion prospects.'

Tilla stirred and murmured something in her sleep. Ruso stared at Priscus, wondering if the man's calm attempt to reason his way out of terrible crimes was a sign of insanity. Wondering, too, if he had collected any more weapons on his way back through the kitchen. 'You expect me to keep quiet about this?'

'Of course.' Priscus' mouth twisted into the wolf smile and for the first time Ruso felt afraid of him. 'What a terrible waste it would be,' continued Priscus, 'to ruin both our careers over something like this. Because no matter what price you get for the girl – and be honest, Ruso, even if you redeem her now, you will have to sell her – it will not make up the deficit in your personal finances, will it?'

'You know nothing about my personal finances.'

'Really? Were you hoping no one would find out? Of course you were. Each of your creditors finding out about the others would cause a total collapse. If my informants are correct, you might be forced to sell that rather lovely farm in Gaul, leaving your brother and his expanding family homeless and penniless.'

'You wouldn't!'

'Only with the deepest reluctance, I assure you.'

One of the candles dimmed and drowned in a pool of

438

wax. Ruso wondered if Valens had got to bed yet. He took a deep breath. 'If I keep quiet now,' he said, 'I'll be in your hands. I'll never know when you might decide to talk.'

'Nor I you,' Priscus pointed out.

'Is that any way to live?'

'On the other hand,' said Priscus, 'as I suggested, we could extend the terms of the loan. I can arrange to mislay the guarantee document. So you can sell your slave whenever you like.'

There was a movement. Before Ruso realized what was happening, Tilla had put one hand to her throat and snapped the twine that held the poison around her neck.

'Stop!' he urged, lunging towards her and freezing a pace away as she put the package to her lips once more. 'Not now, Tilla. Please.'

'Daphne is safe,' said Tilla, looking first at Ruso and then at Priscus. 'Now one of you will sell me. For greed, or for debt.'

He did not dare to move. She could slip the acorn into her mouth and crush it in an instant if he tried to snatch it from her. 'Please, Tilla, don't take whatever it is you've got here.'

Those eyes were looking into his own. The eyes that had first looked at him, unseeing, as she was being dragged down a back street by the greasy Claudius Innocens. 'Daphne does not need me,' she said. 'Why should I not take it?'

And suddenly, clear and so obvious he could not under- stand how he had overlooked it, he knew why. 'Tilla, listen. Do you trust me?'

The poison was held steady. 'You take me in. You mend my arm,' she said.

'Yes. You see?'

'So you can sell me for money.'

439

'No! I had no idea . . .' He was about to say, 'I had no idea you would turn out to be so valuable,' but that was more truthful than helpful. He closed his eyes and prayed for the sort of persuasive powers the gods gave to other men. Men like Valens. When he opened them, no inspiration came. In desperation he whispered, 'You must trust me.' Then he turned back to Priscus. 'I won't keep silent,' he said. 'This has got to stop.'

Priscus frowned. 'I'm offering you your precious slave back, Ruso. Surely you can't be thinking of sacrificing your family to prove a point about a couple of dead whores. There are hundreds of them! You said it yourself: anyone can buy a girl in a back street.'

'Anyone can,' said Ruso, 'but once you have, you're responsible for her.' Without looking, he stretched one hand back towards Tilla, palm open. 'Give me the poison, Tilla.'

The hand remained empty in the air.

A muscle began to twitch in Priscus' cheek. 'You're not seeing things clearly, Ruso,' he said. 'Think about it over night. We'll discuss it in the morning.'

'There's nothing to discuss.'

'Ruso, I am the hospital administrator. I have served with the Legion for fifteen years. You are a visiting medic with record of damaging hospital property, a reputation for lateness and a known penchant for hanging around bars with loose women. Which of us will be believed?'

'I don't know,' said Ruso. 'We'll have to see. Give me the poison, Tilla.' A long streak of muscle in his arm was beginning to ache, and still his hand remained empty.

Priscus was watching Tilla. The wolfish smile began to spread across his face again. 'Have you ever seen a slave market, Tilla? Rows of bodies chained up to be inspected

440

and auctioned to the highest bidder. Of course he wants you to live. I imagine you will fetch quite a price.'

'Don't listen to him, Tilla. Give it to me.' Ruso, not daring to turn, tried not to think about what would happen to her, and to Lucius and the rest of the family, if she did not do as she was told. But then, when had Tilla ever done as she was told?

'She's grown fond of you, Ruso,' said Priscus. 'She doesn't want you to sell her to a stranger. She would rather die. You need to realize that the locals have no fear of death. That's why we have so much trouble with them. They would rather go to the next world than live dishonoured in this one.'

'I think they may have a point.'

'You see, Tilla? Even your Medicus thinks it is shameful to live without honour. Just one little bite, and you can be free.'

'Tilla, please! Trust me.'

'The two of us can come to an understanding, Ruso.' The twitch had begun again in Priscus' cheek. 'For the sake of the medical service.'

Ruso felt something touch the palm of his hand. His fingers closed over three smooth warm shapes.

'It's your duty to support me, Ruso!' cried Priscus. 'They were just slaves! They were of no importance!'

Ruso took Tilla by the arm and helped her to her feet. When he turned back, Priscus was clutching a kitchen knife. Ruso backed away, cursing his carelessness and snatching at the empty space where his own weapon should have been. Stay back, Tilla!'

Instead, Tilla pushed him out of the way and stepped forward, her good arm pointed towards Priscus. In her hand was Ruso's knife, still stained with the blood of the birth.

'Careful, Priscus,' Ruso warned, suddenly inspired. 'Her tribe train all their left-handed people as warriors.'

'I'll have you arrested and sold!' Priscus shouted at Tilla. He waved the kitchen knife towards Ruso. 'He signed the documents!'

'You could do that,' agreed Ruso, moving towards the foot of the bloodstained bed, 'but it wouldn't keep me quiet, would it?'

He opened his hand and placed the poison on the bed covers. Still defended by Tilla, he made for the door. 'Perhaps you're the one who needs to think about it overnight, Priscus,' he said. 'Shut the door behind us, will you, Tilla?'

77

Ruso, hunched in his room with his spare cloak around his shoulders and his feet warmed by a sleeping dog, reached for another tablet of the *Concise Guide*. He flipped it open and squinted at the lettering in the lamplight. Then he breathed on the wax to warm it and ran the flattened end of the stylus across the sheet to wipe away the writing he had spent so many hopeful hours composing.

Stacked at a safe distance from the lamp were the final plan of the *Concise Guide* and a couple of tablets full of notes. These were the only parts he intended to keep. The rest was being finally and irrevocably scrapped. He was never going to finish it: he realized that now. Even if he had not been as tired as he was – and it had taken a lot of night duty to pacify Valens for being left alone on payday – he knew he was not blessed with the powers of concentration that a real author needed. A real author would not have sat for hours in front of an uncompleted work, pondering the answers to irrelevant questions like what had happened to his former servant and whether she was safe. Wondering if she might think of him occasionally. Wondering whether he would ever find out where she was. Wondering whether, if he had been more insistent, she would have stayed. And if she had stayed, what might have happened.

Ruso picked at the twine tying the two leaves of the next tablet, tugged at the end and scowled as it tightened into a knot. He had managed without Tilla before she came. He would manage without her now she was gone. In time –

443

and it was obviously going to take longer than the thirty days he had so far been without her – she would become no more than an interesting memory. In time he would stop feeling a fool for having offered her a choice in the hope that she might want to stay. Perhaps in time he would forget the whole business. Perhaps in time he would even be able to walk the streets of Deva without feeling tainted by the human misery that he now knew lay behind the entertainment of the Legion he served.

He glanced across at the damp stain that had blossomed beneath his bedroom window. Of course she wouldn't have wanted to stay. Even Valens would have had trouble enticing a woman to stay in this mouldering excuse for a home. Ruso, the man who had considered selling Tilla for a profit had not stood a chance. No wonder the last he had heard of her was a message saying she had gone north and taken Phryne with her.

He sliced the tip of his knife through the knot and breathed warmth on to the next sheet. The stylus scraped across the surface, filling the scratches and catching up the misted droplets where his breath had condensed on the cold wax. His careful thoughts on 'Where a broken bone is suspected' sank into the past.

He had signed the death warrant of the *Concise Guide* three weeks ago, when the Camp Prefect had called him and Valens in separately for 'a chat'. The chat had not been a cosy experience. Evidently the Camp Prefect knew more than Ruso would have wished about his performance since joining the Twentieth. There was nothing to be gained by explaining that he was normally very reliable and that the downhill slide was the result of his colleague eating a dish of bad oysters. When the Prefect had said, 'And if you were in charge of the medical service, what would you change he had come up with the brightest idea he could think of at the time, which was that practical first-aid training for every man in the unit would mean faster treatment of injuries, less time off sick and less pressure on the hospital.

The Chief Medical Officer had been appointed the following day. He was a Greek medic from the Second Augusta, based further south. He was generally agreed to possess connections, competence and no charm whatsoever. Unfortunately, though, Ruso's bright idea had not died with his ambitions. The Prefect passed it on to the new CMO, who congratulated Ruso on his initiative and gave him the job of organizing the training. Since no legionary would pay for something the Army would give him for free, Ruso found himself organizing the destruction of the market for his own work.

Valens' response to being overlooked was to announce that he was glad to be able to carry on practising real medicine, instead of being mired in administration like the CMO. Apparently the Second Spear's daughter was very impressed with this devotion to his calling. Ruso was impressed too: not with Valens' devotion but with his ability to weave a useful lie in with the truth. The new man had indeed taken over the reins at a difficult time, following the suicide of the hospital administrator.

It was a month since Priscus' manservant had gone to wake him and found him dead in his bed. A doctor was called. According to Valens, the sight of the administrator's ghastly grimace of pain beneath his beautifully combed hair was the stuff of nightmares. The note on the bedside table had given typically detailed instructions for his funeral — Priscus was an administrator to the last — but no reason for the taking of his own life. The Second Spear, charged with investigating both this death and a murder on the same night in the adjoining bar, dismissed Ruso's suggestion that the two were connected with 'You again! I suppose you're going to tell me you saw him do it?'

'No, sir.'

'Then bugger off and don't come bothering me with any more of this rubbish. The pen-pusher from the hospital killed himself for reasons I know but you needn't, and from what I hear, the doorman was a nasty piece of work who could cheerfully have been knifed by a couple of dozen suspects. And since the woman who owns the place has run off, it's pretty bloody obvious which one of them did it.'

'Sir, with respect −'

But the look on the face of the Second Spear told Ruso that respect was not required. What was required was to shut up, go away and stop being a nuisance.

It occurred to Ruso that only he, Tilla and possibly Merula would ever know the real story behind Priscus' suicide. Ruso had been ignored, Tilla had gone away and Merula, wherever she was, was certainly not going to say anything that would reveal her own failure to protect the Roman citizen whom they had all known as Saufeia. As for Asellina, the slave put to death by her owner for having a fit of the giggles, Ruso tried to find something comforting to say to Decimus, and failed.

In the absence of fact, speculation was both rife and confident. Even Albanus could not resist hinting to Ruso that irregularities had been found in the hospital accounts and in the Aesculapian Fund. 'And when you hear what's in his will, sir, you'll see what I mean.'

At Priscus' request the funeral had been attended by all the hospital staff. As instructed, a clerk read the will to the assembled company. The wish that his manservant be

446

anted his freedom was of scant interest to the mourners. he desire that all his property be sold for the benefit of the esculapian Fund, however, caused raised eyebrows and the change of more than one knowing glance. Ruso caught lbanus looking at him before both resumed a dutifully ipassive funeral expression. The Camp Prefect, who was rning out to be a more perceptive man than Ruso had iagined, described Priscus in his funeral oration as 'an out-anding administrator and a man of many contradictions'.

To Ruso's intense relief, the money loaned to Stichus had een repaid shortly after Stichus and Chloe reappeared from herever they had been hiding. He had waited in vain, ough, for a demand to pay it back to the Aesculapian ind. Finally his conscience sent him to see the unfortunate erk who had been given the task of wrestling Priscus' itstanding administration into a shape presentable to the iperial auditors.

The man hunched over on to one elbow while he ran chewed fingertip down the accounts. Finally the finger used.

'You did have a loan,' he agreed. 'It was paid back on the elfth before the Kalends of October.'

'No, that's not right.'

'Well that's what it says.'

'There must be some sort of mix-up.'

The man sighed, swivelled the record round and slid it ross the desk, the finger pointing to an entry in Priscus' ecisely spaced hand. 'Look.'

Ruso read it twice. The meaning was unmistakeable. round about the same time as the administrator had per-aded him to sign over Tilla as guarantee, Ruso's loan had en repaid in full. There was no mention of a slave in the ind records. The only explanation Ruso could think of

447

was that Priscus had chosen to take over the debt himself. If Ruso failed to pay up, Priscus would take Tilla for his own purposes – and, as he must have guessed, when he tired of her she would still be worth far more than the loan had cost. But if the loan had been paid, Priscus would merely have broken even . . . Ruso paused. He had never been able to settle in his own mind the business of the fire, nor that accident under the bath-house scaffolding. But now that he thought about it, the fire had happened just after he had signed the loan guarantee. Priscus had been in the hospital that night and could have slipped out to push something burning through the shutters of the bedroom window. He had not been on the building site, but he had been a man of wide influence. Perhaps Ruso would go and have a chat about him with Secundus from the century of Gallus. Because of course, if Ruso had burned to death or had his skull split by the trowel, he would never have paid and Priscus would have had his signature on the document handing over Tilla . . . A document which he had not bothered to read before signing it. Had he signed Tilla over to the Fund itself, or to its administrator?

'Satisfied?'

'Mm.' Ruso scratched his ear. 'I suppose,' he said, 'as a Priscus' money was bequeathed to the Fund, I'm morally obliged to consider paying it myself anyway.'

The man looked horrified. 'You can't do that! I've only just got it to balance. You'll mess up the whole system.'

So instead, he had sent the money to another good cause, a family in southern Gaul.

Ruso wiped out the final line of 'In cases of fever' and reflected that truth might be an honourable concept, but very few men actually wanted to hear it. And of those who

448

did, some would regret having asked. He leaned back in his chair and eyed the pile of tablets waiting to be erased. Months of work. Ahead of him, several tedious and penny-pinching hours saving the cost of tablets he would never need again, because he was not going to write a book. Ever. He reached forward, scooped them up, pulled his feet from under the dog and strode into the kitchen.

The embers in the kitchen hearth were still glowing. The first tablets were beginning to smoke as he threw the last one on. A yellow flame popped up through a gap, wavered and grew tall.

The *Concise Guide* was illuminating the kitchen with a merry blaze when the main door scraped open. Valens walked into the kitchen and gave an exaggerated sniff. 'What's that you're burning?'

'Just some rubbish I didn't need.'

'Well burn some more and perhaps we'll be rehoused sooner than we thought.' Valens, his ambition for the CMO's house thwarted, was now eagerly trying to negotiate better lodgings. He bent to peer at the contents of the fire. 'That reminds me. I was supposed to bring you a letter.'

Ruso reached out his hands to warm them over his disappearing masterpiece. 'From?'

'Londinium. That chap you sent to get his cataracts looked at. Albanus gave it to me, and I've left it in the surgery. Big writing. Did it himself, apparently. They're naming their son after you. The worst eye's been done and it seems to have worked.'

'Good.'

'They'll discharge him anyway, you know. The sight will never be up to much.'

'I know,' said Ruso, recalling the battle with Priscus about the cost of the operation. The administrator had been right, but for all the wrong reasons.

Valens lifted the lid of the breadbin.

'It's empty,' said Ruso, reaching for the poker to prod at the settling flames.

Valens lowered the lid with a disappointed sigh. 'I can't eat out, I'm on call. I'll have to wander back to the kitchen and see what I can scrounge. We're going to have to do something about another slave, Ruso.'

'Yes,' agreed Ruso, not adding that they had agreed this more than once, but neither of them had done anything about it. They needed a slave to go and find them a slave.

'Oh, and there was another message. Apparently Albanus thinks I've become his assistant. He said to tell you something about a girl being home safe.'

Ruso stopped. 'Tilla?'

Valens looked pained. 'I would have remembered if it was the lovely Tilla, Ruso, whom you so rashly allowed to abandon us with an empty breadbin. No. This is another of your many women. Let me think . . . something Greek.'

'Phryne?'

'That's it. Phryne.'

'Who brought the message?'

Valens shrugged. 'Some urchin brought it to the gate, apparently.'

The poker clattered back on the hearth. Ruso snatched up his cloak from the chair where he had thrown it. 'I've got to go out.'

'Do I know this Phryne? Can she cook?'

Ruso squeezed the shaft of his cloak-pin into the catch. 'No,' he said, answering both questions with one word on his way out of the house.

78

tichus nodded a greeting from his old place on the door. rom his shadow, a small figure in an identical tunic grinned t Ruso. A quick inquiry confirmed that Lucco had not been ie urchin. He had, as he announced with pride, been at ʹork all day. 'I've been helping the painter.' He pointed at ie outside of the wall beside him. 'Look.' The torch lit up ʹeshly painted lettering. 'I can read all the letters,' added ie boy. 'It says "CHLOE'S".'

'Very good,' observed Ruso, stepping inside. The bar was ʹoing a brisk trade. Ruso nodded to Mariamne, who was ʹrving at the tables. He reached for his purse and waited ʹhile a youth tried unsuccessfully to haggle over the price f the beer. After the youth had lost – but still bought the ʹeer – Ruso asked a girl he did not recognize to pour him large cup of the best wine Chloe's had to offer.

It was the first drink he had ordered here since the day ʹe bought Tilla, and the first time he had been back to the ʹar since the dreadful events of payday. He had just enough ʹoney for the wine. On the way here he had promised ʹimself he was not going to buy anything or anybody else, ʹd if there was the least hint of trouble anywhere near him, ʹe was going to walk away without a second glance.

He was handing over the cash when Chloe's voice cut ʹross the hubbub. 'Don't let him pay for that!' Moments ʹter she was kissing him on the cheek like a long-lost friend. ʹome and see the baby!' she urged. 'Where have you been?'

Steadying his wine as she dragged him by the arm, he

followed her towards the kitchen and a fine smell of stewed lamb. 'I got your package,' he said. 'Thank you.'

Chloe laughed. 'I bet you were worried when you found out we'd gone.'

'Just a little.'

'I told you he'd pay you back.'

Ruso nodded, wondering who really did own the money he had finally sent to Lucius.

Daphne was standing at the kitchen table, cracking brown eggs into a bowl two at a time with a swift and economical technique that made him suddenly nostalgic for Tilla's frustrated struggles to manage his kitchen left-handed. Daphne looked up at his approach, smiled and pointed towards the other end of the table, where a drawer rested on the tabletop. Inside, a small fuzz of dark hair was visible under one end of a blanket.

Ruso said the things people were supposed to say about babies. Indeed, this one was a particular miracle, even though it looked just like all the others and its cloths smelled as though they needed changing.

He glanced from Chloe to Daphne. 'I came to see if you'd heard the news. Phryne is safely home.'

Daphne's thumbs-up sign trailed a long string of egg white.

'Do you know who brought the message?'

Chloe shook her head. 'Nobody's been here.' She took his arm again. 'Come and eat,' she urged, pausing to exchange word with the cook and inspect the contents of a couple of steaming pans before leading him back into the bar and beckoning Mariamne over. 'Whatever the Doctor wants,' she said as the girl gathered empty cups on to a tray. 'And the Falernian. He's our guest of honour. And tell Flora to smile, will you? People come here to enjoy themselves.'

Ruso glanced at the customers and the girls clustered round the lamplit tables and reflected that a couple of months ago, he would have been embarrassed to be made welcome in a place like this. Now he was glad of it. He had nowhere to go this evening and all he had eaten was two sausages scrounged from a patient who was off his food. He placed his drink on the table and settled into an empty seat as Mariamne placed another cup and a brimming wine-jug beside him and went to fetch him a bowl of stewed lamb.

Chloe sat herself beside him, helped herself to his wine and was pouring him a fresh cup from the jug when a large hand landed on the table, and a swaying legionary leaned over her. 'That bitch over there,' he announced, waving at a table across by the bar, 'won't go upstairs with me.'

Chloe put the jug down and placed a hand over his. 'Marcus, I hope you were a gentleman and offered her something nice in exchange?'

'You're in charge. Tell her to do her job.'

Chloe shook her head. 'All our girls work for themselves, Marcus.' She leaned closer to him. 'And they're specially selected and trained by me. You might find she's asking a little bit more than you'd pay somewhere else, but I promise you won't be disappointed.'

The legionary stared at her for a moment. 'She's asking a bloody fortune! Sod her. What else have you got?' He looked her up and down. 'You working tonight?'

Chloe smiled and pointed towards the door, where Stichus was glaring across at them. 'I'm a one-man woman these days, my love. Isidora!' She beckoned over the girl who had turned at the mention of the name. 'Isidora, this is my very good friend Marcus. Marcus, this is the girl for you.' She reached for their hands and joined them.

When they had gone Chloe sank back in her chair with a

sigh of exasperation. 'Silly bitch, I'll have to talk to her. If it's not one thing here, it's another.' She leaned her elbows on the scarred wood and opened her hands to indicate the sweep of the bar. 'Well? What do you think?'

'I take it you're the new Merula?'

'A girl can't keep working for ever, you know. I always wanted to get out before everything started to sag.'

Ruso, not sure if a compliment was expected at this point, mumbled something, took a long draught of the wine she had poured him, then drew back and asked, 'What's this?'

'Weren't expecting that, were you?' inquired Chloe, clearly proud of it. 'It's Falernian. A present from a client. Don't ask, because I won't tell you. We're very discreet here.'

It wasn't, but he didn't have the heart to tell her. At least it was a better imitation than Merula had sold him. He said 'You seem to be doing well.'

She nodded. 'We lost a few girls to start with, people who went back home, but most of us either haven't got home or wouldn't be welcome if we went there. And there's been no trouble recruiting. Not now word's got round that I'm not running things the way that old cow did. The girls work down here for their keep. If they take a customer upstairs they pay me to use the room and they hold on to the rest themselves.'

'I see.'

'It should all work very nicely, if the girls just use a bit of common sense. They provide a good service, they get the cash. Before, everything got handed over to the management.'

'That's very enterprising.'

Chloe grinned. 'And I can tell the tax man we're letting out rooms. So it's all nice and legal.'

Ruso looked at her over the rim of the wine-cup. 'Really?'

She leaned across him and adjusted the fold of his cloak ɔver his shoulder. 'It is unless somebody tells, Doctor.'

'It's none of my business. But someone's going to fathom out before long.'

'From what I heard,' said Chloe, 'the bar wasn't menɔned in Priscus' will.'

Ruso nodded. 'I imagine he didn't trust his witnesses to ɛep it quiet. Being involved in running a, er –'

'Whorehouse,' put in Chloe.

'It wouldn't have done much for his reputation.'

'Exactly,' said Chloe. 'That's why he always let everybody ɪnk the business belonged to Merula. Even a lot of the ɪff didn't realize. So as far as anybody knows – anybody ɛcept you, me and Stich, that is – the name's only been ɪanged because murder's bad for trade, and she's left me ɪ charge till she gets back.'

'Is she coming back?'

'I wouldn't hold your breath. She took all her jewellery ɪth her and she won't want to be tried for what she did to ɪufeia.'

Chloe reached out a manicured fingernail, lifted his chin ɪd pouted a kiss. 'Cheer up, Doctor. Lucco's safe, Daphne's ɪt her baby, and everyone's glad those bastards aren't in ɪarge here any more.'

Ruso took another long drink and swilled the not-quite ɛcious wine dangerously close to the rim of the cup. ɪsellina is dead and her boyfriend doesn't know why. ɪufeia's family will never know where she's buried. And I ɪn't know what's happened to Tilla.'

'Asellina died in an accident, Doctor, still wearing the ɪcklace poor old Decimus gave her as part of their tragic ɪe affair. She loved him to the end. That's what I told him,

455

and if you tell him anything else, we'll have him down here every night getting drunk and picking fights.'

'True.'

'Tilla and Phryne were from the same people, weren' they?'

'The Brigantes.'

'So if one's home safely, then the other must be as well Look, here comes your supper. Now have a taste of tha and tell me if it isn't the best stewed lamb in town. An don't think about Saufeia. You can't tell her family anythin; that'll be of any comfort to them.'

Mariamne placed a steaming bowl on the table. 'Compli ments of the house, sir.'

'When you've finished,' added Chloe, getting to her fee and leaning forward to stroke one fingertip along his cheel 'Choose yourself a girl and tell her Chloe sent you for th special.'

79

Ruso trod heavily down the moonlit street, his stomach full of stew and his mind full of dark thoughts. He had lingered as long as he could over the meal and consumed the entire jug of Chloe's fake Falernian, but he had not taken up the offer of a girl. Even a desperate man had to have standards.

A family group emerged from a side street and joined the road ahead of him. A child who should have been in bed at this hour was perched on its father's shoulders. The mother had a baby cradled against her hip. They seemed to be hurrying somewhere. Moments later they turned off to the right and disappeared.

Ruso walked on, in no particular direction. A rat scurried across the street in front of him and vanished into an alley that smelled of bad drains. Even the rats had somewhere to go and something to do. Whereas he was facing another evening sitting in a cold house with only the dogs and the ashes of his failed work for company.

A man needed a family, Ruso decided. Or a religion. Something to cling to. His own family were far away, and as for religion, he was not sure that he and Aesculapius were on good terms at the moment. Especially if the god had found out that his fund had been short-changed to keep a small farm in Gaul out of debt.

A man needed a family or a religion. He felt a long way from both.

He was thinking about her again. He was thinking that he should have given her instructions about keeping in touch. She was still, technically, his property. But it was obvious that after all that had happened to her in Deva she would not choose to stay here. He had only himself to blame.

He heard voices behind him and turned to see a group of five or six youths striding purposefully down the street. Their conversation was in British. He stepped aside. They passed him without seeming to notice he was there.

He supposed he could go back into the hospital and do a late ward round, but he was more than a little drunk, and, besides, it would only bring out more 'Haven't you got a home to go to?' comments. He had discharged the last patient who had asked that, on the premise that anyone able to sit up in bed and make cheeky remarks was well enough to be sent back to barracks in the morning.

Glancing up to see where he was – it would not be a good idea to wander down the Dock Road at this hour – he was surprised to see the building ahead silhouetted against an orange sky. He drew in a sharp breath and paused to stare. Somewhere towards the distant cemetery, sparks were flying upwards, fading to black specks and floating down through the disturbed air. It was too big for a funeral pyre, and much too late at night. He was too far away to hear the shouting, but he could see well enough. Somebody's house was on fire.

He had promised himself he would walk away from trouble, but this was different. Hurrying through the shadowed streets, he overtook another family group and was surprised to hear, 'Evening, Doctor! Are you going where we're going?'

It was a moment before he recognized the barber, who seemed to be out for a stroll with his family.

'There's a fire,' explained Ruso, wondering how they could have failed to notice.

'Looks good, don't it?' observed the barber. He fell in step with Ruso. 'I wouldn't bother meself, but we'll never hear the last of it if we don't take the ma-in-law.'

Ruso winced. For all they knew, people could be injured or dead. Clearly the barber had been right to assess his mother-in-law as a mad old bitch. 'We'd better hurry,' he said.

'Oh, it'll go on for a bit yet,' observed the barber. 'Mind out!' He pushed Ruso to one side just in time to stop him stepping in a pile of animal droppings. 'Once that lot get going with the dancing and the stories you can be up till daylight.' The man lifted his left hand to reveal the dark shape of a tankard, 'Still, there's usually a good drop of beer to be had.'

Ruso's legs carried on in the same direction while his head rearranged his assessment of where he was going. His suspicions were confirmed when the barber said, 'One thing you can say for the locals, they know how to do a good bonfire.'

Ruso said, 'What's it in aid of?'

'New year.'

'But it's only the end of October!'

'Ah, to you and me and the rest of the Empire, Doc, but he wife's family's off into next year tomorrow. And tonight or one night only – this is according to the old bag, mind – the doors are open between the living and the dead.'

'I see,' said Ruso. They were closer to the fire now. He could hear faint strains of chanting and the wail of pipes, hopefully from the living. He wondered whether, miles away across the damp green hills of Britannia, Tilla was singing one of her interminable ancestor songs beside a bonfire of her own.

*

459

The crowd had gathered on a patch of waste ground between the last houses and the cemetery. The size of the crowd surprised him, but the Twentieth had been here for many years now and he supposed most of their women would be local. People had massed well back from the leaping flames of a colossal bonfire. Those closest to him were silhouettes, and around the fire he could make out pale shapes of faces. The flames lit up the movements of the musicians, who were standing on some sort of platform.

Around him, knots of people were wandering across the grass to where a couple of lamplit carts were serving food and – judging by the numbers of men and women clutching cups – beer. He glanced back at the entrance to the waste ground and saw, as he had expected, a glint of moonlight on polished armour. The legionaries standing guard each side of the gate would be the visible ones. He supposed others would be stationed further back, discreetly positioned so as not to provoke trouble but ready to rush forward and quell it if it seemed to be starting without them. The chances of any trouble here, though, were minimal. Most of these people would have connections with the Army. This, he thought, surveying the crowds, was just the sort of event of which Rome would approve. Happy natives enjoying a night out under the watchful eye of their benevolent imperial guardians. He wondered what the imperial guardians would do if the old woman was right, and the dead decided to walk back through the open door and join in.

The thought reminded him of something. He felt for his purse and fingered the coin inside. Then he strode across to join the queue at the drinks stall.

Ruso disliked talking to people about death. They usually asked questions to which he didn't know the answers.

Wherever possible, he left that sort of thing to the priests. The priests didn't know the answers either, but they thought they did, which usually seemed to please grieving relatives. When there was no priest available, he would trot out some sort of platitude about the deceased having gone to a better place, and being out of pain now. But had they? Were they? How could anyone know?

He had seen many people die, and he could still make no sense of it. One moment the body was a person with a will and a future and a sense of humour and a liking for honeyed dates or goat's cheese or other men's wives. Then – and the change could take a second, or hours, or days, but the end was always the same – the body was just a mass of flesh which had to be disposed of before it stank. And whatever anyone said about ghosts or open doors or crucified Jewish carpenters, nobody had ever come back, so how could anyone say with any confidence that there was a better place – or any place at all?

He knelt, stretched out his hands and let the cold, dry earth run through his fingers. Plants had begun to grow on the grave. He assumed they were weeds, although in the moonlight it was impossible to tell. It had been difficult enough to make out the name burned along the wooden post that was hammered into the top of the grave as a marker, but finally he had picked out all the letters: SAUFEIA. Spelt correctly. One 'f'.

He had never met this young woman in life. He had only seen the battered and decaying husk of a body from which the soul was long gone. He owed her no duty beyond that of a doctor to a patient. He had more than fulfilled that duty. Yet still he felt guilty.

The people who buried Saufeia had not left a spout to connect the dead to the living, so he lifted the cup of wine

461

he had bought from the stall – how Roman these people had become! – and held it at arm's length above the grave. He listened for a moment to the sounds of celebration drifting over from the bonfire. Then he began to tilt the cup until a thin stream of wine ran from it to soak into the soft earth. As it trickled into the ground he said quietly, 'May you rest in peace, sister. If there is a next world, may you enjoy a better life there than you suffered in this one. May you forgive us all for not avenging you sooner, and . . .' He paused to clear his throat, 'And may the dead be kind enough to forgive me for not telling the whole truth, because I have a duty to the living.'

'Sometimes,' murmured a girl's voice, 'is good not to tell too much truth.'

Ruso felt his whole body begin to shake. The night when the doors are open between the living and the dead . . . And yet it was the wrong voice. He knew that voice. He knew it very well indeed. Slowly, he lowered the cup on to the grave and was relieved to press his hands into the solid earth. He told himself he was not losing his mind. He was simply confusing his memories: an understandable mistake brought on by the strange surroundings of the moonlit cemetery and too much free wine at the bar.

'Hail and farewell, Saufeia,' he whispered, then scrambled hastily to his feet.

'Are you finish?' The words were spoken by a woman in native dress with a shawl pulled over her head.

He stared at her, squinting in the moonlight. 'You aren't really here,' he informed her. 'I have had too much to drink. I am going to walk to the real world now, past next year and back into this one, and then I am going to bed and when I wake up tomorrow morning you won't be there.'

The girl eyed him solemnly and then said, 'My lord is afraid he is losing his mind.'

'I'm not losing my mind,' he insisted, 'I'm drunk.'

'My lord is drunk,' she agreed, 'but I am here. She pushed back the shawl and held out one bare arm. 'See.'

He rubbed his eyes and looked at the pale arm. Then he took it and turned it over, marvelling at its straightness.

'I have seen you go to the bar,' explained Tilla. 'I wait outside for a very long time while you drink, and I follow you.'

He had thought many times about what he would say to Tilla if he ever saw her again. He could not remember what he had decided. Instead, he found himself slipping back to the role of doctor. 'The muscles in the arm will be weak,' he heard himself telling her. 'You must do exercises every day to build them up again. Clench your fist for me. Good. Do you have full movement in the hand?'

She gave a deep, throaty chuckle. 'Now will you ask me if my bowels are open today?'

He let go of the arm. 'No. I'm sorry, Tilla, I –' He glanced round them at the deserted cemetery. 'I can't believe you're here. I thought you were never coming back.'

'The first time I meet you,' she said, 'I am thinking I wish to die. I want to go to the next world. You, with your bandages and your exercises and eat your dinner and have you use the pot yet, you keep me here.'

Ruso scratched his ear. 'I'm not sure about the next world,' he said. 'That's why I prefer to keep people in this one, just in case.'

'Then I find out that you want to sell me.'

'That was a mistake,' said Ruso. 'I wasn't thinking straight.'

'A mistake, yes.'

'Did you bring the message about Phryne?'

'I send a boy to the gate. I have to find out what has happened to that Priscus man. To know if it is safe to come.'

'I thought you would stay at home with your people.'

She paused. 'I think about you and the other good-looking doctor,' she said. 'In that terrible house.'

'Valens is negotiating for a better one,' said Ruso.

'My arm is mended,' she said. 'I am still in this world, and I have to thank you. If you sell me, you can get a better house. Then I will find a way to the next world and you will have money.'

He stared at her. 'You mean I sell you, I get lots of money, and if you don't like the new owner you kill yourself? What sort of an arrangement is that?'

'Is honourable.'

'Is ridiculous. I told you, I don't believe in the next world. And I wouldn't dream of sending anyone to it so I can have a better house. That was never what I needed the money for.' He hesitated. 'If you really want to do something for me, come home.'

She looked him up and down. 'You have not shave. There are dark rings under your eyes.' She placed a finger close to the pin on his chest. 'There is a hole in your cloak.'

'I've been doing a lot of night duty.'

The sound of cheering and laughter drifted across from the bonfire. She said, 'Will your better house have mice?'

He took a deep breath. 'If you come back,' he said, 'you will not be sleeping with the mice. You will be sleeping with me.'

Another burst of distant laughter broke the silence. He was beginning to think he had made a serious mistake when she reached forward, took his hand and turned to address the grave.

'We must leave now, sister,' she said. 'We will pray for you. Watch over us in the new year from the next world.'

They were almost back at the fort gates when Tilla said, 'I must tell you some truth, my lord. You could not sell me anyway.'

'Why not?' said Ruso, happy to launch into an argument now that he was assured of her company. 'I have the documents. You told me yourself that Innocens bought you in a legitimate sale.'

There was a slight pause before she replied, 'I told you he pay money for me.'

'Exactly.'

'The woman he pay is not the one who —'

'Stop!' ordered Ruso. 'Whatever it is, I don't want to hear it. I'm tired of the truth. Just carry on the way you are, Tilla. That's an order.'

Author's Note

Ancient accounts of Roman Britain are tantalizingly patchy, and everything we have — even passages purporting to tell us what the Britons were thinking and saying — comes from the conqueror's pen. The earliest British stories were not recorded until an era as far removed from Hadrian as we are from Shakespeare. However, many of the gaps are still being filled by archaeology, and anyone in search of reliable information about our ancestors should most definitely look here rather than within the pages of an entertainment such as this.

The layout and remains of Deva can be seen in the streets of modern-day Chester, although the port silted up many years ago. The Twentieth Legion really did carry out major rebuilding there during Trajan's reign, but the schedule, the delays and the bad behaviour were imposed upon their innocent ghosts by me. I should also confess that, whilst the administration portrayed here was inspired by the Roman army's meticulous record-keeping, some of the arrangements might come as a surprise to scholars. They might be less surprising to anyone who has attempted to plait the fog of public finance for a living.

The word 'Medicus' was used to describe men of various ranks, and the hierarchy Ruso is attempting to climb is pure conjecture. What is not in doubt is that the doctors of antiquity were remarkably skilled. Cataract surgery might have been terrifying, but it was possible. However, there were no modern antibiotics or anaesthetics, and accurate knowledge sat alongside such beliefs as Pliny's suggestions that snake bites could be cured by human ear wax. Small wonder, then, that the sick turned to Aesculapius, the god of healing, who may or may not have had a Thanksgiving Fund but who certainly deserved one.

As for the rescue of Trajan – Cassius Dio records that he was saved from the Antioch earthquake by a mysterious stranger. Whether this stranger was Ruso or the god Jupiter I leave to the reader to decide.

The goings-on at Merula's bar were partly inspired by Pompeii, where the names of long-dead girls remain on the walls of their workplaces. Two thousand years later, of course, we have moved on. Slavery is illegal. Yet I fear that is scant comfort to any young woman a long way from home who is forced to provide 'personal services' while the trafficker who holds her passport pockets her earnings. This appalling trade is going on right now, in our own cities, and it survives because it finds customers. I didn't need to make it up. Unfortunately.